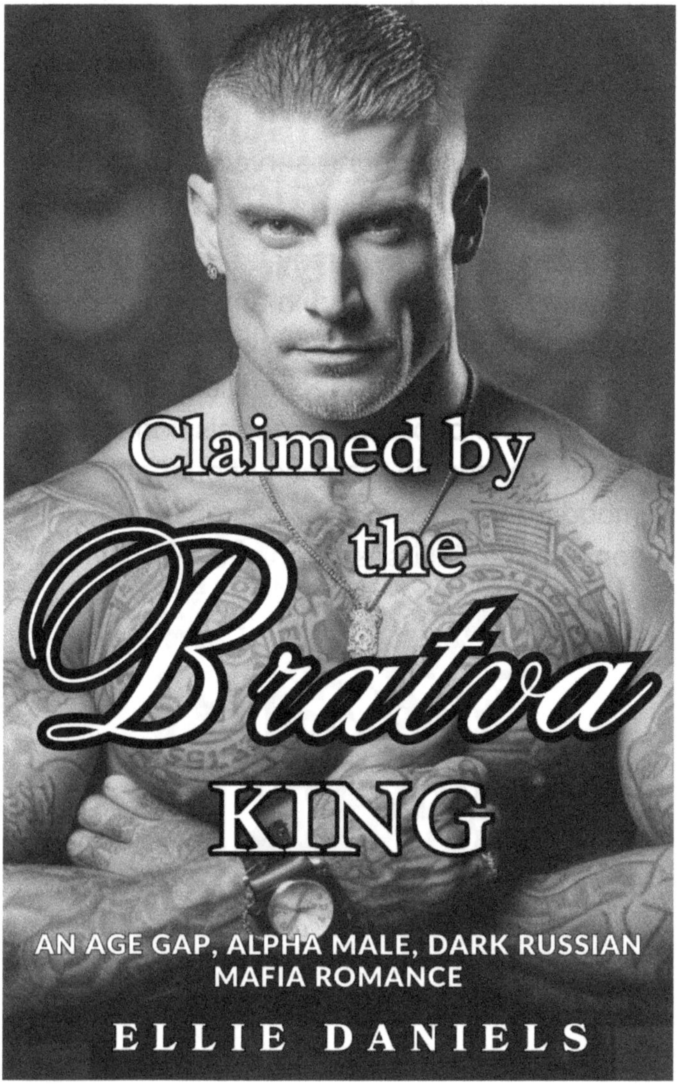

Claimed by the Bratva KING

AN AGE GAP, ALPHA MALE, DARK RUSSIAN MAFIA ROMANCE

ELLIE DANIELS

As Ava walked through the streets of Manhattan, she couldn't help but feel like she was on top of the world. Everything in her life seemed to be falling into place, and it was as if the city was celebrating with her.

She stopped at a quaint little boutique to pick up some final items for the wedding, smiling as she perused through delicate lace garters and sparkling hair accessories. The saleswoman noticed her dress bag and immediately gushed over it, asking about the upcoming wedding.

Ava happily shared all the details, feeling a sense of joy wash over her as she spoke about Derek and their love story. The saleswoman cooed over how romantic it all sounded, making Ava feel even more excited for what was to come.

After paying for her items, Ava continued on her way, feeling almost giddy as she weaved through the bustling crowds. She couldn't wait to show Derek all that she had picked out for their special day.

On a whim, she decided to surprise Derek at his apartment. They had been so busy with wedding preparations that they hadn't had much time to just enjoy each other's company. A surprise visit would be a welcome break from the chaos, a sweet reminder of why they were doing all this.

She fished her key out of her purse, smiling as she thought about Derek's reaction. He would be thrilled to see her, she was sure of it. They would spend the afternoon together, maybe even go out for a quiet dinner, just the two of them. With this image in mind, Ava slipped the key into the lock and quietly opened the door.

Ava stepped into the familiar warmth of Derek's apartment, closing the door softly behind her. Everything was just as she remembered it—the modern furniture, the tasteful art on the walls, the faint scent of Derek's cologne lingering in the air. She set down her things on the kitchen counter, intending to call out to him, but something stopped her. There was a strange, muffled sound coming from the bedroom.

Her heart skipped a beat, a flash of worry crossing her mind. Was Derek hurt? Sick? But no, that didn't make sense. She had just spoken to him an hour ago, and he had sounded perfectly fine. Dismissing the unease, Ava walked quietly down the hallway, her heels clicking softly on the hardwood floor.

The door to the bedroom was closed, but the noises were louder now—sounds she recognized, sounds that sent a cold shock of realization through her body. No. It couldn't be. She refused to believe it.

Her hand trembled as she reached for the door handle. Taking a deep breath, she pushed the door open.

The scene that met her eyes was like something out of a nightmare. There, in the middle of the bed they had shared so many times, was Derek, tangled up in the sheets with another woman. But not just any woman—Melissa, Ava's best friend since college. The woman who had been by her side through every major life event, who had been chosen as her maid of honor.

Ava's breath caught in her throat, suffocated by the raw scene unfolding before her. Derek's body loomed over Melissa, his hips driving into hers with a primal urgency. Melissa's moans filled the room, mixing with the sound of skin slapping against skin as she arched beneath him, lost in the throes of ecstasy. The air crackled with their shared passion, oblivious to Ava's presence as she stood frozen, a silent witness to the brutal betrayal playing out before her.

Ava's heart pounded painfully in her chest, each beat a sharp reminder that this was real. This wasn't a nightmare she could wake up from. She wanted to scream, to cry, to do anything that would break the terrible image happening in front of her, but she was paralyzed with disbelief.

Finally, Derek seemed to sense her presence. He turned his head, and their eyes met. His expression shifted from pleasure to shock to panic in a matter of seconds. He scrambled off Melissa, grabbing at the sheets to cover himself.

"Ava... I... it's not what it looks like," he stammered, but the guilt in his eyes told her everything she needed to know.

Melissa, equally panicked, tried to cover herself with the pillow, her face flushed with shame and fear. "Ava, I—"

"Don't," Ava choked out, finding her voice at last. The single word cut through the air like a knife, silencing whatever pathetic excuses they were about to offer. Her hands clenched into fists at her sides, her whole body trembling with rage and heartbreak.

"How could you?" Ava whispered, her voice thick with emotion. She felt as though the world was crumbling beneath her feet. Everything she had believed in, everything she had built with Derek, was gone in an instant. "How could you do this to me?"

Derek stumbled over his words, trying to explain, trying to reach out to her, but Ava recoiled from his touch. The sight of his face, the same face she had kissed so many times, now filled her with disgust. "Don't you dare touch me!"

She turned to Melissa, her best friend, her confidante, the person she had trusted most in the world next to Derek. "How long?" she demanded, her voice breaking. "How long has this been going on?"

Melissa's eyes filled with tears, and she shook her head, unable to meet Ava's gaze. "It was a mistake, Ava, I swear... it just happened..."

"A mistake?" Ava repeated, her voice rising. "You call this a mistake? How long, Melissa?"

When Melissa didn't answer, Ava felt something inside her snap. The betrayal cut deeper than she could have ever imagined. "I trusted you! Both of you! And this is how you repay me?"

"Ava, please," Derek pleaded, trying to stand, but the sheet tangled around his legs, making him stumble. He looked pathetic, scrambling for some kind of explanation that could make this right, but there was nothing he could say to erase what had just happened.

"Save it," Ava spat, her eyes burning with unshed tears. "There's nothing you can say that will make this okay. You've destroyed everything."

The words hung in the air, heavy and final. Ava looked at the two people who had meant everything to her, and all she felt was a cold, hollow emptiness. This was the end—of her relationship, of her friendship, of the life she had envisioned for herself.

Without another word, Ava turned on her heel and walked out of the bedroom, her movements stiff and mechanical. She grabbed her things from the kitchen counter, barely aware of what she was doing, and headed for the door.

Ava burst out of Derek's apartment, tears streaming down her face as she stumbled into the hallway. Her heart pounded in her chest, each beat echoing the pain and betrayal she had just witnessed. She felt like she was suffocating, like the walls were closing in around her, and she needed to escape—needed to get away from the place where her life had just come crashing down.

She barely noticed the doorman's concerned look as she hurried out of the building and onto the busy Manhattan street. The city's noise and movement felt overwhelming, disorienting her further. She didn't know where she was going; she just needed to get away from the scene she had left behind.

A cab pulled up to the curb, and without thinking, Ava flagged it down. She climbed into the back seat, her hands shaking as she struggled to give the driver her address. Her voice was barely a whisper, choked with emotion.

As the cab pulled away, Ava pressed her forehead against the cool glass of the window, watching the city blur past her. The tears continued to flow, and she made no attempt to stop them. The pain was too much, too raw to hold back.

Her mind replayed the scene over and over, each replay more unbearable than the last. She couldn't understand how everything had gone so wrong, so fast. How could Derek, the man she had loved and trusted, betray her so completely? And with Melissa, of all people? The one person she had counted on to stand by her side through everything?

The questions swirled in her mind, but there were no answers—only the cold, hard reality that her life as she knew it was over.

When Ava finally arrived at her apartment, she felt like a ghost moving through the familiar space. The rooms were dark and silent, but the wedding decorations scattered throughout stood as cruel reminders of what was supposed to be the happiest time of her life. Now, they felt like mocking symbols of her shattered dreams.

She dropped her bags by the door and walked to the living room, collapsing onto the couch. For a long time, she just sat there in the dark, staring at nothing, her mind blank. She felt numb, as if the pain was too much for her to fully process.

Days passed, but Ava barely noticed. The weight of what she had seen pressed down on her, suffocating her. She knew she couldn't stay here, surrounded by the remnants of a future that no longer existed. She had called her wedding planner to cancel the wedding but she couldn't face anyone else, not her family, not her friends. She couldn't bear the thought of explaining what had happened, of seeing their pitying looks and hearing their well-meaning but empty words of comfort.

She needed to get away—far away from everything and everyone. Ava glanced around the room, her eyes landing on the stack of brochures for her honeymoon that she had left on the coffee table. Phuket, Thailand. The trip was supposed to be a romantic getaway with Derek, a celebration of their new life together. Now, it felt like an escape route, a way to distance herself from the pain and betrayal that had consumed her world.

Without giving herself time to second-guess, Ava made the decision. She would go to Phuket alone. It wasn't the honeymoon she had planned, but it was a chance to clear her mind, to figure out what to do next. Maybe some distance would help her make sense of the mess her life had become. Maybe it would give her the strength to face the future, whatever that might look like.

With renewed determination, Ava stood up and began packing. She moved through her apartment like a woman possessed, grabbing clothes, toiletries, and anything else she thought she might need. She threw everything into a suitcase with little care for organization. Her only focus was on getting out as quickly as possible.

As she packed, her emotions began to catch up with her. The numbness faded, replaced by a mix of anger and sorrow that threatened to overwhelm her. She tried to push the feelings down, to focus on the task at hand, but it was impossible to keep them at bay. Every item she packed felt like a reminder of the life she had lost—the life she had thought was just beginning.

Finally, Ava zipped up the suitcase and set it by the door. She took a deep breath, trying to steady herself. There was one last thing she needed to do before she could leave. She walked over to the counter where she had left her engagement ring earlier. The sight of it now made her stomach turn. What had once been a symbol of love and commitment was now a cruel joke, a reminder of the lies she had believed.

Ava picked up the ring, her fingers trembling as she held it in her palm. She stared at it for a long moment, then with a decisive motion, she placed it in a small jewelry box and shoved it into a drawer. She couldn't bring herself to throw it away—at least not yet—but she couldn't bear to look at it anymore, either.

With that final act, Ava felt a sense of closure, however small. She grabbed her suitcase and headed out the door, not looking back.

The airport was a whirlwind of activity as Ava moved through the crowd, her suitcase trailing behind her. The noise, the bright lights, the rush of people coming and going—it all felt surreal, like she was moving through a dream. She had changed her flight online just an hour ago, barely paying attention to the details. All she knew was that she needed to get on that plane and leave everything behind.

As she stood in line to check in, Ava's mind wandered. She couldn't stop thinking about Derek and Melissa, about how they had looked at her with guilt and shame written all over their faces. She couldn't stop hearing their voices, their pathetic attempts at excuses. The pain was still raw, but underneath it was a growing sense of anger—anger at them for betraying her, and anger at herself for not seeing it sooner.

She finally reached the counter and handed over her passport, her hands still trembling slightly. The airline agent smiled at her, asking the usual questions, but Ava barely registered them. She nodded and answered automatically, her thoughts still far away. After what felt like an eternity, she was given her boarding pass and directed to the security line.

The process of going through security was a blur. Ava moved through the motions, taking off her shoes, placing her belongings in the bins, and walking through the scanner. Her mind was on autopilot, focused only on getting to the gate. The weight of everything that had happened pressed down on her, making each step feel heavy and deliberate.

Finally, she reached her gate and found a seat in the crowded waiting area. She dropped her suitcase at her feet and sat down heavily, resting her head in her hands. The reality of what she was doing began to sink in. She was leaving New York, leaving everything she knew, and heading halfway around the world to a place she had never been before. The thought was both terrifying and strangely liberating.

Ava closed her eyes, trying to shut out the noise of the airport and the chaos of her thoughts. She took a deep breath, focusing on the feeling of the air filling her lungs, then slowly exhaling. She repeated the process a few times, trying to calm the storm of emotions swirling inside her.

She didn't know what awaited her in Phuket, but at that moment, it didn't matter. All that mattered was that she was getting away, that she was taking control of her life again—even if just for a little while.

When the boarding announcement came over the loudspeaker, Ava stood up and joined the line to board the plane. She handed her boarding pass to the flight attendant, who smiled and welcomed her aboard. Ava managed a weak smile in return, though it didn't reach her eyes.

She made her way down the jet bridge and onto the plane, finding her seat near the window. As she settled in, she glanced out at the runway, the city she had called home for her entire life stretching out in the distance. The city that now held nothing but painful memories.

As the plane began to taxi down the runway, Ava felt a strange mix of emotions. There was fear, yes—fear of the unknown, of what lay ahead. But there was also a sense of hope, a small glimmer of light in the darkness. Maybe, just maybe, this trip would help her heal. Maybe it would give her the strength she needed to move forward.

As the plane lifted off the ground, Ava closed her eyes, letting the hum of the engines lull her into a state of uneasy calm. She knew she was leaving one life behind, but what waited for her on the other side of the world was still a mystery.

The thought both frightened and excited her, and as she drifted off to sleep, she whispered to herself, "One step at a time, Ava. One step at a time."

And with that, she left New York—and everything it represented—far behind.

20

Chapter 2

The plane touched down on the tarmac with a gentle bump, and Ava Sinclair opened her eyes, momentarily disoriented. The announcement crackled over the intercom in both Thai and English, welcoming passengers to Phuket International Airport. She glanced out the window, seeing the runway bathed in the warm, golden light of the setting sun. The sky was painted in shades of orange and pink, a beautiful contrast to the heavy emotions weighing down her heart.

She had been in a daze since leaving New York, the long flight a blur of sleepless hours and too many thoughts. Now, as the plane taxied toward the terminal, the reality of her situation began to sink in. She was here, halfway around the world, in a place where no one knew her, where she could be alone with her thoughts and perhaps, eventually, find some semblance of peace.

As the passengers began to disembark, Ava slowly gathered her belongings, her movements mechanical. She slung her carry-on bag over her shoulder and stepped into the aisle, following the line of travelers as they made their way toward the exit. The air was thick with anticipation—everyone around her seemed eager to begin their vacations, their voices filled with excitement as they chattered about their plans. Ava felt like an outsider, detached from the joy that seemed to surround her.

Stepping off the plane, Ava was immediately hit by the heat and humidity of Thailand. It clung to her skin, making her feel slightly uncomfortable in her light sweater and jeans. She followed the signs toward immigration, moving with the crowd but feeling utterly alone. The unfamiliar sights and sounds only heightened her sense of displacement. Everything was foreign—this was a place where she didn't belong, at least not yet.

After what felt like an eternity, Ava finally made it through customs and collected her luggage. She pulled her suitcase behind her, navigating the busy terminal as she searched for the exit. The airport was bustling with activity, a chaotic mix of travelers, families, and staff hurrying in every direction. The signs were in both Thai and English, but Ava still felt disoriented, as if she had stepped into a different world.

Outside the terminal, the noise level seemed to rise even higher. Taxis and buses lined the curb, drivers calling out to potential passengers. Tourists milled about, some looking lost, others confidently heading toward their destinations. Ava hesitated, unsure of what to do next. She had arranged for a car from the resort to pick her up, but she had no idea where to find it.

As she stood there, trying to get her bearings, a young man in a crisp white uniform approached her. He held a sign with her name on it, and his smile was warm and welcoming.

"Miss Sinclair?" he asked, his English accented but clear.

"Yes, that's me," Ava replied, relieved that she didn't have to figure this out on her own.

"Welcome to Phuket," the man said, bowing slightly. "I'm here to take you to the resort. Please follow me."

Ava nodded, grateful for his assistance. She followed him to a sleek black sedan parked a short distance away. The driver opened the door for her, and she slid into the cool, air-conditioned interior, immediately feeling a bit more at ease. The driver loaded her luggage into the trunk and then got behind the wheel.

As the car pulled away from the airport, Ava leaned back against the seat, staring out the window at the passing scenery. The road wound through lush green hills, with glimpses of the ocean sparkling in the distance. The beauty of the island was undeniable, but Ava couldn't fully appreciate it. Her mind was still too consumed by the events of the past few days, the betrayal that had shattered her life.

She closed her eyes, trying to block out the memories, but they came rushing back with painful clarity. The sight of Derek and Melissa entwined in her bed, their moans filling the room, the look of shock and guilt on their faces when they realized they had been caught. The emotions she had tried to suppress during the flight—anger, sorrow, disbelief—came flooding back, and Ava felt tears pricking at the corners of her eyes.

No, she told herself firmly. This is why you're here. To get away from it all. To forget.

But forgetting was easier said than done.

The car ride seemed to last forever, though it was probably no more than an hour. The sun had dipped below the horizon by the time they arrived at the resort, leaving the sky a deep shade of purple. As the car turned onto a long, winding driveway, Ava caught her first glimpse of the resort.

It was breathtaking.

The resort was nestled among towering palm trees, with the main building designed in a blend of traditional Thai and modern architectural styles. Soft lighting illuminated the pathways, and the sound of trickling water from nearby fountains added to the serene atmosphere. The entrance was grand, with wide steps leading up to a large open-air lobby that overlooked the ocean. Ava could just make out the silhouettes of other buildings and villas scattered throughout the property, connected by winding paths and lush gardens.

The car came to a stop at the entrance, and the driver quickly got out to open Ava's door. She stepped out, feeling a slight breeze on her face as she took in her surroundings. This was everything she had imagined for her honeymoon—a paradise where she and Derek would have started their new life together. Now, the beauty of the place only served as a painful reminder of what she had lost.

"Welcome to the Orchid Resort," the driver said with a smile. "Your luggage will be brought to your room. Please proceed to the reception desk to check in."

"Thank you," Ava murmured, managing a small smile in return.

She made her way up the steps and into the lobby, where she was greeted by a friendly receptionist. The check-in process was smooth and efficient, with the staff providing her with all the information she needed for her stay. They explained the resort's amenities, dining options, and activities, but Ava barely registered their words. Her mind was elsewhere, lost in a sea of emotions she couldn't escape.

After receiving her room key, Ava was escorted to her suite by another staff member. The walk through the resort was peaceful, with only the sound of crickets and the distant waves breaking the silence. The path was lined with flowering bushes and lanterns that cast a soft, warm glow on the ground. Ava followed in silence, feeling the weight of her exhaustion settle over her like a heavy blanket.

The suite was located in one of the resort's private villas, tucked away from the main building. It was everything Ava had dreamed of—a spacious, elegantly decorated room with a king-sized bed draped in mosquito netting, a seating area with plush sofas, and a large bathroom with a deep soaking tub. The sliding glass doors led out to a private terrace with a plunge pool and a view of the ocean.

Ava stepped inside, her eyes taking in every detail. The room was filled with thoughtful touches—a vase of fresh flowers on the table, a bottle of chilled champagne, and a handwritten note welcoming her to the resort. The honeymoon package, she realized, meant for a couple, not for someone who had just had her heart broken.

The staff member who had escorted her set down the keycard on the dresser and smiled warmly. "If you need anything, Miss Sinclair, please don't hesitate to call the front desk. We're here to make your stay as comfortable as possible."

"Thank you," Ava replied, trying to keep the emotion out of her voice.

The door closed softly behind him, leaving Ava alone in the quiet of her suite. She stood there for a moment, feeling a strange mix of awe and sadness. This place was supposed to be the start of her new life. But now, standing there in that beautiful room, she felt more alone than ever.

Ava sat on the edge of the bed, her body heavy with fatigue. She knew she should unpack, but the thought of opening her suitcase and seeing the clothes she had packed for her honeymoon—dresses meant for romantic dinners, swimsuits for lounging by the pool with Derek—was too much to bear.

Instead, she got up and walked over to the sliding glass doors, pulling them open to let in the night air. The sound of the ocean filled the room, a soothing rhythm that helped to calm her racing thoughts. She stepped out onto the terrace, the cool breeze brushing against her skin as she gazed out at the moonlit water.

The view was stunning. The ocean stretched out before her, its surface glittering under the light of the full moon. The sky was clear, and the stars seemed to shine brighter here than they ever had in New York. It was peaceful, a world away from the chaos she had left behind.

But the beauty of the scene did little to ease the ache in her chest. Ava wrapped her arms around herself, feeling the tears welling up again. She had come here to escape, but there was no escaping the pain. It was with her, no matter where she went.

She turned and walked back into the suite, closing the doors behind her. The room was dimly lit, the only light coming from the bedside lamps. Ava felt an overwhelming urge to do something, anything, to distract herself from her thoughts. She glanced at the bottle of champagne on the table, but the idea of drinking alone didn't appeal to her.

Instead, she went to the bathroom and turned on the taps, filling the tub with hot water. The steam filled the room, and the scent of the bath salts she added was soothing, a blend of lavender and eucalyptus that promised a brief escape from the turmoil in her mind. Ava stripped off her travel-worn clothes, letting them fall to the floor in a heap, and stepped into the tub. The hot water enveloped her, easing the tension in her muscles as she sank down, closing her eyes.

For a few moments, Ava allowed herself to simply be, focusing on the warmth of the water, the soft flicker of candlelight she had lit on the counter, and the gentle sound of the ocean outside. But even here, in this serene environment, her thoughts kept circling back to Derek and Melissa. The image of them together, the raw intensity of their betrayal, replayed in her mind like a cruel movie she couldn't turn off.

Ava tried to push the thoughts away, to focus on the here and now, but it was impossible. The pain was too fresh, too deep. She had loved Derek—trusted him—and he had destroyed everything they had built together. The anger bubbled up again, hot and fierce, mixing with the sadness that threatened to overwhelm her.

She let out a shaky breath, feeling the tears she had been holding back start to spill over. They mingled with the bathwater, unnoticed as Ava allowed herself to cry, the sobs wracking her body in the privacy of the bathroom. It was the first time she had truly let herself break down since she had caught them, and the release was both painful and necessary.

She cried until there were no more tears left, until the water had cooled and her body felt drained of all energy. Only then did she pull herself out of the tub, wrapping a towel around her as she stared at her reflection in the mirror. Her eyes were red and puffy, her face pale, but there was something else there too—determination.

Ava knew she couldn't keep going like this, letting the pain consume her. She had come to Phuket to escape, to heal, and that's what she needed to focus on now. She wasn't sure how, but she was determined to find a way to move forward, even if it meant starting over completely.

With that resolve, Ava dried off and changed into a light sundress. The fabric felt cool and soft against her skin, a small comfort in the otherwise overwhelming loneliness she felt. She wasn't ready to sleep, not yet. The thought of lying in that massive bed, alone and surrounded by memories of what was supposed to be, was too much.

Instead, she decided to go for a walk, hoping that the fresh air would help clear her mind. She slipped on a pair of sandals, grabbed her room key, and stepped out into the warm night.

The resort was quiet at this hour, most of the other guests either asleep or tucked away in their rooms. The pathways were lit by lanterns, casting a soft, golden glow on the surrounding foliage. Ava walked slowly, taking in the sounds of the night—the distant hum of crickets, the rustle of leaves in the breeze, the ever-present whisper of the ocean.

She followed the path that led down to the beach, her footsteps light on the sand as she approached the water's edge. The beach was nearly empty, save for a few couples strolling hand in hand in the distance. Ava kept to herself, letting the cool sand sift between her toes as she walked along the shoreline.

The ocean stretched out before her, vast and endless, the waves rolling gently onto the shore. The moon hung low in the sky, its reflection shimmering on the water's surface. It was a beautiful night, peaceful and calm, a stark contrast to the storm raging inside Ava's heart.

She walked aimlessly, lost in thought, trying to make sense of everything that had happened. The questions kept swirling in her mind, each one more painful than the last. Why hadn't she seen the signs? How long had Derek and Melissa been lying to her? What had she done to deserve this?

But there were no answers, only the cold, hard reality of her situation. She had left everything behind—her life, her friends, her plans for the future—and now she was here, in a place that was supposed to be paradise, feeling more lost and alone than ever.

Ava stopped walking and stared out at the ocean, the waves lapping gently at her feet. She wrapped her arms around herself, trying to ward off the chill that had nothing to do with the temperature. She was so tired of feeling this way—so tired of the sadness, the anger, the emptiness. She wanted to feel something else, anything else, but she didn't know how.

As she stood there, lost in her thoughts, Ava noticed a figure in the distance, near the far end of the beach where the resort's lights didn't reach.

The area was darker, more secluded, with the shadows of palm trees swaying gently in the breeze. She squinted, trying to make out who it was, but the figure was too far away to see clearly.

A strange feeling of curiosity washed over her, mixed with a hint of wariness. It was late, and she was alone on a beach in a foreign country. She knew she should probably turn back, return to the safety of her suite, but something about the figure intrigued her. There was an air of calm and confidence in the way they stood, their silhouette outlined against the backdrop of the ocean.

As Ava hesitated, the figure began to move toward her, stepping out of the shadows and into the moonlight. She could see now that it was a man, tall and broad-shouldered, with a strong, commanding presence. He was dressed casually in a light shirt and pants, his hands in his pockets as he walked slowly, almost leisurely, along the shore.

Ava's heart began to race, a mix of nervousness and something else she couldn't quite place. She wasn't sure if she should feel threatened or intrigued. The man didn't seem dangerous—at least, not in the way she had expected. There was something about the way he moved, the way he carried himself, that made her feel both cautious and drawn to him.

When he was close enough, the man stopped, his gaze meeting hers. Ava's breath caught in her throat as she took in his features. He was strikingly handsome, with sharp, chiseled features and piercing eyes that seemed to see right through her. His hair was dark, slightly tousled by the breeze, and there was a hint of stubble on his jaw. Everything about him exuded confidence and control.

"Good evening," he said, his voice deep and smooth, with a slight Russian accent that Ava found captivating. There was a hint of a smile on his lips, but his expression was otherwise unreadable.

"Good evening," Ava replied, her voice barely above a whisper. She felt a strange flutter in her chest, a mix of anxiety and something else—something that made her feel alive in a way she hadn't in days.

The man's smile widened slightly, and he took a step closer, though he maintained a respectful distance. "What brings you out to the beach so late at night?" he asked, his tone casual but with an undercurrent of curiosity.

Ava hesitated, unsure of how much she wanted to reveal to this stranger. But there was something about him that made her want to open up, to share the pain she had been carrying alone. "I couldn't sleep," she admitted, her voice soft. "I thought a walk might help clear my head."

He nodded, as if he understood. "It's a beautiful night for a walk," he said, glancing out at the ocean. "The moon is especially bright tonight."

Ava followed his gaze, the waves glistening under the moonlight. "Yes, it is," she agreed, feeling a little more at ease.

The man turned back to her, his eyes locking onto hers. "My name is Nikolai," he said, his voice low and smooth. "And you are?"

"Ava," she replied, feeling a strange sense of vulnerability as she spoke her name.

"A pleasure to meet you, Ava," Nikolai said, his voice like a warm caress. "Are you staying at the resort?"

"Yes," Ava said, nodding. "I just arrived today."

"Ah, a newcomer to paradise," Nikolai said, his smile widening. "I hope you find what you're looking for here."

Ava wasn't sure what to make of his words. There was something almost teasing in his tone, as if he knew more about her than he was letting on. But she found herself wanting to know more about him, too. There was an air of mystery about him, something that both intrigued and unsettled her.

"What about you?" Ava asked, trying to shift the focus away from herself. "Are you staying at the resort as well?"

Nikolai's smile didn't waver, but there was a flicker of something in his eyes—something dark and guarded. "I'm here on business," he said, his tone still casual but with a hint of something more. "But I like to take advantage of the peaceful nights when I can."

Ava nodded, though she couldn't shake the feeling that there was more to his story than he was letting on. But she didn't press him. There was a part of her that was content to let the mystery linger, to enjoy the strange connection she felt with this man she had just met.

They continued talking, the conversation flowing easily despite the tension that lingered in the air. Nikolai was charming, attentive, and seemed genuinely interested in what Ava had to say. He asked her about her travels, her life back in New York, and even the reasons that had brought her to Phuket—questions that were both casual and probing. Ava found herself opening up more than she intended, sharing snippets of her life with a stranger who seemed to listen more closely than anyone had in a long time.

"I was supposed to be here on my honeymoon," Ava said softly, the words slipping out before she could stop them. She immediately regretted it, the pain of her broken engagement still too raw, too close to the surface.

Nikolai's expression didn't change, but there was a softness in his gaze, a subtle shift in his demeanor that told her he understood. "And yet, here you are alone," he said, his voice low, almost a whisper against the sound of the waves. "That must be difficult."

Ava nodded, biting her lip to keep the tears at bay. She hadn't wanted to admit it, hadn't wanted to appear vulnerable in front of a stranger, but there was something about Nikolai that made her feel safe, even in her sadness.

"It is," she admitted, her voice trembling slightly. "But I needed to get away, to clear my head and figure out what to do next."

Nikolai studied her for a moment, his gaze intense but not judgmental. "Sometimes, distance is the only way to find clarity," he said. "To see things for what they really are."

His words resonated with her, striking a chord deep within. Ava nodded again, grateful for his understanding. There was something comforting about Nikolai's presence, something that made her feel like she wasn't as alone as she had thought.

They continued walking along the beach, the conversation shifting to lighter topics. Nikolai spoke of his travels, the places he had seen, and the people he had met. His stories were captivating, and Ava found herself drawn into his world, momentarily forgetting her own troubles.

But as they neared the resort once more, the weight of reality began to settle over her again. The night was coming to an end, and with it, the temporary reprieve she had found in Nikolai's company.

The path leading back to the resort was quiet, the only sound the gentle rustling of palm leaves in the breeze. The lights from the resort were now visible in the distance, casting a soft glow on the surroundings. As they approached the entrance to Ava's suite, an awkward silence fell between them, the charged energy of their earlier conversation lingering in the air.

Ava hesitated at the door, unsure of what to say or do. Nikolai had been a welcome distraction, but she wasn't ready to let go of the connection they had formed, however fleeting it might be. Yet, she also knew that she was standing on the precipice of something unknown—something that both intrigued and frightened her.

Nikolai stopped a few feet away from her, his hands still in his pockets, his gaze steady and unreadable. There was a moment of hesitation, a brief pause where neither of them moved or spoke. The tension between them crackled, palpable and intense.

"You've had a long day," Nikolai said finally, his voice low and measured. "You should get some rest."

Ava nodded, though she couldn't help but feel a pang of disappointment. She didn't want the night to end, didn't want to return to the solitude of her suite. But she knew he was right. She was exhausted, emotionally and physically, and she needed time to process everything that had happened.

"Thank you," she said softly, her hand resting on the door handle. "For the walk, and for listening."

Nikolai inclined his head, a small smile playing at the corners of his lips. "It was my pleasure, Ava," he replied, his tone warm and sincere. "Perhaps we'll meet again."

Ava wasn't sure if that was an invitation or simply a polite farewell, but she found herself hoping it was the former. There was something about Nikolai that intrigued her, something that made her want to know more, even if she couldn't quite put her finger on what it was.

"Perhaps," she said, her own smile tentative. She turned the key in the lock and pushed the door open, stepping inside the cool, dark room. She paused in the doorway, glancing back at Nikolai one last time. He was watching her, his expression still unreadable, his presence commanding even in silence.

"Goodnight, Nikolai," she said softly.

"Goodnight, Ava," he replied, his voice a soft rumble in the night air.

With that, Ava closed the door behind her, leaning against it for a moment as she let out a breath she hadn't realized she'd been holding. Her heart was still racing, the encounter with Nikolai leaving her both exhilarated and unsettled. She hadn't expected to feel this way, hadn't expected to be drawn to a stranger so quickly, especially after everything she had been through.

But there was no denying the connection she felt, no matter how fleeting it might have been. Nikolai was different—different from anyone she had ever met. There was a darkness about him, a depth that intrigued her even as it made her cautious. She knew she should be careful, knew that diving into something new so soon after her heartbreak might not be the best idea.

But as she climbed into bed, pulling the soft sheets around her, Ava couldn't stop thinking about him. His voice, his eyes, the way he seemed to see right through her—all of it lingered in her mind, refusing to be ignored.

She fell asleep with thoughts of Nikolai swirling in her head, her dreams filled with images of the dark, mysterious man who had walked with her under the moonlit sky. And as sleep finally claimed her, she couldn't help but wonder if their paths would cross again.

Chapter 3

Nikolai Volkov sat in the darkness of his private villa, the cool glass of whiskey held loosely in his hand as he stared out at the moonlit ocean. The waves crashed rhythmically against the shore, their soothing sound doing little to calm the turbulence in his mind. He should have been focused on the business at hand—the deal that had brought him to Phuket, the negotiations that needed to be finalized, and the ever-present threat of rivals looking for any sign of weakness.

But instead, his thoughts kept circling back to her.

Ava.

He hadn't expected to meet someone like her here. He hadn't expected to meet someone who could distract him so completely from his carefully controlled world. Yet there she was, slipping into his thoughts with the ease of someone who belonged there, despite everything that told him otherwise.

He took a slow sip of his whiskey, savoring the burn as it slid down his throat. Ava was different from the women he was used to. She had a softness, a vulnerability that intrigued him. When they had walked along the beach, the sadness in her eyes had called to something deep within him, something he had thought long buried. She was hurting, that much was clear, but there was also a strength to her—a resilience that he found unexpectedly captivating.

Nikolai leaned back in his chair, the leather creaking softly under his weight. He knew better than to let himself get too involved, especially with someone outside of his world. His life was dangerous, full of secrets and shadows. The people he surrounded himself with were all too aware of the risks, and they had made their choices. Ava was different. She was an innocent, and his attraction to her could only lead to complications—complications he didn't need.

Yet, he couldn't deny the pull he felt toward her. There was something about Ava that had gotten under his skin, something that made him want to know more about her, despite the voice in his head warning him to keep his distance.

He drained the rest of his whiskey and set the glass down on the table beside him. The ice clinked softly as it settled, the sound almost lost in the night. Nikolai stared at the glass for a moment, his thoughts shifting to the business that had brought him to Phuket. He had come here to finalize a deal with a local politician—a deal that would expand his influence in Southeast Asia and secure his position as the head of the Volkov Bratva. It was a delicate operation, one that required his full attention.

But now, with Ava in the picture, he found it harder to focus.

Nikolai stood and walked over to the large windows that opened onto the balcony. He pushed them open, stepping out into the warm night air. The villa was situated on a hill overlooking the ocean, offering a stunning view of the water stretching out to meet the horizon. The sky was clear, the stars bright against the inky blackness, and the breeze carried the faint scent of salt and tropical flowers.

He rested his hands on the railing, his gaze fixed on the distant waves. The resort was quiet at this hour, most of the guests asleep or enjoying the nightlife elsewhere. The Russian language was everywhere here—in the menus, the signs, the conversations of the expats who had made Phuket their home. It was a reminder of the world he came from, the world he still controlled from afar.

Phuket had become a haven for those fleeing the chaos of Russia, especially after the war with Ukraine had begun. Wealthy Russians had poured into the island, bringing their money and influence with them. It was one of the reasons Nikolai had chosen this place for the meeting. It was familiar territory, a place where he could move with relative ease, blending into the expatriate community without drawing too much attention.

But even in this sanctuary, danger was never far away. Nikolai knew that his enemies were always watching, always waiting for an opportunity to strike. He had built his empire on a foundation of power and ruthlessness, and he had no illusions about the lengths others would go to in order to bring him down.

He turned away from the ocean, his thoughts returning to Ava. She was a distraction, yes, but she was also something more. Nikolai wasn't sure what it was that drew him to her—her vulnerability, her beauty, or perhaps the way she had looked at him with those sad, questioning eyes. Whatever it was, it had left an impression on him, one that he couldn't easily shake.

Nikolai knew he should forget about her, focus on the deal that needed to be closed and the threats that needed to be neutralized. But the thought of Ava lingered in his mind, a persistent presence that refused to be ignored.

The following morning, the villa was bathed in the soft light of dawn. Nikolai stood in front of the large mirror in his bedroom, adjusting the cuffs of his tailored shirt. The suit he had chosen was a deep charcoal gray, impeccably cut to fit his muscular frame. Every detail was perfect, from the polished shoes to the silk tie. Nikolai understood the importance of appearance—it was a tool, just like any other, in his arsenal of power.

As he fastened the cufflinks, his thoughts drifted back to the meeting scheduled for later that day.

The politician he was set to meet was a key player in the region, someone who could open doors that would otherwise remain closed. The man had connections, influence, and most importantly, a price. Nikolai knew that everyone had a price; it was simply a matter of finding it.

His phone buzzed on the nightstand, breaking the silence. Nikolai picked it up, his eyes narrowing as he read the message from Viktor, his second-in-command.

Viktor: Deal confirmed for noon. Intel suggests possible interference from the Petrov faction. Security is in place, but we need to stay vigilant.

Nikolai's jaw tightened. The Petrov faction had been a thorn in his side for years, always looking for a way to undermine his operations. They were ambitious, ruthless, and dangerously unpredictable. The fact that they had intel on this meeting was troubling, but not entirely unexpected.

Nikolai typed a quick response.

Nikolai: Understood. Double the security at the venue. No mistakes.

He set the phone down, his mind already calculating the possible scenarios. The meeting was crucial, and he couldn't afford any disruptions. The Petrov faction might try something, but Nikolai was confident in his ability to handle whatever they threw his way. He had been in this business long enough to know that threats were part of the game, and he played to win.

Yet, even as he prepared for the day ahead, his thoughts kept returning to Ava. He wondered what she was doing, if she was thinking about him as much as he was thinking about her. It was a foolish distraction, one that he couldn't afford, but the more he tried to push her from his mind, the more she seemed to cling to his thoughts.

With a final glance in the mirror, Nikolai turned and left the bedroom, ready to face whatever the day would bring.

***

The living area of the villa was spacious and elegantly decorated, with high ceilings and large windows that let in the morning light. Viktor was already there, waiting for Nikolai with his usual stoic expression. He was dressed in a dark suit, his broad shoulders and solid frame giving him an imposing presence. Viktor had been with Nikolai for years, and their relationship was built on trust, loyalty, and a shared understanding of the brutal world they inhabited.

"Morning," Viktor greeted as Nikolai entered the room. His voice was deep, with a slight gravelly edge that came from years of barking orders and making threats.

"Morning," Nikolai replied, nodding as he approached the table where Viktor had spread out a map of the city and a folder of documents.

Viktor got straight to the point, as always. "The venue is secure, but I've increased the number of men on site. The Petrov faction's presence here complicates things, but we're ready for any interference."

Nikolai studied the map, his eyes narrowing as he considered the layout. The restaurant where the meeting would take place was strategically chosen—discreet, with multiple exits and a private room that offered both luxury and security. It was a favorite among the Russian expat community, known for its fine dining and discretion. But with the Petrov faction in play, nothing could be left to chance.

"Good," Nikolai said, his tone measured. "We can't afford any mistakes. This deal is too important."

Viktor nodded, but there was a hint of hesitation in his eyes, something that Nikolai didn't miss. "There's something else," Viktor said, his voice lowering slightly. "You seem... distracted."

Nikolai stiffened, his gaze snapping to Viktor's. "I'm focused on the task at hand," he replied, his tone cold. "Nothing more."

Viktor didn't back down. He was one of the few people who could challenge Nikolai without fear of reprisal. "Is it the woman you met last night?" Viktor asked, his voice carefully neutral. "Ava?"

Nikolai's eyes narrowed, a flash of annoyance crossing his features. Viktor had always been perceptive, too perceptive at times. "What about her?"

"You're letting her get to you," Viktor said, crossing his arms over his chest. "She's not part of our world, Nikolai. She's an outsider," Viktor continued, his voice steady but laced with concern. "Bringing her into your life, even for a brief distraction, could be dangerous. Not just for her, but for you as well."

Nikolai felt a surge of irritation at Viktor's words, but he couldn't entirely dismiss them. Viktor was right—Ava was an outsider, someone who had no idea about the darkness that surrounded him. But there was something about her that he couldn't ignore, something that pulled at him in a way he hadn't felt in years.

"I'm aware of the risks," Nikolai replied, his tone firm. "But she's just a woman, Viktor. She doesn't need to know anything about our business."

"And what happens if she does?" Viktor pressed. "What happens when she starts asking questions, when she gets too close? You know what's at stake, Nikolai. The Petrov faction isn't going to wait for you to deal with a personal complication. They're waiting for any sign of weakness."

Nikolai clenched his jaw, his frustration growing. Viktor was right—he knew that.

Viktor studied him for a moment, his expression unreadable. "Just be careful," he said finally, his voice softer. "I've seen what happens when people get too close to us. It doesn't end well."

Nikolai nodded, his mind already turning back to the business at hand. "I'll handle it," he said, the conversation effectively closed. "Now, let's focus on the deal."

Viktor gave a curt nod, understanding that the subject was dropped for now. He turned his attention back to the map and the details of the meeting, but Nikolai could tell that his second-in-command wasn't entirely convinced.

***

The upscale restaurant was located in a quiet corner of Phuket, away from the bustling tourist areas. It was the kind of place that catered to the wealthy and powerful, with private dining rooms and a reputation for discretion. The interior was dimly lit, with dark wood accents and plush furnishings that exuded luxury. It was a place where deals were made and secrets were kept.

Nikolai arrived at the restaurant shortly before noon, his senses on high alert. Viktor and a few of his trusted men had already secured the area, blending in with the other diners while keeping a close watch on the entrances and exits. The tension in the air was palpable, but Nikolai remained calm, his expression unreadable as he was led to the private dining room at the back.

The politician was already there, seated at the head of the table, a glass of expensive wine in hand. He was a middle-aged man with thinning hair and a paunch that spoke of a life of indulgence. His suit was well-tailored, but there was something oily about him, a sense of corruption that clung to him like a second skin.

"Nikolai," the politician greeted with a slick smile, standing to shake his hand. "I'm glad you could make it."

"Minister," Nikolai replied, his voice cool as he took the man's hand. The handshake was firm, calculated—neither too strong nor too weak. A show of respect, but not submission.

They took their seats, and the door to the private room was closed, sealing them off from the rest of the restaurant. The waitstaff brought in a selection of dishes, each more decadent than the last, but Nikolai barely glanced at the food. He was here for business, not pleasure.

The conversation began politely enough, with the minister making small talk about the island, the influx of Russian expatriates, and the economic opportunities that had arisen as a result. But Nikolai knew this was all prelude, a dance of words meant to soften the ground before the real negotiations began.

Finally, the minister leaned back in his chair, his smile slipping slightly as he got to the point. "As you know, the arrangement we're discussing is mutually beneficial," he said, his tone carefully measured. "But I believe there's room for further negotiation on the terms."

Nikolai raised an eyebrow, his expression betraying nothing. "Further negotiation?" he asked, his voice smooth but with an edge that warned against pushing too far. "I was under the impression that the terms had already been agreed upon."

The minister chuckled, a sound that grated on Nikolai's nerves. "You know how these things are, Nikolai," he said, waving a hand dismissively. "There are always last-minute adjustments, especially when new factors come into play."

"New factors?" Nikolai's tone was deceptively calm, but his eyes were cold as ice. He didn't like surprises, and he especially didn't like being played.

The minister leaned forward slightly, his smile widening. "The Petrov faction has been making some interesting offers," he said, his voice lowering as if they were sharing a secret. "They're very interested in the same opportunities you are, and they've shown a willingness to... sweeten the deal."

Nikolai felt a surge of anger, but he kept it tightly controlled. "And what is it they've offered you?" he asked, his voice deadly quiet.

"More," the minister said simply, his smile turning smug. "They've offered more. And in our line of work, more is always better, wouldn't you agree?"

Nikolai's expression didn't change, but his mind was already calculating the situation. The Petrov faction was trying to undercut him, to steal the deal out from under him by offering the minister a better price, more influence, more of everything. It was a bold move, but also a dangerous one. They were gambling that Nikolai wouldn't retaliate, that he would back down and let them take what they wanted.

They were wrong.

"I understand your position, Minister," Nikolai said, his tone smooth and controlled. "But I believe you've underestimated the value of what I'm offering. The Petrov faction may offer you more now, but they lack the stability and the reach that I can provide. Their influence is limited, their connections unreliable. What I offer you is not just more, but better."

The minister's smile faltered slightly, a flicker of uncertainty in his eyes. Nikolai pressed on, his voice low and commanding. "The Petrov faction is ambitious, yes, but ambition without a strong foundation is a recipe for disaster. You align yourself with them, and you risk losing everything when they inevitably fall. Align yourself with me, and you secure your position, your wealth, and your influence for the long term."

There was a long pause as the minister considered his words, the smugness slipping away as he realized the truth of what Nikolai was saying. The Petrov faction was powerful, but unstable, their reach not as deep as they wanted others to believe. Nikolai, on the other hand, had built his empire on a foundation of power, loyalty, and ruthless efficiency. He was a man who didn't make promises lightly, but when he did, he kept them.

Finally, the minister nodded, his expression serious. "You make a compelling case, Nikolai," he said, his tone respectful. "Perhaps I was too hasty in entertaining other offers. Let's proceed with the original terms."

Nikolai inclined his head, a small smile of satisfaction playing at the corners of his lips. "A wise decision, Minister," he said smoothly. "I look forward to our continued partnership."

The rest of the meeting proceeded without incident, the deal finalized and the terms agreed upon. But as they shook hands at the end, Nikolai knew that this wasn't the end of the Petrov faction's interference. They had made their move, and now it was his turn to respond.

Back at his villa later that evening, Nikolai poured himself another glass of whiskey and sat down on the balcony, his thoughts once again drifting to Ava. The deal had gone as planned, but the Petrov faction's attempt to undermine him had left him on edge. He knew they wouldn't stop—they were too hungry for power, too eager to expand their influence. It was only a matter of time before they tried something else.

But despite the tension of the day, it was Ava who occupied his thoughts. He couldn't stop thinking about her, about the way she had looked at him with those sad, searching eyes. There was something about her that drew him in, something that made him want to know more, to see her again.

Nikolai swirled the whiskey in his glass, watching the amber liquid catch the light. He knew he should let it go, focus on the business at hand, but the pull he felt toward Ava was too strong to ignore. It was more than just attraction—there was something about her that called to him, something that made him want to protect her, to pull her into his world despite the dangers.

He pulled out his phone, tempted to find out more about her. It would be easy—too easy, really. A few calls, a little digging, and he could know everything there was to know about Ava Sinclair. But he hesitated, his thumb hovering over the screen. He wasn't sure why he was hesitating—he had done this countless times before, gathering information on people who interested him or who posed a threat. But with Ava, it felt different. It felt wrong.

Nikolai set the phone down, his frustration mounting. He didn't like feeling this way—torn between his desire for control and the unpredictable pull of his emotions. Ava was a wild card, and Nikolai had never been one to gamble on unknowns. His life had been meticulously constructed, every piece carefully placed, every decision weighed and calculated. But Ava was different. She wasn't a piece on his chessboard—she was something, someone, entirely outside of his control. And that was both thrilling and terrifying.

He took another sip of whiskey, letting the warmth
spread through his chest as he tried to sort through
his conflicting emotions. This was a dangerous
game he was playing, and he knew it. Ava was not
like the women he was used to—women who
understood the rules, who knew what was expected
of them and who never crossed the lines he drew.
Ava didn't know those rules, and she had no
reason to follow them.

Nikolai stared out at the ocean, the dark waves
crashing against the shore, their rhythm almost
hypnotic. He could picture her now, walking along
the beach with the moonlight in her hair, her
sadness and vulnerability mingling with a quiet
strength that made her all the more captivating. It
was that strength that intrigued him the most. Ava
had been hurt, deeply, but she hadn't let it destroy
her. Instead, she had chosen to flee, to seek solace
in a place far from the source of her pain. That
decision, that resilience, drew him to her like a
moth to a flame.

But there was more to it than that. Nikolai knew he
was playing with fire, and yet he couldn't bring
himself to stop. The danger of it, the risk of bringing
her into his world, only made the pull stronger.
There was something exhilarating about the
thought of Ava in his life, of the possibility of
something real, something unscripted. He hadn't
allowed himself that kind of vulnerability in years,
and the idea of it both excited and unnerved him.

He could try to justify it by telling himself that it was just curiosity, that he was merely interested in her because she was different. But deep down, he knew it was more than that. Ava had gotten under his skin in a way that no one else had, and the more he tried to push her out of his mind, the more she seemed to take root there.

Nikolai set down his glass and ran a hand through his hair, frustrated by his own inability to control his thoughts. He wasn't a man who was easily swayed by emotions, and yet here he was, obsessing over a woman he had just met, a woman who had no place in his world. It was foolish, and he knew it. But it didn't matter.

He wanted to see her again.

The realization hit him with the force of a freight train, and Nikolai cursed under his breath. He couldn't afford this distraction, not now, not with the Petrov faction breathing down his neck and the deal hanging in the balance. But no matter how much he tried to convince himself that this was a bad idea, the desire to see Ava again was overwhelming.

He stood up abruptly, the decision made before he could talk himself out of it. He would see her again. Just once, he told himself. Just to satisfy his curiosity, to put these thoughts to rest. After that, he would focus on the deal, on the business that needed to be handled. Ava would be a fleeting distraction, nothing more.

But even as he made the decision, Nikolai knew it wouldn't be that simple. Ava had already gotten under his skin, and seeing her again would only deepen that connection. But the thought of walking away now, of never seeing her again, was unbearable. He had to see her. He had to know if the connection he felt was real, or if it was just a figment of his imagination.

Nikolai walked back inside the villa, the decision solidifying in his mind. He was going to pursue Ava, no matter the risks. He had spent his life calculating every move, weighing every decision against the potential consequences. But with Ava, he was willing to take the gamble. He was willing to risk the unknown.

He pulled out his phone again, this time with a clear purpose. His fingers moved quickly over the screen as he sent a message to Viktor.

Nikolai: Have someone discreetly find out more about Ava Sinclair. No deep dive, just the basics.

He hit send, knowing that Viktor would question the request but would follow through without hesitation. Viktor was loyal to a fault, and while he might not understand Nikolai's interest in Ava, he would do what was asked of him. Nikolai trusted him with his life, and in this moment, with something almost as valuable—his curiosity about Ava.

As he waited for the response, Nikolai paced the room, his mind racing. He knew this was a dangerous path he was heading down, but he couldn't stop himself. There was something about Ava that had hooked him, and he needed to know more. She was an enigma, a puzzle he couldn't quite solve, and he had always been drawn to challenges.

His phone buzzed with Viktor's reply.

Viktor: Understood. I'll have the information within the hour.

Nikolai felt a surge of anticipation, mixed with something he hadn't felt in a long time—excitement. The kind of excitement that came from not knowing what was going to happen next, from stepping into uncharted territory. It was dangerous, exhilarating, and completely unlike him.

As he waited for the information, Nikolai stepped out onto the balcony once more, the cool night air brushing against his skin. The ocean stretched out before him, vast and endless, much like the possibilities that lay ahead. He knew that pursuing Ava could complicate his life in ways he couldn't predict, but the thought of walking away from her, of letting her slip through his fingers, was something he couldn't bear.

She had sparked something inside him, something
he hadn't felt in years. It was a dangerous spark,
one that could ignite a fire that would consume
everything in its path. But Nikolai had always been
drawn to fire, to the heat and the risk that came
with it. He was a man who thrived on challenges,
and Ava was the most intriguing challenge he had
faced in a long time.

He stood on the balcony for what felt like hours, his
mind a whirlwind of thoughts and emotions. When
his phone finally buzzed again, signaling the arrival
of the information he had requested, Nikolai took a
deep breath before reading the message.

Viktor: Ava Sinclair. 23 years old. Originally from
New York City. No criminal record. Engaged until
recently to a Derek Thompson, broke off the
engagement last week. She's here in Phuket alone,
staying at the resort for what was supposed to be
her honeymoon.

The mention of her broken engagement made
something tighten in Nikolai's chest. So, that was it.
She had come here to escape the pain of a failed
relationship, to find solace in a place far from home.
He could understand that—he had seen enough
heartbreak in his life to recognize the signs. But
there was something more, something about Ava
that called to him in a way he couldn't explain.

Nikolai set the phone down, his decision made. He
was going to see her again, to pursue whatever it

was that had ignited between them. He didn't know where it would lead, but for once, he was willing to step into the unknown.

He wasn't sure what the future held, but he knew one thing for certain—Ava Sinclair had become more than just a fleeting distraction. She was a fire that had been lit inside him, and he was ready to see where it would take him, no matter the risks.

Chapter 4

Ava Sinclair stood in front of the mirror, her hands smoothing down the fabric of her dress as she took in her reflection. The pale blue material clung to her curves in a way that was both flattering and modest, the hem brushing just above her knees. She had chosen the dress carefully, wanting to strike the right balance between casual and elegant. Tonight, she was planning to have dinner alone at the resort—a quiet evening to reflect and clear her mind after the whirlwind of emotions she had experienced over the past few days.

As she adjusted her hair, letting the loose waves fall over her shoulders, a soft knock at the door interrupted her thoughts. Ava's heart skipped a beat, and she quickly made her way to the door, wondering who could be visiting her at this hour. When she opened it, she found a resort staff member standing there, a polite smile on his face and a small envelope in his hand.

"Miss Sinclair, this is for you," the young man said, extending the envelope toward her.

"Thank you," Ava replied, taking the envelope with a slight frown. She closed the door and turned the envelope over in her hands, her curiosity piqued.

There was no name on the outside, just a simple, elegant piece of stationary.

She opened it carefully, unfolding the note inside.

Dinner. 7 PM at the private dining room near the west garden. I'll be waiting.
—Nikolai

The message was brief, the handwriting bold and precise. There was no question of who it was from or where she was expected to be. The tone was clear—dominant, with a hint of command that sent a shiver down her spine. Ava's pulse quickened as she read the note again, her fingers trembling slightly. There was something thrilling about the way Nikolai had assumed she would come, as if there was no other possibility. It was a level of confidence that bordered on arrogance, but instead of being put off by it, Ava found herself intrigued.

She had never met a man who was so sure of himself, so certain of what he wanted. The thought of dining with him, of being in his presence again, made her heart race with a mix of excitement and nerves. Nikolai was in his 40s, a full two decades older than her, and he carried himself with a confidence and strength that was both intoxicating and intimidating. There was something about him that made her feel small, vulnerable even, in a way that no one else had ever made her feel. But there was also a strange sense of security in his presence, as if he could shield her from the world with just a look.

The realization that she was genuinely excited to see him again sent a flutter through her chest. Despite her reservations, despite the nagging voice in the back of her mind telling her to be careful, she knew she couldn't resist the pull she felt toward Nikolai. There was something about him that drew her in, that made her want to know more, even though she knew so little about him.

Ava glanced at the clock—she had just enough time to finish getting ready. With a deep breath, she set the note aside and returned to the mirror, determined to push her nerves aside. Tonight was going to be different. She could feel it in her bones, and the anticipation was almost too much to bear.

The private dining area was tucked away in a secluded corner of the resort, far from the bustling restaurants and bars that catered to the other guests. The space was intimate, with a single table set for two, surrounded by flickering candles that cast a soft, golden glow over the room. The sound of the ocean was a constant murmur in the background, a soothing reminder of the paradise they were in.

Ava hesitated at the entrance, her breath catching in her throat as she took in the scene. It was beautiful, romantic even, and she couldn't help but feel a thrill of excitement at the thought of spending the evening here with Nikolai.

He was already there, waiting for her at the table, and the sight of him made her heart skip a beat. Nikolai was dressed in a tailored suit, the dark fabric accentuating his broad shoulders and muscular build. His hair was neatly combed, and his eyes, as they locked onto hers, were dark and intense, holding her in place as if he could see straight through her.

"Ava," he greeted, standing as she approached. His voice was deep and smooth, carrying an authority that sent a shiver down her spine. He stepped forward, taking her hand in his and pressing a kiss to her knuckles. The gesture was old-fashioned, yet it felt entirely natural coming from him, as if he had been doing this for years.

"Nikolai," she replied, her voice trembling slightly as she tried to steady herself. The feel of his lips on her skin sent a jolt of electricity through her, and she found herself wishing he would hold onto her hand a little longer.

But he released her after a moment, gesturing for her to sit. "You look stunning," he said, his gaze lingering on her for a moment longer than necessary. "I'm glad you could join me."

Ava felt a blush creep up her neck, and she quickly took her seat, hoping he wouldn't notice. "Thank you," she murmured, her fingers brushing against the soft fabric of her dress. "This place is beautiful."

"It's one of my favorite spots," Nikolai replied, taking his seat across from her. "Private, quiet—perfect for a conversation."

There was a hint of something in his voice that made Ava's pulse quicken. A conversation. The way he said it made her wonder what kind of conversation he had in mind. She wasn't sure if she was ready for whatever he was about to reveal, but she knew there was no turning back now.

The meal was exquisite, each course more decadent than the last. But as delicious as the food was, Ava found herself more focused on Nikolai than on the dishes in front of her. He was a master of conversation, effortlessly guiding the discussion in whatever direction he chose. He asked her about her life in New York, her interests, and her plans for the future. But even as he questioned her, she could sense that he was holding back, revealing very little about himself in return.

It was clear that he was used to being in control, and while Ava found his dominance intriguing, it also made her uneasy. There was an intensity to him, a subtle pressure that made her feel as if she was being tested, as if he was trying to gauge how far she was willing to go.

She couldn't help but compare him to Derek, her ex-fiancé. Derek had been confident, sure, but not like this. Nikolai's confidence was absolute, almost overwhelming in its certainty. He was a man who knew what he wanted and had no qualms about taking it. The age difference between them was stark, and Ava was acutely aware of the gap in experience and power. She had never been with an older man before, and the way Nikolai carried himself, the way he looked at her, made her feel both vulnerable and incredibly desired.

"Tell me, Ava," Nikolai said, his voice drawing her back to the present. "What are you looking for?"

The question caught her off guard, and she hesitated, unsure of how to answer. What was she looking for? She had come to Phuket to escape, to clear her head after the disaster with Derek, but she hadn't expected to find herself in a situation like this. She hadn't expected to meet someone like Nikolai.

"I'm not sure," she admitted, her voice soft. "I guess I'm still trying to figure that out."

Nikolai nodded, his expression thoughtful. "I see. Sometimes, the answers we're looking for are closer than we think."

There was a weight to his words that made Ava's heart skip a beat. She wasn't sure what he meant, but the way he looked at her made her feel as if he was offering her something, something she wasn't sure she was ready to accept.

As the dinner came to an end, Nikolai stood, offering her his hand. "Would you like to take a walk?" he asked, his voice gentle but firm.

Ava hesitated for only a moment before nodding. "I'd like that."

The night air was warm and fragrant as they stepped outside, the sound of the ocean growing louder as they walked along the dimly lit path. Lanterns cast a soft glow over the greenery, creating an atmosphere of intimacy that made Ava's heart race. She could feel the tension between them, a tension that had been building all evening, and she knew where this was leading.

Nikolai was silent as they walked, his hand resting lightly on the small of her back, guiding her with a touch that was both possessive and protective. Ava found herself leaning into him, drawn to the strength and confidence he exuded. There was something about being with him that made her feel safe, even though she knew very little about him.

As they approached his villa, Ava's nerves began to return. This was it—she was about to cross a line she wasn't sure she was ready to cross. But the thought of turning back now was unthinkable. She wanted this, wanted him, more than she had wanted anything in a long time.

Nikolai opened the door to his villa, gesturing for her to enter. Ava hesitated for only a moment before stepping inside, her heart pounding in her chest. The interior was just as luxurious as the rest of the resort, with high ceilings, plush furnishings, and large windows that offered a stunning view of the moonlit ocean. The space was dimly lit, the soft glow of the lamps casting long shadows across the room. The atmosphere was intimate, almost seductive, and it made Ava's pulse quicken even more.

Nikolai closed the door behind them, the soft click echoing in the silence. He moved with a grace that belied his size, his presence commanding yet somehow calming. Ava stood in the center of the room, feeling a strange mix of excitement and apprehension. She had never been in a situation like this before—so alone, so vulnerable, with a man who was both a mystery and an undeniable force of nature.

Nikolai stepped closer, his gaze never leaving hers. There was something in his eyes, something dark and intense, that made her breath catch in her throat. He reached out, his fingers brushing against her cheek, and the touch sent a shiver down her spine.

"You're beautiful," he murmured, his voice low and husky. "So young, so innocent."

Ava's heart raced at his words, the heat rising in her cheeks. She had never felt this way before—so wanted, so desired. There was a part of her that was scared, that wanted to run, but there was also a part of her that was drawn to him, that craved the attention and the power he exuded.

Nikolai's hand moved to the back of her neck, pulling her closer until their bodies were almost touching. The warmth of his breath fanned across her lips, and before she could think, he kissed her. It wasn't a gentle kiss—it was passionate, demanding, filled with a hunger that made her knees go weak. His lips moved against hers with an intensity that took her breath away, his hands roaming her body, igniting a fire within her that she had never felt before.

Ava melted into the kiss, her hands clutching at his suit jacket as she tried to keep up with the storm of emotions he was unleashing within her. She could feel the strength in his body, the raw power that radiated from him, and it thrilled her in a way that both excited and frightened her. She had never been with a man like Nikolai—so experienced, so dominant—it only heightened the sense of danger and excitement.

His hands moved lower, tracing the curves of her hips before sliding around to the small of her back, pulling her even closer. Ava gasped as he deepened the kiss, his tongue sweeping into her mouth with a possessiveness that left her dizzy. It was as if he was claiming her, marking her as his own, and she found herself responding in kind, her body betraying the fears that lingered in the back of her mind.

When Nikolai finally pulled away, both of them were breathing heavily, their chests rising and falling in unison. He looked down at her, his eyes dark with desire, and she felt a surge of something primal within her—something that told her to let go, to give in to the passion that was crackling between them.

"You have no idea what you do to me," Nikolai whispered, his voice rough with emotion. "I've wanted this since the moment I laid eyes on you."

Ava's heart skipped a beat at his words, her mind reeling with the realization that this powerful, dangerous man wanted her—desired her in a way that was almost overwhelming. She knew she was crossing a line, stepping into something she might not be able to control, but she couldn't bring herself to stop.

She didn't want to stop.

Nikolai's hands moved to her shoulders, his touch firm but gentle as he began to slide the straps of her dress down her arms. Ava shivered at the sensation, her skin tingling under his fingers. He was taking his time, savoring every moment, and the anticipation was almost too much to bear.

As the fabric of her dress slipped lower, revealing the soft curve of her breasts, Nikolai let out a low growl, his eyes darkening with desire. Ava's breath hitched as he leaned down, his lips brushing against her collarbone, the heat of his mouth sending waves of pleasure through her body.

"You're mine now," he murmured against her skin, his voice thick with possession. "Do you understand that?"

Ava's heart pounded in her chest, her mind struggling to process his words. There was something about the way he said it—so matter-of-fact, so confident—that made her knees go weak. She had never been claimed like this before, never felt so utterly desired, and it was both exhilarating and terrifying.

"Yes," she whispered, her voice barely audible. "I'm yours."

The words felt strange on her lips, but they were the truth. She was his, in this moment, and there was no going back.

Nikolai's hands moved lower, sliding the dress down her body until it pooled at her feet, leaving her standing before him in nothing but her bra and panties. He took a step back, his eyes raking over her body with a hunger that made her blush. There was no denying the power he had over her, and she could feel herself surrendering to it, her body responding to his every touch, his every look.

With a deliberate slowness, Nikolai reached behind her, unhooking her bra and letting it fall to the floor. Ava's breath caught in her throat as she felt his hands cup her breasts, his thumbs brushing over her nipples with a touch that was both gentle and possessive. The sensation sent a jolt of pleasure through her, and she couldn't help the soft moan that escaped her lips.

"You're so beautiful," he whispered, his voice filled with awe. "So perfect."

Ava's cheeks flushed with heat at his words, her heart swelling with a mix of pride and desire. She had never felt this way before—so cherished, so wanted—and it made her feel alive in a way she hadn't felt in a long time.

Nikolai's hands moved lower, sliding down her waist, his fingers hooking into the waistband of her panties. He pulled them down slowly, his eyes never leaving hers as he bared her completely to him. The intensity of his gaze made her shiver, the weight of his desire almost too much to bear.

When she was finally naked before him, Nikolai stepped back, his eyes raking over her body with a look of pure hunger. Ava felt a surge of self-consciousness, but the way he looked at her—like she was the most beautiful thing he had ever seen—quickly chased it away.

"Lie down," he commanded, his voice leaving no room for argument.

Ava hesitated for only a moment before obeying, her heart pounding as she lay back on the bed, her body trembling with anticipation. She had never felt so exposed, so vulnerable, but there was also a thrill in surrendering to him, in giving herself over completely to his control.

Nikolai began to undress, his movements slow and deliberate, as if he was putting on a show just for her. Ava's breath caught in her throat as he revealed his powerful physique, the muscles in his chest and arms rippling as he shed his clothing. Tattoos covered his chest, intricate designs that hinted at a life filled with stories she could only imagine. He was older, yes, but his body was that of a man in his prime—strong, powerful, and undeniably masculine.

When he was finally naked, Ava's eyes widened as she took in the sight of him. He was everything she had imagined and more, his body exuding a raw, primal power that made her pulse quicken. But it was his arousal that held her attention, the sight of his engorged cock making her breath hitch with a mix of anticipation and fear. He was large, intimidating even, and she couldn't help but wonder if she could handle him.

Nikolai seemed to sense her hesitation, and a slow, predatory smile spread across his lips as he climbed onto the bed, his body hovering over hers. "Don't be afraid, Ava," he whispered, his voice soothing but laced with a dark promise. "I'll take care of you."

And then he kissed her again, his mouth claiming hers with a passion that made her head spin. His hands roamed her body, exploring every curve, every inch of her skin, as if he was memorizing her. There was no hesitation in his touch, no doubt in his movements—just a deep, burning need that matched her own.

Ava felt herself melt into him, her body responding to his every touch, his every command. She had never felt this way before—so completely at someone's mercy, yet so utterly alive. It was as if he had awakened something inside her, something she hadn't even known was there, and she couldn't get enough of it.

Nikolai's hands moved to her breasts, his fingers teasing her nipples with a skill that made her gasp. The sensation was electric, sending waves of pleasure straight to her core, and she arched into his touch, desperate for more. His mouth followed, his lips wrapping around one nipple while his hand continued to tease the other, and Ava felt a surge of heat pool between her legs.

"Nikolai," she moaned, her hands clutching at the sheets as she tried to keep herself grounded. The pleasure was overwhelming, almost too much to bear, but she couldn't bring herself to ask him to stop. She didn't want him to stop.

His mouth moved lower, leaving a trail of kisses down her abdomen, his breath hot against her skin. Ava's heart raced as she realized where he was headed, and she bit her lip, her body trembling with anticipation.

When he reached her thighs, Nikolai paused, his eyes locking onto hers as he spread her legs wider, his hands firm but gentle as they guided her into position. The intensity of his gaze made Ava's breath hitch, her heart pounding with a mix of anticipation and nervousness. She had never felt so exposed, so vulnerable, yet the way he looked at her—like she was the only thing that mattered in the world—made her feel safe, cherished.

Slowly, deliberately, Nikolai lowered his mouth to her most intimate place, his breath warm against her skin. Ava gasped as she felt the first touch of his tongue, a soft, teasing stroke that sent a jolt of pleasure through her entire body. She couldn't help the moan that escaped her lips, her hips lifting off the bed as she instinctively sought more.

Nikolai responded to her need with a low growl of approval, his hands gripping her thighs to hold her in place as he began to explore her with his tongue.

He moved with precision and purpose, each stroke of his tongue designed to draw out the maximum amount of pleasure. Ava's moans grew louder, her body writhing under his expert touch as he pushed her closer and closer to the edge.

When he added his fingers to the mix, gently slipping one inside her while his tongue continued its relentless assault on her clit, Ava thought she might lose her mind. The combination of sensations was overwhelming. All she could think about was how incredible it felt, how much she wanted—needed—more.

Nikolai seemed to sense just how close she was, and he intensified his movements, his tongue flicking faster and harder against her sensitive nub while his fingers worked their magic inside her. Ava's moans grew louder and more urgent as she felt herself teetering on the edge.

"Nikolai, please," she begged, her voice barely a whisper as she teetered on the brink of release. "I can't… I can't take it…"

He responded with a deep, rumbling chuckle that sent vibrations through her entire body. "You can take it, Ava," he murmured against her skin, his voice low and commanding. "You're going to take everything I give you."

And then he drove his fingers deeper, his tongue moving faster, more insistent, until Ava's entire world exploded into a million pieces. The orgasm ripped through her like a tidal wave, her body convulsing with the force of it as she cried out his name. She had never experienced anything like it, never imagined that pleasure could be so all-consuming, so utterly devastating.

Nikolai didn't stop, didn't let up until she had ridden out every last wave of pleasure, until she was nothing more than a trembling, panting mess beneath him. Only then did he lift his head, his eyes dark with satisfaction as he looked down at her.

"You're beautiful when you come," he said, his voice thick with possessive pride.

Ava could barely form a coherent response, her mind still reeling from the intensity of what she had just experienced. But even in her dazed state, she knew she wanted more. She needed more.

Nikolai seemed to sense her desire, because he wasted no time in positioning himself between her legs, his body looming over hers as he lined himself up with her wet entrance. Ava's breath caught in her throat as she felt the head of his cock pressing against her, the sheer size of him making her momentarily doubt if she could take him.

But before she could voice her concerns, Nikolai captured her lips in a searing kiss, his tongue plunging into her mouth as he began to push inside her. The sensation was intense, almost too much, and Ava cried out against his lips as he filled her inch by inch, stretching her in ways she had never been stretched before.

He was big—bigger than anyone she had ever been with—and the feeling of being so completely filled, so completely claimed, was almost overwhelming. But it wasn't just the physical sensation that had her head spinning; it was the way he made her feel. Like she belonged to him, like she was his in every possible way.

Nikolai's movements were slow, controlled, as if he was savoring the moment, taking his time to fully claim her. Ava's body trembled beneath him, her nails digging into his back as she tried to ground herself in the overwhelming sea of sensations.

"You're mine, Ava," he growled against her lips, his voice rough with possessive intensity. "No one else will ever touch you. No one else will ever make you feel like this."

Ava could only moan in response, her body tightening around him as he began to move with more purpose, his thrusts deep and powerful. Each one drove him deeper inside her, the force of his movements sending shockwaves of pleasure through her entire body.

She couldn't think, couldn't breathe, couldn't do anything but feel. Feel him, feel the way he claimed her with every thrust, the way he possessed her in a way that no one ever had. It was too much, too intense, but she didn't want it to stop. She wanted him to keep going, to keep taking her until there was nothing left of her but the pleasure he gave her.

Nikolai's movements intensified, driving into her with a primal force. His powerful thrusts pushed deep into the wet heat between her thighs, each motion rough and demanding. Ava clung to him desperately, wrapping her legs around his waist, urging him to go further as their bodies collided in a raw display of desire. In the heat of the moment, she gave herself over completely to him, overwhelmed by the intense sensations that coursed through her body. She was lost in him, lost in the pleasure, and she never wanted to be found.

When her second orgasm hit, it was even more powerful than the first, her body shattering around him as she screamed his name. Nikolai followed her over the edge, his own release coming with a guttural roar as he buried himself deep inside her, claiming her in the most primal way possible.

For a long moment, they stayed like that, their bodies tangled together, their breathing heavy and ragged as they came down from the high of their shared release. Ava felt like she was floating, her mind blissfully blank, her body completely spent.

Nikolai finally pulled out of her, his movements slow and careful, as if he didn't want to hurt her. He collapsed beside her on the bed, pulling her into his arms as if it was the most natural thing in the world.

Ava lay in Nikolai's arms, her head resting on his chest as she tried to catch her breath. The room was filled with the scent of sex and the sound of their breathing, and she couldn't help but feel a strange mix of emotions—exhaustion, satisfaction, and a lingering sense of unease.

What had just happened between them had been unlike anything she had ever experienced. It had been intense, overwhelming, and deeply erotic, but it had also left her feeling vulnerable and exposed in a way that she wasn't entirely comfortable with. She had given herself to Nikolai completely, allowed him to claim her in every way possible, and while it had been incredible, it had also been terrifying.

She couldn't help but compare him to Derek, her ex-fiancé. Derek had been kind, considerate, and gentle, but he had never made her feel like this. He had never made her feel so utterly wanted, so completely desired. Nikolai was different—he was older, more experienced, more powerful, and there was an air of danger about him that both thrilled and scared her.

But was this too soon? Was she diving headfirst into something she wasn't ready for, using Nikolai as a way to escape the pain of her recent breakup?

The thought nagged at her, a small voice in the back of her mind that wouldn't be silenced.

Yet, despite her fears, there was something about Nikolai that drew her in, that made her feel safe even in the midst of the storm he had unleashed within her. He was so different from Derek, so much more intense, and while that should have scared her, it didn't. Instead, it made her feel alive in a way she hadn't felt in a long time.

Ava sighed softly, her fingers tracing patterns on Nikolai's chest as she tried to sort through her conflicting emotions. She didn't know what the future held, didn't know what being with Nikolai truly meant, but for now, she was content to stay in this moment, to let herself be held by this powerful, enigmatic man who had somehow captured her heart without even trying.

After what felt like an eternity, Nikolai finally spoke, his voice low and authoritative as he held her close. "You belong to me now, Ava," he said, his tone leaving no room for doubt. "You're mine."

Ava's breath caught in her throat at his words, her heart skipping a beat. There was a finality to the way he said it, a certainty that made her feel both thrilled and frightened. She had never belonged to anyone before, had never been claimed so completely, and the idea of it was both exhilarating and terrifying.

"I… I don't know what that means," she whispered, her voice barely audible.

Nikolai's hand cupped her cheek, turning her face up so that she was looking into his eyes. "It means that no one else will ever touch you, ever make you feel like I do," he said, his voice firm but gentle. "It means that you're mine, and I protect what's mine."

Ava shivered at his words, the possessiveness in his tone sending a thrill through her. She knew she should be wary, should question what it meant to belong to someone like Nikolai, but she couldn't bring herself to do it. There was something about the way he said it, the way he looked at her, that made her want to believe him, that made her want to give herself to him completely.

But there was also a part of her that was scared, that wondered if she was losing herself in him, if she was stepping into something far deeper and darker than she was prepared for. The idea of belonging to someone—of being claimed—was new to her, and it came with a weight that she didn't fully understand.

Ava looked up at Nikolai, searching his eyes for any sign of doubt, any hint that he might not be as certain as he sounded. But all she saw was unwavering conviction, a deep, possessive need that both frightened and thrilled her. There was no doubt in his eyes, no hesitation in his words. He truly believed she belonged to him, and part of her wanted to believe it too.

"I want to believe you," she whispered, her voice trembling with the weight of her emotions. "But I'm scared, Nikolai. I don't know what this means for me… for us."

Nikolai's expression softened slightly, a rare tenderness in his gaze as he stroked her cheek with his thumb. "You don't need to be afraid, Ava," he said gently. "I know this is new for you, but I promise you, I will protect you. I will keep you safe."

Ava's heart ached at the sincerity in his voice, at the way he seemed to understand her fears without her having to voice them. He was so different from anyone she had ever known—so powerful, so sure of himself—and yet, in this moment, he was offering her something she had never had before: a sense of security, of belonging.

But even as she felt the pull toward him, the need to trust him, there was still that small voice in the back of her mind, warning her to be careful. She didn't know Nikolai, not really. She knew he was dangerous, that much was clear, but she didn't know the extent of it. She didn't know what it meant to be with a man like him, what it meant to belong to him.

Yet, despite her fears, she found herself wanting to take the leap, to give in to the feelings that had been building inside her since the moment she met him. She wanted to trust him, to believe that he would protect her, that he would be the anchor she needed in the storm of her emotions.

"I'm yours," she finally whispered, the words slipping out before she could second-guess them. "I don't know what that means, but… I'm yours."

Nikolai's eyes darkened with satisfaction at her words, his grip on her tightening slightly as if to solidify the claim he had just made. "You have no idea how much I wanted to hear you say that," he murmured, his voice filled with a possessive pride that sent a shiver down her spine.

He leaned down, capturing her lips in a slow, passionate kiss that left no room for doubt about the depth of his desire for her. Ava melted into him, her body relaxing against his as she let herself get lost in the moment, in the feel of his lips on hers, his hands on her skin.

For now, in this moment, she allowed herself to believe in the promise he was making her. She allowed herself to believe that she could trust him, that she could belong to him without losing herself completely.

As they lay together in the aftermath of their passion, Ava couldn't help but wonder what the future held for them. She didn't know what it meant to be with a man like Nikolai, didn't know what challenges or dangers lay ahead. But she knew one thing for certain—she had taken a step into a world she didn't fully understand, and there was no turning back now.

Whatever happened next, she was in this with him, for better or worse. And as terrifying as that thought was, it was also strangely comforting. Because for the first time in a long time, she felt like she wasn't alone. She had Nikolai, and as complicated and intense as their relationship was, it was also something she desperately needed.

She needed him, and for now, that was enough.

The night stretched on, the air between them filled with a comfortable silence that spoke volumes. Ava lay in Nikolai's arms, her head resting on his chest, listening to the steady beat of his heart. It was a sound that soothed her, grounding her in a reality that was quickly becoming something entirely new.

She had given herself to Nikolai, surrendered to his dominance, and in doing so, she had found a strange sense of peace. The uncertainty and fear that had plagued her since her breakup with Derek were still there, lingering in the background, but they were overshadowed by the certainty of Nikolai's presence. He was a man who knew what he wanted, who took what he wanted, and she had willingly stepped into his world.

As she lay there, wrapped in the warmth of his embrace, Ava felt a flicker of something she hadn't felt in a long time—hope. It was fragile, tentative, but it was there, growing stronger with each passing moment. She didn't know what the future held, didn't know what it truly meant to belong to Nikolai, but she was willing to find out.

"I want to be yours," she whispered again, her voice barely audible in the quiet of the room. "I don't know what that means yet, but I want to be yours."

Nikolai's arms tightened around her, his lips pressing a gentle kiss to the top of her head. "You already are, Ava," he murmured, his voice filled with a tenderness that surprised her. "You already are."

Ava closed her eyes, letting the warmth of his words wash over her, and for the first time in a long time, she allowed herself to believe that maybe, just maybe, she had found something real. Something worth holding onto.

And as she drifted off to sleep in Nikolai's arms, she couldn't help but feel that she was exactly where she was meant to be.

Chapter 5

Ava awoke to the soft light of morning filtering through the curtains, casting a warm, golden hue over the room. The air was still, and for a moment, she didn't move, savoring the feeling of peace that enveloped her. But as her mind slowly came to life, the events of the previous night rushed back, bringing with them a mix of emotions that made her heart race.

Nikolai's arm was draped possessively over her waist, his body warm and solid beside hers. She turned her head slightly to look at him, taking in the strong lines of his face, softened in sleep. There was something comforting about his presence, something that made her feel safe in a way she hadn't felt in a long time. But alongside that comfort was a nagging sense of unease, a voice in the back of her mind reminding her that she was lying next to a man she barely knew—a man who had claimed her in more ways than one.

The intensity of their connection, both physical and emotional, lingered in her thoughts. She couldn't deny the pull she felt toward Nikolai, the way he made her feel so utterly desired, so alive. But there was also a part of her that was frightened by the speed at which things were progressing. She had always been cautious, always taken her time to understand someone before getting involved. But with Nikolai, everything was different. He had swept into her life like a storm, and she wasn't sure if she was strong enough to withstand the force of it.

Ava shifted slightly, trying not to wake him as she carefully extricated herself from his grasp. The cool morning air brushed against her bare skin as she slipped out of bed, wrapping a sheet around herself as she made her way to the window. She needed to clear her head, to make sense of the whirlwind of emotions that threatened to overwhelm her.

As she stood by the window, looking out at the serene landscape of the resort, Ava couldn't help but wonder if she was getting in too deep, too fast. There was so much she didn't know about Nikolai, so much that he kept hidden behind that calm, controlled exterior. She had glimpsed the power he wielded, the dominance that radiated from him, but there was more—so much more—that she couldn't see. And it was that unknown, that darkness, that both intrigued and terrified her.

But despite her fears, Ava couldn't deny the way she felt when she was with him. There was a strange sense of security in his presence, as if he could shield her from the world with just a look. It was a feeling she had never experienced before, and it both thrilled and unnerved her. She knew she should be cautious, that she should take her time to understand who Nikolai really was, but there was a part of her that wanted to throw caution to the wind, to dive headfirst into whatever this was between them.

A soft rustling behind her made Ava turn, and she saw that Nikolai was awake, his dark eyes watching her from the bed. There was a softness in his gaze that she hadn't expected, a warmth that made her heart skip a beat.

"Good morning," he murmured, his voice still rough with sleep.

"Good morning," Ava replied, her voice barely above a whisper. She tightened the sheet around her, feeling suddenly self-conscious under his gaze.

Nikolai sat up, the sheet falling away to reveal the powerful muscles of his chest and arms. The tattoos that crossed his chest seemed even more pronounced in the morning light, adding to the air of danger that surrounded him. But despite his intimidating appearance, there was something almost tender in the way he looked at her, something that made her feel as if she was the only person in the world who mattered.

"Come back to bed," he said softly, extending a hand toward her.

Ava hesitated for a moment, her mind warring with her heart. But the pull she felt toward him was too strong to resist. She let the sheet fall to the floor and slowly made her way back to the bed, slipping under the covers and into his waiting arms.

Nikolai pulled her close, his hand sliding down her back in a soothing gesture. "Are you okay?" he asked, his voice laced with concern.

Ava nodded, resting her head against his chest. "I'm just... thinking."

"About what?"

"About us. About last night. About everything."

Nikolai's hand stilled for a moment before he resumed his gentle caress. "Do you regret it?"

"No," Ava said quickly, lifting her head to look at him. "I don't regret it. I just... I don't know what this is, Nikolai. I don't know where we go from here."

Nikolai's expression softened, and he reached up to cup her cheek, his thumb brushing lightly over her skin. "We don't have to have all the answers right now," he said gently. "All I know is that I want you, Ava. I want you with me."

Ava's heart swelled at his words, the sincerity in his voice making her chest tighten with emotion. She wanted to believe him, wanted to believe that this could be something real, something worth holding onto. But there was still that nagging voice in the back of her mind, warning her to be careful, to protect herself from getting hurt.

But as she looked into Nikolai's eyes, she couldn't bring herself to listen to that voice. Not now. Not when he was holding her so tenderly, as if she was the most precious thing in the world.

"I want to be with you too," she whispered, her voice trembling with emotion. "But I'm scared, Nikolai. I'm scared of what this means."

Nikolai's grip on her tightened slightly, his eyes darkening with intensity. "You don't have to be scared, Ava," he said firmly. "I will protect you. I will always protect you."

Ava closed her eyes, letting his words wash over her. She wanted to believe him, wanted to trust him. But there was so much she didn't know, so much she couldn't see. And it was that uncertainty, that darkness, that made her heart race with both excitement and fear.

But for now, in this moment, she would push those fears aside. She would let herself be with him, let herself feel the warmth of his embrace and the comfort of his words. She would let herself believe that maybe, just maybe, this could be something real.

After a long, quiet moment in his arms, Nikolai gently pulled away, pressing a kiss to Ava's forehead before sliding out of bed. "Let's have breakfast," he said, his voice back to its calm, controlled tone.

Ava watched as he pulled on a pair of loose pants and made his way to the door, her heart still fluttering with the remnants of their conversation. She took a deep breath, trying to steady herself before following him into the dining area.

The table was already set, a beautiful spread of fresh fruits, pastries, and steaming coffee waiting for them. The room was bright and airy, the morning sun filtering in through the large windows, casting a warm glow over the space. It was a stark contrast to the intensity of the night before, and Ava couldn't help but feel a sense of calm as she sat down at the table.

Nikolai poured them both a cup of coffee before taking a seat across from her, his expression relaxed and unreadable. They ate in comfortable silence for a few moments, the clinking of silverware the only sound in the room. But despite the peaceful atmosphere, Ava couldn't shake the tension that lingered between them, the unspoken questions that hung in the air.

Finally, she couldn't take it anymore. She set down her fork and looked up at Nikolai, her heart pounding with the weight of her thoughts. "Nikolai," she began, her voice hesitant, "can we talk about… last night?"

Nikolai looked up from his plate, his dark eyes locking onto hers. "Of course," he said calmly, setting down his own fork and giving her his full attention. "What do you want to talk about?"

Ava swallowed hard, suddenly unsure of how to put her thoughts into words. "I just… I don't know where we go from here," she admitted, her voice barely above a whisper. "I don't know what this means for us."

Nikolai's gaze softened slightly, and he reached across the table to take her hand in his. "Ava, you don't have to have all the answers right now," he said gently. "All I know is that I want you with me. I want to be with you."

Ava's heart swelled at his words, but there was still a part of her that was hesitant, that was afraid of what being with Nikolai truly meant. "But what does that look like?" she asked, her voice trembling. "What does it mean to be with you, Nikolai? What does it mean for me?"

Nikolai was silent for a moment, his expression thoughtful as he considered her questions. Finally, he sighed and gave her hand a gentle squeeze. "It means that I want you in my life, Ava. I want you by my side. But I won't lie to you—it won't be easy. My life is complicated, and there are things about me that you may not understand."

Ava's heart skipped a beat at his words, the fear that had been lingering in the back of her mind suddenly coming to the forefront. "What kinds of things?" she asked, her voice barely above a whisper. The uncertainty in her voice was unmistakable, and she felt a cold knot of anxiety forming in her stomach as she waited for Nikolai's response.

Nikolai's expression darkened slightly, and for a moment, Ava wondered if she had pushed too far. But then he sighed, his grip on her hand tightening as if to reassure her. "Ava, there are parts of my life that are… not easy to explain. My work, the people I deal with—it's not something that everyone would understand or accept. But I need you to trust me when I say that I will always keep you safe."

Ava wanted to trust him, wanted to believe that he could protect her from whatever dangers lurked in his world. But the more he spoke, the more she realized just how little she knew about the man sitting across from her. The air of mystery that had initially drawn her to Nikolai now felt like a wall between them, a barrier she wasn't sure she could break through.

"What exactly do you do, Nikolai?" Ava asked, her voice trembling slightly. "I know you're successful, that you have businesses, but… what does that really mean?"

Nikolai hesitated, his dark eyes searching hers for a long moment before he finally spoke. "I have many interests, Ava. I'm involved in various industries—real estate, finance, logistics. My work often requires me to make difficult decisions, and sometimes, those decisions involve dealing with people who aren't always... agreeable."

Ava's heart pounded in her chest as she processed his words. He was being deliberately vague, and she could sense that he was holding back, not giving her the full truth. But she also knew that pressing him for more answers might push him away, might make him retreat further into the shadows.

"Does that mean you're in danger?" Ava asked, her voice barely above a whisper. "Are you involved in something dangerous?"

Nikolai's jaw tightened, and for a moment, she thought he might refuse to answer. But then he leaned closer, his gaze intense as he spoke. "I am no stranger to danger, Ava. It's a part of my life, a part of who I am. But you need to understand that I would never let anything happen to you. As long as you're with me, you're safe."

Ava's heart ached at the conviction in his voice, the determination in his eyes. He believed every word he was saying, and she wanted so badly to believe him too. But the fear that had been gnawing at her since the moment she met him was only growing stronger, and she wasn't sure if she could ignore it any longer.

"Nikolai… I'm scared," she admitted, her voice trembling. "I don't know if I'm ready for this. I don't know if I can handle being a part of your world."

Nikolai's expression softened, and he reached out to cup her cheek, his thumb brushing gently over her skin. "Ava, I won't force you into anything you're not ready for," he said softly. "But I'm asking you to trust me, to trust that I will protect you. You don't have to be a part of my world if you don't want to be, but I want you in my life. I need you in my life."

Ava's heart swelled at his words, but the fear still lingered, a cold knot in her stomach that refused to go away. She wanted to trust him, wanted to believe that he could keep her safe, but she also knew that being with Nikolai meant stepping into a world she didn't understand, a world that could be filled with dangers she couldn't even imagine.

"I want to be with you, Nikolai," she whispered, her voice trembling with emotion. "But I'm so scared of what that means. I'm scared of what might happen."

Nikolai's grip on her hand tightened, and his eyes bore into hers with an intensity that made her breath catch in her throat. "I understand your fear, Ava," he said softly. "But I promise you, I will do everything in my power to keep you safe. You are important to me—more than you know. And I would never let anything happen to you."

Ava closed her eyes, letting his words wash over her. She wanted to believe him, wanted to trust that he could protect her from whatever dangers lurked in the shadows of his life. But there was still that lingering doubt, that fear that she was stepping into something far more dangerous than she could handle.

But as she opened her eyes and looked into Nikolai's, she saw something there that made her heart swell—a vulnerability, a need that she hadn't seen before. He needed her, just as much as she needed him, and that realization made her resolve to trust him, at least for now.

"I'll try," she whispered, her voice barely audible. "I'll try to trust you."

Nikolai's eyes softened, and he leaned forward, pressing a gentle kiss to her forehead. "That's all I ask, Ava," he murmured against her skin. "Just trust me."

Ava nodded, her heart aching with the weight of her emotions. She knew that being with Nikolai wouldn't be easy, that it would come with challenges and dangers she wasn't sure she was ready for. But for now, she was willing to try, to trust him, and to see where this path would lead them.

They finished their breakfast in relative silence, the tension between them easing slightly but still present, like a shadow that lingered just out of sight. Ava couldn't shake the feeling that there was still so much she didn't know, so much that Nikolai was keeping from her, but she pushed those thoughts aside for now. She needed to focus on the present, on the man sitting across from her who was offering her a chance at something she hadn't had in a long time—connection, passion, and a sense of belonging.

After breakfast, Nikolai led her to his office within the villa. The room was as she imagined—dark wood, leather furniture, and a large, imposing desk that spoke of power and control. It was the kind of room that seemed to be a perfect reflection of the man who occupied it.

Nikolai gestured for her to sit in one of the leather chairs across from his desk, and Ava did so, her eyes roaming the room as she took in her surroundings. There was something both comforting and intimidating about the space, a reminder of the power that Nikolai wielded and the world he was a part of.

"I wanted to show you something," Nikolai said, breaking the silence as he moved behind his desk. He opened a drawer and pulled out a folder, placing it on the desk in front of her. "This is a small glimpse into my world. I want you to understand that I have responsibilities, obligations, that come with risks."

Ava's heart pounded as she reached for the folder, her fingers trembling slightly as she opened it. Inside were documents, contracts, and business agreements that were far more complex than anything she had ever seen before. She could tell from a quick glance that Nikolai was involved in multiple industries, each one more intricate and far-reaching than she had imagined.

But what caught her attention the most was a photo that had been tucked into the back of the folder. It was an old photograph, slightly worn around the edges, showing a young boy standing next to a man who bore a striking resemblance to Nikolai. The man's expression was hard, almost cold, as he held the boy close to his side. There was something about the image that sent a chill down Ava's spine, a sense of foreboding that she couldn't shake.

"Who is this?" Ava asked, her voice barely above a whisper as she held up the photo.

Nikolai's expression darkened slightly as he looked at the picture, his jaw tightening. "That's me, and my father," he said quietly. "It was taken a long time ago, before… before everything changed."

Ava's heart ached at the pain she saw flicker across Nikolai's face, a rare glimpse into a past that was clearly difficult for him to speak about. She wanted to ask more, to understand what had happened, but she hesitated, afraid of pushing too far.

"What happened?" she asked gently, her voice trembling with uncertainty.

Nikolai was silent for a long moment, his gaze distant as he stared at the photo. "My father was a powerful man," he said finally, his voice laced with bitterness. "He made a lot of enemies, and he paid the price for it. I was just a boy when it happened, but I learned quickly that power comes with a cost."

Ava's heart broke at the pain she heard in his voice, and she reached out to take his hand, squeezing it gently. "I'm so sorry, Nikolai," she whispered, her voice filled with empathy. "I can't imagine how hard that must have been."

Nikolai's grip on her hand tightened, and he looked up at her, his eyes filled with a mixture of pain and determination. "It was a long time ago," he said quietly. "But it shaped who I am today. It taught me that power is the only thing that can protect you, the only thing that can keep you safe."

Ava nodded, understanding dawning on her as she realized just how much Nikolai's past had influenced the man he had become. He had built his life around the need for power, the need to protect himself and those he cared about. And now, she was a part of that, a part of his world.

But as much as she understood his need for power, it also frightened her. The more she learned about Nikolai and his world, the more she realized how dangerous it could be. Power came with risks, with enemies, and with a constant need to stay one step ahead. Ava couldn't shake the feeling that by being with Nikolai, she was stepping into a life that was far more complex and perilous than she had ever imagined.

Nikolai seemed to sense her unease. He reached out, gently cupping her cheek and drawing her gaze back to him. "Ava, I know this is a lot to take in," he said softly. "I didn't want to burden you with my past, but I need you to understand why I am the way I am. Why I'm so protective of you."

Ava leaned into his touch, closing her eyes as she tried to steady her racing thoughts. She could feel the sincerity in his words, the depth of his need to keep her safe. But she also knew that being with him meant accepting all of him—his past, his present, and the dangerous world he inhabited.

"I do understand, Nikolai," she whispered, opening her eyes to meet his intense gaze. "I just… I need time to process all of this. I need to figure out if I'm strong enough to be a part of your world."

Nikolai's expression softened, and he nodded slowly. "Take all the time you need, Ava. I'm not going anywhere. And I promise you, I will do everything in my power to make sure you feel safe and protected."

Ava managed a small smile, though her heart was still heavy with uncertainty. She wanted to believe him, wanted to trust that he could shield her from the dangers that came with his life. But she knew that trust wasn't something that could be given lightly—it had to be earned.

They sat in silence for a moment, the weight of their conversation settling between them. Ava's thoughts swirled with a mix of fear, curiosity, and a deepening sense of connection to the man in front of her. She could feel herself being drawn deeper into Nikolai's world, despite her reservations, and she couldn't deny the powerful pull he had over her.

Finally, Nikolai broke the silence. "I have some business to attend to this morning," he said, his tone returning to its usual calm, controlled cadence. "But I want you to make yourself comfortable here. This villa is as much yours as it is mine."

Ava nodded, appreciating his gesture, though she couldn't shake the feeling of unease that lingered in her chest. "Thank you," she replied softly.

Nikolai stood, giving her one last lingering look before he turned and left the room. Ava watched him go, her heart heavy with the knowledge that while he might be physically leaving her alone, his presence—and the weight of his world—would never truly be far from her.

Left alone in the silence of Nikolai's office, Ava couldn't help but let her curiosity get the better of her. The photo she had seen, the look in Nikolai's eyes when he spoke of his father, had left her with more questions than answers. She found herself drawn to the drawer where the folder had been, wondering if there were more clues hidden within its depths.

She hesitated, her fingers hovering over the handle of the drawer. She knew it was a violation of Nikolai's trust to go snooping through his things, but the need to understand the man she was falling for was too strong to ignore. With a deep breath, she pulled the drawer open.

Inside, she found more documents, each one filled with information she couldn't fully comprehend. Business contracts, financial statements, and legal papers were neatly organized, but they all hinted at a life that was far more complicated than she had imagined. Ava's eyes scanned the pages, her mind racing as she tried to piece together the puzzle of Nikolai's life.

But it wasn't the documents that caught her attention—it was another photograph, this one even older than the first. It showed a younger Nikolai standing next to a man who looked every bit as intimidating as the older version of Nikolai she knew now. The man's expression was stern, almost cold, as he stood with his hand on Nikolai's shoulder.

Ava stared at the photo, her heart aching with a mixture of sympathy and fear. This was a side of Nikolai she had never seen before—a side that hinted at a past filled with pain, loss, and perhaps even danger. She couldn't help but wonder what had happened to the man in the photo, and how it had shaped the man Nikolai had become.

As she stared at the image, lost in thought, the sound of the door opening behind her made her jump. She quickly shoved the photo back into the drawer and closed it, her heart racing as she turned to see Nikolai standing in the doorway.

He watched her with an unreadable expression, his eyes flicking to the drawer she had just closed before settling back on her. "What were you doing?" he asked, his voice calm but with an edge that made her stomach twist.

Ava swallowed hard, her mind racing for an explanation. "I... I was just trying to understand," she admitted, her voice trembling slightly. "I saw the photo earlier, and I wanted to know more about you. About your past."

Nikolai's expression softened slightly, though there was still a trace of tension in his eyes. He stepped further into the room, closing the door behind him. "Ava, my past is not something I share lightly," he said quietly. "There are things I've been through, things I've done, that I'm not proud of. But I don't want those things to scare you away."

Ava felt a pang of guilt at his words, realizing that her curiosity had crossed a line. But she also knew that if they were going to have any kind of future together, she needed to understand the man he truly was.

"I'm not scared of you, Nikolai," she said softly, stepping closer to him. "I just want to know you. All of you."

Nikolai's eyes searched hers for a long moment before he finally sighed, his shoulders relaxing slightly. "I want that too, Ava. But there are parts of my life that I'm not ready to share yet. I need you to trust me when I say that everything I do is to protect you. To keep you safe."

Ava nodded, reaching out to take his hand in hers. "I do trust you, Nikolai. But I also need you to trust me. Trust that I can handle whatever you're hiding from me."

Nikolai looked down at their joined hands, his thumb brushing over her knuckles in a gentle, reassuring gesture. "I want to protect you from the darkness in my life, Ava. But I know I can't keep you in the dark forever. When the time is right, I'll tell you everything. But for now, please… be patient with me."

Ava's heart swelled with emotion at his words, and she squeezed his hand gently. "I'll be patient, Nikolai. I promise."

Nikolai leaned down, pressing a tender kiss to her lips. "Thank you," he whispered against her mouth. "That's all I ask."

Ava melted into the kiss, letting herself get lost in the warmth of his embrace. For now, she would trust him. She would be patient. But she also knew that the time would come when she would need to know the full truth—when she would need to confront the darkness that lurked in Nikolai's world.

And when that time came, she could only hope that she would be strong enough to face it.

Chapter 6

It had been several days since that first night together, and in that short time, Ava's world had completely shifted. She had moved her belongings from her room at the resort to Nikolai's villa without a second thought, as if it had been the most natural decision in the world. They had been inseparable ever since.

Their days were spent in blissful simplicity, walking along the pristine beaches, the soft sand between their toes, and the sound of the Andaman Sea crashing gently beside them. The warm tropical breeze carried with it a sense of freedom that Ava hadn't felt in years. There was something surreal about those walks—how Nikolai's presence by her side made her feel both incredibly safe and undeniably alive. The way he'd reach for her hand, his touch firm but tender, sent shivers down her spine every time.

During the afternoons, they swam in the clear, warm waters of the sea. The water sparkled in the sunlight, wrapping around them like a silken sheet as they waded farther from shore, laughing, teasing, and enjoying the kind of peace Ava hadn't known she needed. The simplicity of their time together felt like a dream—one she didn't want to wake from. But always, in the back of her mind,

there was the knowledge that their time here was
fleeting.

Their nights were filled with luxury and indulgence.
Nikolai took her to the most beautiful restaurants
the island had to offer, places she never would
have dreamed of going on her own. He had a way
of making every moment feel extravagant, from the
private dinners on candlelit terraces to the soft
music playing in the background as they talked late
into the evening. But the best part of every night
came when they returned to his villa.

In his bed, they lost themselves in each other. Ava
felt a physical connection to Nikolai that was unlike
anything she'd experienced before. He made her
feel desired, cherished, and consumed by an
intensity she hadn't known was possible. Each
touch, each kiss, left her breathless, as though
every moment with him was charged with a raw,
electric energy that threatened to overwhelm her
senses.

What surprised her most wasn't just how drawn she
was to him—it was how safe she felt in his
presence. Nikolai's dominance, his control over
everything around him, should have scared her.
Instead, it made her feel protected, as if nothing
could touch her so long as she was by his side.
That sense of security, along with the growing
physical attraction, only deepened her attachment
to him in a short amount of time.

But as the days passed, Ava couldn't shake the feeling that something was coming. Despite the warmth and ease of their days together, there was always an undercurrent of tension surrounding Nikolai. She could see it in the way he would glance at his phone, frown at a message, or disappear for brief moments to take a call. His world was complicated, and though he hadn't told her everything, she sensed that their time in this paradise was temporary.

And then, that morning, everything shifted.

Ava sat at the edge of the terrace, watching the waves crash gently against the shore as the warm breeze swept through the villa. The beauty of the island surrounded her, a peaceful contrast to the storm of emotions brewing inside her. It felt surreal, almost as if this little pocket of paradise had temporarily suspended time, keeping reality at bay. But now, that illusion was shattering.

Nikolai's voice had broken the stillness of the morning, "We need to return to New York," he'd said with a calm certainty that left no room for discussion. "I have business to attend to."

She had expected this moment, leaving Thailand and returning to the real world, but somehow hearing it out loud shook her. New York. She hadn't allowed herself to think about it much since arriving in Phuket. The city represented everything she'd been trying to escape—the heartbreak, the betrayal, the chaos. And now, the idea of returning with Nikolai brought with it a tangle of emotions she wasn't prepared for.

Her heart raced as she processed his words. He stood behind her, his presence as commanding as always, waiting for her answer. She knew what he wanted—to leave together. Nikolai had made that clear in his own quiet, unspoken way. But going with him meant stepping further into his world, a world that was growing more complex and dangerous with each passing day. She could feel the weight of his gaze on her back, waiting for her response.

"You'll come with me, on my private plane." he repeated, his voice deep and unwavering. It wasn't a question—it was a statement, as though her decision had already been made. And yet, there was something in the way he said it, a hint of vulnerability beneath the certainty, that made her pause.

Ava turned to face him, her heart pounding. Nikolai stood in the doorway, the sunlight catching the sharp angles of his face, making him look both impossibly handsome and untouchable. His dark eyes, intense and steady, held hers, and in that moment, she knew that this wasn't just about returning to the city. It was about more than that—about what it meant to continue on this path with him.

Her mind raced. Going back to New York wasn't just going home—it was choosing to follow Nikolai deeper into the life he had only begun to reveal. She didn't know what that life fully entailed, but she was starting to understand that it wasn't just glamorous or exciting. It was dangerous, shadowed by the unknown forces that required him to have so much protection and secrecy.

"I... suppose it makes sense," she said softly, her voice catching slightly as she tried to make sense of it all. "I do live there, after all."

Nikolai's lips curved into a faint, satisfied smile, as if her answer had been exactly what he expected. He took a step closer to her, his presence filling the space between them, the air suddenly thick with the unspoken energy that always seemed to surround them. His proximity made her pulse quicken, the heat of his body almost overwhelming, as if the very air around him vibrated with power.

"Good," he said, his tone low and steady. "We'll leave soon. Everything is arranged."

Ava swallowed, trying to calm her nerves. The way he said it—calm, confident—made it sound so simple. As if all she had to do was pack her things and go with him, no questions asked. And in a way, that was true. But what would leaving with him really mean? She wanted to believe that he could protect her, that being with him would keep her safe from the mess her life had become. But there was so much she didn't know—so many secrets he hadn't shared yet.

Her mind flashed back to New York, the city she called home. She had fled from the chaos of her own life, from Derek's betrayal, from everything familiar. And now, the thought of going back was tangled with the idea of entering Nikolai's world. But, as much as she feared what lay ahead, she also knew she couldn't stay in this dreamlike escape forever. Returning to New York with Nikolai felt like the next step in a journey she was already on, one she was too deep into to turn back from now.

"I'll pack," she said, her voice quiet but resolute. She turned and headed toward the bedroom, her heart still racing as she tried to make sense of the emotions swirling inside her.

Each piece of clothing she folded felt like a step toward something unknown. She was no longer the woman who had arrived in Phuket, seeking solace from a shattered engagement. She had changed. Nikolai had changed her. Their connection had developed faster than she had ever expected, its intensity sweeping her off her feet, leaving her dizzy with both desire and fear.

Packing her belongings felt heavier than just closing a chapter on this brief island escape. It felt like she was sealing her fate, choosing to follow Nikolai wherever he led. And that, more than anything, terrified her. Because following him meant trusting him—and not just with her heart, but with her safety, her future.

The suitcase clicked shut, and a knock on the door startled her out of her thoughts. She took a deep breath and crossed the room to open it. Nikolai stood there, his expression unreadable, but his eyes locked onto hers with that same quiet intensity.

"Are you ready?" he asked, his voice soft but commanding.

Ava nodded, though her heart still pounded in her chest. "Yes," she said. "Let's go."

The two of them stepped out of the villa, the bright sun hitting them as they made their way to the waiting car. It wasn't until she saw it—sleek, black, and guarded by a man in a suit standing at attention—that the full weight of Nikolai's world crashed over her. Behind the car, another vehicle was parked, identical in every way except for the men inside, whose sharp eyes never left her.

Ava's breath hitched. She had known Nikolai was powerful, but this? She hadn't expected this level of security—guards, drivers, and what looked like a full-on convoy.

Nikolai's hand found the small of her back, guiding her toward the car. "It's just precaution," he murmured, as if he could sense her unease. "I told you, you're safe with me."

The words were meant to reassure her, but they only deepened her apprehension. If he needed this much protection, what dangers were they facing? And more importantly, what dangers was she now a part of?

Ava slid into the backseat of the car, her stomach churning as Nikolai joined her. The door closed with a soft thud, and the car began to move, with the second vehicle following closely behind.

For several minutes, neither of them spoke. Ava stared out the window, watching as the tropical landscape blurred past. The resort had felt like a paradise, a place far removed from the chaos of her life back in New York. But now, she realized that this paradise was nothing more than a brief respite. The real world—Nikolai's world—was waiting for her in New York, and it was a world filled with unknowns.

Nikolai's hand slid across the seat, taking hers in his grasp. His touch was warm, steady, but it did little to soothe the knot of anxiety twisting inside her.

"You're thinking too much," he said, his voice a soft rumble. "You're safe. I'll take care of everything."

Ava wanted to believe him. She wanted to believe that being with Nikolai meant she could relax, that he would shield her from whatever dangers lurked in the shadows. But how could she? Every moment with him only seemed to deepen the mystery surrounding him. The power, the control, the danger—it was all there, just beneath the surface.

"I trust you," she whispered, though part of her wasn't sure if that was true.

Nikolai's thumb brushed over her knuckles in a slow, deliberate movement. "Good."

The airport came into view, a sleek, private airstrip lined with jets. Ava's chest tightened as the car pulled up to one of the larger planes on the tarmac. It was luxurious, gleaming under the midday sun, but the sight of the guard standing near the jet sent a shiver down her spine.

The man's eyes were sharp, scanning the surroundings as if expecting something—someone. Ava's pulse quickened. What kind of life required this much security? What exactly was she getting herself into?

Nikolai stepped out first, holding out his hand to help her from the car. She hesitated for a moment, her heart hammering in her chest, before taking it. The cold, professional atmosphere of the airstrip was a far cry from the warm island air. This was

Nikolai's real world—a world of luxury and danger intertwined.

They boarded the jet in silence. Inside, the space was just as opulent as she had expected—plush leather seats, polished wood, and the faint scent of expensive cologne. Nikolai motioned for her to sit, and as she settled into the seat, the reality of what was happening finally hit her.

She was leaving the safety of the resort. She was flying back to New York with a man she barely knew—a man whose life was shrouded in mystery and risk. She was stepping into his world, and there was no going back.

Nikolai sat across from her, watching her closely. "You're tense," he said quietly.

Ava let out a breath she hadn't realized she'd been holding. "I guess I didn't expect this," she admitted. "The security, the guards… it's a lot to take in."

Nikolai's gaze softened, though his expression remained unreadable. "It's necessary," he said simply. "There are things I haven't told you yet. But you don't need to worry about that now. All you need to know is that I will protect you. Always."

Ava looked into his eyes, searching for some hint of what he wasn't saying. But as always, Nikolai gave nothing away. There was a wall around him—one she couldn't quite penetrate.

"You said there are things you haven't told me," she said, her voice barely above a whisper. "What kind of things?"

Nikolai's jaw tightened slightly, and for a moment, she thought he wouldn't answer. But then he leaned back in his seat, his expression hardening.

"My life isn't simple, Ava. I grew up in a world where power was the only thing that mattered. I had to fight for everything I have. And that comes with risks." His voice was low, controlled. "There are people who don't like that I have what I have."

Ava's heart pounded. She wanted to ask more—wanted to dig deeper into the parts of his life he was keeping hidden. But the look in his eyes stopped her. He wasn't ready to share those details, not yet.

"But you don't have to be afraid," he continued, his gaze locking onto hers. "I will never let anything happen to you. You're mine now. That means I protect you."

The possessiveness in his voice sent a shiver down her spine, but it wasn't fear she felt. It was something else—something deeper, more primal. The way he said it, the way he looked at her, made her feel claimed in a way she had never experienced before.

"I don't want to be afraid," she said softly. "But I need to know… what am I really stepping into, Nikolai? What does being with you mean?"

Nikolai's lips twitched into a small, almost bitter smile. "It means you'll be safe. And it means that you are part of something bigger than yourself now," Nikolai finished, his voice calm but with a distinct edge. "Being with me means accepting that my life comes with dangers, but it also comes with power, protection, and certainty. You'll never have to worry about being hurt or betrayed, by me or anyone else. I won't allow it."

Ava swallowed, her heart beating faster. The words were reassuring on the surface, but there was an unmistakable intensity to them. Power and protection, yes—but also control. Nikolai was not just promising safety; he was claiming her as part of his world, and that world was one where his will dominated all.

"I don't want to live in fear, Nikolai," she said quietly, her voice steady despite the uncertainty swirling inside her. "I'm not someone who can just… follow blindly. I need to understand."

Nikolai leaned forward, his eyes narrowing slightly as he studied her. "I don't expect you to follow blindly. You'll understand in time. But for now, just trust me. Trust that I'll always make sure you're safe."

Ava wanted to trust him. She wanted to believe that she could lean into whatever this was between them, that she could let herself fall into his arms and know that he would catch her. But the deeper she fell, the more dangerous it felt. This wasn't like falling for an ordinary man. Nikolai was anything but ordinary.

The jet flew smoothly through the sky, the hum of the engines the only sound between them for a long moment. Ava stared out the window at the endless blue horizon, her mind spinning with thoughts of what awaited her in New York. She had come to Phuket to escape her life, and now she was returning not just to the city she knew but to a future she couldn't predict.

New York had always been home. She knew its streets, its rhythms, its energy. But returning with Nikolai would change everything. She wouldn't be going back to her old life. She'd be stepping into his—a life full of wealth, power, and danger.

And that meant she wasn't just going home. She was walking into a completely different reality.

As if sensing her thoughts, Nikolai broke the silence. "You're thinking too much, Ava," he said, his voice soft but firm. "I can see it in your eyes."

Ava glanced at him, surprised by how easily he seemed to read her. "I can't help it. This… everything about you, about us, is overwhelming."

Nikolai leaned back in his seat, his gaze never leaving hers. "You'll get used to it."

"I don't think I want to get used to it," she admitted, her voice barely above a whisper. "It feels like I'm losing myself."

Nikolai's expression hardened slightly, and for a moment, she thought she had crossed a line. But then he softened, his hand reaching out to touch hers, his thumb brushing over her skin in a slow, soothing gesture. "You're not losing yourself, Ava. You're finding something new. Something stronger."

His words lingered in the air, and despite her apprehension, there was a part of her that wanted to believe him. Being with Nikolai made her feel alive in a way she hadn't before. The intensity of their connection, the way he looked at her, touched her—it was electrifying. But it also terrified her, because she knew that once she stepped fully into his world, there would be no turning back.

Nikolai's phone buzzed, interrupting the tension between them. He glanced at it, his expression shifting to one of focus as he read the message.

"Business," he muttered, almost to himself. "We'll be landing soon."

Ava looked out the window again, her heart skipping a beat as the skyline of New York came into view. The tall buildings stood like sentinels against the horizon, familiar and yet distant. She had always considered this city home, but now, it felt like she was seeing it for the first time.

"We'll go straight to my penthouse," Nikolai said, snapping her attention back to him. "You can rest there while I handle a few things. My security team will be with us the entire time."

Ava nodded, though the mention of security only reminded her of the danger lurking beneath the surface of Nikolai's world. She wasn't naïve enough to believe that his business was entirely aboveboard, not with the kind of protection he required. But she didn't press him for more details. Not yet. She knew she would have to tread carefully if she wanted to get the full picture of who Nikolai really was.

The jet descended smoothly, and Ava's stomach twisted with a mix of excitement and anxiety. She had agreed to this—agreed to follow him back to New York—but now that they were almost there, the reality of it was hitting her all at once. This wasn't just a trip home. It was a turning point.

When the plane touched down, Ava's breath caught in her throat. They were on a private airstrip, far from the bustling terminals of the city's main airports. As they taxied to a stop, Ava caught sight of more security waiting near the runway. A black SUV sat parked near the exit stairs, two men in suits standing beside it, their eyes scanning the tarmac with a practiced air of vigilance.

Nikolai stood, extending a hand to help her up. "Come on. Let's go home."

Home. The word sent a shiver through her. She wasn't sure what "home" meant anymore. Her apartment in New York? Or was she now part of Nikolai's world, with all its uncertainties?

Ava followed him off the plane, the cold air of New York biting into her skin as they stepped onto the tarmac. She wrapped her arms around herself, wishing she had something warmer, but before she could say anything, Nikolai was leading her toward the waiting SUV.

The guards moved with precision, opening the door for them and standing by as they climbed inside. Once they were seated, Nikolai glanced at her, his face calm but his eyes sharp, always watching, always calculating.

As the SUV pulled away from the airstrip, Ava stared out the window at the city she had called home for years. But now, everything felt different. The familiar streets, the towering buildings—it all seemed like a backdrop to a life that no longer belonged to her.

The car wound through the streets, taking a route that kept them away from the busiest parts of the city. Ava recognized some of the areas they passed, but everything felt distant, as if she were watching from behind a glass wall.

Eventually, the SUV pulled up to an upscale building, and Ava's breath caught as she realized they had arrived at Nikolai's penthouse. The towering structure loomed above them, sleek and modern, a testament to the wealth and power he commanded.

The door opened, and once again, Nikolai was there to guide her out. Ava stepped out of the car, her breath catching as she looked up at the towering structure before her. Nikolai's penthouse loomed above, an imposing fortress of glass and steel nestled in one of New York's most exclusive buildings. The city buzzed below them, but from up here, it felt distant, removed—like another world.

She had expected grandeur. Nikolai had that aura about him—everything around him spoke of wealth and power. But the sheer scale of it all, the polished opulence, took her breath away. Even the understated details—like the sleek black SUVs parked discreetly outside or the subtle but constant presence of bodyguards—were a reminder that Nikolai's world was unlike any she had ever known.

As they entered the building, the cool, marbled lobby greeted them, vast and echoing in its emptiness. Her eyes flicked to the bodyguards stationed around the entrance, their expressions unreadable, their postures rigid. They were always watching, always present. Ava had noticed them at the resort, but here in New York, their presence felt more intense, more necessary.

"You live here?" Ava asked, her voice sounding small in the cavernous space.

Nikolai gave her a faint smile. "I do," he said simply, as if living in such luxury was as natural as breathing for him. "It's home."

Home. The word settled heavily in Ava's chest. She had never imagined anything like this. Her own apartment in the city—tiny, cramped, filled with mismatched furniture—felt like a distant memory now, something from a different life. And maybe it was. Because being with Nikolai was transforming her in ways she hadn't anticipated. His world was consuming hers, swallowing up everything she once knew.

The elevator doors slid closed, and with them, Ava felt the last vestiges of her old life fall away. There was no turning back now. She had made her choice.

And she would have to live with whatever came next.

Chapter 7

They ascended in silence, the only sound the soft whir of the elevator as it climbed to the top of the building. Ava's thoughts swirled, her emotions conflicted. She couldn't deny the excitement she felt being with him, the thrill of stepping into his world, but there was something else too—an underlying tension, a sense of foreboding. She had learned more about Nikolai in these last few days than she had about anyone else in her life, and yet, it still felt like he was keeping a part of himself hidden. A part she wasn't sure she was ready to see.

When the elevator doors slid open, Ava's breath caught in her throat. The penthouse was more than she had imagined—sprawling and impossibly luxurious. Floor-to-ceiling windows wrapped around the living room, offering an unobstructed view of the New York skyline, the city lights twinkling like stars in the distance. The furniture was sleek, modern, and clearly expensive, each piece carefully curated to fit the aesthetic of understated opulence.

Ava stepped inside, her heels sinking into the thick carpet as she took it all in. The scale of the space was overwhelming. It felt more like a gallery than a home. She could see reflections of herself in the glossy surfaces, looking almost out of place among the pristine, high-end furnishings.

Nikolai moved with ease through the space, his presence commanding but relaxed. He belonged here, in this world of luxury and power. Ava, on the other hand, felt like she was standing on the edge of something much larger than herself, unsure whether to step forward or retreat.

"This place…" she murmured, still trying to process the grandeur of it all.

"It's home," Nikolai said simply, as if the opulence was nothing more than functional.

Home. The word felt heavy in Ava's chest. Her own apartment—a tiny, cramped space on the other side of the city—felt like a distant memory, a relic of a life she had left behind. Being here with Nikolai, in this lavish penthouse, made her realize just how far from that life she had already come.

But it wasn't just the luxury that unsettled her—it was the constant, subtle presence of the bodyguards. Even here, in his own home, Nikolai was surrounded by security. They stood at attention, discreet but ever-present, their eyes scanning the perimeter, always watching. Ava couldn't help but feel their gaze on her, a reminder of the world she was now a part of. A world where danger was never far away.

She turned to Nikolai, the question burning in her mind. "Why all the security? Even here, in your home… Do you really need this much protection?"

Nikolai's gaze remained steady, but there was a flicker of something in his eyes—something guarded. He didn't answer immediately, instead walking over to the bar and pouring them both a drink. The crystal decanter caught the light, casting soft reflections on the polished surface as he handed her a glass.

"Let's not dwell on that tonight," he said finally, his voice smooth but evasive. "There are things you don't need to worry about. Things I handle."

Ava's fingers tightened around the glass. She had expected that answer, but it didn't make it any easier to accept. Nikolai was always like this—just out of reach, revealing enough to draw her in but never enough to let her fully understand.

"I just want to know," she said quietly, "what kind of business requires this kind of protection?"

Nikolai smiled, but it didn't quite reach his eyes. He took a step closer, his body radiating that quiet intensity that always left her breathless. "I told you, Ava. I have business interests. Some people don't like the way I run things. They'd prefer to see me fail. That's not something I allow."

Ava's heart raced at his words. They were vague, but the meaning behind them was clear. Nikolai wasn't just a businessman—he was someone powerful, someone with enemies. She had known that on some level, but hearing it spoken aloud made the reality of it sink in.

"I protect what's mine," he continued, his voice softening as he reached out to tuck a strand of hair behind her ear. "That includes you."

A shiver ran down Ava's spine at the possessiveness in his tone. There was something dark in the way he said it—something that should have made her feel uneasy. But instead, it sent a thrill of excitement through her. The thought of being Nikolai's, of being protected and claimed by him, made her pulse quicken, even though a part of her knew it wasn't that simple.

Without another word, Nikolai took her hand, leading her toward the living room. They settled onto the plush leather couch, the city skyline stretching out before them like a painting. The lights of the buildings glittered in the distance, casting a soft glow over the room.

For a while, they sat in comfortable silence, sipping their drinks and enjoying the view. The tension that had lingered between them in the car began to melt away, replaced by the familiar pull of their chemistry. Every glance, every subtle touch, seemed to spark something between them, an unspoken connection that neither of them could ignore.

Nikolai turned toward her, his eyes dark and focused. "You're quiet tonight," he observed, his voice low.

Ava shrugged, though her mind was still racing. "There's a lot to take in," she admitted.

Nikolai's hand found hers, his thumb brushing over her knuckles in a slow, deliberate gesture. "You're safe with me, Ava. You know that, don't you?"

Ava nodded, though the truth was more complicated than that. Yes, she felt safe with him, but she also felt the weight of the unknown pressing in on her. She was drawn to him, consumed by him, but at the same time, she knew that being with Nikolai meant giving up a part of herself—maybe more than she realized.

The tension between them grew, a slow, steady buildup that neither of them tried to fight. Ava could feel it in the way his gaze lingered on her, the way his hand tightened ever so slightly around hers. She could feel it in the warmth spreading through her body, in the flutter of anticipation that always seemed to accompany their moments alone.

Nikolai stood suddenly, offering his hand. "Come with me," he said, his voice a quiet command.

Ava hesitated for only a second before taking his hand, letting him guide her through the penthouse. The bedroom was just as grand as the rest of the space—spacious, with a massive bed at its center, framed by soft lighting and floor-to-ceiling windows that offered a breathtaking view of the city below.

Nikolai turned to face her, his eyes dark with desire. He stepped closer, his hand sliding around her waist as he pulled her against him. The kiss was deep, hungry, filled with the kind of urgency that always seemed to simmer between them. Ava's body responded instantly, her hands finding their way to his chest, feeling the warmth of his skin beneath his shirt.

He broke the kiss just long enough to pull her dress over her head, the fabric falling to the floor in a soft whisper. His eyes roamed over her, dark with need, before his hands followed suit, tracing the curves of her body, his touch igniting a fire beneath her skin.

"Beautiful," he murmured, his voice a low growl as his lips found her neck, trailing kisses down to her collarbone.

Ava's breath hitched as his hands moved lower, his fingers hooking into the waistband of her panties and sliding them down, leaving her completely exposed before him. She stood there, trembling with anticipation as Nikolai's hands explored her body, his touch both rough and gentle, commanding and possessive. Every touch sent a

shiver of pleasure through Ava's body, igniting a fire
that seemed to burn hotter with each second. Her
pulse quickened, her breath hitching as his hands
roamed over her skin, leaving a trail of heat in their
wake.

Nikolai pulled her closer, his lips capturing hers in a
deep, intense kiss that left her gasping. His fingers
slid up her spine, tangling in her hair as he tilted her
head back, his mouth moving to the sensitive skin
of her neck. Ava moaned softly, her body arching
into his touch, desperate for more of him.

But Nikolai, as always, was in control. He took his
time, teasing her, exploring her body with deliberate
slowness. His lips moved lower, trailing kisses
down her chest, his tongue flicking over her nipple,
sending jolts of pleasure through her. Ava's hands
gripped his shoulders, her nails digging into his skin
as he continued his slow assault on her senses.

"You belong to me, Ava," he murmured against her
skin, his voice low and possessive. "Every inch of
you."

The words sent a thrill through her, a mix of fear
and excitement that only heightened her arousal.
She couldn't deny it anymore—she wanted this,
wanted him, more than she'd ever wanted anything.

Nikolai's hands moved lower, his fingers brushing
against the sensitive skin between her legs, teasing
her until she was trembling with need. He kissed

his way down her stomach, his lips trailing over her hips as he knelt before her. Ava's breath caught in her throat as his mouth found her, his tongue stroking her clit with slow, deliberate precision.

Ava's knees buckled, her hands gripping the edge of the bed as waves of pleasure rolled through her. Nikolai's hands tightened on her thighs, holding her in place as he continued to pleasure her with a skill and intensity that left her gasping for breath. His mouth worked her clit in slow, deliberate circles, his tongue swirling around the sensitive bundle of nerves with just the right amount of pressure. He alternated between flicking his tongue in quick, teasing motions and dragging it slowly, making her body tremble with need.

She could feel herself getting wetter with each passing second, the heat between her legs building as Nikolai took his time, savoring her reactions. He licked her in long, sensual strokes, sometimes flattening his tongue and pressing it firmly against her clit, then switching to light, teasing flicks that had her entire body tingling with desire.

He took her to the edge, bringing her closer and closer to release, only to pull back just before she could fall. It was torturous, the way he kept her hovering on the brink of climax, never quite letting her reach it. Ava whimpered in frustration, her body shaking with need, desperate for the release he was so expertly denying her.

She tried to shift her hips, to push herself closer to his mouth, but Nikolai's strong grip held her in place. His fingers dug into her thighs, firm and unyielding, reminding her who was in control. Every time she thought she might reach the peak, he slowed down, teasing her, his mouth moving deliberately, driving her insane with the need for more.

"Not yet," he growled, his voice rough with desire as he paused to look up at her, his lips glistening. "You'll come when I say."

The command sent a shiver through her, her body responding to his dominance in ways she hadn't expected. She felt herself surrender completely to him, giving up any notion of control. She was at his mercy, and though it frustrated her, it also thrilled her. There was something intoxicating about the way he controlled her pleasure, about how he seemed to know exactly what she needed before she even realized it herself.

Nikolai returned to her with renewed fervor, his tongue lapping at her slick folds, dipping lower to taste every part of her. His mouth moved expertly, alternating between her clit and the soft, sensitive skin around it, making her body tremble with each stroke. Ava's breathing became shallow, her fingers digging into the sheets as her mind became lost in the overwhelming sensations.

Just as she thought she might fall apart from the intensity of it all, Nikolai shifted, moving back up her body. His mouth found her breast, his tongue flicking over her hardened nipple before sucking it deep into his mouth. Ava gasped, her back arching as the sensation sent jolts of pleasure through her, combining with the heat still pulsing between her legs.

Nikolai sucked harder, his teeth grazing her nipple in quick, tantalizing nips that left her panting. He tugged at her breast with his mouth, pulling her nipple taut before releasing it and moving to the other, repeating the motion with the same intensity. His lips were hot, his tongue skillful, and every movement sent electric shocks through her already overstimulated body.

At the same time, his hand slid between her legs, his fingers slipping through her wetness, spreading it over her swollen clit. He teased her at first, his thumb brushing lightly against the sensitive nub, sending shudders up her spine. Ava's hips bucked involuntarily, her body aching for more of him, desperate for the release that was still just out of reach.

Then, without warning, Nikolai thrust one finger inside her, his thumb pressing firmly against her clit. Ava cried out, her head falling back as the sudden intrusion sent a wave of pleasure crashing over her. He moved his finger slowly at first, pushing in deep before pulling out almost entirely, only to thrust back in again, setting a steady, maddening rhythm.

Her wetness coated his hand as he added a second finger, stretching her, filling her completely. The combined sensation of his fingers thrusting inside her and his thumb swirling over her clit was almost too much. Ava's body trembled violently, her legs shaking as the pleasure mounted, her breath coming in short, ragged gasps.

Nikolai didn't relent. His fingers worked her expertly, thrusting deep, curling inside her, hitting that spot that made her entire body tighten with anticipation. His thumb moved in tight circles over her clit, applying just the right amount of pressure to drive her wild. At the same time, his mouth continued its assault on her breasts, his lips sucking and nipping at her nipples with a relentless intensity.

Ava could feel the tension building inside her, her body teetering on the edge of release. Her moans grew louder, more desperate, as she writhed beneath him, her mind lost in the haze of pleasure he was giving her. She felt herself falling apart, her muscles tensing as the climax built, each thrust of his fingers pushing her closer and closer to the brink.

"Nikolai... I can't... please," she whimpered, her voice breaking as her body shook with need.

But Nikolai only growled in response, his fingers thrusting harder, faster, his thumb swirling over her clit with brutal precision. He wasn't letting her off easy—he was going to make her beg for it, make her feel every second of pleasure before he allowed her release.

His mouth moved from her breast back up to her neck, his teeth grazing the sensitive skin just below her ear as he whispered, "You're mine, Ava. Every inch of you."

The possessiveness in his voice sent a shiver through her, her body responding to the dominance in his words as if it had no choice. She was his. Completely.

Finally, just as Ava thought she might break from the intensity, Nikolai pressed his thumb harder against her clit, his fingers curling inside her one last time, hitting the perfect spot. The pleasure hit her like a tidal wave, her body convulsing as the orgasm tore through her. She cried out his name, her hands fisting in the sheets as she came hard, her inner walls tightening around his fingers.

Nikolai didn't stop, his hand continuing to work her through the orgasm, his mouth claiming hers in a rough, demanding kiss. The pleasure seemed to go on forever, rolling through her in waves, leaving her breathless and trembling.

When she finally collapsed against the bed, her body spent and shaking, Nikolai pulled his fingers from her slowly, his hand moving to cup her cheek. His lips brushed against hers, softer now, as he murmured, "You're mine, Ava. Never forget that."

Finally, after what felt like an eternity, Nikolai stood, his eyes dark with lust as he lifted her onto the bed. He positioned her on her hands and knees, the cool air brushing against her skin as she waited, her body trembling with anticipation.

Nikolai moved behind her, his hands gripping her hips as he teased her entrance with the tip of his cock. Ava moaned softly, her body aching for him, desperate to be filled.

"Please, Nikolai," she whispered, her voice barely above a breath.

He didn't make her wait any longer. With one swift, powerful thrust, he buried himself inside her, his cock stretching and filling her completely. Ava cried out, her body arching as the sensation of him inside her sent waves of pleasure crashing through her.

Nikolai set a slow, deliberate pace at first, his grip on her hips tightening as he drove deeper with each thrust. Ava's fingers clenched the sheets, her body rocking back to meet his movements, the pleasure building with every stroke.

But it wasn't long before his pace quickened, his thrusts becoming harder, more urgent, as the tension between them reached a fever pitch. Ava's moans filled the room, her body quaking as the pleasure built and built, pushing her closer to the edge.

"You're mine, Ava," Nikolai growled, his voice rough and possessive. "Every inch of you."

His words, the intensity of his thrusts, the feel of him claiming her so completely—it was too much. Ava's body tensed, her breath catching as the pleasure overwhelmed her, sending her spiraling into an intense, all-consuming orgasm.

She cried out, her body shaking as the waves of pleasure crashed through her again, her muscles tightening around him as she came hard, her vision blurring as the orgasm wracked her entire being.

Nikolai didn't slow down. He continued to thrust into her wetness, his pace relentless as he chased his own release. His hands gripped her hips tightly, pulling her back to meet his thrusts as he pounded into her, each movement sending another wave of pleasure through her already spent body.

Finally, with a low, guttural growl, Nikolai thrust deep one last time, his body tensing as he came inside her, his cock pulsing as he filled her. Ava gasped at the sensation, her body trembling as she felt him empty into her, the intimacy of the moment almost too much to bear.

For a long moment, they stayed like that, both of them catching their breath, the room filled with the heavy scent of sex and sweat. Nikolai's hands slowly loosened their grip on her hips, his fingers trailing gently over her skin as he pulled out of her and collapsed beside her on the bed.

Ava lay there, her body spent, her mind spinning. She could still feel the lingering heat between her legs, the soreness from where his hands had gripped her so tightly. The intensity of what they had just shared left her breathless, her thoughts swirling as she tried to make sense of everything that had just happened.

Nikolai's arm slid around her waist, pulling her close to him. His body was warm and solid beside hers, his presence grounding her as the fog of pleasure slowly began to lift.

"You're mine, Ava," he whispered again, his voice softer now, filled with something deeper, more intimate. "Never forget that."

Ava closed her eyes, leaning into his embrace. She knew there were still so many questions, still so much she didn't understand about Nikolai, about the life he lived. But in this moment, lying in his arms, she felt safe. She felt claimed. And for now, that was enough.

But even as she lay there, content in the warmth of his arms, a small part of her couldn't shake the feeling that this was only the beginning. That the intensity of what they shared, the dark passion that seemed to bind them together, was only going to grow. And with it, the danger that surrounded Nikolai's world would become more real, more immediate.

Ava wasn't sure if she was ready for what came next. But she knew one thing for certain—she couldn't walk away now. She was already in too deep.

As sleep slowly overtook her, her last conscious thought was of Nikolai's words, echoing in her mind.

You're mine.

Chapter 8

The soft morning light filtered through the vast floor-to-ceiling windows, casting a golden glow over the luxurious bedroom. Ava blinked against the brightness, her body heavy with the exhaustion of the previous night. She felt the soreness in her muscles—a reminder of how thoroughly Nikolai had claimed her. Her limbs ached, but it wasn't just physical fatigue that weighed on her. The emotional whirlwind of the past few days lingered in her chest, leaving her feeling both exhilarated and confused.

For a moment, Ava stayed still, letting herself sink into the softness of the sheets, cocooned in the comfort of the bed. Nikolai lay beside her, his presence a constant, magnetic force even in sleep. She turned her head slightly to watch him, her eyes tracing the sharp angles of his face, the strong lines of his jaw. There was something undeniably compelling about him, even in these rare moments of stillness. His power was ever-present, like an aura that surrounded him, and it drew her in like a moth to a flame.

But with that power came a sense of uncertainty that gnawed at her. She was in awe of him, yes, but there was also a growing unease inside her—an awareness that the intensity of their connection came with consequences she hadn't yet fully comprehended.

Ava slowly shifted, careful not to disturb Nikolai as she slid out of bed. Her feet sank into the plush carpet as she stood, feeling the cool morning air against her bare skin. She walked quietly toward the windows, her fingers trailing over the glass as she gazed out at the city below. From here, the world seemed so distant, so far removed from the chaos and danger that surrounded Nikolai's life. Yet, in this very moment, she couldn't shake the sense that she was teetering on the edge of something far bigger than herself.

She had never been one to shy away from passion, but this—whatever this was between her and Nikolai—was different. It consumed her in ways she hadn't expected, leaving her vulnerable in a way that made her both excited and terrified.

As she stood there, lost in her thoughts, she heard the soft rustle of sheets behind her. Nikolai stirred, waking slowly, his movements deliberate and unhurried. When Ava turned back to look at him, she found his eyes already on her, watching her with that same intensity that always made her heart skip a beat.

"Good morning," his voice was deep and smooth, sending a shiver through her.

"Morning," Ava replied, her voice soft. She tried to smile, but it felt fragile, like a mask she wasn't sure she could hold in place.

Nikolai sat up, the sheets falling away to reveal the muscular lines of his chest and shoulders. He stretched slightly, then patted the space beside him. "Come back to bed."

For a moment, Ava hesitated. It would be so easy to slip back into his arms, to lose herself in the warmth and comfort of his embrace. But something held her back—a quiet voice in the back of her mind that whispered of the uncertainty still lingering between them.

Instead, she shook her head gently. "I think I need a shower first," she said, trying to keep her tone light.

Nikolai raised an eyebrow but said nothing, his gaze following her as she moved toward the bathroom. Ava could feel the weight of his stare, could feel the way it pulled at her, but she pushed it aside, stepping into the cool marble bathroom and closing the door behind her.

Inside, the quiet was almost deafening. Ava turned on the shower, letting the hot water steam up the room as she leaned against the sink, staring at her reflection in the mirror. Her hair was tousled, her cheeks flushed, her lips still swollen from Nikolai's kisses. She looked different—older, somehow.

Worn. And yet, there was something else too, something she hadn't seen in herself before. A kind of rawness, a vulnerability that had been exposed since she'd met Nikolai.

She stepped into the shower, letting the hot water cascade over her skin, washing away the remnants of the night before. As the water pounded against her, she closed her eyes, trying to clear her mind, but it was no use. The thoughts kept coming, swirling around her like a storm.

She thought about the way Nikolai made her feel—how safe and protected she felt in his presence, but also how small and powerless she felt sometimes. He had a way of taking control, of making decisions for her without even asking. At first, it had been intoxicating, thrilling even. But now, she wasn't so sure.

Was this really what she wanted? To be swept up into someone else's world, with no say in how things unfolded? To be kept in the dark about the dangers that lurked just beyond the surface?

Ava leaned her forehead against the cool tile, her mind racing. She couldn't deny her feelings for Nikolai—the attraction, the desire—but there was more to it than that. There was a part of her that craved independence, that wanted to be more than just someone's possession. She wasn't sure how much longer she could live like this, constantly waiting for answers that never came, constantly feeling like she was walking on the edge of a cliff.

When she finally stepped out of the shower, she felt no clearer than before. She wrapped herself in a plush towel and took a deep breath before heading back into the bedroom.

Nikolai was sitting on the edge of the bed, fully dressed now in dark jeans and a fitted shirt that did little to hide the power in his body. He looked up as she entered, his eyes narrowing slightly as he took in her expression.

"Are you all right?" he asked, his voice laced with concern.

Ava nodded, though she wasn't sure if it was the truth. "Yeah. Just… thinking."

Nikolai studied her for a moment longer, as if trying to read her thoughts, but then he stood and crossed the room to her. He reached out, his hand gently brushing a strand of damp hair from her face.

"Let's have breakfast," he said, his tone light but firm.

Ava didn't argue. She followed him to the kitchen, where the scent of freshly brewed coffee and warm pastries greeted her. The space was just as luxurious as the rest of the penthouse—modern, sleek, with stainless steel appliances and marble countertops that gleamed in the morning light.

They ate in relative silence, the clink of silverware against plates the only sound between them. Ava picked at her food, her appetite waning as her thoughts continued to swirl.

Finally, she couldn't take it anymore. She set down her fork and looked up at Nikolai, her brow furrowing with uncertainty. "Nikolai… I need to ask you something."

He glanced up from his coffee, his expression unreadable. "Go on."

Ava hesitated, unsure of how to phrase what was on her mind. "Why do you need so much protection? Even here, in your own home… There are always bodyguards around. You talk about your business, but you never really tell me anything. What exactly do you do?"

Nikolai's gaze hardened slightly, though his tone remained calm. "I've told you before, Ava. I have business interests. Some people don't like how I operate, and they would prefer to see me fail."

"But who are these people?" Ava pressed, her frustration bubbling to the surface. "What are they trying to do? Why won't you tell me more?"

Nikolai's jaw tightened, and for a moment, Ava thought he might shut her down entirely. But then he sighed, setting his cup down on the table.

"It's not that I don't want to tell you," he said, his voice softer now. "It's that there are things you're better off not knowing."

Ava's chest tightened at his words. She had expected more evasion, but there was something about the way he said it that made her heart race with a mix of fear and curiosity. "Why?" she asked quietly. "Why am I better off not knowing?"

Nikolai leaned back in his chair, his eyes fixed on hers. "Because the less you know, the safer you are."

Ava stared at him, her mind racing. Safe. That word again. It was always about safety with Nikolai—keeping her protected, shielding her from the dangers of his world. But what kind of life was that? A life where she was constantly in the dark, where she had no control over her own fate?

"I don't want to be kept in the dark, Nikolai," she said softly, her voice barely above a whisper. "I don't want to be just another part of your world that you control."

Nikolai's eyes narrowed slightly, and for a moment, the tension between them crackled like electricity. "Ava," he said slowly, "I'm trying to protect you."

"But I don't want protection," Ava replied, her voice stronger now. "I want answers. I want to know what I'm getting into. I deserve that, don't I?"

Nikolai didn't respond immediately. Instead, he stood up from the table, pacing slowly to the window, his back to her. He stood there for a long moment, staring out at the city as if he were weighing his words carefully.

When he finally spoke, his voice was quiet, almost distant. "Ava, my life is… complicated. I have enemies—people who would hurt me, hurt those close to me, to get what they want. That's why the bodyguards are always there. That's why I keep certain things from you," Nikolai continued, his voice low, almost regretful. "It's not because I don't trust you. It's because the more you know, the more danger you're in. The people I deal with… they don't play by the same rules as everyone else."

Ava stared at his back, trying to process what he was saying. She had known from the beginning that Nikolai wasn't an ordinary man. He had wealth, power, and an air of danger that had drawn her in from the start. But hearing it laid out like this—hearing the reality of the risks she faced by being with him—it was something else entirely.

"What kind of people?" she asked, her voice trembling slightly. "What are they trying to do to you?"

Nikolai turned back to face her, his expression unreadable. "There are factions, enemies from both inside and outside of my business. It's a constant struggle for control, for power. And if they see a weakness, they will exploit it. That's why I need you to be safe, Ava. That's why you can't know everything."

Ava's mind raced. She understood what he was saying, but it didn't make her feel any better. If anything, it only made her feel more trapped. "But how long can we live like this, Nikolai?" she asked, her voice tinged with frustration. "How long can I stay in the dark, not knowing what's coming, not knowing who's out there waiting for us?"

Nikolai stepped forward, his hands reaching for hers. His touch was warm, reassuring, but it didn't dispel the knot of anxiety that had taken root in her chest. "I know it's not easy," he said softly. "But I need you to trust me. Trust that I'm doing everything I can to protect you, to keep us safe."

Ava looked into his eyes, searching for something—anything—that would make her feel secure. But all she saw was the same darkness that had been there from the beginning. The same danger that had always lurked just beneath the surface. And for the first time, she wondered if she could really handle it.

She pulled her hands from his, stepping back slightly. "I need time to think," she said quietly. "I need to figure out if this is something I can do."

Nikolai's jaw clenched, but he didn't argue. He simply nodded, his eyes never leaving hers. "Take all the time you need."

The words were simple, but Ava could hear the weight behind them. He was giving her space, but it felt like an ultimatum. Either she accepted the life he offered—danger, secrecy, and all—or she walked away.

The thought of leaving him, of walking away from the intensity of what they had, made her chest tighten with a pang of longing. But the alternative—living in a constant state of fear, always wondering what dangers were lurking around the corner—was equally unbearable.

She needed to clear her head.

"I'm going to take a walk," Ava said, turning toward the door. "I just... need some fresh air."

Nikolai didn't try to stop her. He simply nodded again, his expression unreadable. "Take the security with you," he said. "You're not safe without them."

Ava felt a flash of irritation. Even now, he couldn't let her leave without some form of control. But she bit back her retort, knowing that arguing with him would get her nowhere.

She grabbed her coat and left the penthouse, her mind still spinning. Two of Nikolai's bodyguards followed her out, their presence a constant reminder of the world she had stepped into. As she walked through the streets of Manhattan, the cool breeze biting at her skin, Ava tried to think, but her thoughts were a jumbled mess of emotions.

She had fallen for Nikolai—there was no denying that. He was everything she had ever wanted in a man: strong, protective, passionate. But the cost of being with him was becoming clearer with each passing day. Could she live like this? Could she live in the shadows, never fully knowing the dangers that surrounded them?

Ava found herself wandering aimlessly, her feet carrying her through the crowded streets as her mind whirled with unanswered questions. She didn't know how long she walked, but eventually, she found herself in a small park, the quietness of the space a stark contrast to the chaos inside her.

She sat down on a bench, pulling her coat tighter around her as she stared at the trees swaying gently in the breeze. She needed to make a decision. But no matter how hard she tried, she couldn't see a way forward that didn't involve sacrifice.

Being with Nikolai meant giving up a part of herself—her independence, her sense of control over her life. But walking away from him meant giving up the passion, the connection, and the sense of safety she felt when she was in his arms. It was a choice between two halves of herself, and she wasn't sure which one would win out.

Ava sat there for what felt like hours, the weight of the decision pressing down on her. She knew she couldn't stay in limbo forever. Sooner or later, she would have to choose.

Her phone buzzed in her pocket, snapping her out of her thoughts. She pulled it out and saw a message from Nikolai: "I'll be home late tonight. We need to talk."

The words sent a chill down her spine. Ava didn't know what he wanted to talk about, but she knew it wouldn't be easy.

She stood up from the bench, her legs feeling heavy as she made her way back toward the penthouse. The bodyguards followed at a respectful distance, but their presence was a constant reminder of the life she had chosen. A life that, no matter how much she wanted to deny it, was filled with danger and secrets.

By the time she reached the building, the sun was beginning to set, casting a soft golden light over the city. She stepped into the elevator, her stomach churning with anxiety as she thought about what awaited her upstairs.

When she entered the penthouse, the space was empty, save for the soft hum of the city outside. Nikolai wasn't back yet, and the silence only amplified her growing sense of unease.

Ava sank onto the couch, her mind racing as she tried to prepare herself for whatever conversation Nikolai wanted to have. But no matter how hard she tried, she couldn't shake the feeling that things were about to change—irrevocably.

The hours ticked by, and with each passing minute, the knot of anxiety in her chest tightened. By the time the door finally opened and Nikolai stepped inside, Ava was practically vibrating with tension.

He didn't speak at first. He simply crossed the room to her, his expression unreadable as he sat down beside her on the couch.

For a long moment, they just sat there in silence, the weight of the unspoken words hanging heavily between them.

Finally, Nikolai turned to her, his eyes dark and serious. "We need to talk," he said, his voice low. "About us. About the future."

Ava's heart pounded in her chest, but she nodded, bracing herself for whatever came next. She knew, deep down, that this conversation would define everything that followed.

And no matter how much she tried to prepare herself, she wasn't sure she was ready for it.

Ava's breath caught in her throat as Nikolai's words hung in the air between them. The future. The weight of that single word seemed to settle heavily on her chest, as if everything that had transpired between them—the intensity, the passion, the danger—was now being thrust into stark reality.

She had been trying to avoid thinking about it for days, perhaps even weeks. It had been easier to live in the moment, to let herself be swept away by Nikolai's magnetism. But now, sitting here beside him, the cold truth was unavoidable. There was no way forward without confronting the difficult questions. And no way to keep avoiding the fact that her life had changed irrevocably since she had met him.

Ava shifted on the couch, suddenly feeling small in the presence of Nikolai's towering, intimidating aura. She wasn't sure she was ready for this conversation, but there was no escaping it now. Nikolai was watching her closely, waiting for her to respond.

"What about us?" she asked softly, trying to keep her voice steady, though her heart was pounding.

Nikolai's gaze never wavered. He leaned back slightly, his hands clasped in front of him as he exhaled slowly, thoughtfully. "I need you to understand something, Ava," he began, his voice steady, but there was an underlying tension that told her this wasn't easy for him either. "This life… my life… it's not simple. It never will be. And if you're with me, you'll always be part of that life."

Ava swallowed hard, her throat dry. She had known, on some level, that being with Nikolai meant stepping into a world she had never truly understood. But hearing him say it, so plainly, felt like a door closing. "What does that really mean?" she asked, her voice barely above a whisper. "I need to know what I'm getting into, Nikolai. I don't want to be kept in the dark anymore."

Nikolai shifted slightly, his eyes narrowing as he considered her words. "I've kept things from you to protect you," he said. "But you're right. You deserve to know more."

He stood abruptly, pacing the length of the room with long, purposeful strides. Ava watched him, feeling her anxiety rise as she waited for him to continue.

"You've seen the security, the bodyguards. You've sensed the danger around me," he said, turning to face her once more. "It's because of who I am. I'm not just a businessman, Ava. My family… we have a long history. A history of power, of control, of dealing with those who would take what we have built."

Ava's mind whirled, trying to make sense of his words. She had suspected that Nikolai wasn't simply wealthy—that there was something darker, more dangerous about him. But now, hearing him admit it, she realized just how little she truly knew.

"What are you saying?" she asked, her voice trembling slightly.

Nikolai's gaze locked onto hers, his eyes intense. "I'm part of the Bratva, Ava. The Russian mafia."

The words hit her like a punch to the gut. Ava's breath caught in her throat as her mind scrambled to process what he had just said. The Bratva. She had heard of them before—stories whispered in the shadows, rumors about their ruthlessness, their reach, their power. And now, the man she had fallen for, the man she had shared her body and soul with, was a part of that world.

"I didn't tell you before because I wanted to keep you safe," Nikolai continued, his voice softer now. "But I can't hide it from you any longer. If you're with me, you're part of this. There's no escaping it."

Ava sat in stunned silence, her mind racing. She felt like the ground had been ripped out from beneath her. Everything she had thought she knew about Nikolai had been turned on its head. And

now, she was faced with a decision she wasn't sure
she was ready to make.

"I… I don't know what to say," she whispered, her
voice barely audible.

Nikolai crossed the room in two quick strides,
kneeling in front of her. He took her hands in his,
his touch warm and steady, but his eyes were filled
with something darker—something that frightened
her. "I need you to understand, Ava," he said, his
voice low and urgent. "This life is dangerous. But I
will protect you. I will keep you safe, no matter
what. You just have to trust me."

Ava's heart raced as she looked into his eyes. She
wanted to trust him. She wanted to believe that he
could shield her from the dangers of his world. But
how could she? How could she willingly walk into
the arms of a man who was part of something so
violent, so dangerous?

"What if I can't do this?" she asked, her voice
trembling. "What if I can't live in that kind of world?"

Nikolai's jaw clenched, and for a moment, Ava
thought she saw a flash of pain in his eyes. "Then
you'll leave," he said, his voice quiet. "And I won't
stop you."

The words hung in the air, heavy with finality. Ava
felt her chest tighten as she realized what he was
saying. If she couldn't handle his world, if she

couldn't accept the danger and the secrets, then he would let her go. But she knew that leaving him wouldn't be simple. She had already fallen for him—deeply, irrevocably. And walking away now felt impossible.

"I don't want to leave," she said, her voice barely above a whisper. "But I don't know how to live in a world like that."

Nikolai's hands tightened around hers. "I know it's not easy," he said, his voice raw. "But I will do everything in my power to keep you safe. I swear to you, Ava. No one will touch you. No one will hurt you. You just have to trust me."

Ava felt tears prickling at the corners of her eyes, the weight of the decision pressing down on her. She didn't want to walk away from Nikolai. She didn't want to lose the connection they had. But could she really live with the constant danger, the secrets, the fear?

"I love you, Ava," Nikolai said suddenly in his beautiful accented voice, thick with emotion. "I've never felt this way about anyone before. And I can't lose you. Not now. Not when we've just begun."

Ava's heart ached at his words. She had never heard him speak so openly, so vulnerably. And in that moment, she realized how deeply he cared for her—how much he was willing to sacrifice to keep her by his side.

"I love you too," she whispered, her voice trembling.

The admission was both freeing and terrifying. She loved him. She couldn't deny it any longer. But loving him meant accepting everything that came with him—the danger, the secrets, the fear. And she wasn't sure if she was strong enough to do that.

Nikolai pulled her into his arms, holding her tightly against his chest. Ava closed her eyes, letting herself sink into the warmth of his embrace, the steady rhythm of his heartbeat against her cheek. She wanted to believe that they could make this work, that love would be enough to overcome the challenges they faced. But deep down, she knew it wouldn't be that simple.

Nikolai pulled back slightly, his hands cupping her face as he looked into her eyes. "You don't have to decide right now," he said softly. "Take your time. But know this—I'm not giving up on us. I'll fight for you, Ava. I'll fight for us."

Ava nodded, though the tears were already slipping down her cheeks. She wanted to believe him. She wanted to trust him. But the path ahead of them was dark, and she wasn't sure where it would lead.

For now, all she could do was hold onto him and hope that, somehow, they would find a way through.

Chapter 9

Ava sat on the edge of the bed, her mind spinning in a hundred directions. The events of the last twenty-four hours were still fresh in her mind. Nikolai's revelation had shaken her more than she had expected. Head of the Bratva. The words echoed in her head like a heavy, reverberating toll. It was one thing to know Nikolai wasn't just any businessman, but it was something else entirely to confront the fact that he was the head of one of the most powerful and dangerous criminal organizations in the world.

She loved him, there was no doubt about that. The pull between them had always been undeniable. But now, the stakes felt different. Being with Nikolai meant living in a world she had never imagined herself being a part of—a world filled with violence, control, and shadows that could swallow her whole.

But it also meant something else. Safety. With Nikolai, she had never felt safer. His arms around her made her feel invincible, like nothing could touch her. He had power—more than anyone she had ever met. And he used that power to protect her, to shield her from the very dangers his world created.

Ava buried her face in her hands, feeling the weight of the decision pressing down on her. Could she live in a world like that? A world where her every move might be watched, where danger lurked around every corner? The rational part of her screamed to run, to get out while she still could. But another part—the part that loved Nikolai, that was drawn to his intensity, his passion—wanted to stay. To dive deeper into the world he lived in, to see where it would take her.

She sighed, standing up and crossing the room to the large floor-to-ceiling windows that overlooked the city below. New York sprawled out before her, the streets bustling with life, but up here in Nikolai's penthouse, it felt like another world. A world where she was removed from everything ordinary, everything safe.

Behind her, the door opened softly, and she turned to see Nikolai enter the room. He looked calm, composed, but there was an intensity in his eyes that made her heart quicken.

"We're going out tonight," he said, his voice smooth but with an edge of authority. "There's a club I want to take you to. It's a place where I handle business from time to time."

Ava nodded, though her heart fluttered nervously at the thought of entering that world. The places where Nikolai conducted his "business" weren't exactly ordinary. They were filled with dangerous people, men who operated on the fringes of the law, who respected Nikolai for his power and control.

Nikolai crossed the room, his eyes scanning her as if assessing her readiness. Then, with a small, almost imperceptible smile, he handed her a large black box. Ava blinked in surprise, her fingers brushing over the smooth surface of the box before she slowly opened it.

Inside was a dress. But not just any dress. It was sleek, tight, and made of the softest fabric she had ever touched. The black material shimmered in the light, and the neckline plunged daringly low, while the hem barely skimmed her thighs. It was stunning, beautiful even—but it was also incredibly revealing. Accompanying the dress were a pair of black stilettos, impossibly high and gleaming under the light.

"I want you to wear this tonight," Nikolai said, his voice low as he watched her reaction.

Ava felt her pulse quicken as she held the dress up against her body, glancing at herself in the mirror. It was undeniably beautiful, and there was no doubt that it would turn heads. But there was something else too—a feeling that the dress wasn't just for her. It was for him. Nikolai wanted her to wear it, not just because he thought it was beautiful, but because it was part of his control.

"You'll look perfect," Nikolai continued, his eyes dark and commanding. "I want to show you off."

Ava swallowed hard, feeling a wave of conflicting emotions crash over her. Part of her bristled at the idea of being "shown off," of being a display for others to see. But another part of her—one she didn't want to admit—felt flattered. The thought of walking into the club on Nikolai's arm, dressed in something so striking, sent a thrill through her. She had never been the kind of woman who turned heads, who drew attention. But with this dress, with Nikolai by her side, she would be impossible to ignore.

Her fingers brushed over the fabric again, feeling the smoothness under her touch. It was beautiful. It made her feel powerful, sexy, desired. And yet, there was an unease that came with it too—a knowledge that wearing it meant surrendering to Nikolai's control, to his desires.

"I'll wear it," she said softly, meeting his gaze in the mirror.

Nikolai's smile widened slightly, and he stepped closer, his hands resting on her shoulders as he leaned down to whisper in her ear. "Good. You're mine, Ava. And tonight, I want everyone to know it."

The possessiveness in his voice sent a shiver down her spine, and Ava wasn't sure if it was fear or desire that made her pulse race.

The club was like nothing Ava had ever seen before. It wasn't just luxurious—it was opulent, dripping with wealth and power in every corner. The interior was bathed in dim lighting, with sleek black walls and polished chrome accents that reflected the flashing lights from the bar. The music thumped steadily in the background, a deep bass that seemed to pulse through the entire building.

But what stood out to Ava the most were the people. Men and women dressed in designer clothing, sipping on expensive champagne and cocktails, their eyes sharp and predatory. There was a palpable sense of danger in the air, an awareness that the people in this room were powerful, dangerous, and accustomed to getting what they wanted.

Nikolai led her through the crowd, his hand resting possessively on the small of her back. Ava could feel eyes on her—on them—as they walked. The dress clung to her curves, and the high heels made her legs seem impossibly long. She had never felt more exposed, yet at the same time, she had never felt more desired. Men glanced at her as they passed, their eyes lingering for just a moment too long, but they quickly shifted their gazes to Nikolai, as if recognizing the authority he commanded.

She was on Nikolai's arm, and in this world, that meant something. It meant she belonged to him.

They approached a group of men gathered around a private table, each of them standing as they greeted Nikolai with a nod of respect. Ava recognized the power dynamics instantly—these were men who answered to him, who respected him not just for his wealth but for the authority he wielded.

"Viktor," Nikolai greeted one of the men, shaking his hand firmly before gesturing toward Ava. "This is Ava."

Viktor's eyes flicked to her, and he gave her a polite, appraising smile. "A pleasure to meet you, Ava," he said, his voice thick with a Russian accent. "You are as beautiful as I've heard."

Ava felt a flush rise to her cheeks at the compliment, unsure how to respond. Nikolai seemed to sense her discomfort and pulled her slightly closer, his arm wrapping around her waist.

Another man, Sergei, approached, his eyes gleaming with approval as he glanced between her and Nikolai. "You're a lucky man, Nikolai," he said, his gaze lingering on Ava. "She's a rare beauty."

The men exchanged a few more words, mostly business-related, with Nikolai speaking in rapid Russian, his tone calm but authoritative. Ava stood quietly by his side, feeling out of place but also captivated by the interactions. These men weren't just businessmen—they were dangerous, powerful individuals who operated outside the law. And they all answered to Nikolai.

As the conversation continued, Ava felt a strange mix of emotions swirling inside her. She was fascinated by this world, by the way Nikolai commanded respect and fear with just a look or a word. It was intoxicating to be by his side, to feel the power that radiated off of him. But at the same time, she couldn't ignore the unease that lingered just beneath the surface. These men, these people, lived in a world of violence and control. A world where weakness was preyed upon, and power was everything.

Ava took a sip of the champagne Nikolai had handed her, feeling the bubbles fizz against her lips. She glanced around the room again, noticing the way the other women in the club dressed and acted. They were all beautiful, all glamorous, but there was something else too—a certain coldness, a hardness in their eyes. It was as if they had learned how to navigate this world, how to survive in a place where men like Nikolai ruled.

And then there was Ava, standing beside Nikolai, feeling like an outsider in this dangerous, seductive world. Yet, at the same time, she couldn't deny the thrill that ran through her. She was here, with him, and for the first time in her life, she felt like she was part of something larger—something powerful.

The glamorous club, the dangerous men, the power dynamics—it all felt like a whirlwind, and Ava wasn't sure if she was being pulled under or if she was diving in willingly. As she stood beside Nikolai, surrounded by powerful figures and watching the way they deferred to him, she felt the weight of her decision pressing down on her. This was what being with Nikolai meant. It wasn't just about love or passion. It was about power, danger, and control.

She took another sip of her champagne, trying to steady her nerves, when Nikolai's hand slid from her waist to the small of her back, guiding her toward the bar. His touch was possessive but gentle, as if reminding her that she was his.

"Ava," he said softly, leaning in close enough that his breath brushed against her ear. "Are you enjoying yourself?"

She turned to look at him, her heart racing. His eyes were dark, filled with that familiar intensity that always made her weak in the knees. There was something about the way he looked at her—like she was the only person in the room, the only one who mattered. It was overwhelming, the way his gaze made her feel both exposed and cherished at the same time.

"I am," she replied, though her voice was softer than she intended. "It's just… a lot to take in."

Nikolai's lips curved into a small smile, his hand tightening slightly on her back. "You're doing well. Better than I expected."

Ava frowned slightly, feeling the weight of his words. "What do you mean?"

"You're adapting," Nikolai said simply, his eyes never leaving hers. "I know this world is new to you. I wasn't sure how you'd handle it."

She swallowed hard, her thoughts swirling. "It's… different," she admitted. "But I'm learning."

Nikolai's smile widened, a flicker of pride in his expression. "Good. Because there's no turning back now, Ava. You're with me, and that means you're part of this."

The words sent a shiver through her, both thrilling and terrifying. Part of this. It was a statement, not a question. Nikolai wasn't giving her a choice—he was telling her that this was her life now.

Despite the dangerous company, Ava felt a strange sense of belonging. She was beginning to understand the allure of Nikolai's world—the power, the respect, the thrill of living on the edge. It was intoxicating, and she found herself drawn deeper into it.

As the evening wore on, Nikolai stayed close to her, his touch reassuring and possessive. He seemed proud to have her by his side, introducing her as his with a subtle yet unmistakable claim. Ava couldn't deny the flutter of excitement this brought her, even as it highlighted the control he had over her.

The night progressed smoothly, filled with laughter, business discussions, and a sense of camaraderie among Nikolai's circle. Ava was beginning to see the layers of loyalty and danger that underpinned these relationships, and she couldn't help but be fascinated by it all.

As they made their way to the bar for a drink, Ava felt a growing sense of confidence. She was becoming more comfortable in this environment, more at ease with the people around her. But beneath it all, there was a flicker of uncertainty, a recognition of the thin line she was walking between admiration and fear.

The club was pulsing with life, the music pounding against the walls, reverberating through Ava's body as she stood beside Nikolai at the bar. The conversations with his associates had ended, and she had relaxed into the night, feeling more comfortable in her surroundings. She knew she was in dangerous company, but it hadn't felt so pressing until now. The looks she was getting—the respectful nods, the curious glances—were all filtered through the lens of Nikolai's presence, as though everyone knew she belonged to him.

She was part of this world now.

The words had settled into her bones like a promise and a warning. There was no going back. Nikolai hadn't asked her if she wanted to be part of it; he had told her. She was his, and that came with certain realities—power, control, and danger.

Ava sipped her drink, the cool liquid doing little to calm her nerves as she tried to process it all. Despite the excitement of being by his side and feeling desired in a way she never had before, there was a lingering sense of unease. The weight of this decision pressed down on her, the magnitude of it so much greater than she had anticipated.

But before she could follow the thought any further, she caught the eye of a man at the bar. He was swaying slightly, clearly drunk, his gaze locked onto her with an unsettling intensity. She glanced away, hoping he would take the hint, but his eyes remained on her.

A knot of discomfort formed in her stomach. His presence was intrusive, his stare invasive. She shifted closer to Nikolai, hoping the man would back off, but instead, he took a step toward them.

"Hey," the man slurred, his voice rough and overly familiar as he looked Ava up and down. "You're a lucky guy, you know that?"

Nikolai stiffened beside her, and Ava felt the shift in his demeanor immediately. His body tensed, his hand on her lower back tightening ever so slightly. He hadn't turned to face the man yet, but she could feel the storm brewing in him.

The drunk man wasn't finished. He grinned, his eyes lecherous as he let out a low chuckle. "She's something else, isn't she? Must be fun to have her all to yourself."

Ava's skin crawled, heat rising to her cheeks as the man's words sank in. She wanted to disappear, to pull Nikolai away from the situation before it escalated. But she didn't have time.

Nikolai turned slowly, his expression cold and menacing as his gaze locked onto the man. His voice was low, dangerous as he spoke. "What did you just say?"

The man, too drunk to recognize the danger he was in, laughed again, raising his drink in mock salute. "I'm just saying, man. She's a fine piece of—"

Nikolai didn't let him finish. In a flash, his hand shot out, grabbing the man by the collar and yanking him forward. The drink the man had been holding spilled to the floor, forgotten as his eyes widened in shock. He stumbled, trying to regain his footing, but Nikolai's grip was unrelenting.

"You think you can talk to her like that?" Nikolai's voice was barely above a growl, his words dripping with lethal intent. "You think you can look at her, speak about her, like she's nothing?"

The man sputtered, panic flickering in his eyes as he tried to free himself from Nikolai's hold. "I—I didn't mean anything by it," he stammered, his bravado slipping. "I was just—"

But Nikolai wasn't listening. His eyes were filled with fury, his jaw clenched as he pulled the man closer, their faces inches apart. "You don't talk to her. You don't even look at her," he hissed, his grip tightening. "Do you understand me?"

Ava's heart was racing, her hands trembling as she watched the scene unfold. She had never seen Nikolai like this before—so cold, so violent. The tension in the air was suffocating, and she could feel the eyes of everyone in the club turning toward them. People were watching, whispering, but no one dared to interfere.

The drunk man whimpered, nodding frantically as he struggled to find his words. "I'm sorry," he gasped, his voice shaking. "I didn't mean anything by it. I swear."

Nikolai's lip curled in disdain, and for a moment, Ava thought he might let the man go. But then, without warning, he slammed his fist into the man's jaw. The sound of bone cracking against bone echoed through the room, followed by a sickening thud as the man crumpled to the floor.

Ava gasped, her hands flying to her mouth as she stared at the man lying motionless at Nikolai's feet. The club had fallen into stunned silence, all eyes now on Nikolai as he stood over the man, his fists still clenched, his chest heaving with barely restrained rage.

The man groaned, weakly trying to push himself up, but Nikolai didn't give him the chance. He reached down, grabbing the man by the collar again and hauling him to his feet. The man's eyes were wide with terror now, blood dripping from his nose and mouth as he tried to form words.

"I'm sorry," he croaked, his voice hoarse. "Please… I'm sorry."

Nikolai's expression didn't change. His fist connected with the man's face again, harder this time, sending him sprawling across the floor. Blood splattered onto the polished surface, the man's body limp and broken as he lay there, whimpering in pain.

Ava stood frozen, her heart pounding in her chest as she watched the brutal scene unfold. She should have been horrified. She should have felt fear, disgust, something. But instead, she felt… captivated. She couldn't tear her eyes away from Nikolai, from the raw power he exuded as he defended her with such ferocity.

He was terrifying, yes. But he was also intoxicating.

Nikolai took a step toward the man, his voice low and cold as he spoke. "Get out," he growled. "Before I finish this."

The man didn't need to be told twice. He scrambled to his feet, blood still dripping from his nose as he stumbled toward the door, clutching his side in pain. The crowd parted for him, their eyes wide with shock and fear as he disappeared into the night.

For a moment, the club remained silent, the weight of what had just happened settling over the room like a thick fog. Then, slowly, the music resumed, the conversation picking back up, though there was still a lingering tension in the air.

Nikolai turned to Ava, his expression still hard, though his eyes softened slightly when they met hers. He reached for her, his hand gently brushing a strand of hair away from her face. "Are you okay?" he asked, his voice quieter now, though the edge of anger still lingered.

Ava nodded, though her mind was spinning. "I'm fine," she whispered, though she wasn't sure if that was true. She didn't know what to think, what to feel.

Nikolai exhaled slowly, his hand sliding down to her waist, pulling her closer to him. "Let's go," he said quietly, his voice firm. "We're done here."

Ava didn't protest as Nikolai led her out of the club, his arm wrapped protectively around her as they made their way through the crowd. She could feel the weight of the stares, the whispers that followed them, but she didn't care. All she could think about was what had just happened.

Once they were outside, the cool night air hit her like a slap, snapping her back to reality. She shivered slightly, though it wasn't from the cold. Her mind was still reeling, her heart racing as she tried to process the events of the night.

Nikolai was silent beside her, his body still tense with residual anger. They walked in silence for a few blocks before he finally spoke.

"I'm sorry you had to see that," Nikolai said, his voice gruff but sincere. "But I won't let anyone talk about you like that. Ever."

Ava stopped walking, her breath catching as his words settled over her. She tried to breathe, to focus on the simple act of drawing air into her lungs, but her mind was still spinning from what had just happened. The images replayed in her head—the man's body hitting the floor, Nikolai's cold fury, the blood. She had witnessed violence before, but this was different. This wasn't random, this wasn't mindless. This was Nikolai, deliberate and terrifying.

But as her heart raced, fear wasn't the only emotion coursing through her veins.

Desire.

Ava swallowed hard, trying to push it away, but it clung to her, insistent. She should be horrified by what she had just seen—by how easily Nikolai had unleashed his rage, how cold and calculated he had been as he defended her. She should have been disgusted by the brutality, repelled by the violence. But instead, her body was betraying her, drawn to him in ways that confused and unsettled her.

She glanced up at him, catching the hard line of his jaw, the intensity still simmering beneath his calm exterior. He wasn't shaken. He wasn't apologetic. If anything, he was completely in control, just as he had been during the fight. The contrast between the chaos of the scene and the calm assurance he carried now made her stomach twist.

How could she feel safe with a man who was capable of such violence? And yet, she did. She felt protected. Guarded. Like nothing could touch her when Nikolai was there, ready to tear apart anyone who dared come close.

Her heart raced as her mind battled with itself. She should be running—running as far away from this world as she could. But she couldn't. Something deeper, darker, kept her rooted to the spot.

Something that pulled her closer to Nikolai, even as every rational part of her screamed that this was dangerous.

"I don't understand," she whispered, her voice barely audible.

Nikolai's gaze flicked to her, his eyes softening slightly. "Understand what?"

"How can you be so calm?" Ava asked, her voice trembling. "You just..."

She couldn't finish the sentence. The image of the man's blood on the floor, his broken form, flashed through her mind again. It wasn't just the violence that haunted her—it was the way Nikolai had seemed almost detached from it. Like it was second nature to him.

Nikolai exhaled slowly, his hand reaching out to brush a strand of hair behind her ear. "This is my life, Ava," he said quietly, his voice steady. "And if you're going to be with me, you need to understand that."

Ava's breath hitched, her chest tightening as his words sank in. *This is my life.* It was a reminder—a warning—that being with him meant accepting all of it. The power, the danger, the violence. And the cold truth was, she wasn't sure if she could.

But even as fear clawed at her, desire pulsed through her veins. She hated that she wanted him in that moment—hated that the very thing that should have scared her away was the same thing that drew her closer. It was twisted, confusing, and overwhelming, and she didn't know what to do with it.

Ava looked up at him, her voice shaky. "I'm scared, Nikolai."

The admission hung between them, raw and honest. She had never felt more vulnerable in her life.

Nikolai's jaw tightened, but his expression softened as he pulled her closer, his hand resting protectively on the small of her back. "I know," he murmured. "But I'll protect you. Always."

She wanted to believe him, wanted to trust that he could shield her from the dangers that lurked in his world. But there was no escaping the reality that being with Nikolai meant living in the shadow of that danger. The violence would never be far away. It would always be a part of him—a part of them.

They stood there in silence for a long moment, the tension between them thick and heavy. The world around them seemed distant, muted, as though they were the only two people in existence. But Ava's mind was racing, her thoughts tangled in a web of fear and desire, uncertainty and need.

She didn't know how to reconcile the two. How could she be drawn to him when every part of her screamed that this was wrong?

Nikolai's hand tightened on her back, pulling her slightly closer as he lowered his voice. "Let me take you home."

Ava nodded, though her heart was still pounding, her mind clouded with questions she didn't have the strength to ask right now. She needed time to process, time to think.

Without another word, Nikolai led her toward the car, his hand firmly on her waist, guiding her with the same possessive energy he'd shown all night. The air between them was charged with unsaid things, with emotions too complicated to unravel right now.

As they drove back to his penthouse, the city lights flashing by, Ava stared out the window, her mind a whirlwind of thoughts. She should be running—getting as far away from Nikolai's world as possible. But she couldn't shake the feeling that it was already too late. That she was already too deep.

And that terrified her as much as it excited her.

Chapter 10

The ride back to Nikolai's penthouse was silent, but the tension between them was suffocating. Ava could feel every shift of his body beside her in the backseat of the car, the heat radiating from him even though he wasn't touching her. His hand rested on his thigh, but she remembered how it had gripped her waist, the possessive way he had held her as they left the club.

Her mind was still a mess of conflicting emotions—fear and desire warring inside her, and no matter how hard she tried to make sense of it, she couldn't. One minute, she was terrified of what she had seen, of the violence Nikolai was capable of. The next minute, she was drawn to him, to the power and control he wielded so effortlessly. She wanted to get away from it, from the blood and the danger, but at the same time, she craved the safety he provided.

She glanced over at him, her breath catching in her throat as she took in his profile. Even now, after everything, he was so calm. His face was impassive, his jaw tight, but there was no trace of the anger she had seen earlier. He wasn't rattled. He wasn't even remotely fazed. And that scared her more than the violence itself.

Ava turned her gaze back to the window, the city lights blurring together as they sped through the streets. Her heart was still racing, her palms clammy as she tried to process everything that had happened. She had never been in a situation like that before—never been so close to something so dangerous.

But Nikolai had been there, right in the middle of it, and it hadn't shaken him at all. In fact, it seemed like he had expected it. Like it was just another part of his life.

And now, that life was bleeding into hers.

A knot formed in Ava's stomach, her mind spinning with questions she didn't know how to ask. She didn't want to think about what it meant—what being with Nikolai really entailed. But she couldn't ignore it anymore. Not after tonight.

They pulled up to the penthouse, the driver silently opening the door for them. Nikolai stepped out first, his movements smooth and controlled, before turning to offer her his hand. Ava hesitated for a fraction of a second before taking it, allowing him to help her out of the car.

His grip was firm, steady, as if nothing had happened. As if he hadn't just beaten a man within an inch of his life in front of her.

They made their way into the building, Nikolai leading her through the lobby, past the guards who nodded respectfully as they passed. Ava barely noticed them, her thoughts still swirling as they stepped into the elevator and rode up to his penthouse in silence. The soft hum of the elevator was the only sound, and Ava's heart pounded in her chest as the tension between them continued to build.

When the doors slid open, Nikolai stepped out first, his hand still resting on the small of her back as he guided her into the expansive space. The penthouse was dimly lit, the city lights casting a faint glow through the floor-to-ceiling windows, but the quiet luxury of the space did little to soothe her nerves.

Ava walked into the living room, her movements slow and deliberate as she tried to gather her thoughts. She could feel Nikolai's presence behind her, the weight of his gaze heavy on her shoulders.

Finally, she turned to face him, her heart hammering in her chest as she searched for the right words.

"I need to know," she said, her voice barely above a whisper. "I need to understand what happened tonight."

Nikolai's expression didn't change, but there was a flicker of something in his eyes—something guarded. He stepped closer, his movements deliberate, his gaze never leaving hers. "What do you want to know?" he asked, his voice calm, controlled.

Ava swallowed hard, her throat dry. "All of it," she whispered. "What does it mean to be with you? What does it mean to be the head of the Bratva?"

Nikolai's eyes darkened slightly at her words, and he let out a slow breath. "It means power," he said simply. "Control. And yes, sometimes it means violence."

Ava felt her stomach churn at his admission, but she didn't look away. "Is that just part of your life?" she asked, her voice trembling. "Beating people like that?"

Nikolai's gaze remained steady. "It's part of my world, yes," he said, his tone matter-of-fact. "But I don't resort to violence unless I have to. Tonight, that man disrespected you. He crossed a line."

Ava shook her head, her hands trembling as she took a step back. "But it's not just about tonight, is it?" she whispered. "It's not just about some drunk guy at a club. This is who you are, Nikolai. This is your life."

Nikolai's jaw tightened slightly, and he took another step toward her, closing the distance between them. "You knew who I was," he said quietly. "You knew I wasn't a saint."

"I didn't know it would be like this," Ava said, her voice shaking. "I didn't know it would be..."

She trailed off, unable to find the right word. Violent. Dangerous. Terrifying. It was all of those things, and yet, she couldn't bring herself to say it out loud.

Nikolai's expression softened slightly, but his gaze remained intense. "Ava," he murmured, his voice low, "I told you from the start that my world is dangerous. I told you there would be risks."

Ava shook her head, her heart racing. "I didn't realize what that meant," she whispered. "Not until tonight."

Nikolai reached out, his hand gently cupping her cheek, and Ava's breath hitched at the contact. His touch was warm, familiar, but the intensity of the moment made her feel vulnerable in a way she hadn't expected.

"I will always protect you," he said quietly, his thumb brushing lightly over her skin. "No matter what."

Ava's heart fluttered at his words, but the fear still lingered, gnawing at the edges of her desire. She wanted to believe him. She wanted to trust that he could keep her safe. But after tonight, she wasn't sure if she could.

"I don't know if I can do this," she whispered, her voice trembling.

Nikolai's hand tightened slightly on her cheek, his eyes darkening. "You can," he said firmly. "I'll make sure of it."

Ava shook her head, stepping back from his touch. "You can't just... make me okay with this," she said, her voice breaking slightly. "You can't just fix this with promises."

Nikolai's jaw clenched, but he didn't argue. Instead, he took a step closer, his gaze never leaving hers. "I'm not asking you to be okay with everything," he said quietly. "But you need to understand that this is part of my life. It's not going to change."

Ava's chest tightened at his words. She had known that being with Nikolai meant accepting certain things—danger, control, power. But she hadn't realized just how deeply ingrained those things were in his life.

She looked up at him, her heart pounding in her chest. "And what if I can't accept that?" she whispered.

Nikolai's gaze darkened, his hand reaching out to grip her waist, pulling her close. "Then you'll walk away," he said quietly. "But I don't think you want that."

Ava's breath hitched as his words sank in. He was right. She didn't want to walk away. Despite the fear, despite the uncertainty, she didn't want to leave him. She couldn't.

But that didn't mean she wasn't terrified.

Her body trembled as she looked up at him, her emotions a tangled mess of fear, desire, and confusion. "I'm scared, Nikolai," she whispered.

Nikolai's grip tightened on her waist, his eyes burning with intensity. "I know," he murmured. "But I'll protect you. Always."

Ava's heart raced, her body betraying her as desire pulsed through her veins. She hated that she wanted him, hated that even now, with all the fear and uncertainty, she couldn't pull away from him.

"I don't know if that's enough," she whispered, her voice barely audible.

Nikolai's jaw clenched, his eyes darkening. "It will be," he said quietly. "You'll see."

Ava's breath hitched, her heart pounding in her chest as his words sank in. She wanted to believe him. She wanted to trust that he could protect her, that being with him would be worth the risk. But the fear still lingered, gnawing at the edges of her desire.

Nikolai's hand slid up to her cheek, his thumb brushing lightly over her skin. "You're mine, Ava," he murmured, his voice low and possessive. "And I'll never let anything happen to you."

Ava's heart fluttered at his words, the conflicting emotions inside her swirling into a chaotic storm. She knew she should be scared. She knew she should be pulling away from him, walking out of this penthouse, leaving behind the dangerous world he inhabited. But she couldn't. Something deeper, something more primal, kept her anchored to him, her body betraying her mind. Despite the fear gnawing at her, despite the uncertainty that clouded her thoughts, she couldn't bring herself to walk away from Nikolai.

Ava felt her pulse quicken, her heart hammering in her chest as she searched his face for answers. But all she found was his unwavering gaze—dark, intense, and full of the same possessiveness that had drawn her in from the start. It was overwhelming, the way he looked at her, as if she were the only thing that mattered in his world. But it was that same possessiveness that scared her the most.

"I don't know if I'm strong enough," Ava whispered, her voice trembling. "To handle all of this. Your world. The violence. It's... it's too much."

Nikolai's eyes softened, but only slightly. His hand, still cupping her cheek, slid down to her neck, his thumb brushing lightly over her collarbone. "You're stronger than you think," he murmured, his voice low and rough. "I've seen it."

Ava swallowed hard, her throat tight as her mind raced. She wanted to believe him, wanted to trust that she could handle being part of his world. But tonight had shaken her. She had never been so close to danger, never seen the raw brutality that Nikolai was capable of. And yet, standing here in his penthouse, with his hand on her skin, she felt safe. Protected.

And that scared her more than anything else.

"I don't know how to feel," she admitted, her voice barely above a whisper. "I'm scared, Nikolai. But... I don't want to leave."

Nikolai's jaw tightened slightly, but his hand remained gentle as he caressed her skin. "Then stay," he said quietly, his voice steady. "Stay with me."

Ava's breath hitched, her heart racing as his words sank in. *Stay.* It sounded so simple, so easy. But it wasn't. Staying with Nikolai meant accepting everything that came with him—his power, his control, the violence that followed him like a shadow. It meant living in constant fear of the dangers that lurked in his world.

But walking away? That seemed impossible now. She was too far in, too wrapped up in him to turn back. Despite the fear, despite the uncertainty, she couldn't walk away from Nikolai. She didn't want to.

Ava closed her eyes for a moment, trying to calm the storm of emotions swirling inside her. When she opened them again, she met Nikolai's gaze, her voice steady despite the tremor in her chest.

"I don't want to leave you," she whispered.

Nikolai's hand slid back up to her cheek, his thumb brushing over her lower lip. His gaze darkened, his voice low and commanding. "Then don't."

Ava's heart pounded as she stared up at him, her mind a whirlwind of fear and desire. She was still scared—terrified, even—but the pull she felt toward Nikolai was stronger than anything she had ever known. The danger, the power, the possessiveness—it all terrified her, but it also drew her in like nothing else.

"I... I don't know what to do," she admitted, her voice trembling.

Nikolai's expression softened slightly, but there was still an edge of steel in his voice as he spoke. "You don't have to decide right now," he murmured. "But know this, Ava: I will protect you. Always."

Ava's breath caught in her throat, her body trembling as Nikolai's words settled over her. She wanted to believe him—wanted to trust that he could keep her safe. But tonight had shown her just how dangerous his world was. It wasn't just about him anymore—it was about the violence that surrounded him, the constant threat that loomed over their lives.

And yet, despite the fear gnawing at her, she couldn't deny the pull she felt toward him. The tension between them was electric, humming in the air like a live wire. She was caught between wanting to run as far away from this life as she could, and the overwhelming need to be close to him, to feel his arms around her, protecting her from the very dangers he represented.

The room fell into a thick silence, and for a moment, all Ava could hear was the pounding of her own heart, the soft hum of the city outside. She looked up at Nikolai, her gaze locking with his, and the intensity of the connection between them was almost too much to bear.

Without a word, Nikolai stepped closer, his eyes dark and filled with something primal, something that mirrored the turmoil swirling inside her. He reached for her, his hands rough and urgent as they slid around her waist, pulling her against him. Ava's breath hitched as their bodies collided, the heat of his touch searing through the fabric of her clothes.

Then, without warning, Nikolai's lips crashed down onto hers in a feverish, desperate kiss.

Ava gasped into his mouth, her fingers tangling in the fabric of his shirt as she clung to him. The kiss was wild, filled with all the unresolved tension from their argument—anger, fear, desire, and need, all crashing together in a fiery explosion. His hands moved over her body with a fierce intensity, pulling her closer, as though he couldn't get enough of her.

Ava's mind raced, her emotions a tangled mess as their lips collided again and again, each kiss more desperate than the last. She could feel the fear still gnawing at the edges of her consciousness, but it was drowned out by the overwhelming need that coursed through her veins.

Nikolai's hands moved to the hem of her dress, tugging it over her head in one swift motion. The cool air of the penthouse brushed against her skin, but the heat between them was so intense she barely noticed. His lips moved from her mouth to her neck, leaving a trail of scorching kisses along her throat as his hands slid down to her waist.

Ava's fingers fumbled with the buttons of his shirt, her hands trembling as she tried to keep up with the frantic pace. She was consumed by him—by the sheer power of his presence, the way he made her feel as though nothing else in the world mattered except the two of them. She wanted him, needed him, more than she had ever needed anything in her life.

As they stumbled toward the bedroom, leaving a trail of discarded clothing behind them, Ava's heart raced in her chest, her body aching with desire. Her bra and panties fell to the floor, and she kicked them aside, her bare skin tingling with anticipation as Nikolai's hands roamed over her, his touch possessive and demanding.

By the time they reached the bedroom, Ava was trembling with need, her body humming with a mixture of fear and desire. She knew she shouldn't want this—shouldn't want *him* after everything she had seen tonight. But she couldn't stop herself. She couldn't pull away from the fire that burned between them.

Nikolai pushed her down onto the bed, his eyes dark with lust as he looked down at her. His chest was bare now, his tattooed muscles rippling under the dim light of the room, and Ava's breath caught in her throat at the sight of him. He was raw, primal, and completely in control—and she found herself surrendering to him completely.

Ava knelt before Nikolai, her fingers trembling as they moved to his pants, unbuttoning them with shaky hands. The air between them was thick with anticipation, the tension crackling like electricity as she pulled his pants down, revealing the hard, thick length of him.

Her heart raced, her pulse pounding in her ears as she wrapped her fingers around him, feeling the weight of his cock in her hand. He was already engorged, the thick head of him glistening in the dim light, and Ava felt a thrill of anticipation shoot through her as she leaned forward, her lips parting to take him into her mouth.

Nikolai let out a low groan as her lips wrapped around him, his hands sliding into her hair, gripping it firmly as she began to suck, her tongue swirling around the tip of him. The taste of him was salty, musky, and it ignited a fire deep in her belly, her body responding to the primal need that pulsed between them.

Ava's eyes fluttered shut as she took him deeper, her mouth stretching around him as she bobbed her head, her tongue sliding along the length of him. The sensation of his cock filling her mouth, pressing against the back of her throat, sent a wave of heat rushing through her, and she moaned softly around him, her body trembling with desire.

Nikolai's grip on her hair tightened as he guided her movements, his hips thrusting slightly as she took him in, her lips and tongue working in perfect rhythm. The sounds of his groans filled the room, mixing with the soft, wet sounds of her mouth on him, and the raw intensity of it made her pulse quicken.

Ava felt a strange sense of power as she pleasured him, her hands gripping his thighs as she sucked him harder, her lips sliding up and down his length with increasing urgency. She could feel his cock throbbing in her mouth, could feel the tension building in his body as he neared his climax, but just as she felt him tense, Nikolai pulled away.

His hands moved to her shoulders, lifting her up and pushing her back onto the bed. Ava's breath came in ragged gasps as she looked up at him, her body trembling with need as he stood over her, his chest heaving with the same primal desire that coursed through her.

Nikolai didn't waste any time. He grabbed her hips, pulling her roughly toward him as he positioned himself between her legs. Ava's heart raced, her pulse pounding in her ears as she felt the thick head of his cock press against her entrance, the heat of him sending a jolt of pleasure through her body.

She was already wet, her body aching with need, and when Nikolai plunged into her with one powerful thrust, she cried out, her back arching off the bed as he filled her completely. The sensation of him inside her—stretching her, claiming her—was overwhelming, and Ava's body responded instinctively, her hips rising to meet his every thrust.

Nikolai set a brutal, unrelenting pace, his hips slamming into hers with raw, primal force. The room was filled with the sounds of their bodies coming together—his low, guttural groans, her soft moans, and the wet slap of skin against skin. Ava's hands clutched the sheets, her body trembling as the pleasure built inside her, spiraling higher with every thrust.

The intensity of the moment was overwhelming, the fear and desire blending together into something dark and all-consuming. Ava knew she should be scared—knew that being with Nikolai meant living in a world of danger and violence—but in this moment, none of that mattered. All she could think about was the way he made her feel—like she was his, like she belonged to him completely.

Nikolai's hands gripped her hips tightly, his fingers digging into her skin as he pounded into her with increasing urgency. Ava's body responded to him, her hips rising to meet his every movement, her nails digging into his shoulders as she clung to him, the pleasure building inside her like a wave about to crash.

"You're mine, Ava," Nikolai growled, his voice rough with desire. "Every inch of you."

The words sent a shiver down her spine, the possessiveness in his voice igniting something deep inside her. She was his. Completely. And the knowledge of that—the raw, primal truth of it—pushed her over the edge.

Ava's body tensed, her breath catching in her throat as the pleasure finally crested, sending her spiraling into an intense, all-consuming orgasm. She cried out, her muscles tightening around him as her body shook with the force of it, her vision blurring as wave after wave of pleasure crashed through her.

Nikolai didn't slow down, his thrusts becoming harder, more urgent as he chased his own release. His hands gripped her hips, pulling her closer as he drove into her one final time, his body tensing as he groaned, his cock pulsing inside her as he came, filling her with his warmth.

For a moment, the world was still. The only sound in the room was the ragged breathing of their bodies as they lay together, tangled in the aftermath of their passion. Nikolai's body was heavy against hers, his chest rising and falling as he caught his breath, his arms still wrapped around her as though he couldn't let go.

Ava's mind was spinning, her emotions still raw from the intensity of what had just happened. Her body trembled in the aftermath, still feeling the echoes of their passion, but her mind was caught in the conflicting storm of emotions. Fear lingered at the edges of her thoughts, reminding her of the danger she was tethering herself to by staying with Nikolai. And yet, right now, all she felt was a strange sense of calm, a release of tension that had been building ever since the violent confrontation at the club.

Nikolai shifted beside her, pulling away slightly but keeping his arm draped over her waist, his touch firm and possessive, even in this moment of quiet. His breathing was still heavy, but as his chest rose and fell against her, she couldn't help but feel a certain peace. He had promised to protect her, and though his world terrified her, there was comfort in knowing he would keep that promise.

Ava stared up at the ceiling, her chest still heaving from the intensity of their lovemaking. Her heart was pounding in her ears, her mind a mess of thoughts she couldn't quite organize. She knew this was a temporary reprieve, that the fears she had about Nikolai's world hadn't disappeared just because they had found solace in each other's bodies. But for now, wrapped in the warmth of his arms, she allowed herself to simply exist in the moment.

Nikolai's hand slid up her side, his thumb brushing lazily over her skin, sending soft shivers through her already sensitive body. He didn't speak, but Ava could feel the weight of his presence, the unspoken connection between them as they lay together in the dimly lit bedroom. Despite everything that had happened tonight—despite the fear and the violence—there was an undeniable bond between them that she couldn't ignore.

After a long stretch of silence, Nikolai finally spoke, his voice rough and low, still laced with the remnants of their desire. "I meant what I said, Ava," he murmured, his breath warm against her ear. "You're mine. No one will ever hurt you."

His words should have felt possessive, maybe even controlling. But in this moment, they were a reassurance, a promise she found herself needing more than she had realized. She turned her head to look at him, her eyes locking with his in the dim light.

"I know," she whispered, her voice soft but steady.

Nikolai's gaze softened slightly, his thumb brushing over her cheek in a rare gesture of tenderness. "You don't have to be afraid, Ava," he said quietly. "Not when you're with me."

Ava's heart clenched at his words. She wanted to believe him, wanted to trust that being with him would be enough to keep her safe from the dangers of his world. But she couldn't deny the fear that still lingered, the uncertainty of what lay ahead if she chose to stay by his side.

"I'm trying," she whispered, her voice barely audible.

Nikolai's expression darkened slightly, but there was no anger in his gaze—only understanding. He pulled her closer, his arm tightening around her waist as though he could shield her from the dangers that loomed outside the walls of his penthouse.

"I'll never let anything happen to you," he murmured, his lips brushing against her temple.

Ava closed her eyes, leaning into his touch. She knew that tonight was just the beginning—that being with Nikolai meant accepting the violence, the power, and the danger that came with his world. But as she lay there in the safety of his arms, she felt something else—a deep, undeniable pull toward him, a desire that went beyond just the physical.

It was more than just lust. It was the realization that, despite her fear, despite the uncertainty of what their future might hold, she didn't want to be anywhere else but with him.

The thought both comforted and terrified her.

They lay together in silence for what felt like an eternity, their bodies tangled in the sheets, their breathing finally slowing to a more normal rhythm. Ava's mind was still spinning with everything that had happened tonight, but the warmth of Nikolai's body next to hers kept her grounded, kept her from slipping into the chaos of her thoughts.

She didn't know what tomorrow would bring, didn't know if she was truly strong enough to survive in Nikolai's world. But for now, she allowed herself to simply be. To enjoy the quiet after the storm, to bask in the connection they had forged through both passion and conflict.

Because deep down, she knew that no matter how dangerous his world was, she couldn't walk away from Nikolai. Not now. Not ever.

Chapter 11

The first light of dawn crept through the curtains, casting a faint, warm glow over the bedroom. Nikolai lay still, his head resting against the soft pillow, his gaze fixed on Ava. She was asleep beside him, her chest rising and falling gently with each breath, completely unaware of the thoughts raging through his mind.

In the early morning quiet, he let himself study her. Her hair was spread across the pillow in soft waves, her delicate features softened by sleep. She looked peaceful—untouched by the weight of the world he carried. For a moment, as he watched her, Nikolai felt something that was becoming increasingly rare in his life: peace.

It was strange. No woman had ever affected him like this. He had always kept his personal and professional lives separate, careful to never let anyone get too close. Control had always been his guiding principle—control over his business, his empire, and the people in his life. Emotions were a weakness he couldn't afford. Yet here, in the quiet of the morning, with Ava asleep beside him, he felt that control slipping, and it terrified him.

He reached out, gently brushing a strand of hair from her face, his fingers lingering on her skin for a moment longer than necessary. She stirred slightly but didn't wake. His touch was soft, almost reverent, as though she might disappear if he wasn't careful.

Ava.

Her name echoed in his mind. She had become more than just a fleeting presence in his life—she had become something permanent, something he wasn't sure he could ever let go of. The thought unsettled him, but it also filled him with a fierce, primal need to protect her, to keep her close. In his world, nothing was guaranteed. Safety, security, love—it could all be ripped away in an instant. But with Ava, he wanted to defy that. He wanted to shield her from the dangers lurking in his shadows.

But at what cost?

Nikolai's jaw tightened as he thought about the events of the past few days. The club incident had shaken something loose inside him, a fear he hadn't realized was there until he saw that man look at Ava the wrong way, his words filled with disrespect. It was more than just anger that had driven him to act. It was the realization that in his world, Ava was vulnerable. That she could be hurt, used as leverage, or worse.

That was unacceptable.

He wouldn't let anything happen to her. She was his now, whether she realized it fully or not. And that meant he had to control every aspect of her life to keep her safe. His world didn't allow for weakness, and Ava had become his Achilles' heel. He couldn't afford that vulnerability, but at the same time, he couldn't let her go.

Nikolai let out a slow breath, his fingers trailing down her arm before he pulled back, not wanting to wake her. He swung his legs over the side of the bed and stood, the cool air brushing against his bare chest. He moved toward the large window that overlooked the city, the skyline just beginning to stir with the early morning activity. From up here, everything looked so small, so distant. It was easy to forget how much danger lay hidden beneath the surface of this city. The power struggles, the rivalries, the constant threat of violence.

And yet, here he was, bringing Ava deeper into it. She had no idea what it truly meant to be with him, to be tied to a man like him. He'd told her the basics, but she didn't fully grasp the weight of it. Not yet.

But she would.

He thought back to the moment in the club, the way her eyes had widened in fear when she saw him beat that man so savagely. He didn't regret his actions—he would do it again in a heartbeat—but her reaction had left him uneasy. Was she ready for this? Could she handle the brutality of his world? More importantly, could she handle *him*?

He didn't know. But the thought of losing her, of pushing her away because of who he was, made something dark and possessive twist inside him.

Nikolai sighed, rubbing a hand over his face. He wasn't used to feeling this out of control, and he hated it. His entire life had been built on control—controlling his emotions, his empire, the people around him. And yet, with Ava, that control seemed to slip through his fingers like sand.

He turned away from the window, his mind already shifting to the day ahead. He had business to attend to, meetings to conduct, enemies to keep at bay. But before all of that, there was something else he needed to do—something that had been on his mind for days now.

He needed to claim Ava in a way that no one could mistake. He needed to make her his.

****

The jeweler's showroom gleamed under the bright lights, rows of exquisite diamonds and gemstones displayed with meticulous care. Nikolai wasn't one for sentimentality, but he knew that in his world, symbols mattered. Possession mattered.

He stood at the glass counter, his sharp eyes scanning the display. There were necklaces, earrings, bracelets—all of them stunning, but none of them quite right. None of them had the impact he wanted.

"Mr. Volkov," the jeweler's voice interrupted his thoughts. "I think I have something you'll find... appropriate."

The jeweler reached into a velvet-lined case and pulled out a necklace—a single strand of diamonds that shimmered with an almost otherworldly brilliance. It was bold, elegant, and undeniably luxurious. It would stand out. It would make a statement. But more importantly, it would mark Ava as his.

Nikolai lifted the necklace from the jeweler's hands, inspecting it closely. The diamonds caught the light, reflecting a brilliance that matched the cold fire in his eyes. He imagined how it would look on Ava—how the diamonds would rest against her skin, a constant reminder that she belonged to him.

"She'll love it," the jeweler said, his voice full of practiced confidence.

Nikolai didn't respond. Love wasn't the point. This wasn't just about giving her something beautiful. It was about giving her something that symbolized that she was his. It was a claim, a mark of control. And it was exactly what he needed.

He handed the jeweler his payment, not caring about the exorbitant price. Money meant little to him when it came to Ava. He would give her the world if it meant keeping her close, keeping her *his*.

As he left the store, the necklace safely tucked inside the velvet box, Nikolai's mind was already on the moment he would give it to her. He imagined the way her eyes would light up when she saw it, the way she would look at him, unaware of the deeper meaning behind the gift. She would wear it, and every time someone looked at her, they would know—she was his. And no one else could touch her.

The thought filled him with a fierce sense of satisfaction, but it also left him uneasy. His need to control Ava was growing stronger by the day, and he wasn't sure if he could stop it. Part of him didn't want to.

****

Nikolai sat in his office, staring at the large window that framed the sprawling view of New York City. His mind should have been on the meeting he was in—the business at hand with his Bratva associates, each one waiting for his word. They were discussing important matters, the kind that required his full attention, but his thoughts kept drifting back to Ava.

He had been consumed by thoughts of her since the moment he woke up, and now, sitting in this room filled with men who depended on his authority, he was finding it harder and harder to concentrate.

He hated it—this distraction, this feeling of being unbalanced. Nikolai had always prided himself on being in control, on never allowing anyone to get too close. But with Ava, that control was slipping. The more he thought about her, the more possessive he became. His need to protect her was starting to cross into obsession, and he knew it.

The conversation around him droned on, his men discussing a potential threat from a rival faction. Normally, Nikolai would have been fully engaged, calculating his next move, strategizing how to eliminate the threat. But today, all he could think about was Ava's safety. The incident at the club had shaken him in ways he hadn't expected. It wasn't just the violence or the disrespect. It was the realization that she was vulnerable—dangerously so.

His thoughts were interrupted when one of his men, Viktor, cleared his throat, drawing his attention back to the present. "Nikolai, what's the next step?" Viktor asked, his voice steady but laced with concern. They had noticed his distraction. Nikolai's reputation as a calm, collected leader made any hint of distraction stand out like a beacon.

Nikolai's jaw tightened, his focus shifting back to the men seated around the table. He couldn't afford to be seen as weak, not even for a moment. "Double the security on our businesses," he said, his voice hard and decisive. "I want eyes on everyone who's been in contact with the Leonov family. No one moves without our knowledge."

The men nodded in agreement, but Nikolai's mind was already moving back to Ava. He needed to do more to protect her—more than just a necklace. He needed to ensure that she was safe at all times, even when she wasn't with him.

Nikolai leaned back in his chair, his eyes narrowing as he thought about the steps he would need to take. He would assign bodyguards to her, men who would watch over her discreetly. She didn't need to know she was being protected—it would only make her feel trapped. But she *would* be watched. No one would get near her without his permission.

His phone buzzed on the table, and Nikolai glanced down at the screen. A message from one of his security contacts confirmed that Ava had returned to the penthouse safely. He felt a wave of relief wash over him, but it was quickly followed by something darker—possessiveness. She was his. No one would ever touch her, no one would ever take her away from him.

As the meeting continued, Nikolai's mind remained fixed on Ava. He would need to take more control over her life—monitor her movements, ensure she was never in danger. It wasn't enough to simply protect her when she was with him. He needed to protect her at all times, even from a distance. And that meant watching her every move, even if it meant crossing lines he had once sworn never to cross.

The thought of losing her, of her being harmed, was unbearable. Nikolai clenched his fists under the table, the cold edge of his possessiveness rising once more. Ava was his, and he would protect her—whether she knew it or not.

The penthouse was quiet when Nikolai returned after the meeting, the evening shadows stretching long across the floor. Ava wasn't home yet, but he knew she would be soon. He could already picture her walking through the door, her smile lighting up the room, unaware of the storm brewing inside him.

He set the velvet box on the table and poured himself a drink, the amber liquid swirling in the glass as he sat down on the couch. The silence of the penthouse echoed around him, but his mind was anything but quiet. He couldn't stop thinking about her, about how much she had become a part of his life.

He didn't know when it had happened, when his feelings for her had shifted from desire to something deeper, something possessive and dangerous. But now, the idea of her not being with him, not being *his*, was unbearable.

Nikolai took a slow sip of his drink, the burn of the alcohol doing little to calm the restless thoughts in his mind. Ava would be home soon, and when she was, he would give her the necklace. It was more than just a gift—it was a declaration. A statement. And once she was wearing it, there would be no mistaking that she belonged to him.

He didn't know if Ava understood the full weight of that, but she would. Eventually.

As the minutes ticked by, Nikolai's thoughts shifted. He began to wonder what it would take to keep her in his life permanently. The necklace was a step, but it wasn't enough. He needed something more. Something that would bind her to him in a way that couldn't be undone.

Marriage.

The thought came unbidden, and Nikolai scowled, as though the very idea irritated him. He wasn't the type of man to settle down, to play house. But Ava wasn't just any woman. She had gotten under his skin, wrapped herself around his heart in a way that no one else ever had. The idea of losing her was intolerable, and the more he thought about it, the more the idea of making her his permanently began to appeal to him.

Marriage would mean bringing her fully into his world. It would mean exposing her to the darkness, the violence, and the constant danger that followed him like a shadow. But it would also mean that she would never leave. She would be his, legally, permanently—tied to him in a way that went beyond simple affection or desire. It would be a contract, a bond that no one could break.

But could she handle it? Could she truly understand what it meant to be tied to a man like him? Nikolai wasn't sure. Ava was strong—stronger than he had given her credit for when they first met—but his world wasn't one you simply adapted to. It consumed you. And once you were in, there was no way out.

His thoughts were interrupted by the sound of the door opening. He turned to see Ava walk in, her smile lighting up the room just as he had imagined. She was breathtaking, her presence a sharp contrast to the storm that raged within him. She greeted him with a soft kiss on the cheek, her warmth seeping into his skin, soothing some of the restlessness in his mind.

"How was your day?" she asked, her voice light as she slipped off her coat and set it aside.

Nikolai didn't answer immediately. His eyes lingered on her, taking in the sight of her—so unaware of the thoughts running through his mind, so blissfully ignorant of the dangerous path they were both walking. He stood, the velvet box still sitting on the table between them, a silent reminder of what was to come.

"It was... productive," he finally said, his voice low and measured. "There's something I want to give you."

Ava raised an eyebrow, a playful smile tugging at the corners of her lips. "Oh? What's the occasion?"

Nikolai didn't respond right away. Instead, he picked up the velvet box and opened it, revealing the diamond necklace nestled inside. The stones glittered in the dim light, each one carefully cut and polished to perfection. It was a masterpiece, but it was more than that—it was a symbol.

Ava's eyes widened as she took in the sight of it, her breath catching in her throat. "Nikolai... it's beautiful."

Nikolai's heart clenched at her words, but he kept his expression controlled, his voice steady. "It's yours. I want you to wear it."

Ava reached out, her fingers brushing against the diamonds as if she couldn't quite believe it. She looked up at him, her eyes filled with gratitude, but also with something else—something that made Nikolai's chest tighten.

"It's... I don't know what to say," she murmured, her voice soft.

"You don't have to say anything," Nikolai said, stepping closer to her. "Just let me put it on you."

Ava nodded, turning her back to him as she lifted her hair, exposing the smooth line of her neck. Nikolai's hands were steady as he fastened the necklace around her, his fingers brushing against her skin. He took a moment to admire the way the diamonds sparkled against her flesh, the way the necklace seemed to claim her, mark her as his.

It was perfect.

Ava turned back to face him, her hand reaching up to touch the necklace as she smiled at him. "Thank you, Nikolai. It's stunning."

Nikolai's eyes darkened as he stepped closer, his hand sliding around her waist, pulling her against him. "It's more than just a gift, Ava," he murmured, his voice low and possessive. "It's a mark. A reminder that you're mine."

Ava's breath hitched at his words, her eyes searching his face for a moment before she nodded, her lips parting slightly. "I know," she whispered.

Nikolai's grip tightened on her waist, his chest tightening with something fierce and primal. He wanted her—needed her—in a way that went beyond simple desire. The necklace was just the beginning. He would do whatever it took to keep her by his side, to protect her from the dangers of his world, even if that meant controlling every aspect of her life.

He didn't care if it was possessive. He didn't care if it crossed a line. She was his, and no one else would ever touch her.

***

The city lights cast a soft glow over the bedroom as Ava slept beside him, her chest rising and falling with the same steady rhythm as it had that morning. But now, something was different. She was wearing the necklace, the diamonds shimmering faintly against her skin even in the darkness.

Nikolai lay beside her, his head propped up on one arm as he watched her sleep. She looked peaceful, unaware of the thoughts swirling through his mind.

He had given her the necklace, and she had accepted it without hesitation. She trusted him—trusted that he would protect her, keep her safe. But did she truly understand what that meant? Did she understand that being with him meant giving up a part of herself?

He reached out, his fingers gently brushing against the necklace, his touch light enough not to wake her. The diamonds were cool beneath his fingers, a stark contrast to the warmth of her skin. He watched the rise and fall of her chest, his mind turning over the idea of what it would mean to keep her like this—tied to him, bound by more than just affection.

Marriage.

The word echoed in his mind again, stronger this time. The more he thought about it, the more it made sense. Ava was already his, but marriage would make it official. It would bind her to him in a way that no one could question. And in his world, marriage meant power. It meant security. But it also meant danger.

Bringing Ava deeper into his life, into the world of the Bratva, would expose her to risks she couldn't even begin to imagine. She would be a target—his enemies would see her as leverage, a way to get to him. But what other choice did he have? He couldn't let her go. He couldn't imagine a life without her.

Nikolai's hand slid from the necklace to her shoulder, his fingers tracing the curve of her arm. Ava stirred slightly, murmuring in her sleep, but didn't wake. He watched her, his mind racing with the possibilities.

Could she handle it? Could she survive in his world? He didn't know. But he was willing to risk it. He would protect her, shield her from the dangers that surrounded them. He had the power, the resources, the men to do it. But more than that, he had the need—the overwhelming, all-consuming need to keep her by his side.

Ava was his, and he would never let her go.

As he lay beside her, watching her sleep, Nikolai made a silent promise. He would protect her at all costs. He would keep her safe, no matter what. But more than that, he would make sure she never left. She was already wearing his mark—the necklace was a symbol of that. But soon, it would be more.

Soon, she would be his in every way.

Chapter 12

The penthouse was bathed in the warm, fading light of early evening, the golden glow from the setting sun filtering through the windows and casting long shadows across the floor. The city outside was alive with the hum of activity, yet inside the penthouse, it felt as though time had slowed to a gentle, steady rhythm.

Nikolai sat beside Ava on the sleek leather couch, a glass of whiskey in one hand, while his other rested lazily on the armrest. His presence always commanded the room, even when he was silent, his dark, brooding gaze trained on the skyline as if lost in thought. Ava could feel the tension lingering in the air between them, a quiet heaviness that had been there since the events of the last few days.

She shifted slightly on the couch, her legs curled beneath her as she sipped her wine, feeling the warmth of the liquid ease the knot of tension in her chest. She had been thinking about him—about them—for days now, her mind racing with questions she hadn't yet found the courage to ask. Nikolai was still so much of a mystery to her. She had seen glimpses of the man beneath the power, glimpses of vulnerability he rarely showed anyone, but there was still so much she didn't understand.

Tonight, though, she wanted answers. The tension of the past week had left them both on edge, and Ava couldn't shake the feeling that she needed to know more—needed to understand where Nikolai came from, what had shaped him into the man he was now. The silence between them felt heavy, like an invisible barrier she wanted to break through.

She watched him out of the corner of her eye, the way his fingers tightened slightly around the glass in his hand, his expression unreadable. She could sense that he was lost in thought, probably thinking about the business, the dangers that constantly surrounded him. But she wanted more than just the surface-level version of him tonight.

"Nikolai," she said softly, her voice breaking the silence between them.

He didn't look at her right away, his gaze still focused on the city outside, but she saw the slight tilt of his head, an acknowledgment that he had heard her.

"What is it, Ava?" His voice was deep, gravelly, but there was a softness to it, a hint of affection that he rarely let slip through.

Ava hesitated for a moment, unsure how to phrase the question that had been on her mind for days. But she couldn't hold it in any longer. She needed to know.

"Tell me about your childhood," she said quietly, her fingers tightening around her wineglass. "How... how did you end up here? In this life?"

There was a long, drawn-out silence in response to her question. She watched as Nikolai's body tensed, his fingers stopping their rhythmic tapping against the glass. He didn't move, didn't speak, but the air between them seemed to thicken with the weight of her question.

Ava's heart pounded in her chest, worried that she had overstepped. She knew Nikolai wasn't the type to share personal details easily, and she wasn't sure how he would react to her probing into his past. But she had to ask. She had to know.

Finally, after what felt like an eternity, Nikolai let out a long, slow breath, setting his glass down on the table in front of them. His fingers ran through his hair, his posture slumping slightly as if the very act of thinking about his past was exhausting.

"You want to know about my past?" he said, his voice low, almost resigned. "It's not something I talk about."

Ava bit her lip, her heart sinking slightly at the hardness in his tone. She wasn't sure if he was going to shut her down completely, if he was going to walk away from the conversation like he had done so many times before when things got too personal.

But then, to her surprise, Nikolai turned toward her, his dark eyes locking onto hers with an intensity that made her breath catch in her throat. His expression was hard, but there was something else there too—something vulnerable, raw, like he was weighing the decision of whether to open up to her.

"It's not a pretty story," he said after a long pause, his voice quieter now, more reflective.

"I don't expect it to be," Ava replied gently. "I just... I want to understand you."

Nikolai held her gaze for a long moment, his eyes searching hers as if trying to decide whether he could trust her with this part of himself. Finally, he let out another slow breath and leaned back against the couch, his posture more relaxed but still tense.

"I grew up in a small, forgotten town in Russia," he began, his voice rough, like gravel scraping against stone. "It was cold, harsh... the kind of place that didn't offer you much of a future."

Ava listened intently, her eyes fixed on him as he spoke. She could hear the bitterness in his voice, the way he spoke about his childhood with a detached, almost clinical tone, as if those memories had been locked away in a box for so long that he barely recognized them anymore.

"My father was a cruel man," Nikolai continued, his jaw tightening as he spoke. "He was involved in...

things. Dangerous things. Violence, crime—it was the way of life in our town. You either learned to survive, or you didn't. And my father made sure I learned quickly."

Ava's heart tightened at the coldness in his voice. She could only imagine what it must have been like to grow up in that kind of environment, with a man who saw love as weakness and control as survival.

"He wasn't the kind of man who showed affection," Nikolai said, his voice flat, emotionless. "He believed that power was everything—that love made you weak, and weakness was something he wouldn't tolerate. Not in himself, and certainly not in his son."

Ava swallowed hard, her fingers tightening around her glass. The image of a young Nikolai, growing up under the thumb of a man who saw emotions as a liability, made her heart ache. She had always sensed that there was pain behind Nikolai's cold, hard exterior, but hearing it laid bare like this was almost too much to bear.

"And your mother?" she asked softly, almost afraid to hear the answer.

Nikolai's eyes darkened, his expression hardening. "She died when I was young. I don't remember much about her, just that she was... kind. Too kind for a world like ours. After she was gone, it was just me and my father. And he made sure I understood that kindness had no place in our lives."

Ava felt a pang of sorrow for the boy Nikolai had been, growing up in a world that offered him no softness, no warmth. She couldn't imagine what that kind of upbringing had done to him, how it had shaped him into the man he was now.

"When I was sixteen, I left," Nikolai said, his voice quieter now, more reflective. "I couldn't take it anymore—my father, the violence, the constant pressure to prove I wasn't weak. I ran to Moscow, thinking I could find a better life there."

He let out a humorless chuckle, shaking his head slightly. "I was wrong. Moscow was just as brutal, just as unforgiving. I was a kid with no money, no connections, and no one to turn to."

Ava's heart ached as she listened to him, imagining the fear and desperation he must have felt as a teenager, alone in a city that was as cold and unwelcoming as the town he had fled from.

"That's when I found the Bratva," Nikolai continued, his voice hardening. "Or maybe they found me. Either way, I was pulled into their world. I was young, hungry, and willing to do whatever it took to survive. They offered me a way out, a way to escape my father's shadow. But it came with a price."

Ava felt a chill run down her spine at the weight of his words. She had always known that Nikolai's world was dangerous, but hearing him talk about how he had been pulled into it at such a young age made it feel more real, more terrifying.

"What kind of price?" she asked softly, her voice barely above a whisper.

Nikolai's expression darkened, his eyes hardening as he stared into the distance, as if seeing something only he could see. "Violence. Betrayal. Blood."

He paused for a moment, the silence between them heavy with unspoken memories. Ava could see the tension in his jaw, the way his fingers tightened into fists as if he was trying to hold back the emotions that were threatening to surface.

"I had to prove myself," Nikolai said, his voice rough. "I had to show them I wasn't weak—that I could do what needed to be done, no matter the cost. And I did. I became someone they could rely on, someone they could trust. But it came at a cost. It always does."

Ava's chest tightened as she listened to him. She could hear the pain behind his words, the regret that he tried so hard to keep hidden. But she knew that, despite everything, there was still a part of him that felt the weight of the choices he had made.

"How did you... how did you become their leader?" Ava asked, her voice trembling slightly.

Nikolai let out a slow breath, his gaze still fixed on some distant point beyond the skyline. His expression grew even darker, the shadows in the room seeming to deepen around him as the weight of her question sank in. He ran a hand over his face, pausing before he spoke, as if trying to find the right words to explain something so brutal and defining.

"To rise to the top in the Bratva," he began, his voice low and gravelly, "you don't just take control—you seize it. The men who held power before me weren't leaders. They were tyrants. They ruled through fear, but they had no loyalty. No respect. They were paranoid, always looking over their shoulders, waiting for someone to take them down. And they were right to be afraid."

Ava's breath hitched as she listened, the gravity of what Nikolai was saying settling in her chest like a stone. This wasn't just a story of survival—it was a story of violence and betrayal, a path paved with blood that had led him to the man he was now.

"I didn't set out to take over," Nikolai continued, his voice bitter. "I didn't want to be at the top. But when you're good at what you do, when you're the one they trust to get the job done, they start to look to you for leadership. And when the ones in charge get too greedy, too careless, people start to whisper. They start to wonder if someone else could do it better."

Ava felt a chill run down her spine at the cold detachment in his voice. She could hear the pain beneath it, the way he spoke as if this was just the way things had to be. She wanted to reach out, to touch him, to pull him out of those dark memories, but something told her that he needed to finish this story, needed to lay it all out in the open.

"There were two of them," Nikolai said, his voice tightening. "The men who ruled before me. They were corrupt—stealing from their own, using fear and violence to maintain control. But they were getting sloppy. They thought no one could touch them, that they were invincible. And that's when they made their mistake."

He paused, his jaw clenching as the memory played out in his mind. "They tried to kill me. Saw me as a threat. I was loyal, but they didn't care. To them, I was just another pawn to eliminate before I became too powerful."

Ava's heart pounded in her chest as she listened. "What happened?"

Nikolai's lips curled into a bitter smile, though there was no humor in it. "They underestimated me."

He leaned forward slightly, his voice dropping to a low, dangerous tone. "I fought back. I killed them both. But it wasn't just about survival—it was about sending a message. If you come after me, you better be ready to pay the price."

Ava swallowed hard, her throat dry as the full weight of Nikolai's words settled over her. She had known that Nikolai was a dangerous man, but hearing him talk about the way he had risen to power, about the violence and betrayal that had shaped him, made it all the more real.

"I didn't want the power," Nikolai said quietly, his gaze distant. "But once you've killed for it, once you've taken control, you can't just walk away. There's always someone waiting in the shadows, ready to take your place. And if you show even the slightest hint of weakness, they'll come for you."

Ava's heart ached as she listened to him, realizing just how heavy the burden of leadership must be for him. It wasn't just about power—it was about survival. And in his world, survival came at the cost of everything else.

"Do you regret it?" Ava asked softly, her voice trembling slightly.

Nikolai didn't answer right away. His eyes flicked toward her, his expression unreadable as he considered her question. For a long moment, the silence stretched between them, thick with unspoken emotion.

"Regret?" he repeated, his voice hollow. "I don't have the luxury of regret, Ava. In my world, you don't look back. You can't afford to."

Ava felt a pang of sadness at his words. She could see the weight of his decisions pressing down on him, the toll it had taken on his soul. But she also knew that he wasn't beyond saving. There was still a part of him—buried deep beneath the layers of violence and control—that longed for something more, something better.

"You're not your father," Ava said softly, her voice filled with a quiet determination. "You're not the man he tried to make you."

Nikolai's gaze darkened, his jaw tightening as he looked away. "You don't know me as well as you think you do," he muttered.

"I know enough," Ava replied, her voice steady. "I know you're not just the man who kills and destroys. You're the man who cares about the people in his life, even when you try to hide it."

Nikolai let out a low, humorless chuckle, shaking his head slightly. "You're giving me too much credit."

Ava shifted closer to him, her hand reaching out to rest gently on his arm. "I don't think I am."

For a long moment, Nikolai didn't move. He sat there, staring out at the skyline, his body tense beneath her touch. Ava could feel the conflict inside him, the war he was waging between the man he had been forced to become and the man he wanted to be.

Finally, after what felt like an eternity, Nikolai turned to face her, his dark eyes locking onto hers with an intensity that made her breath catch in her throat.

"You don't understand what you're asking for," he said quietly, his voice rough. "My life... it's not something you can just walk into. It's violent. Dangerous. If you stay with me, you'll be a part of that. You'll be a target."

Ava's chest tightened at his words, but she didn't waver. She had known from the beginning that being with Nikolai came with risks. But what he didn't seem to understand was that she was willing to face those risks, that she wasn't afraid of his world as long as she was with him.

"I'm not afraid," she said softly, her voice steady.

Nikolai's eyes narrowed, a flash of frustration crossing his face. "You should be," he growled. "Do you really think you can survive in my world? Do you think you can handle what comes with being *mine*?"

Ava's heart pounded in her chest at the intensity of his words, but she didn't back down. "Yes," she whispered. "I do."

Nikolai stared at her for a long moment, his dark eyes searching hers as if trying to find some crack in her resolve. But there wasn't one. She was standing her ground, refusing to be pushed away.

"I'll protect you," he murmured, his voice softening as he reached out, his hand brushing against her cheek. "No matter what happens, I'll keep you safe."

Ava leaned into his touch, her heart swelling with a mixture of fear and hope. She knew that being with Nikolai wouldn't be easy, that his world would test her in ways she couldn't even imagine. But she also knew that she couldn't walk away from him. Not now. Not after everything they had been through.

"I'm not going anywhere," she whispered.

Nikolai's gaze softened, a flicker of relief crossing his face as he pulled her closer, wrapping his arms around her as if he was afraid she might slip away. For the first time since she had met him, Ava felt like she had finally broken through the walls he had built around himself. She had seen the man behind the power, behind the violence, and she knew that—despite everything—she wanted to stay.

"I don't deserve you," Nikolai murmured, his voice rough with emotion. "But I'm too selfish to let you go."

Ava smiled softly, her hand resting gently against his chest. "Then don't."

Nikolai pulled her closer, pressing his forehead against hers as they sat there in the quiet of the penthouse, the weight of the past finally lifting, if only for a moment.

And in that moment, Ava knew that she was exactly where she was meant to be.

Chapter 13

The room was dimly lit, casting long shadows over the faces of the men gathered around the sleek wooden table. Nikolai sat at the head, his posture relaxed, but there was a tension in the air, the kind that only came when danger was near. The soft glow of a single overhead lamp illuminated the table, but beyond that, the room was cloaked in shadow—just as Nikolai preferred it. Shadows and silence, that's where the real power was wielded.

Viktor, his second-in-command, sat to his right, his fingers drumming lightly against the polished surface of the table. He was the only one who appeared at ease, though Nikolai knew better. Viktor's calm was a well-practiced mask, one he had learned to wear over the years of working alongside Nikolai in the world of the Bratva.

"The Morozovs are pushing in," Viktor began, breaking the heavy silence. His voice was low but carried the kind of weight that made every man in the room sit a little straighter. "They've been moving more men through Little Odessa, and there's been an increase in traffic at the docks. We've had eyes on them for a few weeks now. They're testing the boundaries."

Nikolai's gaze shifted to the map spread out on the table in front of him, the entire city of New York laid out like a chessboard. Red lines marked his territories, the zones of control he and his men had painstakingly carved out over the years. Little Odessa was one of those territories—a key part of his operation—and now, the Morozovs were sniffing around it like wolves circling their prey.

"They're not just testing boundaries," Nikolai said, his voice cold and measured, the calm before a storm. His dark eyes flicked up to meet Viktor's, and for a moment, the room seemed to hold its breath. "They're looking for weaknesses."

There was a murmur of agreement from the other men at the table—his lieutenants, each one loyal to him, each one aware of the precarious situation they found themselves in. The Morozovs were a problem that couldn't be ignored, but it was more than just a territorial dispute. It was personal. And Nikolai knew exactly what they were after.

"They've been watching," Nikolai continued, his voice dropping lower, colder. "They saw Ava with me at the restaurant. They know what she means to me. They think she's my weakness."

The weight of his words settled over the room like a heavy fog. His men exchanged uneasy glances, but no one spoke. They knew better than to interrupt when Nikolai was laying out his thoughts. The tension in the air thickened, the quiet murmur of the city beyond the walls of the penthouse seeming miles away from the reality of the threat that loomed over them.

Ava. The thought of her name alone made his chest tighten with both affection and fear. Nikolai had kept his emotions tightly guarded for most of his life, but Ava had slipped past those defenses, and now, she was more than just a lover or a companion. She was his. And that made her a target.

"They think she's your weakness?" one of the lieutenants, Alexei, asked from across the table, his brows furrowed. "They're idiots if they think they can exploit that."

"They're not idiots," Viktor cut in, his voice sharp but controlled. "The Morozovs know exactly what they're doing. They wouldn't make a move unless they thought they had an edge."

Nikolai's gaze flicked toward Viktor. His second-in-command had a point. The Morozovs had been biding their time, probing for vulnerabilities. The increased activity in Little Odessa wasn't just a show of force—it was a diversion. They wanted Nikolai focused on the surface-level skirmishes so they could plan something bigger.

"Viktor's right," Nikolai said, his voice steady. "They're not making random moves. They're preparing for something. And they think Ava is the way to get to me."

He let the words hang in the air, the weight of them pressing down on everyone in the room. Ava had become more than just a part of his life—she was woven into the very fabric of his existence. And that made her both a strength and a liability. The Morozovs had picked up on it, and now they were preparing to strike.

"They're watching her," Nikolai continued, his hands curling into fists at the thought. "They've been watching her every move. She doesn't know it yet, but they're circling."

The men at the table shifted uneasily. There were murmurs of discontent, some of them cursing the audacity of the Morozovs. But Nikolai stayed quiet for a moment, his mind running through every possible scenario. The Morozovs wouldn't stop. They'd try to break him through her, and the thought of that sent a wave of fury through him, colder and sharper than anything he had felt in a long time.

"We make sure they know that coming after her is a mistake," Nikolai said, his voice like steel, cutting through the tension. "And we make sure she's protected at all times."

He straightened in his seat, his gaze sweeping across the room, meeting the eyes of each man sitting at the table. He had handpicked each one of them, and he trusted them with his life. But Ava... she was something different. She was his heart, and no one—no one—would be allowed to touch her.

"Viktor," Nikolai said, turning his full attention to his right-hand man. "I want increased security on Ava. No exceptions. She doesn't go anywhere without protection, and I want eyes on her 24/7. I don't care if she's going to the store or taking a walk in the park—I want to know where she is at all times."

Viktor nodded, already making notes on his phone, his expression grim. "I'll handle it personally."

The other men exchanged glances, their tension palpable. They knew the situation was serious. The Morozovs had been a thorn in their side for months, but this... this was crossing a line. Targeting Nikolai's woman was an act of war, and everyone in the room knew it.

"And if they make a move?" one of the younger lieutenants, Dmitri, asked from the far end of the table. His voice was tense, his hand gripping the armrest of his chair a little too tightly.

Nikolai's lips curled into a dangerous smile, the kind that sent a chill down the spines of everyone in the room. His eyes gleamed with a cold fire, a promise of what was to come.

"If they make a move," Nikolai said, his voice low and deadly, "I'll make sure they regret ever laying eyes on her."

The room fell into a heavy silence, the weight of his words sinking in. No one doubted him. They had seen firsthand what Nikolai was capable of—what lengths he would go to when pushed. And the Morozovs were pushing.

Viktor glanced up from his phone, his eyes meeting Nikolai's. "We'll have men in place by tonight. She won't take a step without us knowing."

Nikolai nodded, satisfied but still seething inside. It wasn't enough to have her watched, guarded. He wanted to crush the Morozovs before they even had a chance to get close to her. But that would come later. For now, he had to focus on keeping Ava safe—keeping her in his world, but protected from the violence that threatened to tear it apart.

"She doesn't need to know the details," Nikolai said, his voice firm. "Keep everything discreet. She'll resist the extra security, but I don't care. This isn't about what she wants. It's about what's necessary."

Viktor nodded again, understanding the unspoken command. Ava was stubborn, independent, and Nikolai knew she would push back against the increasing restrictions. But she didn't understand the full scope of the danger yet, and until she did,

Nikolai would have to enforce control. Control was the only way to keep her safe.

Nikolai rose from the table, signaling the end of the meeting. The men stood with him, gathering their belongings, but Viktor lingered for a moment longer.

"We'll handle this," Viktor said quietly as the others filed out of the room. "No one will get close to her."

Nikolai nodded, his gaze hard as he met Viktor's eyes. "Make sure of it."

Viktor gave a curt nod before turning and leaving the room, the door clicking shut behind him. Nikolai remained standing by the table, his hands resting on the edge of the polished wood as he stared down at the map of the city.

Ava. She was the center of everything now. His love for her was the one thing that made him human—and the one thing that could destroy him if he wasn't careful.

But he would not allow the Morozovs, or anyone else, to take her from him.

They wanted to exploit his weakness. They'd learn soon enough that Nikolai Volkov had no weaknesses. Not when it came to her.

Nikolai entered the penthouse later that evening, the familiar quiet of the space welcoming him like a sanctuary. The city lights flickered through the massive windows, casting a warm glow across the sleek, modern furniture and the artfully arranged decor that Ava had added since moving in. It felt more like home now with her touch on it—softer, more lived-in. But tonight, the tension that had followed him from the meeting seeped into the room, tightening the air around him.

Ava was curled up on the couch, reading a book, her hair falling in soft waves over her shoulder. She glanced up as he entered, her eyes lighting up at the sight of him. But even in her smile, Nikolai could see the questions that lingered there, the concern she hadn't yet voiced.

"You're late," she said, closing the book and setting it aside. She sat up, tucking her legs beneath her as he walked over to her.

"Business," Nikolai replied, his voice clipped, though he softened as he looked down at her. "You know how it is."

Ava tilted her head, her eyes narrowing slightly. "Is everything all right?"

Nikolai hesitated for a fraction of a second before he nodded. He didn't want to burden her with the full weight of what he was dealing with. She didn't need to know the specifics of the Morozov Bratva's plans. It was enough that he knew, enough that he could handle it.

But the truth was, everything wasn't all right. Not in the way he wanted it to be. The world outside this penthouse was filled with danger, threats lurking around every corner, and Ava... Ava was the one thing that made him vulnerable. The one thing that could bring him to his knees.

"I'm handling it," he said, his voice firmer now as he took a seat beside her. He reached out, brushing a strand of hair behind her ear, his fingers lingering on her skin.

Ava leaned into his touch, her eyes searching his face as if she could see the storm brewing inside him. "Nikolai," she said softly, "you don't have to do this alone."

He looked at her, the sincerity in her words catching him off guard. She had no idea what she was asking, no idea what it would mean for her to be fully involved in his world. He would never let that happen—never let her see the darkest parts of his life. She needed to stay sheltered from the worst of it.

"I know," he replied, his voice softening for her. "But I have to protect you."

Ava's brow furrowed, her eyes flicking down to his hand on her arm. "I can take care of myself, Nikolai. You don't have to keep me locked up in this penthouse like a prisoner."

His jaw tightened, the word *prisoner* hitting him harder than he expected. Was that what she thought? That he was keeping her here, trapping her in his world against her will?

He leaned in closer, his hand gripping her arm just a little tighter. "You don't understand," he said, his voice low and intense. "This isn't just about keeping you safe. It's about survival. If something happens to you, it will destroy me. And I can't let that happen."

Ava's eyes widened slightly at the intensity of his words, but she didn't pull away. Instead, she leaned closer, her hand resting on his chest. "You won't lose me, Nikolai," she whispered, her voice filled with emotion. "I'm not going anywhere."

But her words, while comforting, didn't ease the knot in his chest. He knew better than to believe that everything would be fine just because she promised it would. In his world, promises meant nothing. Only action, only control, could guarantee her safety.

And he would do whatever it took to make sure she stayed safe.

The next morning, Nikolai stood by the windows, watching the city come alive beneath him. The skyline stretched out before him, a mixture of power and chaos that mirrored his own life. He had slept little the night before, his mind too consumed with plans, strategies, and the constant need to stay one step ahead of his enemies.

He turned as Viktor entered the room, his second-in-command as stoic and efficient as always. Viktor wasted no time with pleasantries, getting straight to business as he laid a tablet on the desk, displaying the updated security plans for Ava.

"We've doubled the detail," Viktor said, swiping through the data. "She won't go anywhere without eyes on her. I've personally vetted the team. These men are the best."

Nikolai nodded, his eyes scanning the details. "And if something goes wrong?"

"It won't," Viktor replied, his tone confident. "But if it does, we'll be ready."

Nikolai's gaze flicked up to meet Viktor's. He trusted Viktor, but trust in his world was a fragile thing, easily shattered. Trust wasn't enough when it came to Ava's safety—it was only a piece of the puzzle.

He paced around his desk, his mind racing. Viktor's assurances were solid, but Nikolai had learned that no plan was foolproof. There was always something—a misstep, a miscalculation, a blind spot—that could unravel everything. And he couldn't afford mistakes. Not with her.

"I want every movement monitored," Nikolai said, his voice sharp as he stared at the security details on the screen. "No exceptions. If she even steps outside the penthouse, I want to know. If she leaves a room, someone should be on her. I want them invisible but close. Understood?"

Viktor nodded, his eyes dark and serious. "Understood, boss. The men know what's at stake."

Nikolai's eyes flickered with something cold and dangerous. "Do they? Because if one of them slips up, I will not hesitate to make them regret it."

He wasn't just issuing a threat—it was a promise. Nikolai had built his empire by being ruthless, and that ruthlessness extended to the men who worked for him. They knew what was at stake, but even more than that, they knew the consequences of failure.

Viktor didn't flinch. He had been at Nikolai's side for years, long enough to understand the gravity of his words. "It won't come to that. I'll make sure of it."

Nikolai nodded but remained tense. "Good. But I want contingency plans. If something goes wrong—if the Morozovs try anything, I need to know we can get her out immediately."

"She won't leave the city," Viktor replied, though there was an unspoken question in his eyes. Nikolai had kept Ava close, but he hadn't mentioned taking her out of the country or to a safe house. It was clear he didn't want her far from him, no matter how dangerous things became.

"She won't," Nikolai agreed, his voice quieter now, but no less firm. "I'll keep her with me. She'll be safer here, where I can control the situation."

Viktor nodded again, though it was clear he had reservations. "I'll have the men on standby."

Nikolai stood by the windows again, watching the city as Viktor left. He could see the busy streets below, cars and people moving about, living their lives without the constant threat of violence hanging over them. Ava had once been like that—free from this world of blood and power. But now, she was part of it, even if she didn't fully realize the depth of the danger she was in.

He gritted his teeth, his hands curling into fists. The Morozov Bratva thought they could use her to get to him, to exploit his one weakness. But they had no idea what he was capable of when it came to her.

They'd learn soon enough.

Later that evening, as the sun set behind the city skyline, the tension in the penthouse was palpable. Ava moved around the living room, her restlessness evident in the way she fidgeted with the cushions and straightened the books on the coffee table. Nikolai watched her from the other side of the room, his hands in his pockets, his jaw clenched tight.

He had expected this. He had known it was coming.

"Ava," he said, his voice low, but firm. She stopped moving, turning to face him, her expression filled with frustration.

"You're suffocating me, Nikolai," she blurted out, the words sharp and laced with emotion. "I can't breathe with all these guards following me everywhere. I can't leave without feeling like I'm being watched. What happened to my life?"

Her voice cracked on the last word, and Nikolai felt a pang of guilt twist in his chest. But it was quickly swallowed by the overwhelming need to protect her, to keep her safe. He had to make her understand, even if she hated him for it.

"This isn't about your life, Ava," he replied, his voice harder than he intended. "This is about keeping you alive."

She crossed her arms over her chest, her eyes narrowing at him. "I'm not a prisoner, Nikolai. You can't just lock me away and expect me to be okay with it."

His temper flared at her defiance, but he pushed it down, trying to keep his cool. "I'm not locking you away," he said, stepping closer to her. "I'm protecting you."

"By putting me in a cage?" she shot back, her voice rising. "Because that's what this feels like. A cage."

Nikolai took another step toward her, his eyes flashing with something dark and dangerous. "I would rather you be in a cage and alive than free and dead, Ava. You have no idea what the Morozovs are capable of. You don't know what's at stake."

She faltered for a moment, the reality of his words sinking in. But she didn't back down. "Then tell me. Tell me what's at stake. Tell me why you think controlling every aspect of my life is the only way to protect me."

Nikolai's jaw tightened, the muscles in his neck tensing as he tried to rein in his frustration. He couldn't tell her. He couldn't burden her with the full scope of the danger she was in. It would only terrify her, make her feel even more helpless. And he couldn't stand to see her like that.

"You don't need to know the details," he said, his voice low and dangerous. "You just need to trust me."

Ava stared at him for a long moment, her chest rising and falling with shallow breaths. Her eyes searched his face, looking for something—some sign that he was willing to bend, to let her have even a shred of control over her own life.

But she found nothing.

"I do trust you, Nikolai," she said quietly, her voice filled with emotion. "But I need to be more than just someone you keep in a glass box. I need to live."

Her words struck a chord deep inside him, one he hadn't expected. He wanted her to live, to be happy, but he also knew that his world didn't allow for freedom. Not the kind of freedom she was asking for.

"I won't let you die," he said, his voice rough with emotion. "I can't."

She sighed, her shoulders sagging as the fight drained out of her. "But what kind of life is this?"

Nikolai didn't have an answer for her. He couldn't offer her the life she deserved, not with the danger they faced. All he could do was protect her the only way he knew how—through control.

It was later that night when Nikolai received the news he had been dreading. The Morozov Bratva had made their move. Viktor called him with the information, his voice calm but as he detailed the intercepted intel.

"They're planning something big," Viktor said over the phone, his voice crackling through the speaker. "We don't have all the details yet, but it's clear they're targeting you—and Ava."

Nikolai's blood ran cold at the mention of her name. He had expected this, had known it was coming, but hearing it confirmed made the threat all too real.

"How soon?" Nikolai asked, his voice like ice.

"Could be days, could be hours," Viktor replied. "But we're ready. The men are in place."

Nikolai's grip tightened on the phone, his knuckles turning white. "Increase security around the penthouse. No one gets in or out without my authorization."

Viktor hesitated for a moment. "And Ava? What do you want us to do if they make a move?"

Nikolai's jaw clenched, his mind racing with a thousand possibilities, each one darker and more dangerous than the last. He couldn't let anything happen to her. Not now. Not ever.

"If they touch her," he said, his voice low and deadly, "I'll burn their entire world to the ground."

When Nikolai returned to the penthouse that night, the weight of the Morozov threat sat heavy on his shoulders. Ava was already asleep, her soft breaths filling the quiet of the room. He stood in the doorway for a long time, watching her, his chest tight with a mix of fear and determination.

He couldn't tell her. He wouldn't. She didn't need to know the full extent of the danger they were facing. It would only scare her, make her feel even more trapped. He had to protect her from that, had to shield her from the worst of it.

But the thought of keeping her in the dark, of not giving her the chance to understand the world she was now a part of, tore at him. He wanted to be honest with her, wanted her to trust him completely. But honesty was a luxury he couldn't afford—not in this world.

He stepped closer to the bed, his eyes tracing the curve of her body as she slept peacefully, unaware of the storm brewing around them. He had brought her into his life, into his world, and now it was his responsibility to keep her safe. Even if it meant controlling her every move. Even if it meant making decisions she would never understand.

"I won't let them touch you," he whispered, his voice barely audible in the dark room. "I'll keep you safe, Ava. No matter what."

With one last look at her, Nikolai turned and left the bedroom, his steps slow and deliberate as he made his way to the balcony. The cool night air hit his face, but it did nothing to ease the heat of anger and fear simmering in his chest. He gripped the railing, his knuckles whitening, as his mind ran through every possible scenario, every move the Morozovs could make to get to Ava.

They thought they had found his weakness. They thought that by going after her, they could control him. They were wrong. He would do whatever it took to protect her, no matter the cost.

He took a deep breath, the cold air stinging his lungs as he tried to calm the storm inside him. He knew what he had to do—he had always known. His life was one of control, and control was the only way to ensure survival. Ava wouldn't understand it. She would fight against it. But she was too important to lose. Too precious.

Nikolai closed his eyes, letting the silence of the night wrap around him like a blanket. His enemies were getting closer, and the noose was tightening around his empire. But he wasn't afraid. Not of them. The only fear he allowed himself was the thought of losing Ava.

And he couldn't lose her. Not now. Not ever.

With a final glance toward the city, Nikolai turned back into the penthouse, his resolve hardening with every step. The Morozovs would come for her, and when they did, they would see the full extent of his wrath.

He would protect her with everything he had.

Even if it destroyed him in the process.

Chapter 14

Nikolai sat in his office, the morning light filtering in through the tall windows that overlooked the city skyline. The usual noise of New York was muffled by the thick glass, leaving only the low hum of the world outside. He leaned back in his chair, eyes narrowing at the papers and maps spread across his desk. His mind was focused, calculating the next move. Viktor stood in front of the desk, his posture relaxed but his expression hard.

"The Morozovs aren't just sniffing around the edges anymore," Viktor said, his voice calm but filled with a cold undercurrent. "They're moving. There's been increased activity at the docks, and they're eyeing one of the clubs in Little Odessa."

Nikolai's jaw tightened as he shifted his attention to Viktor. The Morozov Bratva had been a problem for months, testing boundaries, probing for weaknesses. But now, it seemed, they were preparing to act. They weren't content with just poking around the edges anymore. They were ready to strike.

"Which club?" Nikolai asked, his voice low but firm.

"The Empire," Viktor replied, crossing his arms over his chest. "One of our strongest fronts."

Nikolai exhaled slowly, his fingers drumming on the arm of his chair. The Empire wasn't just a nightclub—it was a hub for his operations in that part of the city. Losing it, or even having it threatened, would be a significant blow to his network. But more than that, it would be a public show of weakness, and Nikolai couldn't afford to appear weak—not with the Morozovs breathing down his neck.

"What's their endgame?" Nikolai asked, though he already had a good idea. The Morozovs had always been opportunistic, always looking for a crack in the armor. But they were also smart. They wouldn't make a move unless they believed it would work in their favor.

"They think they've found a weakness," Viktor replied, his eyes darkening as he glanced down at the map on the desk. "They know you've been more focused on your personal life lately. They're banking on that. They're assuming you're distracted."

Nikolai's gaze sharpened. Ava. The Morozovs weren't just coming for his businesses—they were coming for him through her. He could feel the rage simmering beneath the surface, the cold, controlled fury that had driven him for years. It was the same fire that had built his empire, the same drive that had crushed anyone who dared to stand in his way.

And now, they were trying to exploit the one thing that mattered most to him.

"They think she's my weakness," Nikolai said, his voice barely above a growl.

Viktor nodded, his eyes meeting Nikolai's. "They think you've gone soft."

The words hit Nikolai harder than he expected. Soft. It wasn't a word he'd ever associated with himself, not in this life. But he knew what Viktor meant. He'd seen it coming. The more time he spent with Ava, the more he felt like he was slipping into a world that didn't belong to him—a world where love and happiness could exist without the constant threat of violence hanging overhead. But he was a fool if he believed that for even a second. His world didn't allow for those luxuries, and now, the Morozovs were planning to remind him of that fact.

"They're wrong," Nikolai said, his voice cold and hard as steel. "Ava isn't a weakness."

Viktor smirked slightly, though there was no humor in his expression. "They don't need to be right to try."

Nikolai leaned forward, his fingers steepled under his chin as he considered their options. He needed to protect Ava, to make sure she was out of harm's way, but he also knew he couldn't afford to appear weak by running from a fight. He had built his empire on strength and control, and if the Morozovs saw an opportunity to exploit what they perceived as a vulnerability, they would seize it. The game they were playing wasn't just about territory—it was about power. And they thought they could take his by going after Ava.

"We'll reinforce security at all the key locations," Viktor continued, his tone matter-of-fact. "Double the men at The Empire, and I'll personally oversee the operation at the docks. But I think it's best if you step back for a few days. Remove yourself from the line of fire while we deal with this."

Nikolai's jaw clenched. Stepping back wasn't in his nature. He didn't hide from threats—he faced them head-on, crushed them before they had a chance to grow. But Viktor had a point. If the Morozovs were targeting him directly, putting Ava in the crosshairs, then it was time to rethink the plan.

"And Ava?" Nikolai asked, though the answer was already forming in his mind.

Viktor glanced at him, reading the unspoken question. "Take her somewhere safe. Somewhere off the radar. Let us handle things here while you keep her protected."

Nikolai nodded slowly, the wheels in his mind already turning. A retreat wasn't something he would normally consider, but this wasn't about him.

This was about Ava. She had been feeling suffocated in the penthouse for weeks now, and a break from the city might give her the space she needed while also keeping her out of harm's way.

"There's a cabin upstate," Nikolai said after a moment, the plan solidifying in his mind. "We'll go there for the weekend. It'll give you time to secure things here."

Viktor's expression shifted slightly, a flicker of approval in his eyes. "It's a good move. We'll make sure you're covered."

Nikolai stood, his decision made. "I'll tell her today. We leave tonight."

As Viktor nodded and turned to leave the office, Nikolai's thoughts drifted back to Ava. She had become the center of his world, the one thing he couldn't lose. The Morozovs thought they could exploit that, thought they could use her to weaken him. But they didn't know what he was capable of—what he would do to protect her.

Let them come.

They'd regret it.

As the door to the office clicked shut behind Viktor, Nikolai stood in the lingering silence, his mind still racing. The cabin upstate wasn't a place he visited often—isolated, surrounded by thick forest, and off the radar of anyone looking to track him. It had been used before for business, as a location to meet with allies or lie low when things in the city got too heated. But this time, it wasn't business that drove him there. It was her.

Ava.

She had been struggling lately, the tension evident in every glance she threw his way. She hadn't voiced her frustrations outright, but Nikolai had seen it—the way her shoulders tensed, the way her eyes flicked to the door every time a guard passed through the penthouse. She was suffocating, and it was his doing.

He ran a hand through his hair, exhaling sharply as he pushed away from the desk. The lines between his two worlds—business and personal—had become increasingly blurred. When Ava first entered his life, he hadn't anticipated how deeply she would affect him. Now, it felt like every decision, every action, was motivated by the need to protect her. It was an instinct he couldn't shake, one that had grown stronger with each passing day.

But how could he protect her from the very world he ruled?

The thought weighed heavy on him as he crossed the room, grabbing his phone from the corner of the desk. The contact list scrolled quickly until he found the name he needed.

"Gennady, prep the cabin," Nikolai said as soon as the call connected. His voice was steady, but there was an underlying urgency to it. "We're leaving tonight. Make sure everything's in place."

Gennady, one of Nikolai's trusted security men, responded immediately. "It'll be ready, boss. Should I send additional security?"

"No," Nikolai replied, his tone firm. "Keep it low-key. I don't want to draw attention. Just make sure the area is secure."

The call ended as quickly as it began, and Nikolai tucked the phone back into his pocket, his gaze shifting toward the door that led to the rest of the penthouse. Ava was just beyond that door, most likely curled up with a book or trying to distract herself with something mundane. She had never been one to complain, but Nikolai knew she was struggling. The weight of their situation—the constant surveillance, the never-ending threat—it was wearing her down.

It was wearing him down too.

With a deep breath, Nikolai pushed open the door and stepped into the hallway. The penthouse was quiet, save for the soft hum of the air conditioning and the distant sounds of the city beyond the windows. He found Ava in the living room, exactly as he'd imagined—sitting on the couch, her legs tucked beneath her, a book resting in her lap. Her hair fell in soft waves around her face, and she looked peaceful, though Nikolai knew that peace was a fragile thing these days.

She glanced up as he approached, a small smile tugging at the corners of her lips. "Hey," she said softly, her voice carrying the warmth he had come to crave. "You're done with work early."

Nikolai smiled back, though his mind was already racing ahead to what he needed to say. He didn't want to worry her, didn't want to alarm her with the real reason for the trip, but he needed to make sure she understood that this was important.

"I thought we could use a break," he said, his voice smooth but firm. He sat down beside her, one hand resting on her knee as he met her gaze. "How do you feel about a weekend getaway? Just the two of us."

Ava's eyes brightened at the suggestion, her smile widening as she straightened up. "Really? Where?"

"Upstate," Nikolai replied, his tone casual. "I have a cabin there—secluded, quiet. It'll give us a chance to get away from all this."

Ava's expression softened, her shoulders visibly relaxing as she considered the idea. "That sounds perfect," she said, her voice laced with relief. "I've been feeling... a little trapped lately."

Nikolai's heart tightened at her words. He had known it, but hearing her admit it made the weight of it even heavier. He hated that she felt this way, hated that his world had forced her into a corner where she couldn't even breathe freely.

"We'll leave tonight," he said, squeezing her knee gently. "I'll take care of everything."

Ava nodded, her excitement palpable. She leaned in, pressing a soft kiss to his lips before standing. "I'll start packing."

As she disappeared into the bedroom, Nikolai remained on the couch for a moment longer, his mind drifting back to the conversation with Viktor. The threat was real. He couldn't afford to relax, couldn't afford to let his guard down, even for a second. The cabin would give them both some space, but he knew better than to think they were truly safe.

Still, it was better than staying here in the city, where the walls seemed to close in more with every passing day.

Pulling out his phone again, Nikolai quickly typed out a message to Viktor: Everything's set. We leave in a few hours. Let me know if there's any movement.

Viktor's response came almost immediately: Understood. I'll keep you updated.

Nikolai slipped the phone back into his pocket and stood, heading toward the bedroom where Ava was already gathering her things. The penthouse felt more like a fortress these days—impenetrable, but suffocating. The weekend trip was a necessity, a chance to reset, if only for a moment. But Nikolai knew that the shadows of his world would follow them, no matter how far they ran.

Stepping into the bedroom, he watched as Ava moved around the room, tossing clothes into a small suitcase with a sense of ease that Nikolai hadn't seen in weeks. She looked up at him, her smile warm and genuine.

"I can't wait to get out of here," she said, her voice light, as if the weight of their life had already lifted.

Nikolai smiled back, though the heaviness in his chest remained. He would do whatever it took to keep her safe. Even if that meant running. Even if that meant fighting.

Because no matter where they went, the danger would always be there, lurking just out of sight.

The drive upstate was long but peaceful, the miles slipping by as the city fell behind them and the landscape shifted from the urban sprawl to the rolling hills and dense forests of the countryside. Ava leaned her head against the window, watching as the sun began its slow descent behind the trees, casting a golden hue over the winding roads. She seemed more relaxed than she had been in weeks, and for a moment, Nikolai let himself believe that this trip might actually provide them with the respite they both needed.

But his thoughts never strayed far from the danger. His mind remained alert, focused on the road and the quiet conversations happening through the earpiece tucked discreetly in his ear. His security team, though invisible to Ava, wasn't far behind. They were traveling in separate vehicles, keeping their distance but always within reach. Nikolai had made sure of it.

Still, he kept it all from Ava. She didn't need to know about the precautions, didn't need to see the full extent of the shadows that followed them. It was better this way—letting her believe they were just two people on a peaceful getaway. For her sake, he would keep the darkness at bay for as long as he could.

As the car turned off the main road onto a narrow, unmarked path, Ava stirred beside him, blinking away the remnants of a nap. She sat up, rubbing her eyes and looking around, her expression shifting from groggy to curious.

"Are we almost there?" she asked, her voice still soft from sleep.

Nikolai glanced at her, a small smile tugging at the corner of his mouth. "Almost. Just a few more minutes."

The path was lined with towering trees, their branches casting long shadows over the road as the sun sank lower. The air here was different—cleaner, fresher, filled with the scent of pine and earth. It was a world away from the constant noise and chaos of the city, and Nikolai could feel the weight of it beginning to lift from Ava's shoulders.

As they rounded the final bend, the cabin came into view—a rustic structure nestled between the trees, its dark wooden exterior blending almost seamlessly with the surrounding forest. The cabin wasn't large, but it was perfect for what they needed—secluded, quiet, and far removed from the eyes of anyone who might be looking for them.

Ava's eyes widened as she took in the sight, a genuine smile spreading across her face. "It's beautiful," she whispered, her voice filled with awe. "It's so... peaceful."

Nikolai pulled the car to a stop in front of the cabin, his gaze lingering on her for a moment before he turned off the engine. "It is," he agreed, though the peace she spoke of felt fragile to him—like something that could be shattered at any moment.

As they stepped out of the car, the cool evening air greeted them, crisp and fresh in a way that was unfamiliar after the smog-filled city. Ava took a deep breath, closing her eyes for a moment as she soaked it in. Nikolai watched her, his heart tightening. He wished he could give her more of this—more moments of peace, of freedom—but he knew better. This wasn't their life. It was a temporary escape, nothing more.

"Let's get inside," Nikolai said, nodding toward the cabin as he grabbed their bags from the trunk. His eyes scanned the perimeter out of habit, always assessing, always alert. He couldn't let his guard down, not even here. Especially not here.

Ava followed him to the front door, her excitement evident as she glanced around at the surroundings. The forest stretched out in every direction, dense and quiet, with only the faint sound of birds in the distance. It was the kind of place where time seemed to slow down, where the rest of the world faded away.

Inside, the cabin was just as rustic and charming as the exterior. The interior was all warm wood and stone, with a large fireplace dominating the living room and a cozy kitchen tucked off to the side. A few windows let in the last light of the day, casting a soft glow over the simple furnishings.

Ava set her bag down, her eyes wide as she took it all in. "This is perfect," she said, turning to Nikolai with a look of pure gratitude. "I didn't realize how much I needed this until now."

Nikolai's chest tightened at her words. He knew she was right—she needed this break, this space to breathe. But he also knew it wouldn't last. His world had a way of intruding, no matter how far they ran. But for now, he would let her have this moment, this brief illusion of normalcy.

"I'm glad you like it," Nikolai said, his voice softer than usual as he stepped closer to her. He brushed a strand of hair behind her ear, his fingers lingering on her skin. "I wanted to give you something different, even if it's just for a little while."

Ava's eyes softened, her smile warm as she leaned into his touch. "It's perfect," she repeated, her voice barely above a whisper. "Thank you."

For a moment, they stood in the quiet of the cabin, the world outside forgotten. The fire crackled softly in the fireplace, casting a warm glow over the room as the shadows lengthened. It felt like a sanctuary—a place where the chaos of their lives couldn't reach them.

But Nikolai knew better. He always knew better.

As night fell, they settled into the cabin, unpacking their bags and preparing dinner together. Ava moved around the small kitchen with ease, her earlier tension fading as she joked and laughed with Nikolai. The food wasn't extravagant—just a simple meal of grilled vegetables and pasta—but it felt special, if only because it was something they hadn't done in a long time.

For a few hours, they forgot about the dangers that lingered beyond the walls. They forgot about the men who were always watching, the enemies who were always plotting. It was just them, in this small cabin, far from the city and the weight of the life they lived.

But as they sat together by the fire, Ava curled up against Nikolai's side, he couldn't shake the feeling that it wouldn't last. This moment, this peace—it was temporary. The world would catch up to them eventually.

And when it did, Nikolai knew he'd be ready.

As the evening wore on, the cabin grew even quieter, the sounds of the forest fading with the setting sun. The soft crackle of the fire in the living room was the only noise, a steady, comforting rhythm that filled the space as Ava nestled into Nikolai's side. She was wrapped in one of the thick blankets from the cabin, her head resting on his shoulder as she let out a contented sigh.

"I could stay here forever," Ava murmured, her voice low and drowsy.

Nikolai's arm tightened around her, though he didn't respond right away. He stared into the flames, the warmth from the fire seeping into his skin, but the tension in his chest hadn't faded. The quiet of the cabin felt too fragile, too easily broken. The moment felt borrowed, like something that wasn't really theirs to keep.

"I wish you could," he finally said, his voice softer than usual. But even as the words left his mouth, he knew it wasn't possible. This wasn't their life—this wasn't the reality they lived in. The peace they found here was temporary, a fleeting illusion that would dissolve the moment they stepped back into the real world.

Ava shifted beside him, tilting her head up to look at him. Her eyes were soft, filled with something he couldn't quite name—affection, gratitude, maybe even love. It twisted something inside him, something that had been growing ever since she entered his life. A part of him wanted to believe that they could have more of this—that they could find a way to live in this quiet, isolated world without the constant threat of violence hanging over their heads.

But he wasn't that naïve. Not anymore.

"I know we can't stay forever," Ava said, her voice cutting through his thoughts. "But it's nice to pretend for a little while."

Her words hit him harder than she probably realized. She knew, just as he did, that their time here was limited. She wasn't as oblivious to the dangers as he liked to think. But she never complained, never voiced her fears or frustrations in a way that made him feel like he was failing her. She always found a way to stay strong, even when the world they lived in threatened to tear her apart.

Nikolai turned slightly, brushing a strand of hair behind her ear. His fingers lingered on her skin, and for a moment, he allowed himself to forget the outside world—the threats, the enemies, the violence. Here, in this moment, it was just them. Just Ava.

"You deserve more than this," he said quietly, his thumb tracing the curve of her jaw.

Ava's eyes softened, her hand reaching up to cover his. "I have more than I ever thought I would," she whispered, her voice filled with sincerity. "I have you."

The words sent a wave of emotion crashing through him, something fierce and uncontrollable. He didn't deserve her—he knew that. He didn't deserve the loyalty, the trust, the love she offered him so freely. Not after everything she had been through. Not after everything he had brought into her life.

But there was no escaping it now. She was his. And he would protect her, no matter what it took.

"I'm sorry," Nikolai said, the words catching in his throat. "I'm sorry for all of it."

Ava frowned, her head tilting slightly as she looked at him with confusion. "Sorry? For what?"

"For this," Nikolai said, gesturing vaguely to the cabin, to the life they had found themselves in. "For making you live like this. Trapped. Always looking over your shoulder. You deserve better."

Ava's hand tightened on his, her expression softening. "Nikolai," she said gently, "you didn't make me do anything. I'm here because I want to be. Because I love you."

The words hung in the air between them, heavy with meaning. Nikolai's chest tightened, his heart pounding in a way that felt unfamiliar, almost foreign. He wasn't used to this—wasn't used to feeling so exposed, so vulnerable. But with Ava, it was different. She had a way of breaking down his walls without even trying.

"I love you too," he finally said, the admission slipping past his defenses before he could stop it. It was the truth—raw, unguarded, and terrifying. He had spent so much of his life closing himself off, protecting himself from the vulnerability that came with love. But with Ava, it was different. She made him feel things he hadn't allowed himself to feel in years.

Ava's eyes brightened at his words, a soft smile spreading across her face. She leaned in, pressing a gentle kiss to his lips, and for a moment, the world outside the cabin disappeared. It was just them, wrapped in the warmth of the fire and the comfort of each other's presence.

When the kiss broke, Ava rested her head against his chest, her breathing slow and even. Nikolai held her close, his hand stroking her hair as he stared into the flames. The fire crackled softly, the logs shifting and settling as the heat continued to rise.

It was peaceful. Too peaceful.

The thought crept in before he could stop it. He couldn't relax—not entirely. Not when he knew the world they had left behind was still waiting for them, still watching. He had taken every precaution, made sure they were protected even here in this secluded place, but his instincts told him that danger was never far away.

Ava's soft breathing was a steady rhythm against his chest, and for a moment, he let himself enjoy the quiet. But it was a fragile thing, and Nikolai knew better than to believe it would last.

He shifted slightly, his mind already moving to the logistics of the weekend. He needed to check in with his men, to make sure everything was in place. The security around the cabin was tight, but Nikolai was never one to trust a plan blindly. He needed confirmation—reassurance that Ava was as safe as she could be.

"Get some rest," he murmured, his lips brushing against her hair. "I'll be back in a few minutes."

Ava stirred slightly, her eyes fluttering open as she looked up at him. "Where are you going?"

"Just need to check on something," he replied, his voice soft but firm. "I'll be right back."

Ava nodded, though her eyes remained heavy with sleep. She nestled back into the blanket, her body relaxing as Nikolai carefully disentangled himself from her embrace. He stood, glancing down at her one last time before moving toward the door.

Nikolai stepped out into the night, his breath misting in the cool air as he moved away from the cabin. The silence was almost oppressive, broken only by the soft rustling of leaves in the breeze. He glanced around the perimeter, his eyes scanning the dark shadows between the trees, his instincts on high alert. He had told himself this was just a precaution—that everything was secure—but deep down, he knew better. The tension that had been coiling inside him all evening hadn't eased, and now it was beginning to gnaw at him.

He tapped Viktor's number into his phone, holding it to his ear as he paced the gravel path in front of the cabin. After a few rings, Viktor's familiar gruff voice came through.

"Everything quiet on your end?" Viktor asked, skipping pleasantries.

"Too quiet," Nikolai muttered, his eyes never leaving the treeline. "No signs of movement?"

"None," Viktor replied. "The perimeter is clear. I've got men stationed nearby, but there's been no activity."

Nikolai exhaled slowly, but it did little to settle the unease simmering inside him. He trusted Viktor—trusted his men—but the sense of impending danger refused to loosen its grip on him.

"Good. Stay alert," Nikolai said. "I'll check in again soon."

Viktor grunted in acknowledgment before the line went dead. Nikolai pocketed his phone, his gaze lingering on the dark woods around the cabin. Something wasn't right. His gut told him that, and he had learned long ago never to ignore that instinct.

He turned to head back inside, the chill of the night biting at the back of his neck. Just as his hand reached for the door handle, the sharp crack of gunfire shattered the silence.

Nikolai's body reacted instantly, every muscle tensing as he ducked low and turned toward the direction of the shots. His heart pounded in his chest, his mind already calculating the next steps. The gunfire hadn't come from far. They were here. The Morozovs.

Ava.

Without hesitation, Nikolai darted back inside the cabin, his movements swift and silent. The cabin was dark, the only light coming from the dying embers of the fire. Ava was still curled up on the couch, her eyes fluttering open at the sound of the door slamming behind him.

"Nikolai?" Her voice was thick with sleep, but there was a hint of alarm in it now, as if she could sense the sudden shift in the air.

Nikolai was already moving, crossing the room in two quick strides. He grabbed her by the arm, pulling her to her feet as her eyes widened in confusion.

"Ava, listen to me," he said, his voice low but firm. "Stay in the bedroom. Don't come out, no matter what you hear."

Ava blinked, her face pale as the weight of his words sank in. "What's happening?"

"Just stay down," Nikolai repeated, pushing her toward the hallway that led to the bedroom. "I'll handle it."

Before she could protest, he was already gone, disappearing down the hall toward the main part of the cabin. His movements were calm, calculated, but his heart raced with the knowledge of what was coming. The Morozovs had found them. He didn't know how, but it didn't matter now. All that mattered was keeping Ava safe.

Nikolai reached the kitchen, grabbing the gun he had stashed in one of the drawers. The cold metal felt familiar in his hand, the weight of it grounding him as he listened to the sounds outside. More gunfire, closer this time. He could hear the distant shouts of his security team, engaging with the attackers in the woods.

But then, a new sound reached him—footsteps. Inside the cabin.

Nikolai's grip on the gun tightened, his muscles coiled and ready as he pressed himself against the wall, just out of sight. The footsteps were slow, methodical, moving through the cabin with purpose. Someone had made it inside.

His mind raced. Ava was in the bedroom, out of harm's way for now. But whoever was inside the cabin was hunting, and it wouldn't be long before they reached her.

Nikolai didn't wait.

He moved swiftly, rounding the corner of the kitchen just in time to catch a glimpse of the intruder—a tall, broad-shouldered man dressed in black, his gun raised as he swept the room. Nikolai didn't hesitate. He fired a single shot, but the man was quick, dodging behind a piece of furniture as the bullet shattered the glass window behind him.

The cabin erupted into chaos. The intruder fired back, and Nikolai ducked behind the kitchen island, the sound of gunfire ringing in his ears. Glass shattered, wood splintered, but Nikolai's focus remained razor-sharp. He couldn't let this man get any closer to Ava.

The gunfire stopped for a moment, a brief lull in the battle, and in that second, Nikolai moved. He lunged from behind the island, firing again as he closed the distance between them. The intruder grunted in pain as one of Nikolai's bullets found its mark, but he didn't go down. Instead, he rushed forward, tackling Nikolai with surprising strength.

They crashed into the counter, the impact knocking the gun from Nikolai's hand. The two men grappled, the kitchen filling with the sounds of their struggle—the sharp grunts of pain, the thud of fists meeting flesh. Nikolai's body screamed in protest, but he didn't relent. He couldn't. Not while Ava was in danger.

The intruder threw a punch that landed hard against Nikolai's ribs, but Nikolai twisted, using the man's momentum against him. They slammed into the counter again, and in the chaos, Nikolai's hand found a kitchen knife. He didn't hesitate.

With a swift, brutal motion, Nikolai drove the knife into the intruder's chest. The man's eyes widened in shock, his body stiffening as blood bloomed across his shirt. For a moment, everything went still. The world narrowed to just the two of them, locked in that final, terrible moment.

Then the man collapsed, his body crumpling to the floor with a heavy thud.

Nikolai staggered back, his breath coming in ragged gasps as he wiped the blood from his hands. His muscles ached, his ribs throbbed from the blows he had taken, but none of that mattered. He was alive. And more importantly, Ava was safe.

The cabin was eerily quiet now, the gunfire outside having died down. Nikolai glanced down at the man on the floor, then back toward the hallway where Ava was hidden. Relief washed over him, but it was tinged with something darker—something colder.

He had protected her. But the danger was far from over.

Ava appeared in the doorway then, her face pale, her eyes wide with fear and concern. "Nikolai?" Her voice trembled, her gaze sweeping over him, taking in the bruises, the blood.

"I'm fine," he said quickly, moving toward her, his focus entirely on her. "Are you hurt?"

She shook her head, but her eyes never left his. "What about you?"

Nikolai brushed a hand over his ribs, wincing slightly. "I'm fine," he repeated, though the strain in his voice betrayed the pain he was in. "It's over."

But even as the words left his mouth, he knew they weren't true. It wasn't over. Not yet.

Ava rushed toward Nikolai, her eyes wide with panic as she took in the scene. The man lay dead at Nikolai's feet, blood pooling around his body, the knife still clutched in Nikolai's hand. The sight of it—the brutality, the violence—sent a shudder through her, but it was Nikolai's injuries that kept her focus. His face was pale, his jaw tight as he braced himself against the counter, the tension in his body barely masking the pain he was clearly in.

"Nikolai, you're hurt," Ava breathed, her voice trembling as she reached out to him.

But Nikolai shook his head, waving her off. "It's nothing," he said, his voice strained. "I'm fine."

She could see the bruises forming on his ribs, the way he winced with every movement. Blood was smeared across his shirt, but it wasn't his. Ava's heart pounded in her chest as she closed the distance between them, her hands trembling as she gently touched his arm.

"You're not fine," she insisted, her voice firm but laced with worry. "You need to sit down."

Nikolai's eyes softened slightly at her concern, but there was still that edge of steel in his gaze, the unyielding strength that he always carried with him. He straightened, shaking off her touch as he turned to the security guard who had entered the cabin.

"What's the situation outside?" Nikolai asked, ignoring the pain in his voice.

The guard stood at attention, his expression professional, though there was a slight tension in his stance. "The perimeter is secure," he said. "We've taken care of the other two attackers. They won't be getting back up."

Nikolai nodded, satisfied. He stepped away from Ava, moving toward the door with a calculated calm that made her heart ache. He was always in control, always thinking ahead, but she could see the toll it was taking on him now. His body was battered, and the lines of pain etched into his face were impossible to ignore.

Ava's gaze flicked to the man on the floor, her stomach twisting at the sight of his lifeless body. She had never seen anything like this up close—the violence, the death. It made everything feel so much more real, so much more dangerous than she had ever imagined.

This wasn't just a world Nikolai lived in—it was his reality. And now, it was hers too.

She wrapped her arms around herself, suddenly feeling cold despite the warmth of the cabin. The adrenaline was still coursing through her veins, but there was a heaviness settling in her chest, a fear that gripped her in a way she hadn't felt before.

"Nikolai," she whispered, her voice small, almost lost in the chaos of the moment. "What if they come back? What if they—"

"They won't," Nikolai cut her off, his voice hard and sure. He turned to her then, his dark eyes locking onto hers with an intensity that sent a shiver down her spine. "This was a warning. They thought they could come after us, but they underestimated what they were up against. I'm going to make sure they don't make that mistake again."

Ava swallowed hard, her throat tight. She wanted to believe him, wanted to trust that he could keep her safe. But the reality of the situation was sinking in, and it terrified her. She had known that being with Nikolai meant danger—he had never hidden that from her—but she hadn't understood just how close that danger would come.

Nikolai crossed the room in a few swift strides, his hands coming to rest on her shoulders as he pulled her close. "Look at me," he said, his voice low but commanding. "I won't let anything happen to you. You're safe with me."

Ava searched his eyes, her heart pounding in her chest. She believed him—she had to. There was something in the way he looked at her, the way he held her, that made her feel safe, even in the midst of all this chaos. But the fear lingered, gnawing at the edges of her mind.

"I don't know if I can do this," she whispered, her voice breaking. "I don't know if I'm strong enough."

Nikolai's grip on her shoulders tightened, his gaze fierce. "You're stronger than you think," he said, his voice steady. "You've survived everything they've thrown at you so far. And you'll survive this too."

Tears pricked at the corners of Ava's eyes, but she blinked them away, refusing to break down in front of him. She nodded, taking a deep breath to steady herself. She had to be strong—had to be the person Nikolai believed she could be. There was no room for weakness in this world. Not if she wanted to survive it.

"Come here," Nikolai murmured, pulling her into his arms. She went willingly, pressing her face against his chest as he wrapped her in his embrace. His heartbeat was steady beneath her ear, the strong, reassuring rhythm calming the storm of emotions swirling inside her.

For a long moment, they stood like that, the world outside forgotten. It was just them, wrapped in the warmth of each other's presence, holding on to the one thing that kept them grounded in the midst of the chaos.

But even as they stood there, Ava couldn't shake the feeling that this was far from over. The Morozovs had sent a message tonight, and it was clear they weren't going to stop until they got what they wanted.

She pulled back slightly, looking up at Nikolai with wide eyes. "What do we do now?"

Nikolai's expression darkened, his jaw tightening. "We go on the offensive," he said, his voice like steel. "They came for us tonight, but next time, we'll be ready. They won't catch us off guard again."

Ava nodded, though her heart raced at the thought of what that meant. She didn't want more violence, more bloodshed, but she knew there was no escaping it. Not in this world. Not with Nikolai.

The security guard cleared his throat, stepping forward. "We've swept the area, and everything's clear now," he said. "We'll take care of the mess in here" he said while glancing at the man's body on the kitchen floor," and have a team stationed outside for the night, just in case."

"Good," Nikolai said, his tone clipped. "I want updates every hour. If there's any movement, I want to know immediately."

The guard nodded and left the room, leaving Ava and Nikolai alone once again.

Ava looked at him, her heart aching with a mix of fear and love. She knew he would protect her—she had no doubt about that. But the cost of that protection was becoming more and more evident. The man standing in front of her, bruised and bleeding, had killed to keep her safe. And he would do it again if he had to.

"Nikolai," she said softly, her voice trembling. "What if this never ends?"

Nikolai met her gaze, his expression unreadable. "It won't," he said quietly. "Not as long as we're together."

The weight of his words hung between them, heavy and unyielding. Ava knew what he meant—that their love came with a price, a constant danger that would never truly go away. But she also knew she couldn't walk away from him. Not now. Not ever.

"I'm not going anywhere," she whispered, her voice filled with quiet resolve.

Nikolai's eyes softened, his hand brushing a strand of hair from her face. "Neither am I."

Chapter 15

Ava stood in the kitchen, her entire body humming with adrenaline as she watched Nikolai lean against the counter, his shoulders heavy with exhaustion. The room still carried the scent of blood, the aftermath of the attack hanging in the air like a dark cloud. Every muscle in her body felt tense, her mind spinning as she tried to make sense of what had just happened.

Her eyes were locked on Nikolai. His shirt was smeared with blood—some of it from the dead man on the floor, some of it his own. The fight had left its marks on him, his face bruised, his knuckles raw from the blows he'd delivered. And yet, despite the violence, despite the fact that he had just killed a man to protect her, Nikolai stood tall, unbroken.

Ava's heart clenched. She should be scared—any normal person would be terrified after what she had just witnessed. But all she could feel was an overwhelming sense of love and gratitude for the man standing before her. The fear, the danger—they were real, and she couldn't ignore them. But there was something else, something deeper that pulled at her. A sense of safety, even in the chaos, that only Nikolai could give her.

He had fought for her. Risked his life for her. And now, despite his own pain, despite the bruises and cuts that marked his body, his only concern was her.

"Ava," Nikolai's voice cut through the silence, low and gruff. "Are you okay?"

His question broke her out of her daze, and she blinked, her eyes meeting his. There was worry in his gaze, a flicker of vulnerability that she hadn't expected. He was bleeding, beaten, and yet here he was, asking her if she was okay.

"I'm fine," Ava whispered, though her voice shook. "What about you?"

Nikolai pushed away from the counter, wincing slightly as he moved, but his eyes never left hers. "It's nothing," he said, brushing it off as though he hadn't just been in a life-or-death fight. "I'm more worried about you."

Ava's throat tightened, her emotions swirling into a tangled knot. How could he still be thinking about her after everything that had just happened? He had been hurt—badly—and yet he was brushing it off like it didn't matter. Like she was the only thing that mattered.

"I... I can't believe this just happened," Ava murmured, her hands trembling as she took a step closer to him. Her eyes flicked to the body on the floor, her stomach churning at the sight of it. "I've never... I've never seen anything like this."

Her voice cracked on the last words, but Nikolai reached out, his hand gently cupping her cheek, pulling her gaze back to him. "You don't have to think about that," he said, his voice soft but firm. "It's over. You're safe. That's all that matters."

Ava stared up at him, her heart pounding. She could still feel the fear coursing through her veins, the remnants of the adrenaline that had surged through her when the gunfire first erupted. But beneath that fear was something else—something stronger. Her eyes traced over Nikolai's face, over the bruises and cuts that marred his skin, and her heart ached with a sudden, fierce love.

He had fought for her. He had killed for her. And she wasn't running.

In fact, if anything, she felt more drawn to him than ever.

Ava's hands trembled as she reached for Nikolai, her fingertips brushing against his chest, feeling the warmth of his skin beneath his bloodstained shirt. He was hurting—she could see it in the tightness of his jaw, the way he winced when he moved—but he was trying to hide it. Trying to stay strong for her.

"Nikolai, you're hurt," Ava said softly, her voice filled with concern. "You need to sit down. Let me take care of you."

He shook his head, dismissing her words. "I'm fine," he said, his tone firm, but there was a flicker of something in his eyes—pain, exhaustion, maybe even vulnerability. "I need to make sure everything is secure first."

Ava's chest tightened. He was always like this—always putting her safety first, always acting like nothing could break him. But she could see the cracks now. She could see the toll this life was taking on him, even if he refused to admit it.

"Nikolai, please," she whispered, her hand pressing more firmly against his chest, feeling the steady beat of his heart beneath her palm. "Just stop for a minute."

For a moment, he didn't move, didn't speak. He just looked at her, his dark eyes searching hers as if trying to figure out what she was really asking. Then, with a slow, controlled breath, he nodded.

Ava felt a rush of relief as she gently guided him toward one of the kitchen chairs, her hands still trembling as she helped him sit. Her heart was pounding, her mind racing with everything that had just happened, but all she could think about was him. The man who had risked everything for her. The man who was now sitting in front of her, bruised and bleeding, yet still so strong, so powerful.

Her fingers traced along the edge of his shirt, carefully lifting it to reveal the bruises that were already forming on his ribs. Her breath hitched at the sight of him, her heart aching at the thought of the pain he must be in. But as her fingers brushed over his skin, something shifted inside her. Something deep and primal.

She wasn't just worried about him. She wanted him.

The thought hit her like a wave, unexpected and intense. She should be scared, should be thinking about how close they had come to death tonight. But all she could think about was how much she wanted to be close to him, how much she needed to feel him, to know that he was real and alive and hers.

Ava's hands moved of their own accord, sliding up over Nikolai's chest, feeling the hard muscles beneath her touch. His body was a canvas of strength and power, even bruised and battered as it was. And as she ran her hands over him, a heat began to build in her core, a need that she couldn't ignore.

"Nikolai," she whispered, her voice trembling with both fear and desire. "I don't know what I'd do without you."

His gaze softened, his hand reaching up to cup her face. "You'll never have to find out," he said quietly, his thumb brushing over her cheek. "I'll always protect you."

Ava's heart swelled at his words, her body leaning into his touch. She could feel the tension still thrumming through him, could see the weight of the night's events in his eyes. But beneath that, she could see something else—something raw and powerful. Desire.

He wanted her too.

Without thinking, Ava leaned forward, pressing her lips to his in a soft, lingering kiss. It was gentle at first, tentative, as if testing the waters. But the moment Nikolai responded, the kiss deepened, and all the fear, all the tension of the night melted away. It was just the two of them now—alive, together, and connected in a way that went beyond words.

As her hands moved lower, tracing the line of his bruised torso, Ava felt that familiar heat building inside her. She knew this moment shouldn't be about desire, not after everything that had just happened. But she couldn't help it. She needed him. Now more than ever.

And judging by the way Nikolai's hands gripped her waist, pulling her closer, he needed her too.

Ava's lips lingered on Nikolai's as the kiss deepened, a hunger building inside her that she couldn't deny. She pulled back slightly, just enough to look into his eyes, her breath coming in shallow gasps. His dark gaze held hers, a flicker of surprise there, but more than that—desire. It mirrored her own, a reflection of the intensity that coursed between them like a live wire, sparking with every shared look, every touch.

Her heart pounded in her chest as her hands moved along his bruised torso, her fingers brushing over the lines of his tattoos and the ridges of his muscles. The feel of him beneath her touch, so strong yet vulnerable in this moment, sent shivers down her spine. He was hurt, beaten, and bleeding, yet all she could think about was how much she needed him.

She leaned forward again, pressing her lips to his neck, feeling his pulse quicken beneath her mouth. Nikolai groaned softly, his hands gripping her waist as she kissed a trail down his jaw, her body leaning into him as though she couldn't get close enough. The danger, the violence, the near-death experience—it should have made her pull away, should have made her run. But instead, it made her want him more.

Ava could feel the tension still humming through his body, the remnants of the fight clinging to him. But beneath that was something else—a primal need, a raw desire that mirrored her own. He had fought to protect her, had risked everything for her. And now, here they were, alone in this moment, the world outside forgotten.

"Nikolai," she whispered, her breath warm against his skin. "I need you."

He tensed beneath her, his hands tightening on her hips as if trying to keep control. His gaze was dark, filled with an intensity that made her pulse quicken, but there was something softer beneath it, something vulnerable. "Ava," he murmured, his voice rough with both desire and hesitation. "You don't have to—"

"I want to," Ava cut him off, her voice firm despite the tremor in her chest. She needed him to know—needed him to understand that this wasn't just about the heat of the moment. This was about everything. The fear, the love, the need that had been building inside her from the moment she had met him. "I want this. I want you."

Her fingers moved to the hem of his shirt, lifting it slowly, revealing the hard planes of his chest. His bruises were dark, the purple and blue marks standing out against his skin, but it didn't deter her. If anything, it made her feel more for him—made her want to show him just how much she cared, how much she loved him despite everything.

Nikolai exhaled sharply as her hands brushed over his skin, her fingers tracing the outline of his tattoos, lingering on the bruises as if trying to ease his pain with her touch. His body was a map of strength, power etched into every line, every muscle, but right now, he felt so human to her. So real.

Her hands moved higher, pushing the shirt up and over his head, revealing the full expanse of his chest. Nikolai watched her, his eyes dark and unreadable, but there was something raw in his gaze—something that told her he was just as affected by this moment as she was.

"Ava," he said again, his voice rough as his hands moved to her waist, pulling her closer. "You don't have to—"

"I know," she whispered, her fingers trailing over his chest, feeling the heat of his skin beneath her touch. "But I want to."

She kissed him again, her lips soft but insistent, her body pressing against his as she let herself fall into the moment. His hands slid up her back, pulling her tighter against him, and she could feel the tension melting away, replaced by something deeper, something more primal. It wasn't just about desire—it was about the connection between them, the need to be close, to feel each other in every way possible.

As Nikolai's hands roamed over her body, Ava could feel the heat building inside her, the intensity of their connection making her breath come faster, her skin tingling with anticipation. His fingers found the edge of her shirt, and with a quick, deft movement, he pulled it over her head, tossing it aside without a second thought.

For a moment, they just looked at each other, the weight of everything that had happened hanging between them. Ava's chest rose and fell with quick breaths, her heart pounding in her ears as she waited, unsure of what would happen next. But Nikolai's gaze was steady, his eyes locked on hers as if he was trying to memorize every detail of her, as if he was seeing her for the first time.

His hand moved slowly, gently, sliding up her side until it rested just beneath her breast. The touch was soft, almost hesitant, and for a moment, Ava could feel his restraint—the way he was holding himself back, afraid of hurting her, afraid of doing too much. But she didn't want him to hold back. Not now. Not when they were both so close to the edge.

Her hand covered his, guiding him as she leaned in to kiss him again, her lips moving against his with a slow, deliberate passion. Nikolai responded immediately, his grip tightening on her as the kiss deepened, their bodies pressing together with a need that couldn't be denied.

As they stumbled toward the bedroom, their movements became more urgent, more desperate, clothes falling to the floor in a trail of discarded fabric. Ava's fingers traced the lines of Nikolai's body, her heart racing as she felt the strength beneath his skin, the power that radiated from him even in his most vulnerable moments.

He was bruised, battered, but still so strong. So undeniably Nikolai.

And she wanted him. All of him.

By the time they reached the bed, Ava's body was humming with desire, her skin flushed and sensitive to every touch, every caress. Nikolai's hands were everywhere, sliding over her curves, teasing her, making her ache with need. But there was a tenderness to his touch, a carefulness that told her he was still thinking of her, still protecting her, even in the heat of the moment.

As he laid her down on the bed, his body hovering over hers, Ava felt a shiver of anticipation run through her. She could see the raw need in his eyes, the hunger that mirrored her own, but beneath it all, there was love. Pure, unfiltered love.

And that was all she needed.

"Nikolai," she whispered, her voice trembling with both fear and desire. "Please."

He didn't need any more encouragement.

Ava's breath came in shallow gasps as she lay beneath Nikolai, the warmth of his body hovering over hers like a protective shield. The room was bathed in the soft glow of the firelight from the living room, casting flickering shadows across their skin. Her heart raced in her chest, a wild drumbeat that echoed the rush of desire coursing through her veins.

Nikolai's dark eyes held hers, the intensity of his gaze making her pulse quicken even more. His fingers trailed down her side, the lightest touch, but it left a trail of heat in its wake, her skin tingling with anticipation. He was being careful with her, his touch slow and deliberate, as if savoring every moment, every inch of her body. But there was also a raw need in his movements, an undercurrent of passion that simmered just beneath the surface.

Ava's hands moved to his chest, her fingers sliding over the hard muscles and the lines of his tattoos. His skin was warm beneath her touch, the bruises darkening against the strong planes of his torso. She could feel the power in him, the strength that made her feel both safe and exhilarated all at once. Her hands lingered on his bruises for a moment, her heart aching with the knowledge of the pain he must be feeling, but even now, he showed no sign of weakness.

"Nikolai," she whispered, her voice trembling as her fingers traced the edge of one of his tattoos. "Are you sure you're okay?"

He didn't answer right away, his hand slipping from her waist to cup her cheek. His thumb brushed lightly over her skin, his gaze softening as he looked down at her. "I'm fine, Ava," he murmured, his voice low and rough. "All that matters is you."

Her heart swelled at his words, a flood of emotion crashing over her. He always made it about her, always put her first, even when he was the one who had risked everything. It was that unwavering devotion, that protective instinct, that made her fall even deeper for him. The love she felt for him was overwhelming, an all-consuming force that left her breathless.

"I love you," she whispered, her voice barely above a breath, but the weight of the words hung between them, heavy and real.

Nikolai's eyes darkened, his hand sliding down her body with slow, deliberate precision, stopping at the curve of her waist. "I love you too," he said, his voice thick with emotion. Then, with a low groan, his lips crashed against hers in a kiss that was anything but gentle.

It was hungry, raw, filled with all the passion they had been holding back, and it sent a jolt of heat straight through Ava's body. Her fingers tangled in his hair as she pulled him closer, needing more, wanting to feel every inch of him. His mouth moved over hers with a sense of urgency, their tongues tangling as the intensity between them grew, building with every touch.

Nikolai's hands slid up her body, his fingers grazing her breasts, teasing her until she moaned into his mouth. Her nipples hardened under his touch, the sensation sending a wave of pleasure through her. He broke the kiss, his lips moving to her neck, sucking and nipping at her skin as his hands continued their slow, torturous exploration of her body.

Ava's back arched beneath him, her breath coming in short, sharp gasps as his hands cupped her breasts, his thumbs brushing over her hardened nipples. The pleasure was almost too much, her body trembling as he took his time with her, teasing and testing her limits. She could feel the wetness pooling between her legs, her core throbbing with need as his mouth moved lower, trailing kisses down her chest.

"Nikolai," she gasped, her fingers gripping his shoulders as his lips closed around one of her nipples, sucking gently before flicking his tongue against it. The sensation sent a shockwave of pleasure through her, and she couldn't help but moan, her hips bucking up instinctively.

He groaned against her skin, the sound vibrating through her body as his hands moved lower, tracing the curve of her waist, the dip of her hips. His fingers slid between her thighs, parting them as he settled between her legs. Ava's breath hitched, her entire body tense with anticipation as his hand dipped lower, brushing against her wetness.

"Oh God," she whimpered, her eyes squeezing shut as his fingers circled her clit, the sensation sending sparks of pleasure shooting through her. Her hips moved against his hand, desperate for more, and Nikolai didn't make her wait. His fingers slid inside her, thrusting slowly as his thumb continued to circle her clit, building her pleasure higher and higher.

Ava's body trembled beneath him, her breath coming in ragged gasps as the pleasure mounted, her muscles tightening around his fingers. She was so close, her entire body aching for release, but Nikolai was taking his time, driving her to the edge and pulling her back again and again.

"Nikolai, please," she begged, her voice trembling with need.

He grinned against her skin, his lips brushing her ear as he whispered, "I'll give you what you need, baby. Just be patient."

Ava whimpered in frustration, her body shaking with desire, but she knew better than to argue. Nikolai was in control, and she was at his mercy. But the way he touched her, the way he teased her, made it clear that he was enjoying every second of it.

He pulled his fingers out slowly, drawing a soft moan from her lips, and Ava opened her eyes just in time to see him strip off the rest of his clothes. Her heart raced as she took in the sight of him, his body a masterpiece of strength and power. His cock was hard, thick, and ready, and the sight of him made her mouth go dry with anticipation.

Nikolai settled between her legs, his body pressing against hers as he leaned down to kiss her again, the weight of him pinning her to the bed in the most delicious way. Ava wrapped her legs around his waist, pulling him closer, her hips bucking up as she silently begged him to take her.

"Please," she whispered, her voice filled with need. "I need you."

Nikolai groaned, his hands gripping her hips as he positioned himself at her entrance, teasing her with the tip of his cock. The sensation sent a shiver down her spine, her body arching beneath him as she waited, her breath catching in her throat.

And then, with one slow, powerful thrust, he buried himself inside her, the fullness of him overwhelming her senses. Her body arched beneath him, her hands gripping his shoulders as she struggled to catch her breath. The slow burn of anticipation finally gave way to a rush of pleasure that sent shockwaves through her, the feel of him deep inside her lighting every nerve on fire.

Nikolai stilled for a moment, his body pressed against hers, his breathing ragged as he allowed her to adjust to the sensation. His hands slid up her sides, fingers tracing the curve of her waist, before they settled on her hips. He held her there, his grip firm but careful, as if he was trying to hold back, to maintain some semblance of control. But Ava could see the tension in his jaw, the strain in his muscles, and she knew he was fighting a losing battle.

She didn't want him to hold back.

Ava's hips lifted instinctively, her body moving against his as she encouraged him to keep going. "Nikolai," she whispered, her voice trembling with need. "Please..."

Nikolai groaned in response, his grip tightening on her hips as he pulled back slightly, then thrust into her again, harder this time. The movement sent a jolt of pleasure through Ava's body, her breath catching in her throat as her nails dug into his shoulders. She could feel the raw power in his movements, the way his body responded to hers, and it drove her wild.

He thrust into her again, his pace steady but deliberate, each movement designed to push her closer to the edge. Ava's moans filled the room, her body moving in rhythm with his as the pleasure built higher and higher, her mind spinning with the intensity of it. Every thrust, every brush of his skin against hers, sent her spiraling further into a world where only the two of them existed.

Nikolai leaned down, his lips brushing against her neck, sucking gently at the sensitive skin there as he continued to move inside her. His breath was hot against her skin, his body trembling with the effort to hold back, but Ava could feel the urgency in him, the need that mirrored her own. She tilted her head, giving him more access as her hands slid down his back, feeling the hard muscles ripple beneath her touch.

"I need more," she gasped, her voice filled with desperation. "Nikolai, I—"

Her words were cut off as he thrust into her harder, the sudden force of it drawing a sharp cry from her lips. The pleasure was overwhelming now, her body trembling beneath him as the intensity of the moment consumed her. She could feel the heat building inside her, the tension coiling tighter and tighter until she thought she might break apart from it.

Nikolai groaned, his hands moving up to cup her breasts, his thumbs brushing over her nipples as he thrust into her again, each movement sending another wave of pleasure crashing over her. Ava's back arched, her body pressing against his as her hands moved down to grip his hips, trying to pull him even closer.

The sensation of his cock filling her, stretching her, was almost too much to bear. Every thrust was a delicious torment, her body aching for release but held captive by the slow, deliberate rhythm he set. She could feel the heat pooling between her legs, her muscles tightening around him as her hips bucked up to meet his, her breath coming in short, ragged gasps.

"Nikolai," she moaned, her fingers digging into his back. "I'm so close."

He growled low in his throat, the sound sending a shiver down her spine as he picked up the pace, thrusting into her with more urgency now, his movements more primal, more raw. The control he had been holding onto so tightly was slipping away, and Ava could feel it in the way his body trembled, in the way his hands gripped her hips as if he was afraid to let go.

Her own body responded in kind, the tension building to an unbearable level as she felt herself teetering on the edge of release. Every nerve in her body was on fire, every touch, every kiss, driving her closer and closer to the brink. She could feel her muscles tightening around him, her breath coming in short, sharp gasps as the pleasure mounted higher and higher.

And then, with one final thrust, she fell.

Ava cried out, her body shaking as the orgasm ripped through her, wave after wave of pleasure crashing over her as she clung to Nikolai, her nails digging into his skin. Her muscles clenched around him, drawing him deeper inside her as her vision blurred, her mind lost in the overwhelming sensation.

Nikolai followed her over the edge, his body tensing as he thrust into her one last time, his cock pulsing as he came inside her. Ava gasped at the sensation, her body trembling with the aftershocks of her orgasm as she felt him fill her, the intimacy of the moment almost too much to bear.

For a moment, they were both still, their bodies pressed together as they caught their breath. The air around them was thick with the scent of sex and sweat, their skin slick and glistening in the dim light of the room. Ava's heart raced in her chest, her body still trembling from the intensity of the release, but there was a strange sense of peace that settled over her.

Nikolai collapsed onto the bed beside her, his chest heaving as he tried to catch his breath. He reached out, pulling her into his arms, and Ava went willingly, curling up against him as they lay together in the quiet aftermath of their lovemaking.

The adrenaline from the attack, the fear, the danger—it all seemed so far away now, replaced by the warmth of Nikolai's body and the steady rhythm of his breathing. Ava closed her eyes, resting her head against his chest, feeling the rise and fall of his breaths beneath her cheek.

She should have been scared. She should have been questioning everything—her decision to stay with him, the danger that came with being a part of his world. But all she felt was a deep, overwhelming love for the man who held her in his arms. He had risked everything for her, and despite the violence, despite the danger, she knew she would never leave him.

"I love you," she whispered, her voice barely audible in the quiet of the room.

Nikolai's hand stroked her hair, his lips brushing against her forehead. "I love you too, Ava," he murmured, his voice rough but filled with emotion. "Always."

Ava smiled against his chest, her body relaxing into his as the last remnants of tension melted away. Whatever came next, whatever danger lay ahead, she knew she wouldn't face it alone.

As the quiet settled around them, Ava lay nestled in Nikolai's arms, her body still humming from the intensity of what they'd just shared. The room was warm, cocooning them in a moment of peace that felt almost surreal after the violence and chaos that had unfolded earlier. Nikolai's fingers lazily stroked her back, the gentle rhythm soothing her, but her mind was still racing.

Ava's thoughts swirled in a mix of love, fear, and confusion. She had never felt so close to someone, so irrevocably connected, but at the same time, the reality of what had just happened—the violence, the danger—was settling deep into her bones. She had watched a man die tonight, had seen Nikolai take a life with his own hands, and yet here she was, wrapped in his arms, feeling more safe and loved than she had ever thought possible.

It didn't make sense. The world outside—the one filled with blood and betrayal—should have scared her away. But instead, it drew her closer to Nikolai. She couldn't deny the pull he had over her, the way his presence made her feel both vulnerable and protected, even in the face of danger. Her body still tingled from the raw passion they had just shared, but her heart ached with the weight of the choice she knew she was making.

There would be no turning back now. This wasn't just a temporary escape, a fling she could walk away from when things got tough. Being with Nikolai meant accepting his world, with all its violence and danger. It meant accepting him—every dark, brutal part of him—and knowing that there would always be risks, always be threats lurking in the shadows.

But despite everything, despite the fear that twisted in her chest, she couldn't imagine leaving him. The thought of walking away, of not feeling the strength of his arms around her or hearing the steady beat of his heart beneath her cheek, was unbearable. She loved him—deeply, fiercely—and that love, no matter how complicated or dangerous, was something she couldn't deny.

Ava shifted slightly, turning her head to look up at Nikolai. His eyes were closed, his breathing steady, but his grip on her tightened as if he knew she was watching him. She smiled softly, reaching up to brush her fingers through his hair, marveling at the way this man—this powerful, dangerous man—could make her feel so cherished, so safe.

"I'm not going anywhere," she whispered, more to herself than to him, the words a quiet promise to both of them. No matter what came next, no matter how dangerous things became, she knew she couldn't walk away from him. She wouldn't.

Nikolai stirred slightly, his arm pulling her closer as if in response to her unspoken vow. Ava closed her eyes, allowing herself to sink into the warmth of his embrace, knowing that whatever came next, they would face it together.

Chapter 16

Nikolai paced back and forth across the sleek marble floor of his penthouse, his hands clenching and unclenching at his sides as his thoughts raced. It had been only two days since the attack at the cabin, but the anger still simmered beneath his skin, pulsing through him like a slow-burning fire. The scene kept replaying in his mind—the sound of gunfire, the bodies falling, Ava's terrified eyes as he fought to protect her.

His jaw tightened as he glanced around the room. Everything in the penthouse was pristine and calm, a stark contrast to the storm brewing inside him. The familiar skyline of New York City stretched beyond the floor-to-ceiling windows, but even that view couldn't soothe him tonight.

The Morozov Bratva had crossed a line.

Nikolai had never felt vulnerable before. He was always ten steps ahead, always anticipating every move his enemies made. But this time, they had known exactly where he would be—exactly when to strike. The cabin was supposed to be secluded, a place he had chosen carefully. No one should have known they were there. No one except his most trusted men.

Which meant only one thing: there was a mole.

The thought gnawed at him, a bitter taste in the back of his throat. Someone within his own Bratva had betrayed him, and that betrayal burned worse than any physical wound. Trust was the foundation of the organization he led, and to have it broken in such a way felt like a personal attack. It was unforgivable.

He stopped pacing, his eyes narrowing as he stared out at the city. The Morozovs had made a calculated move, and it nearly cost him everything. He hadn't just been concerned for his own life that night—he had been terrified for Ava. The thought of her being caught in the crossfire, of her being hurt or worse, made his blood run cold. She had become his greatest weakness, and his enemies knew it.

His hands curled into fists, his knuckles white. That couldn't happen again. He wouldn't allow it.

Nikolai's mind raced with possibilities. The Morozovs had grown bolder, their attacks more brazen, but this was different. This was targeted, precise. They knew exactly where he would be, and that was no coincidence. It had taken careful planning, coordination, and most of all, insider information.

He could feel the tension coiling in his muscles, every instinct screaming at him to take action. He had to root out the mole—had to find the traitor and make an example out of them. He needed to send a message to his enemies, to the Morozovs, that this kind of betrayal would not be tolerated.

But more than that, he needed to protect Ava.

His gaze drifted to the closed door of the bedroom, where she was resting. Since their return to the city, she had been quieter than usual, the events at the cabin clearly weighing on her. He had seen the fear in her eyes that night, and it had shaken him more than he cared to admit. She hadn't signed up for this—hadn't asked to be pulled into the violent world he lived in. And yet, here she was, caught in the crosshairs of his enemies because she had fallen in love with him.

Nikolai let out a slow, controlled breath, his anger simmering just beneath the surface. His enemies had underestimated him, underestimated his resolve. He would find the mole, eliminate the threat, and make sure Ava was never in danger again. He couldn't afford to show weakness—not to his enemies, not to his men. Weakness was a death sentence in his world, and he had no intention of dying anytime soon.

His phone buzzed in his pocket, pulling him from his thoughts. He glanced at the screen, seeing Viktor's name flash across it. He answered quickly, his voice low and tense.

"What do you have for me?"

There was a pause on the other end before Viktor's deep voice replied, steady and calm as always. "I've started looking into the possibility of a mole. It's too early to have any definitive answers, but I've narrowed down a few leads."

Nikolai's grip on the phone tightened. "I don't want leads, Viktor. I want results. Find the traitor and deal with them."

"I know," Viktor said, his tone carefully measured. "But this isn't something we can rush. If we move too quickly, we could tip our hand and scare off whoever's feeding information to the Morozovs. We need to be sure before we act."

Nikolai's jaw clenched. He hated waiting, hated feeling like his control was slipping. But Viktor was right. As much as he wanted to put a bullet in the traitor's head right now, they had to be smart about this. One wrong move could make things worse.

"Fine," he said, his voice cold. "But don't take too long. The longer we wait, the more danger Ava's in."

There was another pause on the line, and Nikolai could hear the unspoken concern in Viktor's silence. "I understand," Viktor said finally. "We'll get this handled. You have my word."

Nikolai ended the call without another word, his frustration mounting. He trusted Viktor more than anyone else, but even that trust had limits. The betrayal had shaken him to his core, and he couldn't help but wonder who else might be lying to him, hiding behind a mask of loyalty while selling him out to his enemies.

He exhaled sharply, running a hand through his hair as he tried to clear his mind. There was too much at stake to let paranoia take over. He needed to stay sharp, stay focused. The Morozovs had made their move, but Nikolai wasn't about to back down. He would hunt down the mole, destroy the rival Bratva, and secure his place at the top.

But most of all, he would keep Ava safe. No matter what it took.

With renewed determination, Nikolai crossed the room and headed for his office. There were plans to be made, enemies to crush, and a traitor to find. The city outside his windows glittered in the night, but all Nikolai saw was a battlefield waiting for his next move.

Nikolai sank into the leather chair behind his desk, the weight of the day pressing heavily on his shoulders. He had been through countless wars, fought more battles than he could remember, but this felt different. This betrayal was personal. It was one thing to face enemies head-on, but having a traitor within his ranks—a rat feeding information to the Morozovs—was like a knife in the back.

He poured himself a glass of whiskey, his hand steady despite the storm raging inside him. The amber liquid sloshed against the sides of the glass as he took a slow sip, letting the burn spread through his chest. His mind was still racing, still calculating. Viktor would handle the investigation, but even he knew that finding the mole wasn't going to be easy. The Bratva was built on loyalty, a loyalty that was earned through blood and sacrifice. For someone to betray that meant they were either very desperate or very greedy. Either way, their time was running out.

The sharp knock on the door broke through his thoughts. "Come in," Nikolai called, his voice steady, though tension still coiled in his gut.

Viktor stepped inside, his expression as serious as ever, though there was a subtle tightness in his eyes that only someone like Nikolai would notice. The man was a fortress of calm, but even fortresses had cracks.

"Sit," Nikolai ordered, gesturing to the chair opposite him. Viktor obliged, folding his large frame into the seat with a quiet grace that belied the violence he was capable of.

"We need to talk," Nikolai said, swirling the whiskey in his glass. "I can't afford to wait much longer.

Whoever this mole is, they're putting everything at risk. That attack at the cabin... they knew where we were. They knew when to strike."

Viktor's jaw tightened, his eyes darkening with understanding. "I've narrowed it down to a few people," he said, his voice low and controlled. "But we need to be careful. If we move too fast, we risk tipping them off. They'll disappear, and we'll be left in the dark."

Nikolai took another slow sip of his whiskey, his gaze sharp as he studied Viktor. He knew the man was right, but patience wasn't a virtue Nikolai had ever possessed in abundance. Especially not when the stakes were this high. He couldn't shake the image of Ava's face, pale with fear, as the gunshots rang out at the cabin. He couldn't let that happen again.

"I don't want careful, Viktor," Nikolai said, his voice like steel. "I want results."

Viktor held his gaze, unflinching. "And you'll get them. But we need to do this right. We can't act on suspicion alone. I need more time to dig, to make sure we find the right person. If we make a wrong move..."

Nikolai cut him off with a wave of his hand. "I know. I know what's at stake. But time is a luxury we don't have. The Morozovs are making moves. They're growing bolder. If they sense weakness..."

He didn't finish the sentence, but he didn't need to. Viktor understood. The Bratva was built on power, on fear. If Nikolai showed any sign of weakness, his enemies would seize the opportunity to destroy him. Worse than that, his own men might begin to question his ability to lead, and that was something he couldn't allow. The Bratva had to believe in him, had to know that he was the one in control.

Viktor leaned forward, his elbows resting on his knees as he lowered his voice. "I've already started investigating the people closest to you. We'll find them, Nikolai. But you need to let me handle this."

Nikolai's eyes narrowed, his mind already racing through the possibilities. He trusted Viktor more than anyone, but trust didn't come easily to him. The betrayal cut deep, and it made him question everyone around him.

"Fine," he said after a long pause. "But when we find them, I want them dealt with. No second chances. No mercy."

Viktor nodded, his expression hardening. "Understood."

Once Viktor left, the quiet of the penthouse seemed to press down on Nikolai even harder. The weight of his responsibilities felt suffocating, but the fire of anger burned hot enough to keep him sharp. He couldn't afford any missteps. One wrong move and his entire empire could crumble. Worse than that, Ava could be caught in the crossfire.

Nikolai drained the rest of his whiskey and set the glass down with a soft clink. There was no time to wallow in frustration. He had to act, and he had to act now. Waiting for the mole to reveal themselves was one part of the plan, but that wouldn't stop the Morozovs. They had made their move, and it was time for him to make his.

He stood, moving with purpose toward his desk. His phone buzzed with a message from one of his lieutenants, confirming that the arrangements had been made. Nikolai's jaw clenched. Tonight, there would be blood.

Sitting behind the large mahogany desk, Nikolai dialed a number, his voice low and deadly when the line was answered. "Everything is ready?"

"Da, everything's in place. Just waiting on your word."

Nikolai's grip tightened around the phone. "Good. Proceed. I want them to know what happens when they cross me."

The man on the other end didn't ask questions. He knew better than that. The conversation ended quickly, and Nikolai sat back, exhaling slowly as he steeled himself for what was to come. The

Morozovs had made a mistake attacking him at the cabin, and now they would pay for it.

He wasn't one to back down from a fight, and he wasn't one to wait for his enemies to strike again. This was his city, his empire, and he wasn't about to let anyone—even a rival Bratva—challenge his authority. The hits would be swift, precise, and brutal. Key members of the Morozov family would fall, and the message would be clear: Nikolai Volkov was not to be underestimated.

His thoughts flickered to Ava, a wave of protectiveness sweeping through him. The danger had become all too real for her, and while she didn't know the full extent of his world, she was now undeniably a part of it. That fact gnawed at him, his heart torn between the life he'd built and the woman he loved.

As much as he wanted to shield her from all of this, he knew that wasn't possible. The world he lived in was violent, unpredictable, and anyone close to him was a target. That was why he needed to act decisively. There could be no loose ends, no lingering threats. The Morozovs had crossed a line, and Nikolai would show them just how far he was willing to go to protect what was his.

He dialed another number, this time reaching one of his trusted captains. "We move tonight," he said, his voice cold, every trace of emotion carefully controlled. "I want hits on the Morozovs' top men. No survivors. Make sure it sends a message."

The captain on the other end of the line didn't hesitate. "Understood, boss."

Nikolai ended the call and leaned back in his chair, his eyes drifting to the city skyline beyond the window. He couldn't afford any more weakness, any more threats to his empire. The Morozovs would be dealt with, and the mole would be found.

He wouldn't stop until every last enemy was eliminated.

The orders had been given, the plans set in motion. Nikolai knew that within hours, blood would spill in the streets of New York, and the Morozovs would feel the full weight of his wrath. Yet, despite the satisfaction that usually came with executing his strategy, tonight, there was a gnawing discomfort that he couldn't shake.

Ava.

His eyes flicked toward the closed door of the bedroom, the faint glow of light from beneath it telling him she was still awake. He had told her to rest after the chaos of the last few days, but she had been quiet, too quiet. He knew the attack at the cabin had affected her more than she was letting on. It was one thing to know Nikolai's world was dangerous—it was another thing entirely to witness it firsthand. To see the violence, to hear the gunfire. To watch him kill a man with his bare hands.

A dark part of him had expected her to run after that night. He wouldn't have blamed her if she had. Any sane person would have. But Ava was still here. And that only made the fear of losing her more acute.

The attack had exposed a vulnerability Nikolai hadn't anticipated. Not in himself—he had lived his life in constant danger, walking the fine line between power and death. But with Ava, the stakes had changed. She was a target now, not just by proximity but because she was the one thing in his life that could truly hurt him.

And his enemies knew that.

The Morozovs had always been bold, but attacking him while he was alone with Ava? That was calculated. It wasn't just an attempt to kill him—it was a message. They were willing to go after her to weaken him. To make him afraid.

And it was working.

Nikolai clenched his jaw, the anger and fear twisting in his gut. He had never felt this way before, never allowed anyone to become such a part of his life that they could be used against him. But Ava… she had slipped past his defenses. He hadn't seen it coming, and now it was too late to undo.

She was his. His to protect. His to keep safe.

But how could he protect her from this world? The life he lived was dangerous by its very nature. There would always be enemies, always be threats lurking in the shadows. He could keep her surrounded by bodyguards, confine her to the penthouse, but was that really a life for her?

Would she hate him for it?

The thought gnawed at him as he stood, his fingers tightening into fists at his sides. He had already ramped up security, ordering his men to watch over her every moment of the day. But that wasn't enough. He knew it wasn't enough. If the Morozovs—or any of his enemies—wanted to get to Ava, they would find a way. Unless he crushed them first.

Nikolai crossed the room in a few quick strides, pausing in front of the bedroom door. He hesitated for a moment, his hand resting on the doorknob. He didn't want her to see him like this, so wound up, so consumed with fear. She had seen enough violence already. But he couldn't keep avoiding the conversation, couldn't keep pretending everything was normal.

He needed her to understand.

With a slow exhale, he turned the knob and stepped inside. Ava was sitting up in bed, a book in her lap, but her eyes weren't focused on the pages. She looked up as he entered, her gaze searching his face for answers he wasn't sure he had.

"You okay?" she asked softly, her voice breaking the silence that had settled between them since they returned from the cabin.

Nikolai closed the door behind him, leaning against it for a moment before crossing the room to sit on the edge of the bed. His hand found hers, and he gave it a gentle squeeze, though the tension in his body remained.

"I should be asking you that," he said quietly, his eyes locking onto hers.

Ava's lips curved into a faint smile, but it didn't reach her eyes. "I'm fine," she said, though he could hear the hesitation in her voice. "I just... I keep thinking about what happened at the cabin."

Nikolai's jaw tightened. He had known this conversation was coming, but it didn't make it any easier. The image of her standing in that cabin doorway, watching as he ended the life of a man who had come to kill them, was burned into his memory. He had wanted to shield her from that part of him, but there was no going back now.

"I'm sorry," he said, his voice rough. "I didn't want you to see that. Any of it."

Ava shook her head, her hand tightening around his. "Don't apologize. You were protecting me. I understand that."

"But it's not fair to you." The words came out harsher than he intended, the frustration bleeding into his tone. "You shouldn't have to live like this—constantly looking over your shoulder, wondering if someone's going to try and kill you because of me."

Her expression softened, her eyes searching his. "Nikolai, I chose to be with you. I know what that means. I'm not naïve."

Nikolai exhaled, his hand running through his hair as he looked away, the weight of her words pressing down on him. She didn't understand. Not fully.

"I don't think you do," he said, his voice quieter now. "This world... it doesn't just touch you. It consumes you. And now that they know you're with me, you're a target."

Ava was silent for a long moment, her eyes fixed on him as she processed what he was saying. He could see the fear in her gaze, the way her fingers trembled slightly in his. But she didn't pull away. Instead, she moved closer, resting her hand on his chest, over his heart.

"I'm not going anywhere," she whispered, her voice steady despite the fear he knew she must be feeling. "I love you, Nikolai. I'm not afraid of your world."

Her words sent a strange mix of emotions surging through him—relief, gratitude, but also a deep, gnawing fear. She didn't know what she was saying. She didn't know what it really meant to be with someone like him, someone whose entire life was built on violence, on power, on blood.

But she was here. She had stayed.

And for the first time in his life, Nikolai realized that he couldn't do this alone. He didn't want to.

Nikolai felt her hand against his chest, the warmth of her touch grounding him, even as his thoughts spun wildly out of control. Ava's gaze was steady, unwavering as she pressed closer to him, her words a quiet promise that she wasn't going to leave, no matter what danger his world held. It should have comforted him, but instead, it terrified him more.

He had expected her to run, or at least to demand answers, to ask why she had been dragged into this brutal world. But instead, she was sitting here with him, offering nothing but her love. It felt like both a gift and a burden. The weight of his responsibility to protect her was growing heavier by the minute.

Nikolai let out a slow breath, his hand resting over hers on his chest. He stared down at the bed for a long moment, his mind racing through everything that had happened in the last few days—the attack, the bloodshed, the constant threat that hung over them. His enemies weren't going to stop until they found a way to weaken him, and they had already figured out that Ava was the key.

But how could he protect her from the inevitable danger that came with being part of his life? Keeping her close wasn't enough, and the more he tried to shield her, the more suffocated she might feel. Still, it was better than the alternative.

"I should never have let you get this close to me," Nikolai finally murmured, his voice low and gruff. His hand slid down to cover hers, his grip firm but gentle. "It would have been safer for you if I had kept my distance."

Ava frowned, her eyes searching his face. "But you didn't. And I'm not going to let you push me away now."

Nikolai's heart clenched at her words. How could she stand there, so certain, when everything about him should send her running? His life was violence, control, and power. It was all he had known. He was no hero, no savior. He was a man shaped by blood and darkness.

And yet, she stayed.

He lifted his gaze to meet hers, the soft glow of the bedroom light casting her features in a warm glow. Her face was etched with concern, but there was also a quiet strength in her eyes, a resilience that made him love her even more. She was stronger than he had ever given her credit for, braver than he could have imagined. But even bravery had its limits.

"Ava," he said softly, his voice filled with the weight of unspoken fear. "You don't know what you're asking for."

She shifted closer, her fingers tracing the line of his jaw, her touch sending a wave of warmth through him. "I know enough," she replied, her voice firm. "I know what kind of man you are, Nikolai. And I'm not afraid."

Her words echoed in his mind, but they did little to ease the growing fear that gnawed at him. She had seen glimpses of his world—just enough to know it was dangerous. But she hadn't seen everything. She didn't know the depths of what he was capable of, the lengths he was willing to go to protect her. There was a part of him that was afraid she would eventually come to hate him for it.

"I would do anything for you," he whispered, his voice rough with emotion. "But I can't promise you safety. Not in this life. Not with the enemies I have."

Ava didn't flinch. Instead, she leaned forward, pressing her forehead against his, her breath warm against his skin. "I'm not asking for promises," she whispered. "I'm just asking you to let me stay. I can handle this. I can handle you."

Her words washed over him, calming the storm that had been raging in his chest. How could she have this much faith in him? How could she look at him, knowing the violence and danger that surrounded him, and still want to stay? It was beyond anything he had ever experienced before. She didn't see him as a monster. She saw him as a man—a man who loved her fiercely, even if it meant dragging her into his world of blood and betrayal.

He closed his eyes, letting out a shaky breath as his hand moved to cradle the back of her neck. He pressed a soft kiss to her forehead, his lips lingering there for a moment as he tried to memorize the feel of her, the warmth and softness that grounded him in a way nothing else ever had.

"I love you," he murmured against her skin, the words thick with emotion. "More than anything."

Ava smiled softly, her fingers threading through his hair as she kissed him gently, the tenderness of the moment easing some of the tension that had coiled so tightly inside him. She shifted in his arms, settling against his chest, and for a moment, Nikolai allowed himself to relax. The weight of the world outside their bedroom seemed to fade, leaving only the two of them in the quiet intimacy they shared.

He knew it couldn't last. The reality of their situation was too dangerous, too unpredictable. But in this moment, with Ava wrapped in his arms, he allowed himself to believe that maybe, just maybe, they could find a way to survive this together.

But as much as he wanted to hold on to that hope, the fear still gnawed at him. The attack at the cabin had shown him how vulnerable he was—how vulnerable they both were. If the Morozovs found another opening, another way to strike at him through Ava, he wasn't sure he would survive it.

He needed to act, to ensure that nothing like that would happen again. He had already put things in motion, but the danger wasn't over. Until he found the mole and eliminated every threat, Ava would never be safe.

"I'm going to protect you," he said softly, his voice carrying the weight of a promise. "No matter what."

Ava looked up at him, her eyes filled with a quiet understanding. She didn't need to say anything. He could see the trust in her gaze, the way she had already accepted whatever came with being by his side. It was that trust that terrified him the most, because it meant he had more to lose than ever before.

Nikolai pressed another kiss to her forehead before leaning back against the pillows, pulling her closer as he cradled her against his chest. The quiet of the room wrapped around them, and for the first time in days, he allowed himself to close his eyes, letting the steady rhythm of Ava's breathing lull him into a brief moment of peace.

But even as sleep began to pull him under, the weight of the world outside their bedroom lingered, reminding him that this fragile peace could be shattered at any moment.

Chapter 17

Ava stood by the window, staring out at the Manhattan skyline, the city glittering beneath the pale winter sun. The beauty of the scene felt distant, muted by the tension that had wrapped itself around her like a thick fog. It had been a week since the night at the cabin, a week since she had watched Nikolai kill a man with his bare hands. In that time, everything had changed.

The war with the Morozov Bratva had escalated quickly. Nikolai had been relentless, ordering hit after hit on key members of the rival family. Each night, he would leave the penthouse late, returning in the early hours of the morning, often covered in the scent of smoke and blood. Ava didn't need to ask what he was doing. She already knew. She could see the toll it was taking on him—the sleepless nights, the tension in his muscles, the cold distance that had settled between them.

She understood why he was doing it. The Morozovs had made their move, and Nikolai wasn't one to sit idly by and wait for another attack. He was going on the offensive, making sure they paid for what they had done. But as the violence escalated, so did the distance between them. Ava had known from the beginning that Nikolai's world was dangerous, that it was filled with violence and betrayal, but seeing it firsthand was different. It was real now, in a way it hadn't been before.

She turned away from the window, wrapping her arms around herself as she paced the living room. The tension in her chest hadn't eased since that night at the cabin. No matter how much she tried to tell herself that she was safe here, that Nikolai was doing everything he could to protect her, the fear lingered. The violence was all around them now, creeping into the corners of her life, and there was no escaping it.

Ava couldn't shake the feeling that she was losing him. The more Nikolai was pulled into the war, the more distant he became. He had always been guarded, always kept parts of himself hidden, but now it felt like he was shutting her out completely. She missed the way things had been before, when it had just been the two of them, wrapped up in their own little world. Now, it felt like they were on opposite sides of a widening chasm, and she wasn't sure if they would ever find their way back to each other.

The worst part was that she didn't know how to talk to him about it. Every time she tried to bring it up, every time she tried to tell him how she was feeling, Nikolai would change the subject or brush her off with a cold, distant look. He wasn't the same man she had fallen in love with. At least, not the one she had thought she knew.

She sank onto the couch, her fingers twisting in her lap as her mind raced. The uncertainty of it all was driving her mad. She had always been someone who craved stability, who needed to feel in control of her own life. But being with Nikolai meant giving up that control, trusting him to protect her in a world that seemed determined to destroy them both.

And she wasn't sure if she could do it anymore.

A soft knock on the door pulled Ava from her thoughts. She looked up, surprised to see one of Nikolai's men standing in the doorway. He was one of the newer ones, a tall, quiet man with a stern expression that never seemed to change.

"Miss Sinclair," he said, his voice as rigid as his posture. "Mr. Volkov wanted me to inform you that he has a meeting tonight. He'll be leaving shortly."

Ava frowned. "A meeting? Where?"

The man shifted uncomfortably, as if he wasn't used to being questioned. "At one of his clubs, ma'am. He asked me to tell you that he won't be long."

Ava's heart sank. She knew what that meant. Nikolai had been spending more time at his clubs recently, using them as neutral ground to meet with his lieutenants and strategize their next moves against the Morozovs. Normally, he would take her with him, keeping her by his side as a way to reassure her that everything was under control. But lately, things had changed.

"Why can't I come with him?" Ava asked, her voice quieter now.

The man hesitated, his eyes flickering toward the floor. "It's not safe right now. Mr. Volkov wants you to stay here until things settle down."

Of course, she thought bitterly. Stay home. Stay safe. Always left behind while Nikolai went off to fight his wars. She knew it was irrational, that Nikolai was only trying to protect her, but it still hurt. She hated feeling like a liability, like someone who had to be kept in the dark for her own good.

"Fine," she said, her voice tight with frustration. "Tell him I understand."

The man nodded and left, the door closing softly behind him. Ava leaned back against the couch, her mind racing with a thousand different thoughts. She understood why Nikolai wanted her to stay home, but that didn't make it any easier to accept. She wanted to be part of his life, all of it—not just the parts he thought were safe for her to see. But with the war raging all around them, she wasn't sure if that was even possible.

Hours passed after Nikolai's man had delivered the message, and the penthouse had fallen into an almost unbearable silence. Ava moved restlessly from room to room, her mind heavy with thoughts she couldn't escape. She had tried to distract herself—picked up a book, scrolled through her phone—but nothing worked. All she could think about was Nikolai out there in the dangerous world he refused to let her into.

He had promised to protect her. And she knew, in her heart, that he was doing just that. But it didn't stop the gnawing sense of isolation, the feeling that she was slowly being pushed to the sidelines of his life. The violence was getting worse. Every day brought new headlines about shootings, about mob wars erupting in dark alleys and underground deals. Every night, Nikolai left her behind to dive deeper into that world, and every morning, he returned just a little more distant.

Ava stood in front of the mirror in the bedroom, staring at her reflection. The woman looking back at her seemed like a stranger—pale, anxious, nothing like the confident woman she used to be. She was slipping, piece by piece, into Nikolai's world of secrets and danger, but the worst part was how powerless she felt to stop it.

She had thought she could handle it. When they first met, she had been drawn to him, not just because of his power, but because he made her feel alive, protected, like nothing in the world could touch her as long as she was by his side. But now...

now it felt like being close to him only made her more vulnerable.

The door to the closet was slightly ajar, and Ava found herself drifting toward it. She pulled the door open, her eyes scanning the rows of clothes—expensive dresses, shoes, everything Nikolai had bought for her. At first, it had felt like a dream—being spoiled, cherished, like she was something precious. But now... now it just felt like a gilded cage.

She reached for one of the dresses, a sleek black number that clung to her curves in all the right places. She had worn it the last time Nikolai had taken her to one of his clubs, and she remembered the way he had looked at her that night—like she was the only woman in the room. She had felt powerful then, secure in his gaze, in the way he had wrapped his arm around her waist, as if daring anyone to even think about approaching her.

But that was before everything had spiraled out of control. Before the attack at the cabin. Before the war between the Bratvas had escalated to the point where she was no longer safe, even standing next to him.

Ava slipped the dress back onto the hanger, her heart sinking. She wanted that feeling back—the feeling that she was part of his world, not just an observer. But with each passing day, she felt more and more like a spectator, watching as Nikolai fought battles she would never truly understand.

She closed the closet door and made her way to the kitchen, her fingers trailing along the sleek countertops. Everything in the penthouse was immaculate, untouched, as if life itself had been paused in this space while chaos raged outside. The only sound was the faint ticking of the clock on the wall, marking the minutes as they dragged by.

Ava poured herself a glass of wine and sat at the kitchen island, her thoughts still circling the same question: What had changed? When had she become someone he had to protect from his own life?

It hadn't always been this way. At the start, Nikolai had been open, or at least more open than he was now. He had shared parts of his world with her, shown her glimpses of what it meant to be with a man like him. She had known there would be danger, but there had also been a sense of partnership—like they were in this together. He had taken her with him to meetings, to dinners, to clubs where she had seen his world firsthand. He had trusted her to stand by his side, to be part of it all.

But now, everything had changed. The war with the Morozovs had shifted something in him. He was more guarded, more distant, as if he was shutting her out to protect her. And maybe he thought he was. Maybe he believed that leaving her at home while he went to fight his battles was the best way to keep her safe. But it didn't feel like protection. It felt like abandonment.

She took a sip of her wine, her fingers trembling slightly as she set the glass back down. The bitterness of the drink mirrored the bitterness that had settled in her chest.

The thought of Derek flashed in her mind. The last time she had felt like this, left behind, wondering what was happening behind closed doors, it had been Derek—her ex-fiancé—who had shut her out. She had trusted him too, believed that he was someone who cared about her. And in the end, he had betrayed her with her best friend.

Ava shook her head, pushing the memory away. Nikolai wasn't Derek. He wasn't. She knew that. But the creeping doubt was hard to ignore. What if history was repeating itself? What if she was just another woman, another conquest for him, someone he could set aside when things got too dangerous?

She finished her glass of wine, trying to steady her nerves. She knew she was overthinking it. Nikolai had told her he was protecting her, and she believed him. She knew he would never intentionally hurt her. But that didn't stop the fear from creeping in, the fear that she was being left behind, that she was losing him to a world she could never fully understand.

The hours ticked by, and the penthouse grew darker as the evening settled in. Ava stood by the window again, her arms wrapped around herself as she stared out at the city. She had hoped Nikolai would come back soon, that he would walk through the door, sweep her into his arms, and remind her that everything was going to be okay. But the minutes turned into hours, and there was no sign of him.

She sighed, feeling the weight of the week pressing down on her shoulders. She wasn't just tired of waiting. She was tired of feeling like she didn't belong. Like she was a guest in Nikolai's life, instead of someone who was truly part of it.

As the city lights flickered below, Ava made her way to the bedroom, her steps heavy with disappointment. She didn't know how much longer she could keep doing this—waiting, wondering, hoping that things would go back to the way they were.

But deep down, she knew the truth. Things had changed. And they weren't going back.

The next morning dawned overcast, the gray light filtering into the penthouse through the large windows. Ava woke up alone in the bed, the sheets cool beside her. She sat up slowly, glancing at the clock on the nightstand. It was later than she had realized—Nikolai still wasn't home. The disappointment she had tried to push away last night rushed back with full force, a dull ache settling in her chest.

She pulled on a robe, tying it around her waist as she padded barefoot into the kitchen. The air felt heavy, the silence oppressive as she moved through the empty space. She had grown used to waking up like this, to finding herself alone after Nikolai disappeared into the night. But that didn't make it any easier.

Ava poured herself a cup of coffee, her mind still tangled with the same thoughts that had plagued her the night before. She took a seat at the kitchen island, flipping through her phone absently, waiting for a text or a call from Nikolai. Nothing.

Her gaze drifted to the stack of newspapers on the counter, delivered every morning even though she rarely bothered to read them. She reached for the top one, more out of habit than interest, flipping it open to the lifestyle section.

And then she froze.

Her breath caught in her throat, her heart slamming against her ribs as her eyes locked onto a photograph splashed across the page.

Nikolai.

He was standing at one of his clubs, looking devastatingly handsome in a tailored suit, the dim lights casting shadows over his sharp features. But it wasn't just him in the photo.

There was a woman beside him—a beautiful, raven-haired woman, her body pressed close to Nikolai's as they stood together near the bar. She was stunning, her figure wrapped in a tight dress that clung to every curve, her lips painted a deep shade of red. But it wasn't her appearance that made Ava's stomach twist into knots. It was the way Nikolai had his hand on the woman's waist, his fingers resting possessively on her hip, as if he had every right to touch her like that.

The caption beneath the photo was even worse.

"Nikolai Volkov spotted with a mystery brunette at an exclusive NYC club. Could the Russian billionaire have found himself a new flame?"

Ava's blood ran cold. She stared at the picture, her mind racing as a wave of betrayal washed over her. It felt like the air had been sucked out of the room, leaving her struggling to breathe, her heart pounding in her chest. She couldn't believe what she was seeing. She didn't want to believe it.

But there it was, right in front of her. Proof that Nikolai had been out with another woman while she had been sitting here, waiting for him. It felt like a punch to the gut, the familiar sting of betrayal that she had thought she'd never feel again. Not after Derek.

Her mind flashed back to that awful moment, months ago, when she had walked in on Derek and her best friend tangled together in bed. The shock, the disbelief, the pain—it had all come rushing back now, triggered by the sight of Nikolai with that woman. She had trusted him. She had let herself believe that he was different, that he wasn't like every other man who had hurt her. And now, here she was, staring at the proof that he had betrayed her too.

Ava's hands shook as she set the paper down on the counter, her vision blurring with unshed tears. She tried to breathe, tried to calm the storm raging inside her, but it was no use. The hurt, the anger, the humiliation—it all came crashing down on her at once, leaving her reeling.

How could he do this to her? After everything they had been through, after everything he had promised her, how could he be out with another woman? And not just any woman—someone who looked like she belonged on the cover of a magazine, someone who looked like she fit perfectly into Nikolai's world.

The tears finally spilled over, burning hot as they slid down her cheeks. Ava wiped them away angrily, refusing to let herself fall apart. She had told herself she would never let a man hurt her like this again. She had promised herself that she wouldn't be the girl left waiting at home while her man was out with someone else.

But that was exactly what had happened. And it hurt more than she had imagined.

Her mind whirled with questions, with doubts that she hadn't dared to entertain before. Had this been going on the entire time? Had Nikolai been seeing other women behind her back, using her to satisfy whatever twisted part of himself that craved control and domination, while he kept someone else on the side? Had he ever really cared about her, or had she just been another conquest, another woman to add to his list?

Ava stood abruptly, her chair scraping against the floor as she pushed it back. She couldn't sit here and stew in her thoughts any longer. She needed answers. She needed to confront him, to demand the truth, even if she wasn't sure she wanted to hear it.

Her chest ached with the weight of her emotions, her heart pounding as she began to pace the kitchen, the paper still lying open on the counter, mocking her with its damning photo. She felt sick, her stomach churning with anger and hurt. She had let herself fall in love with him—completely, recklessly—and now it felt like that love had been nothing more than a cruel joke.

The minutes ticked by, each one stretching painfully
long as she waited for the sound of the front door,
for the moment when Nikolai would walk back into
the penthouse. She didn't know what she would
say, didn't know how she would even begin to
confront him. All she knew was that she needed to.

Ava's heart raced as the front door clicked shut, the
sound reverberating through the silent penthouse.
Every step Nikolai took toward the kitchen felt like a
countdown to something explosive. She stood
frozen by the island, her hands gripping the edge of
the countertop, the crumpled newspaper still lying
open in front of her. Her mind was a whirlwind of
emotions—anger, betrayal, and a deep sense of
hurt. But above all, she was furious.

Nikolai appeared in the doorway, his broad
shoulders filling the space, his eyes locking onto
hers with a calm that only fueled her rage. He
looked pristine, as if the events of the last night
hadn't touched him at all—his tailored suit still
immaculate, his expression unreadable. But Ava
knew better. She had seen the photograph, seen
the woman wrapped around him like a second skin.

Her breath came faster, her chest rising and falling
as she struggled to contain the storm brewing
inside her. How could he act so normal, so
detached, after what he had done? After the
betrayal he had committed right under her nose?

"Ava," Nikolai greeted, his voice deep and smooth, as if nothing was wrong. "Why are you up so early?"

The casualness of his tone, the way he spoke to her like everything was fine, snapped something inside her. Ava slammed her palm down on the countertop, her voice trembling with fury.

"Don't do that," she hissed, her eyes blazing. "Don't pretend like nothing's wrong."

Nikolai's expression shifted slightly, his dark eyes narrowing as he stepped further into the room, his gaze flickering to the newspaper on the counter. His calm demeanor began to harden, his lips pressing into a thin line.

"What's going on?" he asked, his voice low and measured, but there was an edge to it now, a hint of tension that told Ava he knew exactly what was coming.

She snatched the newspaper from the counter, holding it up in front of him like a weapon. Her hand shook as she pointed to the damning photograph, her throat tightening as she fought to keep her voice steady.

"This!" she spat, her anger spilling over. "This is what's going on. You, with that woman, at the club last night. You lied to me, Nikolai. You said you were going for business, and then I wake up to find this. Do you have any idea how humiliating this is?"

Nikolai's gaze dropped to the photograph, his face remaining impassive as he took in the image. His silence only stoked the fire inside her, the hurt and anger rising to a fever pitch. How could he just stand there, so unaffected, when her entire world was crashing down around her?

"Ava," he began, his voice firm but calm, "it's not what you think."

"Not what I think?" Ava's voice cracked with emotion, her heart pounding against her ribs. "What am I supposed to think, Nikolai? You're out with another woman, your hands all over her, and you expect me to just believe that nothing happened?"

"It was business," he said coldly, his eyes locking onto hers with that intense, unreadable gaze that both unsettled and infuriated her. "She's a business associate. Nothing more."

Ava let out a sharp, bitter laugh, her hands clenching into fists at her sides. "Business associate? That's what you're going with? How convenient. And I'm just supposed to believe that you, of all people, have no interest in a woman who looks like that? Like I haven't seen the way you look at women when you want something from them."

Nikolai's jaw tightened, his calm exterior cracking as the tension between them escalated. "You're being irrational," he said, his voice growing colder, sharper. "You're letting your emotions cloud your judgment."

"I'm being irrational?" Ava's voice rose, her anger spilling over in a torrent of accusations. "You lied to me! You kept me in the dark, left me here while you were out with her, and now you expect me to just sit here and listen to your excuses? You're no different from Derek. No different at all."

The mention of Derek sent a shockwave through the room. Nikolai's expression darkened, his eyes flashing with something dangerous as he stepped closer to her, his presence looming over her like a shadow.

"Don't compare me to him," he warned, his voice low and menacing. "I'm nothing like that man."

"You're exactly like him!" Ava shouted, her voice breaking as the pain and betrayal came pouring out. "You think you can control me, make me believe whatever you want, but I'm not some naive little girl. I trusted you, Nikolai. I thought you were different, but you're just like every other man who's ever lied to me. Just like Derek."

The air between them was electric, charged with the tension of everything they had been holding back. Ava could see the anger in Nikolai's eyes, the

cold fury that simmered beneath his calm facade.
But she didn't care. She was too hurt, too angry to
stop now.

Nikolai took another step forward, his eyes locking
onto hers with an intensity that made her heart skip
a beat. His voice was low, dangerous, as he spoke.

"You're acting like a child," he said, each word
dripping with icy control. "And if you continue to act
like one, I will treat you like one."

Ava's breath caught in her throat, a chill running
down her spine at the cold authority in his voice.
But she didn't back down. She couldn't. The anger,
the betrayal—it was all too much.

"You wouldn't dare," she spat, her voice trembling
with both fear and defiance.

Nikolai's eyes darkened, and before she could
react, he grabbed her arm with a firm, unyielding
grip, pulling her toward him. His hand moved with
swift precision, and in one fluid motion, he bent her
over his knee, his other hand pulling up her
nightgown in a single, commanding gesture.

Ava gasped, her heart racing as she struggled to
process what was happening. But Nikolai didn't
give her time to think. His hand came down hard on
her bare skin, the sharp crack of the spanking
echoing through the kitchen. The sting of it sent a
shockwave through her body, her mind reeling from

the sudden shift from anger to something she didn't want to admit.

"Stop it!" Ava cried, her voice shaking as she tried to push herself up, but Nikolai's grip was firm, his dominance undeniable.

"You need to learn," he growled, his hand coming down again, harder this time. "You don't get to make baseless accusations without consequences."

Ava's mind whirled, a storm of emotions crashing through her as Nikolai's hand came down on her again, harder this time. The sting of his palm against her skin sent a jolt through her, but it wasn't just pain that ignited within her—it was something darker, something she couldn't fully understand. The shame and anger mixed with an undeniable heat, her body betraying her as the line between punishment and desire blurred.

"Nikolai," she gasped, her voice trembling as she tried to wriggle free from his hold. But his grip on her waist was firm, unrelenting, as he held her in place over his knee. His power over her was palpable, suffocating, yet intoxicating all at once. She had never felt so vulnerable, so exposed. And yet, she couldn't deny the rush of arousal that pulsed through her with every strike of his hand.

"You don't get to speak to me like that," Nikolai growled, his voice low and authoritative as he brought his hand down again, the sharp crack of the impact echoing through the kitchen. Ava's body jerked at the contact, her skin tingling from the force of it. "You think you can accuse me of betrayal without consequence? You think you know me, Ava? You don't know anything."

His words cut through her, but instead of retreating into the pain, Ava found herself sinking deeper into the moment. Her breath came in ragged gasps, her heart pounding as her body responded in ways she hadn't anticipated. The heat between her legs was unbearable, an ache that was both shameful and undeniable. She hated him in this moment—hated the way he made her feel powerless, the way he controlled her with such ease. But she also wanted him. Desperately.

Ava's fingers gripped the edge of the kitchen chair, her knuckles white as she tried to steady herself. But she was spiraling, lost in the overwhelming mix of emotions coursing through her—fear, anger, desire. Her mind screamed at her to stop, to fight back, but her body had already surrendered to him.

Nikolai's hand slid lower, brushing over the red, heated skin of her ass before dipping between her legs. Ava sucked in a breath, her entire body going rigid as his fingers found the wetness there, undeniable proof of her arousal. A dark chuckle escaped his lips as he teased her, his fingers sliding through her slick folds with deliberate, taunting strokes.

"Look at you," he murmured, his voice thick with satisfaction. "You're soaking wet. You like this, don't you?"

Ava's cheeks burned with humiliation, but she couldn't deny it. Her body was betraying her in the worst way possible, responding to his dominance, his control, in ways she couldn't comprehend. She hated herself for it, hated that she wanted him even now, after everything that had just happened.

"N-no," she whispered, her voice weak and trembling. But Nikolai wasn't fooled. His fingers continued to slide between her legs, stroking her clit with slow, agonizing precision.

"Liar," he growled, his hand tightening on her waist as he held her in place. "You can't lie to me, Ava. I know exactly what you want."

His words sent a shiver down her spine, her body quaking as he pressed harder, his fingers moving in a rhythm that drove her closer and closer to the edge. She bit down on her lip, trying to stifle the moan that threatened to escape, but it was no use. The pleasure was too intense, too raw, and despite everything—despite the anger, the confusion, the betrayal—she wanted more.

Ava's legs trembled as Nikolai's fingers pushed deeper, the rough pads of his fingertips grazing her most sensitive spots with devastating precision. Her breath hitched in her throat, her body arching involuntarily as he worked her toward a climax she was desperate to resist.

"Please," she gasped, her voice cracking with both desperation and need. "Nikolai... I—"

But before she could finish, Nikolai pulled his fingers away, leaving her panting and aching with unfulfilled desire. She let out a soft whimper, the loss of contact almost unbearable, but he wasn't done with her yet.

Without a word, Nikolai pulled her up from his lap and spun her around, bending her over the kitchen counter. Her chest pressed against the cool surface, her breath coming in shallow gasps as she braced herself for what was to come. Behind her, she heard the sound of his zipper, followed by the soft rustle of fabric as he freed himself from his pants.

Her heart raced, a mix of fear and anticipation swirling in her chest as she felt him position himself behind her. His hand came down on her ass one last time, the sting of the impact sending a jolt through her, before he grabbed her hips, pulling her back toward him.

"Nikolai..." Ava whispered, her voice trembling as she felt the heat of his body against hers. But he didn't respond. Instead, he thrust into her with a single, powerful stroke, filling her completely. Ava gasped, her fingers curling against the countertop as the sensation of him inside her sent shockwaves through her body.

He didn't give her time to adjust. His hands gripped her hips tightly as he began to move, each thrust hard and demanding, as if he was claiming her all over again. Ava's breath came in ragged gasps, her body trembling from the force of it. The anger, the betrayal, the hurt—it all melted away in the face of the raw, physical pleasure that consumed her.

She moaned, her body arching into him as he drove deeper, his cock hitting that perfect spot inside her that made her mind go blank with need. Her hands gripped the edge of the counter, her nails digging into the wood as Nikolai's pace quickened, his breath hot against the back of her neck.

"You're mine, Ava," he growled, his voice rough with possession. "You belong to me. No one else."

His words sent a shiver down her spine, her body clenching around him as the intensity of the moment reached its peak. She was on the edge, teetering between pleasure and pain, her mind and body at war with each other. But in that moment, all she could think about was him—the way he controlled her, the way he dominated her so completely.

With one final thrust, Nikolai pushed her over the edge, her body convulsing as she came hard around him. Her moans filled the kitchen, her vision blurring as wave after wave of pleasure crashed through her. Nikolai followed soon after, his grip tightening on her hips as he came with a low, guttural growl, his cock pulsing inside her.

For a moment, the world went quiet. The only sound was the heavy breathing between them, the heat of their bodies still tangled together. Slowly, Nikolai pulled out of her, his hands loosening their grip on her waist as he stepped back.

Ava collapsed against the countertop, her legs shaking, her heart racing. The intensity of what had just happened left her breathless, her mind reeling from the whirlwind of emotions. She couldn't believe it—couldn't believe how quickly everything had spiraled out of control. And yet, despite the anger and confusion that still simmered beneath the surface, all she could think about was how much she wanted him, how much she needed him, even now.

Nikolai leaned down, his lips brushing against her ear as he whispered, "I won't let anything come between us, Ava. Not ever."

Chapter 18

Ava stood in the kitchen, her body still tingling from the raw intensity of what had just transpired. The cool air of the room brushed against her exposed skin, a stark contrast to the heat that still simmered inside her. She could feel Nikolai's presence behind her, powerful and unyielding, his hand still resting lightly on her waist, a possessive reminder of the control he held over her.

Her breath was shaky, uneven, as she tried to steady herself. The kitchen felt like it was closing in around her, the weight of their argument hanging in the air like a storm cloud. Ava had never felt so conflicted—so torn between anger and desire, between fear and something deeper. She had lashed out at him, accused him of things that weren't fair, things she knew, deep down, weren't true. But in the heat of the moment, all she had been able to feel was the suffocating weight of betrayal.

Nikolai's grip tightened slightly, pulling her closer to him. The warmth of his body pressed against her back, steady and grounding, but it did nothing to calm the whirlwind of emotions raging inside her. She wanted to push him away, to scream at him again, to demand answers that she wasn't sure she wanted to hear. But at the same time, all she wanted was to sink into his embrace, to let him hold her and promise that everything would be okay.

The contradiction of it all made her head spin.

"I won't let anything come between us," Nikolai murmured, his deep voice rumbling against her ear.

The words sent a shiver down her spine, but they didn't soothe the ache in her chest. Ava closed her eyes, trying to block out the overwhelming surge of emotion that threatened to consume her. She wasn't sure what to believe anymore. Everything felt so tangled, so confusing. How had things gotten this far?

Ava had always prided herself on being in control, on knowing where she stood in her relationships, in her life. But with Nikolai, nothing felt certain. The man who stood behind her, the one who had just dominated her so completely, was a mystery she wasn't sure she could ever unravel. One minute, he was protective and caring, holding her as if she were the most precious thing in the world. The next, he was cold, distant, locked away in a world of violence and danger that she couldn't fully comprehend.

And the worst part was that she didn't know how to talk to him about it. Every time she tried, he shut her down, his walls going up so fast she barely had time to process what was happening. She had always known that being with him meant entering a life of uncertainty, but now it felt like she was losing herself in the process.

Ava let out a shaky breath, her hands coming up to cover her face. She didn't want to cry, didn't want to show him how much this was hurting her, but the tears were already pricking at the corners of her eyes.

Nikolai's hand slid from her waist to her shoulder, his fingers gentle as they brushed against her skin. "Ava," he said softly, but there was an edge to his voice that made her flinch.

She pulled away from him, wrapping her arms around herself as if to shield herself from the onslaught of emotions threatening to break free. "I don't know if I can do this," she whispered, her voice trembling.

Nikolai stepped closer, his brow furrowed in concern. "What do you mean?"

Ava shook her head, feeling the tears spill over now, her chest tight with the weight of everything she'd been holding in. "I mean… I don't know if I can handle this, Nikolai. Your world, the danger, the violence. I'm losing myself in it, and I'm scared."

His expression darkened, but he didn't reach for her again. Instead, he stood there, watching her, his eyes unreadable. "You're not losing yourself," he said quietly. "You're mine, Ava. I'll keep you safe."

Safe. The word echoed in her mind, hollow and empty. She wasn't sure if she believed him anymore. Not because she thought he couldn't protect her—she knew Nikolai would go to any length to keep her out of harm's way. But was that really what she needed? To be protected? Or did she need more? More understanding, more connection, more of him?

"You don't understand," Ava said, her voice breaking. "It's not just about being safe. It's about feeling like I belong in your life. Like I'm not just someone you have to keep locked away while you go out and fight your battles."

Nikolai's eyes flashed with something she couldn't quite read—anger, maybe, or frustration—but he remained silent.

Ava swallowed the lump in her throat, her hands twisting together in her lap. "I need more than just protection," she continued, her voice growing steadier. "I need to know that I matter to you, that I'm not just someone you're keeping around because it's convenient."

"You do matter," Nikolai said, his voice rough. "You matter more than anything."

"Then why do I feel like I'm always on the outside looking in?" Ava asked, her heart aching as she finally voiced the question that had been gnawing at her for weeks.

Nikolai looked away, his jaw clenched. "Because my world is dangerous," he said after a long pause. "And I won't risk losing you to it."

The words were meant to comfort her, but instead, they only deepened the chasm between them. She understood his need to protect her, but at what cost? How long could she live like this—on the fringes of his life, never fully a part of it, always kept at arm's length?

Ava's tears fell silently now, and she wiped them away with the back of her hand. She wasn't sure what the answer was. All she knew was that, for the first time since she'd met Nikolai, she felt completely and utterly lost.

The silence in the room felt oppressive. Ava sat down heavily on one of the barstools at the kitchen island, her fingers playing absently with the edge of her sleeve as her thoughts churned. She could still feel the lingering warmth of Nikolai's touch on her skin, but it only heightened the strange sense of disconnection growing inside her.

Nikolai stood across from her, his back turned as he leaned against the counter, his broad shoulders tense. It wasn't like him to leave so much unsaid, but that was part of the problem, wasn't it? Lately, he had been pulling away, shutting her out in ways that weren't as obvious but were just as devastating. The subtle distance had crept into their relationship over the past week, and now Ava felt like they were miles apart, even when they were in the same room.

The distant sounds of the city filtered through the large windows, the hum of New York's restless energy a sharp contrast to the suffocating quiet between them. Ava stared at his back, wishing she could see his face, read his expression, but she knew Nikolai well enough by now to understand that he wouldn't show her much. He'd retreat into himself, keep his thoughts and emotions locked away behind those carefully constructed walls.

It was one of the things that frustrated her the most. How could she reach someone who had spent his entire life learning to guard every vulnerable part of himself? She didn't just want to be protected by Nikolai—she wanted to protect him, too. She wanted to be part of his life, not just on the periphery, waiting for scraps of his attention.

"You're always protecting me," Ava said quietly, breaking the silence, though her voice wavered. "But who protects you?"

Nikolai turned his head slightly, his profile sharp in the dim light of the kitchen. "I don't need protection."

"That's not what I mean." Ava's tone was gentle, but there was an edge of desperation in it. "You take on everything by yourself. You bear the weight of the world, and you don't let anyone help. Not even me."

Nikolai was silent for a long moment, and for a second, she thought he wasn't going to respond at all. Then, finally, he turned to face her, his dark eyes locking onto hers with an intensity that made her pulse quicken. "I can't afford to need help," he said, his voice low but firm. "Not in my world."

"And what about me?" Ava asked, her heart aching as she spoke. "Am I supposed to just sit back and watch you carry everything alone? You say you're protecting me, but I feel like you're shutting me out. I'm right here, Nikolai, but you won't let me in."

Nikolai's expression darkened, his jaw tightening. "You don't understand what you're asking, Ava."

"Then explain it to me!" Ava's frustration boiled over, her voice rising slightly as she stood from the stool and took a step toward him. "Stop shutting me out. I can't keep doing this, Nikolai—living in your world without being a part of it."

His eyes flashed with something—anger, maybe, or something darker—but his voice remained calm. "You don't want to be part of my world."

Ava flinched, the words hitting her like a physical blow. "You don't get to decide that for me."

Nikolai's hands clenched at his sides, his gaze piercing as he stared at her, but she refused to back down. She had spent too long feeling like an outsider in her own life, too long letting fear dictate her choices. She wasn't going to let him make this decision for her, not when it mattered so much.

"I know your world is dangerous," Ava continued, her voice softer but no less determined. "I'm not naive. I know what you do, what you're capable of. But I'm not some fragile thing that needs to be locked away for protection. I'm with you because I love you, not because I need to be kept safe."

Nikolai's eyes softened for a brief moment, but it was gone as quickly as it had appeared. "It's not just about keeping you safe, Ava. It's about survival. My enemies wouldn't hesitate to use you against me if they thought for one second that you were part of the game. I can't risk that."

The vulnerability in his words tugged at Ava's heart, but it didn't ease the pain in her chest. She could see how much he believed what he was saying, how deeply rooted his fear for her safety was. But that didn't make the distance between them any less real.

"I get that you're trying to protect me," she said, her voice steady now. "But the more you shut me out, the more alone I feel. And I don't know how much longer I can do this, Nikolai. I don't know how much longer I can feel like I'm losing you."

Nikolai stepped toward her, his eyes never leaving hers. "You're not losing me."

Ava shook her head, her throat tight with the emotions she was barely holding back. "It feels like I am."

They stood in the middle of the kitchen, the tension between them thick and suffocating. Ava wanted to believe him, wanted to trust that their connection was still as strong as it had been in the beginning, but the growing distance between them was hard to ignore.

"I love you," Nikolai said, his voice low and rough. "More than I've ever loved anyone."

Ava's heart clenched at his words, but the doubt still lingered. She loved him, too, with every fiber of her being. But love wasn't enough to erase the fear and uncertainty that gnawed at her. It wasn't enough to close the gap that had been widening between them.

"I love you, too," she whispered, her voice barely audible. "But I need more, Nikolai. I need you to let me in."

He didn't respond right away, his gaze searching hers as if he were trying to figure out what to say. And for a moment, Ava thought that maybe, just maybe, he would let her in. That he would finally open up and show her the parts of himself that he kept so carefully guarded.

But instead, Nikolai simply nodded, his expression unreadable. "I'll try," he said, his voice distant.

It wasn't the answer she wanted, but it was the only one he was willing to give.

The conversation with Nikolai left Ava feeling more unsettled than before. She had poured her heart out, laid her fears and frustrations bare, and all she'd gotten in return was a promise that felt hollow. "I'll try." Those two words had hung in the air long after the conversation had ended, and they offered little comfort.

Nikolai's world was dangerous, unpredictable, and brutal. She understood that. She wasn't asking for a perfect relationship, free from complications. She knew who he was when she'd fallen in love with him, but what she hadn't anticipated was how much his need to protect her would shut her out. It was suffocating, even though she knew it was coming from a place of love.

***

Ava's heart felt heavy as she stood at the window, watching the early morning sunlight cast long shadows over the Manhattan skyline. The city felt distant, cold, just like Nikolai had become over the past week. As the war with the Morozov Bratva escalated, so had the distance between them. Every day, he left earlier and came back later, his face set in a hard line, the weight of violence hanging over him like a storm cloud.

She glanced at the clock. It was only 7 a.m., but Nikolai had already left, just like every other day this week. She hadn't even heard him slip out of bed, his movements as silent as the ghost of their former connection.

Ava's fingers tightened around the mug of coffee she was holding, the heat seeping into her palms. She hadn't realized how cold she felt until now—like there was a chill deep inside her that no amount of warmth could touch.

Her mind wandered back to the previous morning. They had fought, they had made love, and still, she felt no closer to him. The war was pulling him away, consuming his attention, and no matter how hard she tried, Ava couldn't seem to reach him.

Nikolai was slipping into the role he had perfected over the years: the ruthless leader of the Volkov Bratva. The man who wielded violence like a weapon, always calculating, always one step ahead of his enemies. But in that cold, calculated existence, there wasn't room for vulnerability or connection. And that's what scared her the most. As long as he was locked in this war, she was locked out of his heart.

Ava turned away from the window, her footsteps quiet on the hardwood floors as she moved through the penthouse. It felt too big, too empty without Nikolai there. She didn't know how much longer she could handle this—being left behind while he went out to fight battles she could never understand.

The thought hit her like a punch to the gut: What if he never came back?

The idea was ridiculous, but in Nikolai's world, it wasn't. People like him didn't always get to walk away from their wars. They didn't always come home. She knew that. She had known it from the beginning. But knowing it in theory and facing it in reality were two very different things.

Ava sat down on the edge of the couch, her mind spinning with images of Nikolai—images she tried to push away but couldn't. What if something happened to him? What if one night he didn't come back, and all she was left with were memories of a man she could never fully have?

Her phone buzzed on the table in front of her, snapping her out of her thoughts. She reached for it, her heart skipping a beat when she saw Nikolai's name on the screen.

Leaving for a meeting. Stay home. I'll be back later.

The message was brief, to the point, and offered none of the reassurance she craved. He didn't say where he was going or what he was doing, just that he'd be back. But how many times had he said that over the past week, only to return hours later, silent and brooding, his mind clearly elsewhere?

Ava set the phone back down, the knot in her stomach tightening. She knew he was doing what he thought was best—protecting her from the brutal reality of his life. But it felt like he was protecting her from him, from the man she wanted to know more deeply, the man she was desperate to connect with beyond the walls he kept erect around his heart.

She had never felt so distant from him. Every day, it was like watching him slip further into the role of Bratva kingpin, and further away from being the man she had fallen in love with. She loved him deeply, but that love wasn't enough to bridge the gap that was growing between them. It wasn't enough to pull him out of the war that was consuming him, body and soul.

Ava stood, her hands running along the edge of the couch, needing something to ground herself in the moment. Everything felt so uncertain, like the ground beneath her feet was slowly crumbling, and she didn't know how to stop it.

The war with the Morozovs was taking its toll on him, and by extension, on her. She had seen the headlines, the whispers of violence spreading through the streets, the bodies that were piling up as the Bratvas waged their bloody war for control. Every day it got worse, and every day Nikolai became more distant.

She had tried to be understanding, had tried to give him the space he needed to handle his business. But it wasn't space she wanted—it was him. She wanted the man behind the walls, the man she had seen glimpses of when they were alone together, the man who could be soft and caring in the moments between the chaos. But as the war dragged on, those moments had become few and far between.

Ava knew she had to make a decision. She couldn't keep waiting for things to go back to the way they were, because they wouldn't. The violence wasn't going to stop, and Nikolai wasn't going to magically become someone who could walk away from it all. He was who he was—a man born and bred for this life, a man who thrived in the shadows and wielded power like a weapon.

And if she wanted to stay with him, she had to accept that. She had to accept that his world would never be safe, and that the distance between them would always be there, lurking in the background, a reminder of the danger that surrounded them.

Her phone buzzed again, and this time, the message was even shorter.

Be back late. Don't wait up.

Ava stared at the screen, her heart sinking as the words blurred in front of her eyes. She set the phone down, her chest tight with the weight of it all.

She was losing him. And the worst part was, she didn't know if she could stop it.

Ava's heart felt like it was sinking into an abyss, heavy with fear and uncertainty. She stared at the phone, its dull screen reflecting the growing void in her chest. The short, clipped messages from Nikolai had become a daily occurrence, but it wasn't the brevity of the texts that hurt. It was the reminder of how distant he had become, how unreachable.

She placed the phone on the table, its weight far more than the small device deserved. She felt trapped—trapped in the beautiful penthouse that had once felt like a safe haven but now felt like a gilded cage. A part of her wondered if she was being unreasonable, if this was all just the result of her overactive emotions. She knew Nikolai loved her. He had said it, hadn't he? But why did it feel so fragile, like it was slipping away from her no matter how hard she tried to hold on?

Ava exhaled, pressing her fingers to her temples, trying to ease the growing tension in her head. She was overthinking things—she knew she was. But how could she not? Everything about her relationship with Nikolai was unlike anything she had experienced before. The stakes were higher, the risks far greater.

And it wasn't just about Nikolai. The fear, the worry, the doubt—they were all ghosts from her past, shadows of the betrayal she had tried so hard to move on from. But they lingered, creeping in during moments like these, when she felt vulnerable and unsure. Derek had done that to her. He had taken away her ability to trust, to believe in the promises of a man, and left her with scars that hadn't fully healed.

Ava stood up and paced the room, her fingers brushing against the furniture as she walked. The penthouse was too quiet, too empty. She hated it when it was like this, when she was left alone with her thoughts. It gave the past too much room to breathe, to take over her mind. She found herself thinking about Derek more often than she wanted to admit, comparing him to Nikolai in ways that made her stomach turn.

Was she overreacting? Was she letting the past cloud her judgment?

Derek's betrayal had been brutal, a complete blindsiding that had shattered her trust in an instant. She had loved him, or at least she had thought she did. But then she had walked in on him and her best friend, tangled together in bed, a living nightmare she had never anticipated. The memory still stung, raw and painful, as if it had just happened yesterday. The anger, the humiliation, the hurt—they all came flooding back whenever she let herself think about it for too long.

And now, standing here in the penthouse, feeling abandoned by Nikolai, those old wounds started to open again.

She hated that. She hated that Derek still had the power to hurt her, even after all this time. He was out of her life, and yet his betrayal still haunted her, still colored the way she saw relationships, still made her question whether she could truly trust anyone again. Even Nikolai.

Especially Nikolai.

Ava sat down on the couch, her hands resting in her lap as she let out a long, slow breath. She didn't want to compare them. She didn't want to think that Nikolai could be anything like Derek, but the nagging fear wouldn't leave her alone. The photo in the paper, the woman with him at the club—it had triggered something deep inside her, a fear she couldn't shake.

Was she repeating history?

She tried to remind herself that Nikolai wasn't Derek. He hadn't lied to her. He hadn't betrayed her. And yet, there was still a part of her that couldn't help but wonder. What if he did? What if this was just another heartbreak waiting to happen? Another moment where she would find herself standing alone, wondering how she had missed the signs?

Ava closed her eyes, her fingers tightening into fists as she fought against the flood of emotions threatening to overwhelm her. She had promised herself that she wouldn't let Derek's betrayal define her, that she wouldn't let it ruin her ability to trust again. But here she was, letting the past control her, letting it seep into her relationship with Nikolai.

She didn't want that. She didn't want to keep questioning him, doubting him, every time he left the penthouse. She didn't want to keep waiting for the other shoe to drop, for the moment when everything would fall apart. She loved him. She wanted to believe in him. She wanted to trust him with every part of her.

But that was hard when her past kept whispering in her ear, telling her that love wasn't enough. That no matter how much you loved someone, they could still hurt you. They could still betray you.

Ava opened her eyes and stared at the ceiling, her mind still racing. She needed to stop. She needed to pull herself out of this spiral before it consumed her. Nikolai wasn't Derek. She knew that. He was a different man, a man who had shown her love in ways that Derek never had. Nikolai was flawed, yes, but he wasn't a liar. He wasn't someone who would hurt her the way Derek had.

So why was she still so afraid?

The answer hit her like a punch to the gut. It wasn't Nikolai she was afraid of. It was herself. It was her own fear of being hurt again, her own inability to trust completely after what had happened with Derek. She was projecting that fear onto Nikolai, assuming the worst because it was easier than letting herself be vulnerable again.

She pressed her hands to her face, her mind spinning as she realized how unfair she had been to him. Nikolai wasn't the problem. She was. She had been acting out of fear, letting the past dictate her actions instead of trusting the man in front of her.

Ava lowered her hands, her heart pounding as the weight of the realization settled over her. She loved Nikolai. She trusted him. But she had been too caught up in her own fear to see it clearly. She had let Derek's betrayal poison her relationship, and now, if she wasn't careful, she was going to lose the best thing that had ever happened to her because of it.

She couldn't let that happen. She wouldn't.

Ava's chest felt lighter after the realization, like a weight had been lifted. She exhaled slowly, letting the tension seep out of her body. For the first time in what felt like days, her mind was clear, the fog of doubt and fear beginning to dissipate. She sat there in silence, her thoughts no longer racing in endless loops. Instead, a sense of calm washed over her, the clarity of her emotions finally surfacing.

She had been pushing Nikolai away without even realizing it. All this time, she thought it was him building walls, keeping her at arm's length, but now she saw that she had been the one erecting barriers. The fear of being betrayed again had seeped into her relationship, coloring every interaction, every moment they shared. And Nikolai, who had his own world to manage, hadn't known how to reach her, how to pull her out of the darkness she'd built around herself.

But now she knew.

She loved him.

And that love was stronger than her fear. It had to be. She couldn't keep letting the past dictate her future, couldn't keep expecting Nikolai to fail her in the same way Derek had. Nikolai was not Derek.

He was fierce and commanding, yes, but he was
also protective, loyal, and steadfast in his affection
for her. He had never given her any reason to doubt
him. Not once.

Ava got up from the couch, pacing the living room
as the realization settled deeper into her bones.
She could see it all now, the way her fears had
warped her perception, making her suspicious of
Nikolai when all he had ever done was protect her.
He had warned her about his world, told her it was
dangerous, and tried to shield her from it. But
instead of trusting him, she had let her insecurities
cloud her judgment.

She stopped by the window, staring out at the city
once again. The same skyline, the same tall
buildings, but somehow everything looked different
now. Brighter. Less suffocating. She loved New
York, but it had never felt like home until she was
with Nikolai. He had become her anchor, the
person who made her feel safe despite the chaos
surrounding them. He was the one who held her
together, even when she didn't realize she was
falling apart.

And that was what scared her the most. How
deeply she loved him. How much she trusted him
with her heart, her body, her soul. That level of
vulnerability terrified her, and it had been easier to
hold back, to keep him at a distance emotionally,
than to admit how much she needed him. But now

that she was standing on the edge, staring into the abyss of her own fear, she realized that she couldn't keep running.

She had to trust him.

Ava took a deep breath, steadying herself as her mind finally quieted. She thought back to the kitchen, to their argument, and how she had been so quick to lash out at Nikolai, accusing him of things that weren't true. She had been unfair, driven by the same hurt that Derek had inflicted, but now she saw it for what it was—a shadow from her past. A ghost that had haunted her for too long.

But no more.

She wouldn't let Derek's betrayal define her. She wouldn't let it ruin what she had with Nikolai, the man who had shown her nothing but love and loyalty since the day they met. She had to let go. She had to trust in the present, in what was real, instead of letting the past cast its long, painful shadow over her future.

Ava wrapped her arms around herself, closing her eyes as a sense of peace settled over her. She loved Nikolai with everything she had, and she was done letting fear stand in the way of that love. He was dangerous, yes. His world was violent and unpredictable. But he had never been anything but honest with her, never pretended to be something he wasn't. He had always shown her exactly who he was, and it was time she accepted that. All of it.

When she opened her eyes again, the city seemed less foreboding. The skyline shimmered in the winter sun, the same way it always had, but this time Ava felt like she could breathe. Like the walls that had closed in around her were finally falling away.

I trust him.

The words echoed in her mind, solid and true. She trusted Nikolai with her life. With her heart. And that trust wasn't fragile; it wasn't something that could be easily broken. It was strong, like the love they shared. Unshakeable.

A small smile tugged at the corners of her lips as she thought about him—Nikolai, with his fierce eyes and commanding presence, the man who had risked everything to protect her. The man who loved her in ways she hadn't thought possible. He had never faltered, never wavered in his devotion to her. And now, it was time she did the same for him.

She wasn't going to let the past ruin what they had. She wasn't going to let her fear of betrayal hold her back any longer. This was her life, her relationship, and she was going to fight for it.

Chapter 19

Ava woke up to the soft glow of morning light filtering through the heavy curtains of the penthouse bedroom. The golden rays bathed the room in warmth, creating a stark contrast to the cold knot of anxiety that had been lodged in her chest for days. But today, that knot was gone. As she lay there, her head resting on the pillow beside Nikolai, she felt a calmness settle over her, a sense of peace she hadn't known she needed.

She turned her head to look at him, still fast asleep beside her. His strong, angular face looked softer in the early light, the hardness that usually accompanied him in waking hours temporarily absent. His dark hair fell messily across his forehead, his chest rising and falling in the rhythm of deep sleep. He looked so different from the powerful man she had come to know. Right now, he wasn't the head of the Bratva, a man feared and respected in equal measure. He was simply Nikolai—her Nikolai.

Her heart swelled as she watched him, love surging through her in a way that both surprised and comforted her. Just the night before, she had been torn apart by doubt and anger, unsure of everything between them. But something had shifted. Their fight had forced her to confront the ghosts of her past, and in doing so, she had finally understood that those ghosts no longer had a place in her future.

She trusted him. The realization had struck her with a force she hadn't expected. She had been holding onto the hurt Derek had caused her for far too long, letting it dictate how she saw the world, how she saw men. But Nikolai was not Derek. He had shown her again and again that he wasn't the type to betray her, and she finally believed it. Fully. Completely.

The memories of their heated argument, followed by the intense physical connection they had shared, replayed in her mind. Every touch, every whispered word between them, had only solidified what she already knew in her heart: she loved him, and she trusted him not just with her heart but with her life.

Ava shifted slightly in the bed, careful not to wake him as she stared up at the ceiling. It was a strange feeling—this lightness in her chest. For the first time since she had stepped into Nikolai's world, she didn't feel weighed down by fear or uncertainty. She felt free. The past that had once clung to her like a shadow was finally starting to fall away.

She closed her eyes briefly, relishing the moment, letting herself soak in the peace. But as her mind wandered, a lingering thought surfaced—something she had pushed aside for months. The engagement ring. Derek's engagement ring, to be precise. She hadn't thought about it in what felt like forever, but now, it gnawed at her. She had shoved it into a drawer in her old apartment, an apartment she hadn't stepped foot in since she moved in with Nikolai. It had been out of sight, out of mind, but now... now it felt like a loose end she needed to tie up.

Ava sighed softly. She knew what she needed to do. She needed closure, true closure, from that part of her life. Derek had hurt her, yes, but she had let that wound fester for too long. She had held onto the bitterness, the betrayal, thinking it was a way of protecting herself from ever being hurt like that again. But the only thing it had done was build walls between her and the man she truly loved.

It's time to let it go.

She sat up slowly, glancing back at Nikolai. He stirred slightly but didn't wake. A small smile tugged at her lips as she brushed a lock of hair away from his face. She didn't want to disturb him. He had been working late into the night, caught up in the escalating war with the Morozov Bratva, and he needed the rest. She would do this alone.

Slipping out of bed as quietly as she could, Ava padded across the room and grabbed her robe, wrapping it around herself before heading into the adjoining bathroom. The cool tiles under her feet sent a shiver through her, but her resolve stayed firm. She splashed some water on her face and looked at herself in the mirror, her reflection staring back at her with a mix of determination and relief. Today, she would take a step toward fully letting go of her past.

She dressed quickly, throwing on a pair of jeans and a sweater, her mind already focused on what lay ahead. As she moved through the penthouse, the familiar luxury of the space felt comforting. This was her home now—this was where she belonged. But she couldn't truly move forward with Nikolai until she faced the last lingering remnant of her old life.

Ava grabbed her purse from the kitchen counter and slipped out the door, making her way down the elevator. The quiet hum of the city greeted her as she stepped onto the sidewalk, the morning rush just beginning. She hailed a cab, giving the driver the address to her old apartment. It felt strange saying it out loud, like she was going back to a place she no longer recognized. But this time, she wasn't going back to reminisce or to hold onto the past. She was going back to close that chapter for good.

As the cab sped through the city streets, Ava felt a sense of finality settling over her. She wasn't the same person who had lived in that apartment, the person who had clung to the idea of love with Derek even after it had shattered. She was someone new now, someone who had found real love, real trust, in the arms of a man who wasn't afraid to show her all the dark, dangerous parts of himself.

This was just one more step in claiming that new life. One more step toward letting go of everything that had once held her back.

The cab's gentle hum filled the silence as Ava leaned back against the seat, her eyes flicking to the passing cityscape outside. The familiar streets of Manhattan blurred together, yet her mind was somewhere else, wrapped in the memories of her old apartment. She hadn't been there in months, and just the thought of stepping inside again made her stomach tighten. So much had changed since then. She had changed.

But it was necessary. It was time to face the last fragment of her past head-on.

Ava's hand instinctively went to her necklace, her fingers tracing the delicate chain. She closed her eyes briefly, feeling the weight of the decision she was about to make. She wasn't just getting rid of a ring; she was severing ties with a part of herself that had been caught in a spiral of disappointment, pain, and mistrust. Derek had left more than just physical scars—he had left emotional ones, too. But now, those wounds were ready to heal.

The engagement ring had haunted her in a way she hadn't fully realized. She had shoved it into a drawer, hidden it from sight, thinking that would be enough to forget it, to forget him. But she should have known better. It wasn't just the ring—it was everything it symbolized: the future she had once imagined, the lies she had unknowingly believed, and the betrayal that had nearly destroyed her ability to trust. All of it was bound to that small piece of jewelry.

She could still remember the day Derek had proposed, the way his voice had wavered with excitement as he knelt down, the ring glinting in the soft evening light. Ava had been so happy then, so full of hope and dreams. She had said yes without hesitation, believing that her future with him was going to be perfect. How naive she had been.

Now, as she sat in the back of the cab, Ava wondered if she had ever really known him at all. Derek had been charming, loving, and attentive in all the ways a man should be. But it had all been an act, a carefully crafted performance to keep her from seeing the truth. He hadn't been faithful. He hadn't been honest. And she had been too blind to notice.

The memory of walking in on him with her best friend flashed through her mind like a cruel joke, the scene replaying itself with vivid clarity. She had opened the door, expecting to find him waiting for her, only to see the two of them tangled together, their betrayal so blatant and raw that it had left her breathless. That moment had broken something inside her, something that had taken months—years, really—to begin to mend.

But now, as she approached the apartment where all those memories lived, Ava felt stronger than she had in a long time. Nikolai had shown her what real love was supposed to feel like, what real trust was built on. It wasn't about grand gestures or promises made in the heat of passion—it was about actions, about the way someone protected you, cared for you, stood by you through the worst of times.

Nikolai had done that. He had proven himself in ways Derek never could have. And while Nikolai's world was dangerous and unpredictable, while there were things about his life that terrified her, Ava knew one thing for certain: he would never betray her. He had risked everything for her, and that alone meant more than any ring ever could.

The cab slowed to a stop in front of her old apartment building, pulling her from her thoughts. She glanced out the window, staring at the familiar entrance with its chipped paint and worn-out steps. It felt strange to be here, like she was stepping back into a life that no longer fit. But this was the final step. The final goodbye.

"Here we are," the driver said, his voice breaking the silence.

Ava nodded, handing him the fare and stepping out of the cab. She stood on the sidewalk for a moment, taking a deep breath as she looked up at the building. It was just an apartment, just a space filled with old memories. And yet, the weight of what it represented made her heart feel heavy. She had spent so many nights in that apartment, crying over Derek, replaying every moment of their relationship, wondering where she had gone wrong. But none of that mattered now.

She pulled her keys from her bag and made her way up the steps, her feet feeling lighter with every step. When she reached the door, she hesitated for just a moment before pushing it open. The familiar scent of the place hit her immediately, a mix of dust and stale air that hadn't been disturbed in months. She stepped inside, closing the door softly behind her.

The apartment was just as she had left it—empty, quiet, and untouched. It was as though time had stopped here, frozen in that moment when she had walked away, determined never to look back. But now, the space felt cold, devoid of the life she once thought she would live here.

Ava crossed the living room and made her way to the bedroom. Her hand hovered over the doorknob for a brief second before she twisted it and stepped inside. The room was dim, the curtains drawn, and everything was just as she had left it—the bed unmade, a few boxes piled in the corner, and a small dresser in the far corner of the room.

Her eyes immediately went to the drawer where she had stashed the ring. She walked over, her steps slow and deliberate, and pulled it open. The ring was still there, tucked neatly into the velvet box Derek had used when he proposed. For a moment, Ava just stared at it, her heart beating steadily in her chest. There it was—the symbol of all the promises that had been broken, all the dreams that had been shattered.

But now, looking at it, she didn't feel sadness. She didn't feel regret. She felt relief.

Ava picked up the ring box and held it in her hands, her fingers brushing over the smooth velvet. There was no rush of emotion, no surge of longing or heartbreak. It was just a ring, just a piece of jewelry that no longer had any hold on her. She was free from it now.

She opened her bag, taking out an envelope and a small piece of paper. With a steady hand, she wrote a short note to Derek. It was simple, just a few lines thanking him for what they had shared but making it clear that she had moved on. There was no anger in her words, no bitterness. Just finality.

Ava stared at the small, delicate ring resting in the velvet box. The symbol of a future she had once believed in, now reduced to a meaningless trinket.

It no longer held any power over her, no longer represented the love she once thought she had. Slowly, she placed the ring inside the envelope along with the note, sealing it with a quiet sigh of finality.

As she stood there in the dim light of the bedroom, the weight of her past life seemed to fade further away with each passing second. The walls of this apartment, once a place she had shared with her dreams of a different future, now felt cold and foreign. This place no longer felt like hers. It hadn't for a long time, but now it was undeniable—this was just an empty shell of her former self.

Ava closed the drawer with a soft click, her fingers trailing along the wood. The air in the apartment felt thick, unmoving, like a place forgotten by time. The quiet hum of the city outside barely penetrated the silence inside these walls, reminding her how disconnected she had become from this space.

She stood in the middle of the room, her eyes roaming over the remnants of her old life. There wasn't much left. A few pictures in frames still sat on the dresser, untouched, gathering dust. She walked over and picked one up, blowing off the thin layer of dust that had settled over the glass. It was a photo of her and Derek, smiling, carefree, back when everything had felt perfect.

Looking at it now, the image felt foreign—like she was looking at a stranger. The woman in the photo wasn't her anymore. That version of herself was naive, innocent, unaware of the pain that was waiting just around the corner. Ava studied the smile on her face, wondering how she could have been so blind, so oblivious to what was coming.

But she wasn't that woman anymore. She had learned, grown, and become stronger in ways she hadn't even realized until now. And standing here, in the apartment that once held so many memories, she realized something important—she no longer needed to carry the weight of that past. It didn't define her. It didn't hold her back. She had built something new, something stronger with Nikolai, and that was what mattered.

Ava placed the photo back on the dresser, not with sadness or regret, but with acceptance. She wasn't here to mourn the past. She was here to say goodbye to it. She glanced around the room one last time, her gaze lingering on the small personal items she had left behind. The bed, the dresser, the boxes—none of it meant anything anymore. There was nothing here that she wanted to take with her. Nothing she needed.

Her eyes drifted to the closet, the place where she had once kept all her clothes, neatly organized by color and season. Now, the closet was nearly empty, just a few forgotten outfits still hanging on their hangers. She walked over and pulled the door open, staring at the meager collection of clothes that had been left behind. They didn't fit her anymore—literally or metaphorically. The life she had envisioned for herself when she had worn these clothes was long gone.

She inhaled deeply, savoring the sense of closure that settled over her like a warm blanket. She wasn't running from the past anymore. She was walking toward the future. And that future was with Nikolai. He was the one who had shown her what real love looked like, what it meant to be with someone who truly cared about her. He had shown her that trust wasn't something to be feared—it was something to be embraced.

Ava took one final glance around the room before walking toward the door, her steps lighter than they had been in months. She didn't look back as she closed the door behind her, the soft click of the latch sealing the chapter of her life that was now behind her. There was no sadness, no hesitation. She was ready to move forward.

As she made her way back to the living room, she noticed the silence once again. But this time, it didn't feel oppressive. It felt peaceful. The apartment had served its purpose in her life, and now it was time to leave it behind.

Ava grabbed the envelope containing the engagement ring and note to Derek from the table by the door. She had one last thing to do before she could truly close this chapter for good. With the envelope in hand, she walked toward the front door, her heart lighter, her mind clearer than it had been in a long time.

She stepped out of the apartment, the cool winter air greeting her as she descended the stairs to the street. This was it. The final act. She made her way to the corner of the block, where a blue mailbox stood waiting. Ava hesitated for just a second, staring at the envelope in her hand. And then, with a deep breath, she dropped it into the mailbox, watching as it disappeared through the slot.

A small smile tugged at her lips as she turned away. She had done it. She had let go of the last piece of her past. Now, it was time to walk away—literally and figuratively.

The cold air nipped at her cheeks as she turned away from the mailbox, her hands slipping into her coat pockets. It was over. The ring, the note, the apartment—they were all behind her now. And with them, the version of herself that had once been so consumed by pain and betrayal.

As she walked down the familiar street, Ava glanced over her shoulder at the building that had once been her home. It felt distant now, as though it belonged to someone else entirely. The woman who had lived there, who had cried herself to sleep in that apartment, who had given up on love—she was gone. Ava was no longer that person. She had grown stronger, more resilient, and with Nikolai, she had found something far more real and profound than anything she had ever imagined with Derek.

Nikolai.

Even just thinking of him brought warmth to her chest, melting away the cold bite of the winter air. She had been afraid to trust him fully, afraid that history would repeat itself, that he would betray her the way Derek had. But she knew now how wrong she had been to compare the two. Nikolai wasn't just a man who had come into her life—he was the man who had shown her that love didn't have to come with conditions or deceit.

And as much as his world terrified her at times, as dangerous and brutal as it could be, Ava realized she wasn't afraid anymore. Not of him. Not of what they could be together.

There was no going back to her old life, to her old self. And she didn't want to. Nikolai had taught her that love wasn't about safety—it was about trust, about standing by someone's side no matter how dark or uncertain the path ahead might be.

As she walked away from her old life, Ava felt lighter, her steps quicker, more certain. The past was exactly that—the past. And she was ready to leave it behind, knowing that everything she truly needed was waiting for her back at the penthouse.

The thought echoed through her mind with every step she took, and for the first time in what felt like ages, she wasn't haunted by old memories or what-ifs. She had let go of the engagement ring, of the apartment, of Derek. Everything that had tied her to the life she thought she wanted was behind her now. And in front of her was a future she hadn't dared to dream of—a future with Nikolai.

A small smile tugged at her lips as she imagined his reaction when she told him what she had done. He would probably scold her for leaving the penthouse without telling him, without one of his security men trailing behind her. Ava chuckled to herself, already imagining his possessive grumble, but she didn't mind. Nikolai's protectiveness was part of who he was, and though it had taken her time to adjust, she now understood that it came from a place of deep care.

She rounded the corner onto a quieter street, where a few parked cars lined the curb. Her old apartment was in a more residential part of the city, and the morning was still early enough that the street was nearly empty. Ava walked at a leisurely pace, savoring the crisp air and the sense of freedom that filled her.

But then, in a heartbeat, everything changed.

Ava felt the hairs on the back of her neck prickle, a sudden chill sweeping over her that had nothing to do with the temperature. She instinctively glanced over her shoulder, her eyes scanning the empty street behind her. Nothing seemed out of place, but a creeping sense of unease settled in her stomach, causing her to quicken her steps.

Just a few more blocks, she told herself. You'll be fine.

But the nagging feeling didn't go away. Instead, it intensified. She could feel it—the unmistakable sensation of being watched, followed. Her pulse began to quicken, and her eyes darted around, trying to find any sign of danger. She cursed herself for not being more careful, for not listening to Nikolai's warnings about going out alone. She had let her guard down, and now she felt exposed, vulnerable.

Her pace quickened even more, her heart thudding in her chest. Just get to the corner, she thought, glancing ahead to where the main street would be busier, where there would be more people. Her breath came faster, her mind racing as she tried to rationalize the fear building inside her. Maybe it was nothing. Maybe she was just being paranoid.

But as she reached the middle of the block, a black SUV screeched to a stop beside her, the tires skidding on the pavement. Before Ava could react, two men in dark clothing jumped out. Her blood ran cold, panic surging through her as one of them grabbed her arm with a vise-like grip.

"No—" Ava screamed, but the sound was cut off as one of the men clamped a hand over her mouth, dragging her toward the waiting vehicle.

She struggled, kicking and thrashing with every ounce of strength she had, but it was no use. The man's grip tightened painfully around her arms, pulling her into the back seat of the SUV. The other man slammed the door shut behind them, and within seconds, the car sped off down the street, the engine roaring as it merged into traffic.

Ava's heart raced, her breath coming in panicked gasps as she was shoved into the back seat. Her hands were bound quickly, the rope biting into her wrists as one of the men tied her up with practiced efficiency. She fought to stay calm, to think through the terror that threatened to paralyze her, but her mind was spinning out of control.

Who were they? What did they want? And how had they found her?

Her eyes darted wildly around the interior of the SUV, trying to make sense of the situation, but it all felt surreal, like some kind of nightmare. The men didn't speak, their faces hidden behind their masks, but their intentions were clear. They hadn't taken her by mistake. This was planned, deliberate.

The Morozov Bratva.

The realization hit her like a punch to the gut. Nikolai had warned her that the Morozov Bratva was becoming more aggressive, more dangerous. They had already made one attempt on his life, and now... now they were coming after her. This wasn't just about her—it was about hurting Nikolai, about hitting him where it would hurt the most.

Terror washed over her, but alongside it came a fierce determination. She couldn't let them take her without a fight. She couldn't let herself be used as a pawn in their deadly game. Ava wriggled in her seat, testing the bonds around her wrists, but they were tight, and the man sitting beside her kept a watchful eye on her every movement.

The car sped down unfamiliar streets, weaving through traffic as if trying to evade pursuit. Ava's mind raced, trying to think of anything she could do to escape, but the situation felt hopeless. They were moving too fast, too efficiently. She was trapped.

But one thought burned in her mind, sharp and clear despite the chaos around her: Nikolai would come for her.

He would stop at nothing to find her. She knew that with every fiber of her being. Nikolai was a man of power, a man who didn't let anyone take what was his. And she was his—whether she had fully realized it or not, she belonged to him in every sense of the word.

The fear that had gripped her chest slowly began to transform into something else, something fiercer. She wasn't just some helpless victim, and she wouldn't give up. If there was any chance to escape, she would take it.

Ava's eyes darted toward the front seat, where the driver and another masked man sat, their attention focused on the road ahead. She shifted in her seat, trying to move her hands, to loosen the ropes even a little. There had to be a way out.

But for now, all she could do was wait—wait for the moment, the opportunity to fight back. Because she knew that Nikolai wouldn't stop until he found her. And when he did, the men who had taken her wouldn't stand a chance.

Chapter 20

The van skidded to a stop, the harsh sound of tires grinding against gravel snapping Ava back into the present. Her heart raced, and her breath quickened, her eyes darting around wildly as the door was yanked open. Cold, sharp air hit her, biting at her exposed skin. She tried to move, to find any kind of leverage, but her hands remained bound, the ropes cutting into her wrists with every attempt to free herself.

Rough hands grabbed her by the arms, dragging her out of the van and onto the rough, cold ground. Ava stumbled, barely managing to stay upright as they pulled her toward the building looming ahead—a decaying, abandoned warehouse. The structure seemed to rise out of the ground like a monster, the rusted metal doors creaking on their hinges as they were wrenched open. The men didn't speak, but the sinister energy in the air was palpable.

Her shoes scraped against the gravel as they dragged her toward the entrance, her body too weak from exhaustion and fear to put up much of a fight. Her breath came in ragged bursts, her mind racing. Stay calm, she told herself, her thoughts swirling as she tried to figure out a way out of this. Nikolai will come. He will find me.

They pulled her into the warehouse, the smell of
rust and decay immediately overpowering her
senses. Inside, it was dark, save for the faint
beams of sunlight filtering through the cracks in the
walls and ceiling. The sound of their footsteps
echoed off the walls, the hollow emptiness of the
place only heightening her fear.

The men were silent, focused, their faces giving no
hint of emotion. They yanked her forward with
force, and Ava's heart sank as they led her toward
the far end of the warehouse. There, hanging from
the ceiling, were thick metal chains, their purpose
immediately clear. Panic surged in her chest.

"No," she whispered, shaking her head, though her
voice barely rose above a whisper. "No, please—"

Her words were cut off as one of the men grabbed
her wrists, forcing her hands above her head and
shackling them to the chains. She winced as the
cold metal clamped tightly around her already sore
wrists, pulling her arms taut until her toes barely
touched the ground. The strain on her shoulders
was immediate, the pain sharp as her body was
forced to dangle uncomfortably.

Ava struggled against the chains, her breath
coming in short, panicked bursts, but it was no use.
She was completely immobilized, suspended in
midair, her body on full display before her captors.
Her chest heaved as she looked around, desperate
for any way out, but the warehouse was empty,

save for the men who stood before her, watching with cruel, unfeeling eyes.

One of the men stepped forward, his face and body language oozing menace. He reached out, grabbing the front of Ava's shirt with one hand, his fingers digging into the fabric.

"No!" Ava cried, trying to twist away, but it was useless. With a sharp, brutal motion, the man ripped her shirt open, the fabric tearing apart with a loud, violent sound. The cold air hit her bare skin, and a wave of humiliation and fear washed over her.

"Shut up," the man growled, his voice low and menacing. His eyes roamed over her body, and Ava felt her stomach turn as she saw the lecherous way he looked at her. To him, she was nothing more than a piece of meat, a tool to be used. His gaze lingered on her exposed chest, and he smirked beneath his mask. "You're just a pawn. You're nothing to us."

Ava's blood ran cold, her body trembling in the chains as she fought to keep her fear from overtaking her. "Let me go," she whispered, her voice shaking, but she knew it was pointless.

The man reached out, his hand tracing over her bare skin in a way that made her skin crawl. "You think we care about you?" he sneered, his breath hot against her cheek. "You're just here to get Volkov's attention. You're nothing but bait."

The words hit her like a slap to the face, her heart hammering in her chest. This wasn't about her—it was about Nikolai. They didn't care what happened to her. She was just a means to an end, a tool to draw Nikolai into their trap.

But even as the fear gripped her, another thought pushed its way to the front of her mind: Nikolai will come for me. She clung to the thought like a lifeline, holding onto the belief that he would find her. He would stop at nothing to get her back.

"Volkov's going to die for you," the man continued, his hand now trailing down her side, his touch cruel and possessive. "And by the time we're done, you'll be nothing but a message. Maybe we'll send him your fingers first."

Ava's heart pounded in her ears, the horror of his words sinking in. They were willing to mutilate her, to send pieces of her to Nikolai, just to hurt him. She bit down hard on her lip, fighting back the wave of nausea that threatened to overtake her. She wouldn't give them the satisfaction of seeing her break.

The man stepped back, his eyes glinting with malice. "But don't worry, sweetheart," he said with a dark chuckle. "We'll have plenty of fun with you before that."

Ava's body tensed as the other men laughed, their voices echoing off the walls of the warehouse. She was trapped, chained, and helpless, but deep inside her, the anger flared. She wouldn't let them win. She wouldn't give them the satisfaction of breaking her spirit.

Nikolai would come. He had to.

The laughter of the men echoed in the vast emptiness of the warehouse, their voices carrying a chilling, malicious undertone. Ava hung helplessly from the chains, her arms aching from the strain, her body trembling from both fear and the cold. The torn remnants of her shirt fluttered uselessly at her sides, leaving her exposed, vulnerable. But it wasn't just the physical cold that chilled her—it was the ice in their words, the way they spoke about her as if she were nothing more than an object, a tool to be used and discarded.

One of the men stepped closer, his mask hiding his face, but the cruel intent in his eyes was unmistakable. He reached out, his fingers brushing against her bare skin with a deliberate slowness that made her stomach twist. His touch was invasive, violating, a reminder that she was at their mercy. Ava recoiled, her body trying to pull away, but the chains kept her firmly in place.

"Don't like that, do you?" the man sneered, his voice low and mocking. He ran his hand over her side, trailing down to her waist, his fingers pressing into her skin hard enough to bruise. "Too bad. You're ours now. And we'll do whatever we want with you."

Ava's breath hitched in her throat, her heart racing as she struggled to control her fear. She wanted to scream, to fight, to lash out, but she knew it would be pointless. These men were bigger, stronger, and more ruthless than she could ever hope to be. But she refused to let them see how scared she was. I can't break, she told herself, clenching her fists as her wrists chafed against the cold metal shackles. Nikolai will come.

Another man approached, this one taller and broader, his steps slow and deliberate. He circled her like a predator sizing up his prey, his eyes raking over her body with open contempt. Ava's stomach churned, bile rising in her throat as she watched him, her pulse quickening with every step he took. She could feel the danger radiating off him, a cold, calculating cruelty that made her skin crawl.

"You think you're special?" the man asked, his voice dripping with disdain. He stopped directly in front of her, towering over her, his presence suffocating. "You think Volkov cares about you? You're nothing to him. Just a little toy he can toss aside when he's bored."

Ava's jaw clenched, her chest tightening with a surge of anger. She knew Nikolai wasn't like that. She knew, deep down, that he cared about her. But these men... they were trying to break her, to make her doubt everything she believed in, and for a moment, the fear threatened to overwhelm her.

The man leaned in closer, his breath hot against her ear. "We'll see just how much you mean to him when he's watching us carve you up. Piece by piece." He chuckled darkly, the sound sending a shiver down her spine. "Maybe we'll start with that pretty face of yours. Or your fingers. Do you think he'll cry when we send him your hand in a box?"

Ava's blood ran cold, her mind reeling from the horrifying image his words conjured. She tried to swallow the fear, to push it down, but it was too much. The reality of what they intended to do hit her like a freight train. They were willing to mutilate her, to send her body parts to Nikolai just to lure him out. The sickening cruelty of it left her breathless.

"You're nothing but bait," the man continued, his voice growing darker, more threatening. "Volkov will come for you, sure. But not because he cares. He'll come because he can't stand the idea of losing. You're just a piece of his empire, and when we're done with him, you'll be nothing but a pawn that didn't matter."

The words cut deep, even though Ava knew they were lies. Nikolai wasn't like that. He wasn't using her. She knew he cared about her—he had shown it in the way he protected her, the way he kept her close. But doubt crept in, gnawing at the edges of her mind. *What if they're right? What if I'm just a pawn in his game?*

No. She shook the thought away, pushing it to the farthest corner of her mind.

The man stepped back, his cold, calculating eyes scanning her face as if searching for cracks in her resolve. Ava met his gaze with all the defiance she could muster, refusing to give him the satisfaction of seeing her break. She wouldn't let them win. She couldn't.

But even as she fought to keep her emotions in check, her body betrayed her. Tears pricked at the corners of her eyes, and she bit down hard on her lip, drawing blood to keep them from falling. The pain was sharp, but it kept her grounded, kept her from losing control.

The man laughed, clearly enjoying her struggle. "You're stronger than you look," he said, his tone almost admiring. "But strength won't save you. Not here."

One of the other men, growing bored with the taunts, stepped forward, his fists clenched. "Enough talking. Let's see if she's still strong after this." Without warning, he lashed out, his fist connecting with the side of Ava's face with a sickening thud.

The impact sent her reeling, her vision blurring as pain exploded across her cheek. Her head snapped to the side, the force of the blow leaving her momentarily disoriented. She gasped, the metallic taste of blood filling her mouth as her lip split open. For a moment, everything spun, her mind struggling to keep up with the pain radiating through her skull.

But even as the agony tore through her, she forced herself to stay upright, to keep her footing despite the fact that her legs were shaking, her entire body trembling from the force of the hit. She refused to cry out, refused to let them see how much it hurt. I can't let them win, she repeated over and over in her mind, clinging to the thought like a lifeline.

Her breath came in short, ragged bursts as she slowly lifted her head, glaring at the man through the haze of pain. Blood dripped down her chin, her vision still swimming, but she met his gaze with as much defiance as she could muster.

"You're going to die for this," she whispered, her voice hoarse but filled with conviction. "Nikolai will kill you. All of you."

The men around her laughed, their voices cruel and mocking. "We'll see about that," one of them sneered. "But don't worry, we'll have plenty of fun before he gets here."

Ava's stomach churned with revulsion, but she clung to her anger, to the burning hatred she felt for these men. She wouldn't let them break her. Nikolai would come. She just had to hold on until he did.

Ava's vision swam as the pain pulsed through her face, the aftermath of the punch radiating from her cheekbone and jaw. The taste of blood still lingered in her mouth, sharp and metallic, a reminder of how fragile her situation had become. She could feel the slow trickle of blood from her split lip, the warm liquid crawling down her chin and dripping onto her exposed chest. Her body was trembling now, not from the cold but from the shock of the blow, the reality of her captivity settling over her like a thick, suffocating blanket.

The man who had hit her stood back, admiring his handiwork as if she were nothing more than a canvas for his violence. His lips twisted into a cruel smile, his eyes gleaming with sadistic satisfaction. Ava wanted to scream, to curse him, to lash out, but her body refused to obey. She was too weak, too battered, hanging helplessly from the chains that kept her suspended just above the ground.

"Look at you," the man sneered, his voice dripping with condescension. "Not so tough now, are you?"

Ava's breath came in shallow gasps, her chest heaving as she fought to control the pain. The throbbing in her cheek was relentless, every heartbeat sending another pulse of agony through her body. But she refused to cry. She refused to let them see her break.

The other men circled her like vultures, their eyes gleaming with malice as they watched her struggle to stay conscious. One of them reached out, his fingers brushing against the bruise forming on her cheek. The touch was light, almost gentle, but it sent a wave of revulsion through her body.

"Maybe we should send Volkov a picture," the man suggested, his tone casual, as if he were discussing a mundane task. "Let him see what we're doing to his precious little toy."

Ava's stomach twisted at the thought. She could picture it clearly—Nikolai opening a message to find a photo of her, beaten and bloodied, strung up like an offering to his enemies. The thought of him seeing her like this, of him knowing what they were doing to her, made her chest tighten with panic. But would it matter? Would he even care?

No. Ava shook her head, biting down hard on her lip to keep the tears at bay. She couldn't let herself think like that. Nikolai would come for her. He had to. She clung to that belief, holding onto it as if it were the only thing keeping her afloat in the storm of terror that surrounded her.

But as the minutes dragged on, each one stretching longer than the last, doubt began to creep in. The pain in her body was overwhelming, every breath a struggle, every movement sending waves of agony through her limbs. The men continued to taunt her, their voices a constant, mocking presence in the background, but their words had begun to blur together, fading into the haze of her suffering.

The chains around her wrists bit into her skin, the metal cold and unyielding. She could feel the slick warmth of her own blood trickling down her arms, mixing with the sweat and dirt that covered her body. Her muscles screamed in protest, her shoulders burning from the strain of being held in the same position for so long.

Ava's head lolled forward, her strength slowly ebbing away as the physical and emotional toll of the situation weighed down on her. Her vision blurred, the edges of her consciousness dimming as the pain threatened to pull her under.

But even in the haze of her suffering, one thought remained clear: Nikolai will come.

The warehouse seemed to close in around her, the shadows lengthening as the cold, damp air pressed against her skin. Ava's body ached, every nerve on fire from the repeated blows and the constant strain of hanging from the chains. Her wrists throbbed, her shoulders screamed in protest, but the physical pain was nothing compared to the fear gnawing at her insides.

The men moved around her like circling wolves, their eyes gleaming with cruel satisfaction as they admired their work. She could feel their stares crawling over her exposed skin, like insects burrowing into her flesh. But what made it worse—what made her stomach turn—was the casualness with which they spoke about her, as though she were nothing more than an object, a bargaining chip in their war with Nikolai.

The tallest of the men, the one who had hit her last, stepped forward again. He lifted his hand, running his fingers through the blood that trickled down from her lip, his thumb smearing it across her chin as if inspecting his handiwork. The touch made her skin crawl, and she flinched away, the chains rattling as she tried to shift her body.

"She's got fight in her," he said, his tone almost amused. "I like that. Makes it more fun."

His hand trailed lower, across her throat and down to her collarbone, before finally resting on her bare stomach. Ava's breath hitched, her pulse quickening as his fingers pressed into her flesh. The invasion of her personal space felt like another violation, and the helplessness that came with it sent a wave of nausea rolling through her. But she clenched her jaw, fighting back the tears that threatened to spill.

Another man leaned against a nearby pillar, watching the interaction with a smirk. "Don't break her too quickly," he said with a chuckle. "We've got time before anyone gets here. Let's enjoy the show."

Their laughter echoed in the cavernous space, bouncing off the rusted metal walls like the mocking call of vultures. Ava wanted to scream at them, to tell them that Nikolai would tear them apart when he found them, but her throat was too dry, her voice too weak. She could barely keep her head up, the weight of the pain dragging her down, pulling her toward the edge of unconsciousness.

But she couldn't let herself black out. Not yet. She needed to stay awake. She needed to be ready for when Nikolai came.

The man who had been touching her leaned in closer, his breath hot and foul against her ear. "You're going to beg before this is over," he whispered, his voice a sickening mix of promise and threat. "And when you do, I want you to remember that Volkov did this to you. His war, his choices—this is all because of him."

Ava clenched her fists, her nails digging into her palms as she fought to keep her composure. He's lying. She knew that. She knew this wasn't Nikolai's fault. But the seed of doubt had already been planted, and it gnawed at her, tiny roots of uncertainty spreading through her mind. What if he's right? What if this is all because of Nikolai? What if loving him is what brought her to this?

No. She shook her head slightly, trying to dispel the thought. She couldn't afford to doubt him. Not now. Not when everything was on the line.

But even as she told herself that, the fear crept in. What if he doesn't get here in time? What if they kill me before he can reach me?

Ava's heart pounded against her ribs, her breath coming in shallow, rapid gasps as panic set in. She could hear the men talking in the background, their voices fading in and out as the world around her grew darker. The edges of her vision blurred, and for a moment, she wondered if this was it. If this was how it would all end—chained up in a warehouse, waiting for a rescue that might never come.

But then, out of the corner of her eye, she saw movement. One of the men stepped forward, pulling something out of his pocket. It was a phone—a sleek, black device that looked so out of place in the grimy, rusted warehouse. He tapped on the screen a few times before holding it up in front of her face.

"Smile," he said with a cruel grin. "Let's give Volkov a preview."

The flash from the phone's camera was blinding, and Ava squeezed her eyes shut, her body tensing as she heard the shutter click. The sound was like a death knell, a cold reminder that these men were preparing to send Nikolai a message—a message with her bloodied face plastered across it.

They were using her, manipulating her pain to draw Nikolai into their trap. And she could do nothing to stop them.

The man sent the picture, his fingers moving quickly over the phone before tucking it back into his pocket. He gave her one last, smug look before stepping back, as if satisfied with his work. "Now we wait."

Ava's head slumped forward, her chest heaving as the weight of the situation pressed down on her. She was powerless, helpless, and completely at their mercy. But even as the despair threatened to consume her, she clung to one thought, one sliver of hope: Nikolai would come.

She had to believe it. It was the only thing keeping her going.

Chapter 21

Nikolai awoke slowly, his body sinking back into the plush mattress as his mind tried to shake off the remnants of sleep. The morning light filtered through the curtains, casting soft shadows across the room, but something felt off. His hand reached across the bed instinctively, searching for the warmth of Ava's body beside him, but all he felt was the cool, empty sheets.

His eyes snapped open.

The bed was empty.

Nikolai's heart gave an uneasy thud, and he sat up, scanning the room. His mind raced, trying to rationalize her absence, but the gnawing sense of dread that had been growing inside him since last night refused to be ignored. His throat tightened as he glanced toward the bathroom—dark, empty. His pulse quickened.

"Ava?" His voice cut through the silence, but there was no answer. He stood quickly, throwing off the covers and moving through the penthouse with swift, measured steps. His mind struggled to remain calm, to assure himself that there was a reasonable explanation for her absence. But with every empty room he passed, his anxiety spiked higher.

She wasn't in the living room, or the kitchen, or anywhere else in the sprawling penthouse. He checked the guest room, even the bathroom again, but each room remained eerily vacant, as if Ava had simply vanished. His jaw clenched, and the calm mask he'd perfected over years of ruthless control began to crack.

He grabbed his phone from the bedside table and immediately dialed Viktor's number. The phone rang twice before Viktor answered, his voice rough but alert.

"Boss?"

"Ava's gone," Nikolai barked, pacing the bedroom now. "She's not here. Where the fuck is she?"

There was a brief pause on the other end before Viktor responded, his tone shifting into something more serious. "She left the penthouse this morning. I had a security team tailing her, as always. She's safe. Let me call and get an update."

Nikolai didn't respond, his hand tightening around the phone as he paced the length of the room. He hated the surge of panic rising in his chest. He had built his life around control, around making sure every move he made was calculated, planned, and safe. But the thought of Ava out there, exposed, sent a wave of fear crashing through him that he could hardly contain.

He heard Viktor barking orders in the background, followed by the click of another phone call being made. The silence on Nikolai's end felt suffocating, each second that passed making his heart beat faster, harder. He hadn't been this shaken in years—decades, maybe. Not since he had fought his way to the top of the Bratva, back when every corner he turned meant life or death. But this was different. This wasn't about him or his empire. This was about her. Ava.

Where the fuck could she have gone?

Nikolai rubbed a hand over his face, trying to suppress the images of worst-case scenarios flashing through his mind. She wouldn't just leave like that. She wouldn't disappear without telling him. And the fact that she had security with her meant she wasn't stupid—she understood the danger of his world. But the longer Viktor stayed silent, the more that gnawing sense of dread twisted in his gut.

Minutes stretched on, feeling like hours, until Viktor's voice crackled back through the phone. But there was something in his tone now that set Nikolai's teeth on edge. Something cold. Grim.

"Nikolai..." Viktor's voice was strained. "The security team... they were found outside her apartment. They've been shot. Dead. All of them."

The words hit him like a sledgehammer to the chest. Nikolai's breath stalled, his vision narrowing as the world around him blurred. Dead? His men—his highly trained, loyal men—were dead? And Ava...

His grip tightened on the phone until his knuckles turned white. "And Ava?" His voice was barely controlled, a deep, simmering rage underlying the words.

"She's gone," Viktor said, his voice thick with frustration. "She wasn't there when we found the bodies. Whoever took her... they left no trace."

The air in the room grew cold, and for a brief moment, Nikolai felt his world tilt. He couldn't breathe, couldn't think past the single horrifying thought that clawed its way into his mind: They took her.

Before he could respond, his phone buzzed with another notification. He pulled it away from his ear and saw the message—a number he didn't recognize. Frowning, he opened it.

His blood ran cold.

There, on the screen, was a photo. Ava—his Ava—hanging from chains, beaten, bloodied, half-naked. Her face was swollen, bruises darkening her delicate skin, and her eyes... her eyes were closed, her head slumped forward as if she had already accepted her fate.

A low growl built in Nikolai's throat as he stared at the image. Every muscle in his body tensed with rage, with the kind of fury that made men do unspeakable things. They had hurt her. They had taken her. And they were taunting him with it.

His hand shook as he gripped the phone, his entire body trembling with the need to act, to tear whoever was responsible apart piece by piece. But for the first time in years, he felt powerless. He didn't know where she was, who had her, or how much time he had to get to her before...

No. He couldn't think like that. He couldn't let the fear control him. He had to act. He had to save her.

"Viktor," Nikolai's voice was a low, dangerous growl. "I need you to find her. Now. Find out who did this and bring them to me. I don't care what it takes. Do you hear me?"

"Yes, Boss," Viktor replied immediately, his voice steady despite the gravity of the situation. "I'll find her."

Nikolai hung up the phone, his jaw clenched so tightly he thought his teeth might crack. He paced the room, every step filled with barely contained rage. The photo was still on his phone screen, mocking him, daring him to come after her. He would. There was no question about that. But first, he needed information.

Ava's life was on the line, and whoever did this would pay in blood.

Nikolai stormed out of the bedroom, his mind a whirlwind of rage and fear. He could barely contain the storm brewing inside him. The walls of the penthouse felt suffocating, closing in as the weight of what had just happened pressed down on him. Ava was gone. And his men—his trusted, highly trained men—were dead. This wasn't just a message. It was a direct assault on his world.

But more than that, it was a strike against his heart.

He reached the large glass windows that overlooked the city, his hands curling into fists as he stared out at the sprawling skyline. Somewhere out there, Ava was suffering. His Ava, the one woman who had ever truly meant something to him, was at the mercy of his enemies. The image of her bruised, bloodied, and half-naked—chained up like an animal—was burned into his mind, fueling the rage that simmered just below the surface.

He needed to act. Now.

His phone buzzed again, and he swiped it open with more force than necessary, half-expecting another taunting message. But this time, it was Viktor calling back. Nikolai answered immediately, his voice sharp and tense.

"Talk to me."

"The security team was ambushed," Viktor said, his voice calm but laced with an underlying frustration. "Two men, shot dead outside Ava's apartment. They didn't stand a chance. It was clean, professional—whoever did this knew what they were doing."

Nikolai's grip tightened around the phone, his knuckles white. The security team had been some of his best men, trained for scenarios exactly like this. How had they been caught off guard so easily? "And Ava? No sign of her?"

"Nothing. The apartment was empty when we got there. It's possible they took her straight from the street. We're combing the neighborhood and nearby security footage, but nothing solid yet." Viktor paused, the silence on the other end of the line a stark contrast to the chaos swirling in Nikolai's mind. "We'll find her, Boss. I promise."

Nikolai's jaw clenched. He wasn't used to this feeling—this gnawing sense of helplessness. In his world, everything had a price. Everyone had a weakness. But right now, the only thing that mattered was getting Ava back. And the fact that he didn't know who was holding her or where she was being kept made the fury inside him burn even hotter.

"They sent me a message," Nikolai growled, his voice dark. "A photo. Ava... she's chained up, beaten. They're using her to draw me in."

A sharp intake of breath on Viktor's end told him the severity of the situation was sinking in. "Do you know who sent it?"

Nikolai's eyes darkened as he paced the length of the room. His mind flashed to the Morozov Bratva, the rival family who had been breathing down his neck for weeks now. The attacks, the ambushes—it all led back to them. They were trying to weaken him, to push him into a corner. And now they had taken the one thing that could truly destroy him if he let it.

"It's Morozov," Nikolai spat, the name leaving a bitter taste in his mouth. "This is their move. They think they can take me down by using her."

Viktor cursed under his breath. "That bastard Ivan's been making noise ever since we hit their last shipment. This is retaliation. They want to make you suffer before they come for the rest."

"I'm going to kill him," Nikolai said, his voice low, lethal. "Every last one of them."

Viktor's voice remained calm, though the tension was clear. "We'll get her back, Nikolai. But we need to move carefully. They're expecting you to come after them."

Nikolai stopped pacing, his entire body coiled with rage. "I don't care what they expect. They've taken Ava. I'm not going to sit around and play their game. Find her, Viktor. Now."

There was a pause on the other end before Viktor spoke again, his tone measured but firm. "I'm already on it. We're sweeping the entire city. I'll have my men follow every lead we can find. But there's something else. I've been getting whispers... we might have the mole."

Nikolai's breath stilled. "The mole?" The words felt foreign, poisonous. His mind raced through the possibilities, the faces of every man who had served him, each one more loyal than the last. But someone—someone close—had betrayed him at the cabin. And that betrayal had led to Ava's kidnapping.

"Yes. We've narrowed it down to a few suspects. But the way this went down, it was too precise. They knew where she was when she left the penthouse. It wasn't random."

Nikolai's vision blurred with rage. The thought of someone within his ranks feeding information to the enemy made his blood boil. The betrayal was personal now. Whoever had done this had signed their own death warrant. And Nikolai would make sure they suffered before he killed them.

"Find the mole," Nikolai growled. "I want to know who it is, and I want them alive."

"You got it, Boss. I'll handle it."

The call ended, and Nikolai was left standing in the middle of the penthouse, his chest heaving with barely contained fury. Every second that passed was another second that Ava was in danger, another second that they could be hurting her, tormenting her.

He couldn't think about that. He wouldn't. Not yet.

Instead, he focused on the one thing he could control: his vengeance. When he found out who had betrayed him, they would suffer. They would pay for every bruise, every cut, every ounce of pain that Ava had endured.

Nikolai slammed his fist into the wall, the sharp sting of pain shooting up his arm, but it was nothing compared to the storm brewing inside him. This wasn't just business anymore. This was personal. And Nikolai wasn't going to stop until he had Ava back and every man responsible for this was dead.

Nikolai's fists clenched and unclenched as he paced the penthouse like a caged animal. His mind was racing, heart pounding against his chest as images of Ava flashed through his mind—Ava smiling, Ava laughing, Ava sleeping peacefully beside him. Now all of it was tainted by the brutal reality of the image he had seen moments before. That photo of her—bruised, bloodied, chained—burned behind his eyes. His breath came in ragged bursts as he fought to keep his composure, but he was losing the battle.

The phone in his hand was still lit, the photo staring back at him, mocking him. Every instinct in him screamed to throw the device across the room, to smash it into a thousand pieces, but he couldn't. That photo was the only link he had to her right now. It was a taunt, a challenge from his enemies, daring him to come for her. And Nikolai would, without hesitation.

He stared down at the image again, his grip tightening around the phone until his knuckles turned white. Ava was barely recognizable, her face swollen and marked with dark bruises. Her clothes—what little remained of them—were torn, leaving her vulnerable, exposed. The worst part was the look of defeat in her slumped posture, as if she had given up all hope.

Nikolai's jaw clenched painfully, a low growl rising in his throat. He couldn't allow that image to exist in his mind—not of her. Ava wasn't defeated. She wouldn't give up. But the thought of what they might be doing to her, the torture they could be inflicting, made his blood boil. It wasn't just a matter of rescuing her anymore. It was about vengeance. He was going to tear every man involved in this apart.

His phone buzzed again, pulling him from his dark thoughts. He glanced down, half-expecting another taunt from his enemies. Instead, it was Viktor.

"We have the mole" Viktor said the moment Nikolai answered.

Nikolai's heart stilled. The mole. The traitor. The one who had sold him out. "Where is he?"

"We grabbed him just outside the city. He's one of your security detail—Sergei Novikov.

The name hit Nikolai like a punch to the gut. Sergei had been with him for years. Trusted. Reliable. Or so he had thought. The realization that someone so close had betrayed him left a bitter taste in his mouth. How could he have missed this? How had he let someone like Sergei infiltrate his inner circle?

"Is he talking?" Nikolai asked, his voice low, barely contained fury simmering beneath the surface.

"Not yet," Viktor replied, his tone hard. "But he will. We're making sure of that."

Nikolai knew exactly what that meant. Viktor would make Sergei talk—by any means necessary. And once they had the information they needed, there would be no mercy. Sergei had signed his death warrant the moment he betrayed Nikolai, and Nikolai would see to it personally that the punishment was slow and agonizing.

"Good," Nikolai growled, his grip on the phone tightening. "I want him to suffer."

"He will," Viktor assured him. "And we'll get the location of where they're keeping her. I'll call as soon as we have something."

Nikolai ended the call and stood in the middle of the room, his chest heaving with barely suppressed rage. His mind raced with possibilities—where they might be holding her, what kind of condition she might be in. Every second that ticked by felt like a lifetime. He had never been this out of control before. He hated it. Hated that these bastards had gotten the upper hand, even for a moment.

His phone buzzed again, and for a split second, he expected Viktor to have more news. But as he looked down at the screen, his stomach dropped.

Another message.

His fingers trembled as he opened it, and his worst fears were confirmed. A video file. He hesitated for just a moment before tapping the screen, his breath catching in his throat as the footage began to play.

The screen flickered to life, and there she was—Ava, chained to the wall, barely conscious. The camera was shaky, as if whoever was holding it was enjoying the chaos of the moment. Ava's head lolled to the side, her body bruised and battered. But then, her eyes fluttered open, and for a brief moment, she looked into the camera.

Nikolai's heart stopped.

He could see the pain in her eyes, the fear. But there was something else there too—something that ignited a fire deep within him. Defiance.

Ava hadn't given up. She wasn't defeated.

The camera shifted, and one of her captors appeared on screen, a sadistic grin spread across his face. He moved closer to her, brushing a hand against her bruised cheek, and Nikolai's entire body went rigid with fury. Every muscle in his body tensed as he watched, helpless, as the man taunted her.

"Look at you," the man sneered, his voice thick with cruelty. "You're nothing but a pawn. Nikolai won't come for you. You're not worth it."

Ava flinched at his words, but she didn't break. Even through the screen, Nikolai could see her fighting to hold on to whatever strength she had left. The man moved closer, his hand trailing down her neck, and Nikolai's vision blurred with red-hot rage.

"If he doesn't show, maybe we'll have some fun with you," the man continued, his fingers lingering on her throat. "Maybe we'll send him pieces of you, bit by bit."

The video cut off abruptly, and Nikolai was left staring at the blank screen, his heart pounding in his chest. His blood boiled, his entire body vibrating with the need to act. They had touched her. They had hurt her. And they were using her as bait, knowing full well that he would come for her.

But they had underestimated him.

Nikolai's grip tightened around his phone, his breath coming in sharp, controlled bursts as he fought to keep the rage at bay. He had to stay focused. Losing control now wouldn't help Ava. He needed to be smart, calculated. But the image of that man touching her, taunting her, promising to send pieces of her—it was too much.

They were going to pay. Every last one of them. And when he found them, he would make sure their deaths were slow, brutal, and painful.

Nikolai dialed Viktor again, his voice low and deadly as the call connected. "I need the location. Now."

"We've got him. Sergei's been... persuaded to cooperate," Viktor said, his tone cold but satisfied. Nikolai knew exactly what that meant. Sergei had been broken—bruised, bloodied, but broken. There was no room for mercy, not for a traitor. Especially not one who had sold out Ava.

Nikolai's teeth ground together at the thought of Sergei betraying him. The man had been in his inner circle for years, trusted with the most sensitive of details. And now, he had sold Nikolai out to the Morozov family in exchange for... what? Money? Power? Revenge? It didn't matter. Whatever Sergei had thought he would gain from this betrayal was irrelevant. He had betrayed the wrong man, and now, he would die for it.

"What did he say?" Nikolai demanded, his patience wearing thin.

"He gave up the location of a warehouse," Viktor replied, the satisfaction in his voice barely masked. "They're holding her there, using it as a trap. Sergei's been feeding them information for weeks—about your movements, about Ava's schedule. They knew exactly when to strike. That's how they new about the cabin and about Ava this morning."

Nikolai's breath stilled, the full weight of the betrayal settling on his chest like a heavy stone. Weeks. Sergei had been watching him, tracking Ava, planning this ambush with his enemies, all while standing at Nikolai's side. The rage that simmered beneath his skin ignited, hot and vicious, threatening to consume him whole.

"Is Sergei still alive?" Nikolai asked, his voice flat, emotionless.

"For now," Viktor said. "But not for long."

A twisted satisfaction coiled in Nikolai's chest. Sergei's fate was already sealed. He would die for his betrayal, but not before he felt every ounce of pain he deserved. Still, the urge to handle Sergei himself burned inside Nikolai. He wanted to be the one to look the traitor in the eyes as he ended his miserable existence. But that would have to wait.

First, he had to get Ava back.

"Send me the address of the warehouse," Nikolai ordered, his voice sharp and filled with deadly intent. "I want every man we have ready to move. We're going in."

"Understood," Viktor replied. "I'm on my way."

The call ended, and Nikolai stood in the middle of the penthouse, his hands clenched into fists at his sides. His mind raced with the plan forming in his head. They thought they could trap him. They thought they could use Ava to bring him down. But Nikolai Volkov wasn't a man who walked into traps. He was the one who set them.

His enemies had made the gravest mistake of their lives. They had underestimated him, and for that, they would pay with their lives. He was no stranger to bloodshed, no stranger to violence. It was what had made him the man he was today, and it was what would drive him to destroy anyone who dared to touch what was his.

Ava.

He took a deep breath, forcing himself to focus. Ava needed him. Every minute he wasted was another minute they could be hurting her, tormenting her. The image of her bloodied and beaten flashed through his mind again, stoking the fire of rage that had been burning inside him since the moment he'd received that first photo.

Nikolai grabbed his gun from the nightstand and slid it into his holster, his movements sharp and precise.

As Nikolai stepped into the elevator, the metallic walls closed in around him, but his mind was elsewhere—laser-focused on what was to come. His hand brushed the gun holstered at his side, a familiar weight that anchored him to the moment.

Every decision he'd made, every calculated move, had led him to this.

But this time, it wasn't just business. This was personal.

The elevator hummed softly as it descended, the lights above casting harsh shadows across his sharp features. He could feel the pulse of the city beneath his feet, but it felt distant, muted by the storm of emotions swirling inside him. For years, he had built his empire with blood and fear, never letting anyone close enough to threaten the walls he had fortified around himself. And then there was Ava—the only one who had ever slipped past his defenses, the one who made him feel like something more than just the ruthless leader of the Bratva.

But that vulnerability had been exploited, and now she was paying the price for his enemies' ambition.

His chest tightened as he thought of her—bloodied, broken, chained up like an offering to his enemies. The image wouldn't leave him, burned into his mind like a scar. Ava needed him, and he would not fail her.

When the elevator doors slid open to the underground parking lot, Nikolai's steps were sure, his face a mask of calm determination. Viktor was already waiting for him beside one of the black SUVs, the engine idling quietly. As soon as Nikolai approached, Viktor straightened, his expression grim but resolute. He had seen Nikolai like this before—focused, lethal. There was no room for hesitation now.

"She's in a warehouse," Viktor said without preamble, his eyes sharp as they met Nikolai's. "We're ready to move."

Nikolai didn't say a word as he climbed into the vehicle, his mind already mapping out every possible outcome, every potential obstacle. They would get Ava back. And when they did, there would be nothing left of the Morozov Bratva.

Viktor slid into the driver's seat, and as the SUV roared to life, Nikolai's thoughts darkened. He had always been a man of few words, preferring actions over promises. And soon, he would show every man responsible for this mistake exactly what it cost to cross him.

They pulled out of the garage, the city blurring by as they sped toward the warehouse, toward Ava.

He would bring her home. And the streets would run red before the night was through.

Chapter 22

Nikolai's hands clenched into tight fists on his lap as they sped through the dark, empty streets. His mind was a storm of rage and desperation, each passing second stretching unbearably. He could hear the low hum of the engine and the occasional sound of Viktor shifting gears beside him, but everything else faded into the background. All that mattered was Ava—somewhere in that warehouse, bruised and broken—and the men who had taken her. His heart pounded violently in his chest, the tension coiling tighter with every mile they drew closer to her.

As they pulled up to the warehouse, the headlights cut through the dense fog, illuminating the crumbling building that loomed ahead. It was quiet, almost too quiet, the kind of silence that made Nikolai's instincts scream. His heart pounded in his chest, the adrenaline coursing through his veins as he threw the car into park and jumped out. Viktor followed, his gun already in hand, eyes scanning the area for any sign of movement.

Without a word, Nikolai nodded to his men, and they immediately fanned out, moving with the quiet precision of a well-trained team. The air was thick with tension, the kind that could snap at any moment. Nikolai's face was a mask of cold determination as he approached the warehouse, his mind focused on one thing: getting Ava out, no matter the cost.

"Secure the perimeter," he growled to Viktor, his voice low and commanding. "Take out any guards quietly. We don't need anyone alerted to our presence."

Viktor gave a sharp nod, signaling his men to move into position. They disappeared into the shadows, guns drawn, ready to strike. Nikolai didn't wait for confirmation. He knew his men—they were the best, handpicked for their skill and loyalty. They would handle any outside threats. But Nikolai wasn't worried about them. He was worried about Ava.

As he reached the entrance, Nikolai's hand instinctively moved to his gun, the cold metal comforting against his skin. He took a deep breath, forcing the rising tide of anger and fear down. He needed to stay sharp, to stay focused. There was no room for emotion here. Not yet.

With a swift motion, Nikolai kicked open the door, his gun raised, ready for whatever was waiting inside. The dim light inside the warehouse flickered weakly, casting eerie shadows over the cracked concrete floors and rusted metal beams. The air was thick with the stench of mildew and something else—something darker.

Nikolai moved forward, his steps slow and deliberate, every sense on high alert. His heart hammered in his chest, but his expression remained cold, unreadable. He'd been in situations like this before—too many to count. But this time, it was different. This time, it was Ava.

Each room they passed was empty, the silence only amplifying the dread curling in Nikolai's gut. His men moved with lethal efficiency, clearing every corner, every shadow. But they weren't finding anything. No guards, no signs of life. It was as if the warehouse had been abandoned long before they arrived.

But Nikolai knew better.

As they approached the end of the hallway, Viktor signaled for Nikolai to stop. They were close now—Nikolai could feel it. His pulse quickened, his fingers tightening around the grip of his gun. From behind the heavy metal door ahead, faint voices drifted through the cracks. Laughter. The cruel, mocking kind that made Nikolai's blood boil.

Nikolai glanced at Viktor, his eyes dark and filled with an unspoken command. Without hesitation, Viktor moved into position, his gun trained on the door. Nikolai's heart pounded in his ears as he approached the door, every nerve in his body on high alert. His hand reached for the handle, the cold metal biting into his palm as he slowly, silently turned it.

The door swung open with a low creak, and what he saw inside made the world tilt beneath his feet.

Ava.

She was strung up against the far wall, her wrists bound above her head with thick, rusted chains. Her clothes were torn, barely clinging to her battered body, and her face—God, her face—was swollen and bruised, a dark streak of blood trailing from the corner of her mouth. Her head hung limply to the side, her eyes half-closed, barely conscious.

Nikolai's chest tightened, a wave of pure, unfiltered rage crashing through him like a tidal wave. His heart slammed against his ribs, his vision narrowing until all he could see was her—the woman he had sworn to protect, hanging there like a broken doll. Every fiber of his being screamed to run to her, to tear her down from those chains and hold her, to make sure she was okay.

But his instincts kicked in, and he forced himself to hold back. Not yet. He couldn't afford to be reckless, not with her life on the line.

His eyes shifted to the men standing around her—the men responsible for this. One of them was laughing, a sick, twisted grin on his face as he grabbed a fistful of Ava's hair and yanked her head back roughly. The sight of it, the sound of her soft whimper, ignited something dark and vicious inside Nikolai, something he hadn't felt in years.

Without a second thought, Nikolai raised his gun and fired.

The first man went down instantly, a single bullet to the head silencing his laughter forever. The others barely had time to react before Nikolai was on them, his movements swift and deadly. Viktor and his men surged forward, taking down the remaining guards with brutal precision, but Nikolai barely registered them.

His focus was on the man standing closest to Ava—the one who had dared to touch her.

Nikolai moved toward him like a predator stalking its prey, his eyes burning with cold fury. The man's eyes widened in terror as he saw Nikolai coming, but it was too late. There would be no mercy tonight.

Nikolai's fist collided with the man's face again, blood splattering across the concrete floor as the sickening crunch of breaking bones echoed in the cold, dark room. The man let out a pained groan, his legs buckling beneath him, but Nikolai didn't stop. His rage was far from satisfied, and the thought of what this man had done to Ava fueled the violence driving each brutal blow.

The man's eyes were glazed with terror, his hands weakly trying to shield his face, but it was no use. He had no chance. Nikolai was relentless, his grip tightening around the man's throat as he slammed him back against the wall, forcing a choked gasp from his victim.

"You think you can touch her?" Nikolai growled, his voice low and deadly, the words vibrating with barely contained fury. "You think you can hurt her and walk away?"

The man's mouth opened, but no sound came out. His lips were already swollen and bleeding, his nose broken from Nikolai's earlier assault. Desperation flickered in his eyes, but there was no pleading with a man like Nikolai—not after what he had seen, what they had done to Ava.

Nikolai's fist came down again, harder this time, the force of the punch sending the man crashing to the floor in a heap of broken bones and blood. He groaned weakly, struggling to push himself up, but Nikolai kicked him back down, his boot landing squarely in the man's chest.

The man let out a strangled cry, clutching his ribs as he writhed on the ground. His body convulsed with pain, but Nikolai didn't care. All he could see was Ava's battered face, her bruised body hanging limply in those chains. They had done this to her. They had made her suffer. And now they were going to pay.

Nikolai reached down, grabbing the man by the collar and hauling him back to his feet. He slammed the man against the wall again, his fingers tightening around his throat. The man's eyes bulged in fear, his breaths coming in ragged gasps as he clawed weakly at Nikolai's hand, but it was no use. Nikolai's grip was iron, unbreakable.

"You're nothing," Nikolai hissed, his face inches from the man's.

With one swift motion, Nikolai pulled his gun from his holster and pressed the barrel against the man's temple. The man's eyes widened in terror, a strangled whimper escaping his throat.

"N-no, please," the man rasped, his voice barely a whisper.

But Nikolai wasn't listening.

He pulled the trigger.

The sound of the gunshot echoed through the room, the man's body slumping lifelessly to the ground at Nikolai's feet. Blood pooled beneath him, the metallic scent filling the air, but Nikolai didn't flinch. He stood over the body for a moment, his chest heaving with adrenaline, his mind buzzing with the need for more violence, more retribution.

It wasn't enough.

It would never be enough to erase the image of Ava strung up like an animal, helpless and vulnerable, suffering at the hands of these men.

Nikolai's gaze shifted to the last remaining captor, the one cowering in the corner of the room, his face pale with terror. He had seen what Nikolai was capable of, and now it was his turn to face the consequences.

Nikolai's steps were slow, deliberate, as he crossed the room, his gun still clenched tightly in his hand. The man trembled, his back pressed against the wall, his hands raised in a weak attempt to ward off the inevitable.

"Please," the man whimpered, his voice trembling with fear. "Please, I didn't—"

Nikolai didn't let him finish. With a swift, brutal motion, he grabbed the man by the front of his shirt and threw him to the ground. The man cried out, scrambling to his knees as he tried to crawl away, but Nikolai was faster. He stepped forward, driving his boot into the man's ribs, the force of the kick sending him sprawling across the floor.

The man let out a pained wheeze, curling into a ball as he clutched his side. His body shook with fear, but Nikolai showed no mercy. He crouched down beside the man, his hand gripping his hair and yanking his head back to meet his gaze.

"You'll never touch her again," Nikolai growled, his voice low and filled with a deadly promise. "None of you will."

With a final, decisive movement, Nikolai pressed the barrel of his gun against the man's forehead and pulled the trigger. The gunshot rang out, sharp and final, the man's body falling limp beneath him.

Silence fell over the room, broken only by the sound of Nikolai's heavy breathing. He rose to his feet, his chest heaving, his pulse pounding in his ears. His hands were slick with blood, his knuckles raw from the violence he had unleashed, but none of it mattered. All that mattered was Ava.

Turning away from the bodies littering the floor, Nikolai's gaze returned to her. She was still hanging there, her body limp, her head tilted to the side, and a cold fear gripped his heart. He rushed to her, his hands moving with uncharacteristic gentleness as he reached for the chains that bound her wrists.

"Ava," he whispered, his voice rough with emotion. "I'm here."

He freed her wrists from the chains, catching her limp body in his arms as she collapsed into him. Her skin was cold, clammy, and her breath was shallow, but she was alive. That was all that mattered.

Nikolai cradled her against his chest, his heart aching at the sight of her bruised face, the blood that stained her once-pristine skin. He pressed his lips to her forehead, a silent vow passing between them.

"I've got you," he whispered, his voice thick with emotion. "No one will ever hurt you again. I promise."

Nikolai's breath came in heavy, labored gasps as he held Ava tightly against him, her fragile body trembling in his arms. The rage that had fueled his every move, the bloodlust that had driven him to tear through the men who had dared to touch her, was still simmering beneath the surface. But now, cradling her bruised and battered form, something else was rising within him—something far more powerful than fury.

Fear.

For all the violence he had just unleashed, for all the blood he had spilled in his relentless pursuit to protect her, nothing compared to the fear that gripped his heart now. He could feel her warmth against him, hear the faint sound of her breath as it rattled in her chest, but it wasn't enough. He needed to know that she was okay—that she would survive this.

"Ava," he whispered, his voice cracking as he pulled her closer, his hand gently cupping the back of her head. Her hair was damp with sweat, matted against her bruised skin. She didn't respond, her body limp in his arms, and that terrified him more than anything else.

He lowered her carefully to the ground, his coat already draped around her to shield her from the cold air of the warehouse. His fingers trembled as they brushed across her cheek, tracing the angry red marks left by the chains, the blood that had dried on her skin. His heart clenched at the sight, guilt surging through him like a tidal wave.

This was his fault.

He had failed to protect her, had let her slip away from his grasp, and now she was paying the price for his carelessness. The thought of her suffering, of her enduring the cruelty of these men, made him want to rip the entire world apart.

But for now, all he could do was focus on her—on getting her out of this nightmare and making sure she was safe.

"Ava, sweetheart, can you hear me?" His voice was softer now, laced with an emotion he rarely let himself feel—vulnerability. He pressed his forehead against hers, his eyes closing as he listened for any sign that she was still with him.

For a moment, there was nothing but the deafening silence of the empty warehouse. And then, just barely, he felt it—the softest movement, the faintest shift in her breathing.

His heart leapt in his chest.

"Ava," he whispered again, his voice hoarse. "Stay with me, baby. I need you to stay with me."

She stirred in his arms, her eyelids fluttering weakly as she tried to focus. Nikolai could see the confusion in her eyes, the pain that clouded her expression, but he didn't let go. He couldn't. He was terrified that if he did, she would slip away from him again, into a place where he couldn't reach her.

"I'm here," he murmured, his thumb gently brushing across her cheek. "You're safe now. I've got you."

Her lips parted, a soft, barely audible sound escaping her, and for a brief moment, her eyes locked with his. It was enough to make the breath catch in his throat, enough to make the guilt and rage that had consumed him fade, if only for a second.

But then her eyes drifted closed again, her body sagging back against his chest, and the fear came rushing back.

Nikolai's jaw clenched, his arms tightening around her as he rose to his feet, lifting her effortlessly into his arms. He glanced around the room, his men standing silently by, their weapons still drawn, ready for any remaining threat. The sight of them was a stark reminder of the violence that had just unfolded, but all Nikolai could think about was getting Ava out of there, getting her somewhere safe where he could make sure she was okay.

Without a word, he strode toward the exit, his every step filled with purpose. Viktor was at his side in an instant, his face grim but determined. He knew better than to speak right now, to try and offer any words of comfort or reassurance. There was nothing that could ease the weight pressing down on Nikolai's chest, nothing that could erase the image of Ava hanging there, broken and bruised.

As they reached the door, Nikolai paused, his eyes scanning the area for any sign of further danger. His men were already securing the perimeter, ensuring that no one else would come near them. But it wasn't enough. It would never be enough.

"Get the car ready," Nikolai said, his voice cold and commanding, the steel of his usual demeanor slipping back into place. He had to stay focused. He had to keep his head clear, for her.

Viktor nodded and quickly moved to make the arrangements, while Nikolai stood there, cradling Ava in his arms, his mind racing with a thousand different thoughts. He could feel the warmth of her breath against his neck, the slight rise and fall of her chest as she clung to life, but it wasn't enough to calm the storm inside him.

Nothing would be enough until he knew she was truly safe.

"I'm sorry," he whispered, his voice so soft it was barely audible. It wasn't just an apology for what had happened tonight. It was an apology for all the danger he had brought into her life, for the violence that seemed to follow him wherever he went.

But even as the guilt and regret gnawed at him, there was something else beneath it all—a promise. A promise that he would make things right, that he would tear apart anyone who dared to hurt her again.

Because no matter what it took, no matter how many enemies he had to destroy, Nikolai wasn't going to lose her.

Not now. Not ever.

Chapter 23

Ava lay in the king-sized bed, her body sinking into the soft sheets as she stared up at the ceiling. The familiar surroundings of Nikolai's penthouse offered a sense of security, but the events of the past few days weighed heavily on her. She could still feel the dull ache in her muscles, the lingering soreness from the bruises that marred her skin, and the rawness of the memories that refused to fade. Her mind wandered back to the warehouse, the chains biting into her wrists, the cruel laughter of her captors ringing in her ears. But the most vivid memory was of Nikolai—his arrival, his fury, and the way he had torn through her enemies to get to her.

The thought of him filled her with a complex mix of emotions: fear, gratitude, love, and something more primal, something she couldn't quite name. He had been by her side ever since, not leaving for even a moment. She knew that his world was brutal, and she had experienced that brutality firsthand, but there was something deeply comforting about his presence. His protectiveness, though overwhelming at times, made her feel safe in a way she hadn't felt in years.

She turned her head slightly to glance at Nikolai, who sat in the armchair near the window, his dark eyes fixed on her. His posture was rigid, his shoulders tense, as if he were still on high alert, even here in the safety of his penthouse. His gaze softened when their eyes met, but she could see the worry etched into his features, the guilt that weighed heavily on him for not having prevented what had happened.

He had been a constant presence since they returned to the penthouse. He had arranged for a private doctor to come and tend to her injuries, ensuring that she received the best care possible. And though he hadn't spoken much, his actions spoke volumes. The way he gently adjusted her pillows, the way he kept her water glass full, and the way he watched over her with an intensity that bordered on obsessive—it was his way of showing love, a kind of fierce devotion that both reassured and unsettled her.

Ava shifted slightly in bed, wincing as the movement pulled at a sore muscle. Instantly, Nikolai was at her side, his hand gently brushing against her arm.

"Are you in pain?" he asked, his voice low but filled with concern.

She shook her head, though the ache still lingered. "No, I'm fine. Just... tired."

Nikolai's brow furrowed as he studied her, his thumb lightly tracing the edge of a bruise on her shoulder. "You need rest," he said softly, though his voice held the unspoken command she had come to recognize in him. He wasn't asking her to rest—he was telling her to.

Ava managed a small smile, touched by his care even if his possessive nature sometimes felt overwhelming. "I will. I just... I can't stop thinking about everything."

His hand stilled on her arm, and she could see the tension creeping back into his posture. He hated talking about the warehouse, hated the reminder that he had failed to protect her, even though she knew there was nothing more he could have done. She reached up to touch his hand, trying to offer him some comfort in return.

"It wasn't your fault," she whispered, her voice barely audible.

Nikolai's jaw tightened, his eyes darkening as he looked away. "It shouldn't have happened," he said, his voice rough with frustration. "I should have kept you safe."

"You did keep me safe," Ava insisted, squeezing his hand gently. "You came for me. You saved me."

He didn't respond, but she could see the conflict warring in his expression. Nikolai was a man who lived by a code of absolute control, and the fact that he had lost control, even for a moment, weighed heavily on him. Ava knew it would take time for him to come to terms with what had happened, just as it would take time for her to fully recover—not just physically, but emotionally as well.

But she wasn't alone in this. She had Nikolai, and despite the danger that came with being in his world, she knew he would do anything to protect her. That thought alone was enough to ease some of the tension that had been gripping her chest since the moment she had been taken.

"I'm okay," she whispered again, more for his sake than her own. "I'm here, and I'm okay."

Nikolai's eyes finally returned to hers, his gaze softening as he leaned down and pressed a gentle kiss to her forehead. "You are," he murmured, his voice barely above a whisper. "And you always will be."

Ava lay in the bed, feeling the weight of Nikolai's words as he kissed her forehead, but the heaviness in her chest didn't lift entirely. The memories of the past few days lingered like a fog, impossible to fully shake. Every time she closed her eyes, she could still feel the cold metal of the chains, still hear the mocking voices of her captors as they spoke about using her to lure Nikolai into a trap. She shivered, not from the cold, but from the realization that this was the world she had chosen to be part of.

Nikolai stayed close to her, his presence as steady as a fortress, and yet Ava felt an unsettling mixture of emotions bubbling beneath the surface. Her love for him was undeniable, but so was the fear. The violence she had witnessed, the raw brutality of it all, left a scar on her heart that she wasn't sure would ever fully heal.

"I can't stop thinking about it," she said softly, her eyes focusing on the intricate patterns of the ceiling as she spoke. "About what happened... and what could have happened."

Nikolai's hand moved to cup her cheek, his thumb brushing gently over her skin. "You're safe now, Ava. I won't let anything happen to you. Not again."

"I know," she whispered, her voice barely audible. "But I'm scared, Nikolai. I'm scared of how easily things could go wrong. One second everything is fine, and the next... I'm being chained up in a warehouse, waiting to be used as a pawn."

The words came out harsher than she intended, but she couldn't stop them. She needed to say it, needed to acknowledge the terror that had been gnawing at her since the moment she was taken. Nikolai's face hardened at her words, but she knew it wasn't anger directed at her—it was the guilt he carried for not being able to shield her from his enemies.

"Ava..." Nikolai's voice was low, strained, as if he too was fighting to hold back the emotions surging beneath the surface. "I will make them pay for what they did to you. Every single one of them. I swear it."

She believed him. She knew, without a shadow of a doubt, that Nikolai would hunt down every last man who had been involved in her kidnapping and destroy them. But that wasn't what she needed right now. What she needed was to understand how to live in this world—the world Nikolai inhabited, where violence was as natural as breathing, where every step could lead to danger.

"I'm not asking for vengeance," she said, her voice quieter now. "I'm asking for you to be honest with me. About everything. I need to know what this really means, being with you. I need to know what I'm walking into."

Nikolai's grip on her tightened ever so slightly, his jaw clenched as if he were weighing his next words carefully. She could see the hesitation in his eyes, the reluctance to expose her to the darker truths of his life, but Ava knew she couldn't be protected from it forever. If she was going to stay by his side, she needed to understand the full extent of the danger.

"I won't lie to you, Ava," Nikolai finally said, his voice firm but laced with emotion. "My world is dangerous. It's violent. And yes, there will always be people who want to hurt me... and you. But I will never let them touch you again. You will be protected, always."

"But at what cost?" she asked, her voice trembling as the question she had been dreading finally slipped out. "How long can we live like this, always looking over our shoulders? Always waiting for the next attack?"

Nikolai's face darkened, his eyes narrowing as if he too had thought about this. "As long as it takes. Until every last one of them is dead."

Ava swallowed, feeling the weight of his words settle over her. There was no escaping the violence that came with being with Nikolai. This wasn't a life she could walk away from unscathed. And yet, despite everything, despite the terror and the danger, she couldn't bring herself to leave. She couldn't imagine her life without him in it.

"I don't want to lose you," she whispered, her voice raw with emotion. "But I don't know how to live in this world."

Nikolai moved closer to her, his hand sliding down to clasp hers, his fingers wrapping around hers in a gesture of quiet strength. "You don't have to face it alone, Ava. I will be with you. Every step of the way."

Ava's heart swelled at his words, and she felt the familiar pull of love and devotion that had drawn her to Nikolai in the first place. He wasn't perfect—far from it—but he was hers. And for the first time in her life, she realized that she was willing to fight for that. To fight for him.

"I love you," she whispered, the words slipping out before she even had time to second-guess them. "I don't know how, or why, but I do. I love you, Nikolai."

The moment hung between them, heavy and raw with emotion. Nikolai's eyes softened, his expression shifting from one of guilt to something much deeper. He leaned down, pressing his forehead against hers, his breath warm against her skin.

"I love you too, Ava," he murmured, his voice thick with emotion. "More than anything in this world."

Ava's heart swelled as Nikolai's words washed over her, the weight of them sinking in with a finality that left her breathless. His love for her was undeniable, fierce, and all-consuming. She had seen it in his actions, felt it in the way he held her, protected her, and now, hearing him say it, she couldn't help but feel overwhelmed. But there was still fear—fear of the unknown, fear of the dangerous world they inhabited.

As she lay there, wrapped in the warmth of his presence, Ava felt a deep sense of longing rise within her. She didn't want to dwell on the fear anymore. She didn't want to be haunted by the events of the past few days. She wanted to focus on the man beside her, the man who had risked everything to save her.

"I don't know how you do it," she said softly, her voice barely a whisper as she traced the line of his jaw with her fingers. "How you carry so much... and still look at me like I'm the most important thing in your world."

Nikolai caught her hand, bringing it to his lips as he kissed her fingers gently. "Because you are the most important thing in my world, Ava," he replied, his voice steady and sincere. "I've built an empire. I've fought battles most people can't even imagine. But none of it matters if I don't have you."

His words sent a shiver down her spine, but there was still that lingering doubt. Not about his feelings, but about whether she could survive in this world, whether she could thrive in the shadow of his empire. Ava shifted slightly, her fingers curling into the sheets as she searched for the right words.

"I'm scared," she admitted, her voice trembling with vulnerability. "Not just of your world, but of how much I need you. I've never felt like this before... so consumed by someone."

Nikolai's grip tightened on her hand, his gaze locked on hers with an intensity that took her breath away. "I know, Ava. I know it's overwhelming. But you don't have to carry that weight alone. I'm here. I'll always be here."

Ava felt tears pricking the corners of her eyes, a mix of fear and relief bubbling up inside her. "But what if something happens to you?" she asked, her voice cracking as the fear of losing him finally escaped her. "What if you don't come back one day? I don't know if I could survive that."

Nikolai's eyes softened, and he shifted closer, his body pressing against hers as he cupped her face in his hands. "Nothing is going to happen to me, Ava. I swear to you, I will always come back to you."

She wanted to believe him. She wanted to trust in the strength of his words, but the reality of his life—the violence, the danger—was always lurking in the back of her mind. Ava blinked back her tears, trying to push away the dark thoughts that threatened to consume her.

"I don't know how to be strong like you," she whispered, her voice barely audible.

Nikolai's thumb brushed away a stray tear from her cheek, his touch gentle despite the power and strength she knew he possessed. "You're stronger than you think, Ava. You survived what happened at the warehouse. You faced your fears head-on. That takes strength."

Ava shook her head, still unsure. "I only survived because of you. If you hadn't found me... I don't even want to think about what would have happened."

"But I did find you," Nikolai said firmly, his voice filled with conviction. "And I always will. No one will ever hurt you again. I won't allow it."

There was something in his voice, something so sure and unwavering, that made Ava believe him. She wasn't alone in this. She had Nikolai, and though his world was dangerous, though the violence would always be a shadow over their lives, she knew that he would never stop protecting her.

"I need to let go of the past," she said, her voice soft but determined. "I need to stop letting what happened with Derek control how I feel. You're not him. I know that. But sometimes... sometimes the fear creeps in, and I start questioning everything."

Nikolai's gaze darkened at the mention of Derek, his jaw tightening. "I'm nothing like him, Ava. I would never betray you the way he did."

"I know," she whispered, her fingers brushing against his chest. "I know that, but it's hard to forget. I've been hurt before, and I'm scared of being hurt again."

Nikolai's hands slid down to her shoulders, his grip firm but comforting. "You won't be hurt again. Not by me. I promise you, Ava, I will never let you down."

His words were like a balm to the wounds she hadn't even realized were still open. Ava felt the weight of her insecurities slowly begin to lift as she looked into Nikolai's eyes. This was what she had been searching for all along—someone who wouldn't just protect her, but who would love her fiercely, without question, without hesitation.

Ava reached up, cupping his face as she brought his lips to hers in a soft, lingering kiss. It wasn't the fiery, passionate kind of kiss they often shared, but something deeper—something filled with gratitude, love, and the knowledge that they were in this together, no matter what.

When she pulled back, she whispered, "I trust you, Nikolai. With my heart... and my life."

Nikolai's eyes softened, his hands cupping her face as he kissed her again, this time with more intensity. "You're mine, Ava. Always."

As Ava lay in the soft embrace of Nikolai's arms, she felt a sense of calm wash over her that hadn't been there before. The storm of emotions she'd been battling for weeks was slowly beginning to settle. She no longer felt like she was drowning in uncertainty. For the first time, she understood what it meant to truly trust someone, and that trust went beyond her love for Nikolai. It extended to the core of who he was—his dominance, his power, and even the dangerous world he inhabited.

The weight of her confession still hung in the air between them. Telling Nikolai that she loved him, that she trusted him with her heart and her life, was not just a declaration. It was a vow. She had spent so long guarding herself, protecting her heart from the pain of betrayal, but with Nikolai, she knew she didn't need to hide. He wasn't Derek. He was a man of strength, a man who would always put her first. A man who, despite the darkness of his world, had given her a sense of belonging she hadn't realized she was missing.

A soft sigh escaped her lips as she turned her head, resting it against his chest. His heartbeat was steady, grounding her in the present moment. There was something so reassuring about the quiet strength in him, the way he held her as if she were the most precious thing in his life. She felt his hand gently stroking her hair, his fingers threading through the strands with an ease that came from familiarity.

Nikolai shifted slightly beside her, his lips pressing against the crown of her head as he broke the silence. "I've been thinking, Ava," he said, his voice a deep rumble that vibrated through his chest.

Ava lifted her head slightly, tilting her gaze up to meet his. "About what?"

He hesitated for a moment, his expression unreadable as he searched her face. "About us. About everything we've been through."

Her heart skipped a beat, her pulse quickening as she wondered where this conversation was headed. There was something different in his tone, a seriousness that sent a ripple of anticipation through her.

Nikolai sat up, gently pulling her with him until they were both sitting on the edge of the bed. He took her hands in his, his dark eyes locking onto hers with an intensity that made it hard to breathe. "You've been through so much because of me," he began, his voice softer now, but no less commanding. "More than I ever wanted you to. And I know my world... it's not an easy one to live in."

Ava's fingers tightened around his, her heart racing as she tried to find the right words. "I chose this," she whispered. "I chose you."

"I know," he replied, his gaze unwavering. "But that doesn't change the fact that you deserve better. You deserve a life without fear, without constant danger."

Ava shook her head, her heart aching at the thought of losing him. "I don't want anything else. I want you. I don't care about the danger. I know what I'm getting into."

Nikolai's lips curled into a small smile, but there was still something serious in his eyes. "That's why I need to make sure you understand something, Ava. You are mine. You will always be mine. But I want more than that."

Her breath caught in her throat, her pulse racing as she tried to comprehend his words. "More?"

Nikolai let out a soft sigh, his hands tightening around hers as he leaned in closer. "I want you to be my wife."

The words hung in the air, heavy and full of meaning. Ava's heart skipped a beat, her eyes widening in shock. "Wife?" she whispered, her voice barely audible.

Nikolai nodded, his gaze never leaving hers. "I want you to be with me—forever. To stand by my side, no matter what comes. I want to protect you, to take care of you, to make sure that no one ever hurts you again. And the only way I can do that is if you're truly mine. If you belong to me... in every way."

Ava's mind raced, her thoughts spinning in a whirlwind of emotions. Marriage. She hadn't imagined herself wanting to marry again, not after what had happened with Derek. But this... this was different. Nikolai was different. He wasn't offering her a life of security or comfort; he was offering her a partnership, a bond that went beyond mere words. He was offering her a place by his side, in his world, no matter how dangerous or uncertain it might be.

She swallowed hard, her throat tight with emotion as she stared into his eyes. "You... you really want me to be your wife?"

Nikolai's expression softened, and he cupped her face in his hands, his thumb brushing against her cheek as he leaned in closer. "More than anything. I want you to be mine, Ava. Completely. In every way."

Tears welled in her eyes, and she blinked them away, her heart swelling with a love so fierce it almost hurt. This was what she had been searching for—someone who would never let her go, someone who would fight for her, protect her, and love her with everything he had.

"Yes," she whispered, her voice breaking with emotion. "Yes, Nikolai. I'll be your wife."

The smile that spread across his face was breathtaking, a rare glimpse of unguarded happiness that made her heart ache with love. He pulled her into his arms, kissing her deeply, passionately, as if sealing the promise between them with his touch.

In that moment, everything else faded away. The danger, the fear, the uncertainty—all of it melted into the background, leaving only the two of them, bound together by a love that had survived the darkest of storms.

Nikolai's lips moved gently against hers, their kiss deepening as the reality of their new bond sank in. Ava's heart raced, her pulse quickening with every brush of his fingers along her skin. There was a tenderness in his touch, but also a quiet dominance that she had come to crave. He pulled her closer, his hand cupping the back of her neck as his lips began a slow, deliberate path from her mouth down to the curve of her jawline.

A soft sigh escaped her as he kissed along her neck, the heat of his breath sending shivers down her spine. His lips were firm but loving, claiming every inch of her as if he were marking her as his. And she was—she was his in every way now, his wife-to-be, bound to him in love, desire, and trust. There was no more fear, no more hesitation. She wanted him just as fiercely as he wanted her.

Nikolai's hands began to explore, trailing down her sides with a commanding possessiveness. His fingers traced the curve of her waist, then slid lower to grip her hips, pulling her against him as he kissed her collarbone. Each kiss was slow and deliberate, as though he were savoring the moment, the feel of her beneath him. His lips grazed the delicate skin there, teasing her with the softest of touches before his tongue followed, leaving a trail of warmth in its wake.

Ava arched her back, her body already responding to him, her nipples hardening beneath the fabric of her nightgown. Nikolai must have sensed her need because his hands moved up to cup her breasts, his thumbs brushing over her sensitive peaks through the thin material. She gasped, her hands instinctively gripping his shoulders as a rush of pleasure shot through her.

"Nikolai," she breathed, her voice barely a whisper.

He didn't respond with words. Instead, he let his actions speak for him. His hands slipped beneath her nightgown, the fabric sliding up her thighs as he caressed her skin. His touch was firm but gentle, his fingers pressing into her flesh as if he were memorizing every inch of her body. The nightgown was soon bunched around her hips, and Nikolai pulled it over her head, discarding it without a second thought.

Ava was left bare before him, her skin flushed with anticipation. She could feel the cool air against her heated body, but it was nothing compared to the warmth of Nikolai's touch. His hands roamed her now-exposed flesh, his fingers teasing the sensitive skin just beneath her breasts before finally cupping them fully.

His thumbs brushed over her hardened nipples, and Ava moaned softly, her body arching into his touch. He lowered his head, his lips finding the soft curve of her breast before his mouth closed over one nipple. He sucked gently at first, teasing her with the wet heat of his mouth before his teeth grazed her sensitive skin. The sensation sent a jolt of pleasure straight to her core, and she gasped, her fingers tangling in his hair as she pressed him closer.

Nikolai's mouth moved between her breasts, lavishing attention on each one in turn, his tongue flicking over her hardened peaks before he sucked them into his mouth, his lips pulling at her until she was trembling beneath him. His hands slid lower, tracing the curve of her waist, then lower still, until his fingers brushed the inside of her thighs.

Ava's breath hitched, her body already aching for more. He teased her for a moment, his fingers just barely grazing her skin, before finally slipping between her legs to find her wet and ready for him. He groaned softly against her breast, his fingers sliding through her slick folds as he caressed her, his thumb brushing over her clit with slow, deliberate strokes.

"You're so wet for me," he murmured, his voice thick with desire.

Ava could only nod, her mind spinning as he worked her with his fingers, his thumb circling her clit in a way that made her entire body tremble. He thrust one finger inside her, then another, filling her slowly, stretching her with each deliberate movement. She gasped, her hips bucking against his hand as the pleasure built inside her, a slow, burning heat that consumed her completely.

"Nikolai," she moaned, her voice barely audible as he thrust his fingers deeper, his thumb pressing harder against her clit. "Please..."

He didn't need any more urging. With one final thrust of his fingers, he pulled back, leaving her trembling and aching for more. He rose up on his knees, his dark eyes locked on hers as he unbuckled his belt and pushed his pants down, revealing his already hardened length.

Ava's breath caught in her throat at the sight of him. He was so powerful, so commanding, and yet there was a tenderness in his eyes as he looked down at her that made her heart swell with love. She reached out, her fingers wrapping around his cock as she stroked him, her touch gentle but firm.

Nikolai groaned, his hips bucking slightly as she worked him with her hand. His cock was thick and heavy in her grip, and she could feel the tension in his body as he held himself back, his need for her almost palpable. But he didn't rush. He let her touch him, let her explore him, until he was practically trembling with restraint.

When he could take no more, he gently pushed her
hand away and positioned himself between her
legs. His hands gripped her hips, pulling her toward
him as he lined himself up with her entrance. He
paused for a moment, his gaze locking onto hers as
if asking for permission, as if silently telling her that
she was in control.

Ava nodded, her heart pounding in her chest as
she felt the head of his cock press against her slick
folds. He entered her slowly, gently, filling her inch
by inch until she was stretched completely around
him. She gasped, her body trembling at the feel of
him inside her, the way he filled her so perfectly.

Nikolai let out a low groan as he buried himself to
the hilt, his hands tightening on her hips as he
began to move. His thrusts were slow and
deliberate at first, his hips rolling against hers as he
pushed deeper, each stroke hitting that perfect spot
inside her that made her toes curl. Ava moaned,
her fingers gripping his arms as the pleasure built
inside her, her body responding to him in ways she
couldn't control.

"God, Ava," Nikolai breathed, his voice rough with
need. "You feel so good... so perfect."

Ava's only response was a soft moan as he thrust
deeper, his movements becoming more urgent as
the need between them grew. He reached down,
his fingers finding her clit once more as he stroked
her in time with his thrusts, his touch sending

shockwaves of pleasure through her with every movement.

She was close, so close, the tension building inside her until she thought she might break. Nikolai seemed to sense it, his thumb pressing harder against her clit as he thrust into her, each stroke more commanding than the last.

"Come for me, Ava," he growled, his voice thick with desire. "I want to feel you come."

That was all it took. Ava's body tightened around him, her muscles clenching as the orgasm ripped through her, her vision blurring as wave after wave of pleasure crashed over her. She cried out, her fingers digging into his arms as her body convulsed around him, the pleasure so intense it left her breathless.

Nikolai groaned, his hips slamming against hers as he followed her over the edge, his cock pulsing inside her as he filled her completely. He collapsed against her, his body trembling with the force of his release as he held her close, their bodies still intertwined.

For a long moment, neither of them moved, their breathing the only sound in the room as they lay together, completely spent. Nikolai's arms wrapped around her, pulling her close as he kissed the top of her head.

"You're mine, Ava," he whispered, his voice rough with emotion. "Always."

Chapter 24

Ava stood by the tall windows of Nikolai's penthouse, the morning light spilling over the New York City skyline. The city looked as alive as ever, but Ava felt like she was seeing it through new eyes. So much had changed in the past six weeks, more than she could have ever imagined. The woman staring back at her from the glass wasn't the same person who had walked into Nikolai's world with wide eyes and a heart full of uncertainty.

She had thought she would never get used to the constant tension, the undercurrent of danger that seemed to pulse through everything in Nikolai's world. But now, as she looked out over the city, she realized just how much she had adapted. She was no longer afraid. The darkness no longer scared her; in fact, she had come to understand it. There was a power in Nikolai that extended beyond his wealth and influence—it was a power that came from knowing exactly who you were and what you were capable of. And Ava had found her place in that power.

The woman who had once been terrified of the violence, who had hesitated at the thought of being a part of Nikolai's life, was gone. In her place was someone who understood what it meant to be the partner of a man like Nikolai Volkov. She wasn't naive anymore. She knew what it meant to live in a world where control was everything, where strength was survival, and where love had to be fierce and unbreakable.

Ava traced her fingers along the cold glass, watching the movement of the city below. There had been a time when she thought she could never live in this world. That she wasn't strong enough to stand by Nikolai's side. But now, she knew she was exactly where she belonged. She had found her strength, her resilience, in the face of everything they had endured together.

The past weeks had been hard—recovering from her kidnapping, dealing with the lingering fear, and coming to terms with what being with Nikolai really meant. But through it all, he had been there, never wavering, never leaving her side. His love had been the one constant, the one thing she could rely on even when everything else felt like it was slipping away. She had leaned on him more than she ever thought she would, and yet, in that vulnerability, she had discovered something even more profound. She wasn't just Nikolai's lover. She was his equal.

It was a realization that had come slowly, piece by piece, as she healed from the physical and emotional scars left behind by the Morozovs. Nikolai's world was dark, dangerous, and unforgiving, but it was also a world where she had found purpose. She wasn't just a bystander anymore. She wasn't a woman on the outside, looking in. She was fully integrated into his life, a part of everything he did.

As she stood there, watching the city hum beneath her, Ava felt a sense of peace settle over her. She had come a long way from the woman who had been betrayed by her ex-fiancé and left wondering if she would ever trust again. She had learned that love wasn't about safety or guarantees. It was about risk, about diving headfirst into the unknown and trusting that the person standing beside you would be there no matter what.

Nikolai had shown her that. He had shown her what it meant to love without reservation, to give everything without holding back. And now, she was ready to do the same. She was ready to face whatever came next, whether it was more violence, more danger, or more uncertainty. Because as long as she had Nikolai by her side, she knew they could face anything.

The darkness didn't scare her anymore. It was just a part of their world—a world she had finally embraced.

Ava didn't hear Nikolai enter the room, but she felt his presence the moment he stepped behind her. His warmth pressed against her back, his arms slipping around her waist as he pulled her into his chest. She let out a soft sigh, her body relaxing instantly in his embrace. There was something so comforting about the way he held her—strong, secure, as if nothing could ever hurt her when she was wrapped in his arms.

"You're quiet this morning," Nikolai murmured, his lips brushing against her ear as he spoke. His voice was low, filled with the same quiet intensity that always made her heart race.

"I'm just thinking," Ava replied softly, resting her head against his shoulder. She closed her eyes for a moment, savoring the feel of him. She had grown so accustomed to his touch, to the way he seemed to know exactly when she needed him close. "About everything."

Nikolai tightened his grip on her, his hands splayed across her stomach as he held her close. "Is it too much?" he asked, his voice laced with concern. "Do you feel like I've pushed you too far?"

Ava shook her head, turning slightly to look up at him. His dark eyes searched hers, as if he were trying to find the answers she hadn't spoken out loud. She smiled softly, reaching up to touch his cheek, her thumb brushing over the rough stubble along his jaw.

"No," she said, her voice filled with certainty. "I don't feel like you've pushed me. I feel like I've finally found where I belong."

Nikolai's expression softened, his eyes darkening with something she had come to recognize as love—deep, consuming love. It was a look he reserved only for her, and every time she saw it, it made her heart swell with an overwhelming sense of belonging. She knew that no matter how dark his world might be, no matter what dangers lurked around every corner, she would always be safe with him.

He bent down, pressing his lips to her forehead in a gentle kiss. "You've come so far," he whispered against her skin. "More than I could have ever expected. You've become everything I need."

His words washed over her, filling her with warmth. It hadn't always been easy. There were times when she had questioned whether she could handle being a part of his world, whether she could live with the constant danger and the weight of the violence that came with it. But those doubts had faded over time, replaced by the undeniable truth that she couldn't imagine her life without Nikolai.

"I've accepted it," she said quietly, turning fully in his arms so she could face him. "All of it. The danger, the power, the darkness... I've accepted it because I love you. I can't live in fear anymore."

Nikolai's hand came up to cradle her cheek, his thumb brushing over her skin as he gazed down at her. "I never wanted to bring you into this life, Ava. I tried to keep you away from it, to shield you from the worst of it. But now... I can't imagine doing any of this without you."

Ava smiled, feeling a deep sense of contentment settle in her chest. She reached up to take his hand in hers, squeezing it gently as she looked into his eyes. "You don't have to do it alone anymore. I'm with you, Nikolai. In every way. I'm not afraid."

He didn't say anything for a moment, his dark eyes flickering with an emotion she couldn't quite name. But then, without warning, he leaned down and captured her lips in a slow, tender kiss. It was a kiss that spoke of promises made, of love that would endure even the darkest of times. Ava melted into him, her arms wrapping around his neck as she kissed him back with the same intensity.

When they finally pulled apart, Nikolai rested his forehead against hers, his breath warm against her skin. "You're my strength, Ava," he murmured. "I've built my world on power and control, but you... you make it worth it."

Ava's heart swelled at his words. She had always known that Nikolai was a man of power, a man who ruled with an iron fist in a world of violence and danger. But hearing him say that she was his strength, that she was the reason he fought so hard—that was everything she needed to hear.

"You've given me everything," Ava whispered, her fingers tracing the lines of his jaw. "I just want to give you the same."

Nikolai smiled, a rare softness in his expression as he looked at her. "You already have."

Ava leaned into Nikolai's embrace, her head resting against his chest as they stood by the window, watching the city come alive below. The quiet moments between them felt even more precious now, after everything they had been through. Every touch, every kiss seemed to carry more weight, a deeper meaning. Ava had never imagined that she could feel this way about someone, especially someone like Nikolai. He was dark, dangerous, and powerful, but he was also the man who had saved her, protected her, and loved her with a ferocity that left her breathless.

As she stood there, enveloped in his warmth, Ava thought about everything that had led them to this point. The violence, the fear, the uncertainty—it had all been worth it. She had faced her worst fears and come out stronger on the other side, and she had done it with Nikolai by her side. He had been her rock, her anchor, even when the world around them was falling apart. And now, standing here with him, she felt more certain than ever that she had made the right choice.

"I used to be so scared," Ava admitted quietly, her voice barely above a whisper. "Not just of your world, but of letting myself love someone again. After everything that happened with Derek, I thought I would never trust anyone like that again. But then I met you, and... everything changed."

Nikolai's hand gently stroked her back, his touch soothing and reassuring. "You were betrayed by someone who didn't deserve you, Ava," he said, his voice low and firm. "But I'm not that man. I will never betray you. I will never let anyone hurt you again."

Ava nodded, knowing his words were true. Nikolai wasn't Derek. He wasn't like any man she had ever known. He was fierce, protective, and unapologetically dominant, but he was also capable of a kind of love that she had never experienced before. It wasn't just that he protected her physically—it was the way he saw her, the way he valued her as his equal, even in his world of power and control.

"I know," she whispered, looking up at him with a soft smile. "I trust you, Nikolai. I trust you with my heart, and I trust you with my life."

Nikolai's eyes darkened with emotion as he looked down at her, his hand tightening on her waist. "You're mine, Ava," he murmured, his voice a mix of possessiveness and tenderness. "And I'm never letting you go."

Ava's heart fluttered at his words, a familiar warmth spreading through her chest. She knew what it meant to be his, and she accepted it fully. There was no more fear, no more hesitation. She had given herself to him completely, and she had no regrets.

They stood in silence for a few moments longer, the weight of their shared experiences settling between them. Ava couldn't help but think back to everything they had been through—the kidnapping, the violence, the betrayals. It had been more than she ever thought she could handle, but somehow, she had made it through. And it wasn't just because of Nikolai's protection. It was because of the strength she had found within herself.

"I'm not the same woman I was when I met you," Ava said softly, breaking the silence. "I've changed. I've grown stronger. And I think it's because of you."

Nikolai tilted her chin up, forcing her to meet his gaze. His eyes were intense, filled with a depth of emotion that made her breath catch. "You've always been strong, Ava. You just didn't see it. But I did. From the moment I met you, I knew you were different. You have a strength that no one can take from you. Not even me."

Ava smiled, her heart swelling with love for the man standing before her. He had seen something in her that she hadn't even seen in herself, and now, because of him, she had become the woman she was always meant to be.

"I love you," she whispered, the words flowing easily from her lips. "I love you more than I ever thought possible."

Nikolai's expression softened, and for a moment, the dangerous man he was to the world outside disappeared, leaving only the man who loved her, who cherished her. "And I love you, Ava," he said quietly, his voice full of sincerity. "More than anything in this world."

The world outside the penthouse was dangerous and uncertain, but in this moment, everything felt perfect. Ava knew they would face new threats, new enemies, and new battles, but they would face them together.

Ava smiled, knowing that no matter what the future held, they would face it as one. Their love was stronger than the darkness, stronger than the violence, stronger than anything the world could throw at them.

And together, they were unstoppable.

I hope you enjoyed
Claimed by the Bratva
King. Scan the QR code
below and share your love
with a review!

Chapter 1

Tatiana sat at the small kitchen table, her fingers idly tracing the worn edge of the wood. The early morning sun filtered through the lace curtains, casting soft golden light across the room. The kitchen was modest, like the rest of their house, but it had always been her mother's pride. It was the heart of their home—a place where her family gathered every night, where laughter and conversations flowed as freely as the warm meals her mother prepared.

Tatiana's long, dark brown hair cascaded over her shoulders, framing her delicate, pale face. Her skin was smooth and fair, almost porcelain-like, a testament to her Russian heritage. Her large, expressive eyes—pale blue, a striking contrast against her dark hair—were the most captivating feature about her, always shimmering with a mix of curiosity and innocence. Her lips were soft, a light shade of pink, giving her an air of natural beauty that was untouched by the heavy makeup her peers often wore.

She was slender, her figure graceful and elegant, though she had always been shy about the way her body had developed over the years. The curves that now shaped her body had drawn glances from men, but her father's protective eye had always

made sure those glances never lingered too long.
Tatiana had never been allowed to explore the
attention or indulge in the freedom her peers did.
There had always been rules—strict rules. And her
father, Ivan, had made sure she followed them.

Her father had already left for the restaurant, as he
did every morning. He'd built the small Russian
eatery from the ground up, pouring his life into it,
just as he had poured himself into protecting his
family. Tatiana had grown up watching him work
tirelessly, a quiet, determined man who kept his
emotions close. Her mother, on the other hand, had
always been the more expressive one—nurturing,
traditional, and deeply tied to their Russian roots.
Theirs was a family that held onto tradition fiercely,
preserving the old ways in the midst of the bustling,
ever-changing city of New York.

Tatiana had always loved their traditions. Growing
up in a traditional Russian household had shaped
so much of her life. Their community was tight-knit,
and their values strong. Russian holidays were
celebrated with reverence, their customs honored
with respect. They attended church regularly, where
her mother would light candles and whisper prayers
in the soft, lyrical tones of their language. Her father
was strict about preserving their heritage, insisting
that they speak Russian at home and follow the
rules that had been passed down through
generations.

But Tatiana had always been aware of the restrictions that came with those traditions. While other girls her age had boyfriends, went to parties, and experienced the freedom of youth, Tatiana's life was different. She wasn't allowed to date, wasn't allowed to stray too far from the watchful eyes of her family. Her father's rules were rigid, and her mother supported them with a quiet but firm devotion.

Today, however, Tatiana's mind buzzed with anticipation. Tomorrow would be her nineteenth birthday, a milestone she had dreamed of for years. Nineteen—it was a number that carried the weight of possibility. Surely, now she could have the independence she longed for. Surely, her father would loosen his grip, and she could finally experience life beyond the walls of their small, protective world.

About the Author

Ellie Daniels is a Colorado author who ignites passion and desire through her captivating erotic romance novels and sizzling short stories. When she's not crafting worlds of desire and intimacy, Ellie enjoys quiet moments at home with her loving husband, their devoted chihuahua, and four playful cats. A sensualist at heart, she believes in the transformative power of passion and connection. Cherishing close relationships, Ellie finds inspiration in the complexities of love.

www.ingramcontent.com/pod-product-compliance
Lightning Source LLC
Chambersburg PA
CBHW050453160726
48003CB00001B/4